ALSO BY DEBRA MONROE

A Wild, Cold State

The Source of Trouble

Simon & Schuster

A Novel

fangled

Debra
Monroe

SIMON & SCHUSTER
Rockefeller Center
1230 Avenue of the Americas
New York, NY 10020

SIMON & SCHUSTER and colophon are registered
trademarks of Simon & Schuster Inc.

Designed by Sam Potts
Manufactured in the United States of America
1   3   5   7   9   10   8   6   4   2

Library of Congress Cataloging-in-Publication Data
Monroe, Debra.
Newfangled : a novel / Debra Monroe.
p.   cm.
I. Title.
PS3563.O5273N44   1998
813'.54—dc21   97-36281
CIP

ISBN 0-684-81905-8

For

Clara Mae Haskin

and

Arlene Tyman

Newfangled

Ready . . .

The caustic fact of the afternoon, the felt *fact, was the sun. We're* nearer the hot equator, Maidie thought, standing on the border of the graveled plot of her yard, across the street from her neighbor Rona's yard. Rona stood next to Maidie, wearing a straw hat that was indebted to *Little House on the Prairie,* or a series of greeting cards about doll-like women who gardened and had better characters because of it. Rona nodded; her lips moved, speaking. Maidie nodded back, registering the familiar sense that she'd heard it all before out of the mouth of someone a lot like Rona, if not exactly Rona. Or here. The Arizona sun beamed on Maidie's scalp, and she thought about how she'd been warned to wear a hat herself, though it was only May. She had to go back to work in an hour. If she didn't get out of the sun now, all of the style she'd crimped into her hair when she'd blown it dry that morning—smearing it with an expensive product called Humectin Humidifier, meant to provide it with

some of the dew it lacked in this strange desert—would be
singed away. She'd catalogue vases and butter paddles with her
hair as lackluster as dust.

Rona said, "Rex is nice, and you are. But maybe you don't
mix."

Maidie thought again: How similar. Usual.

Rona said, "Like oil and water."

The surprise was hearing this announcement about love, its
dwindling, at 3:00 P.M. on a Monday. And certain word choices,
similes Rona favored, made the moment distinct. Otherwise, it
had come and gone before. Hanging over into the present, it
wasn't mystical like déjà vu, didn't bring with it wisdom. Maidie once read about a Vietnamese woman who, all her life, had
been visited in dreams by ancestors who told her how to pro-
ceed through strife. Then she moved to the United States, and
her ancestors avoided her dreams. What came from Maidie's
past? Mistakes. They hauled themselves out of previous circumstances—not ancient, reincarnated circumstances like, say, the
life of a slave girl from Mesopotamia. Mistakes had been made
in Maidie's life, had evolved into new mistakes according to
contingency and location. Maidie, flailingly at the center of
doubts and arrows, new-made propositions, bungled and took
aim, usually took advice from some slightly older woman who
lived nearby. Staring at Rona's face as she counseled Maidie, put
a flea in Maidie's ear, Maidie thought to herself: It's not like I
want *her* life. A few months earlier, Rona's husband had hit
Rona with a pillow while she was sleeping, which sounds as
harmless as an Elvis Presley movie but was in fact a toned-down
way of not hitting Rona with his fists because he'd promised the
family minister when he and Rona married each other for the
second time that he wouldn't do it again, hit Rona with something hard.

Rona said, "So when Rex left, how mad was he?"

Maidie said, "Maybe just tired." That's what he'd said—tired of listening to Maidie. She'd shouted at him until her throat hurt. That was two days ago; her words seemed corroded now, impossible to reclaim. *Go!* Rex left. Maidie went outside and broke glass against the patio wall. She hoped Rona hadn't heard, that she couldn't see the shards and slivers lying in glinty heaps.

Rona said, "Do you have a number where you can call him?"

"No."

Rona raised her eyebrows. "How long is he going to be gone?"

"Three months."

"Maidie!" Rona said. "And no phone number."

Maidie bristled. She wanted to let the comments forging themselves under the cover of her surface blow: You're repeating yourself! You're reverberating! She said, "I didn't ask for his number."

"Then he'll call, I'm sure." Rona was kind.

Or nosy.

"I'm not in suspense," Maidie said.

But once—in Norfolk, Virginia, with her second husband, Jack Bonasso—Maidie *had* been in suspense. She'd phoned Jack at a hotel where he'd gone for a sales meeting, but no one at the front desk had heard of the meeting. Then she'd phoned his office, where the secretary didn't know about the meeting either. The manager picked up the phone and said, "Mrs. Bonasso, this is the hardest piece of information I've ever passed on to a wife, but I have no idea where Jack is." Maidie and Jack had lived in Virginia for two months, and neither of them had friends yet, familiar neighbors. In the context of dislocation, she and Jack didn't seem to know each other. Did she know herself? She paced through the rented house with its fresh-painted walls, neutral carpet, her old possessions dusted and set on shelves to look better—better!—in new surroundings, a new arrangement. She had a sudden foresight she'd survive Jack's betrayal, already under way. But what were its details? His brother had been arrested in Miami for soliciting a prostitute. Maybe Jack had a noncaloric lover—all pleasure, no toil. Maybe he'd escaped, sleeping on the beach, smoking cigars, placing bets at the track, trying on another life before he came back to his own with Maidie.

It's not the end of the earth, she'd thought, staring out the window at a flock of wrens in the rain. Then she corrected herself: the end of the world, the end of life-as-we-know-it. Because Virginia—after Minnesota, Wyoming, Nebraska, and Arkansas, where Maidie had lived before—was the end of the continent at least. People had stood worse, war and famine, worse, she thought, than not knowing where a husband was. She'd recover. In ten years, this would be a small, bad memory; in ten weeks. In ten days, it would be known and managed. But the next ten minutes would be hell, she'd realized, and the morbid hunch she'd pushed back her whole life came forward, the dead certainty that no one knew where she was, with whom.

Or how she stood it.

She started crying.

Which had its upside and its detriments too. On the one hand, it gave you something to do. There, there, you said to yourself. On the other hand, it could swamp you down, stretch out the period of time you stayed mired in gloom. If only someone could monitor, interpret, advise. A woman should put her foot down, maybe. Or be understanding. As situations go, it wasn't good, or "pretty good." Maybe it was "not bad"? In this robotic state, as if she'd left authentic habits behind, Maidie searched through the Yellow Pages. Once, in Wyoming, she'd called a hot line advertised in the newspaper—PREGNANT? SCARED? FIND HELP!—for her roommate, Laree, who'd sat in a corner incapacitated by panic while Maidie dialed and spoke. "A friend who's pregnant needs to know . . ." The voice on the other end stayed gentle, having assumed, Maidie realized, that

Maidie had invented her friend, Laree, as a privacy tactic because she, Maidie, was pregnant by accident and embarrassed.
She wasn't—pregnant by accident, that is. Maidie had strategy,
maybe too much.

But in Virginia, Maidie had called Jack's mother, who lived in
Florida. "Have you heard from him?" She hadn't. "What do you
think? Why is he being secretive? I know this move has been
hard."

Jack's mother said, "If he phones, I'll let you know."

Maidie asked, "Do you think he's doing something wrong?"

Jack's mother said, "Maybe," in a severed, frosty voice. She'd
withstood her own bad surprises.

Maidie had hung up, paced, flipped through her Rolodex.
Who to call? Saying: I know we haven't spoken in months, or
years, but I can't locate my husband, and while I don't exactly
have an urgent message for him, I feel lopped off. Then she
called a number listed in the Yellow Pages, "Mobile Outreach."
A woman answered, a deep voice with good humor, Maidie felt.
Maidie envisioned her in a swiveling chair, wearing glasses,
chewing on a pencil eraser. Maidie said, "I'm having a small but
serious problem. I don't know if I've called the right place. I just
moved here and don't know anyone." The woman assured Maidie this was typical: "We get a lot of calls from army wives at
the base."

Maidie explained about Jack, the nonexistent sales meeting,
how they'd gotten married in Arkansas, then moved here for
Jack's job. He hadn't liked Arkansas either, where Maidie had
worked on her master's degree in sociology, the study of human
structures. "Hurry so we can move somewhere better," he'd
said.

"Uh huh," the woman said. "You don't know where he is."

"Yes." Maidie waited.

"It takes two to fuss and fight," the woman said.

"Yes," Maidie had said. But what else?

"Maybe you're a bad combination," the woman said.

This sounded systematic, like having your colors done, or deciding what vitamin to take. "How so?" Maidie asked. Maidie had married her first husband, Neville, right after her father divorced her stepmother, Neena—a coincidence Maidie hadn't noticed until years later, even though her sisters, Lucy and Thea, had married a pair of truckdrivers that same month. Anyway, an expert hired for a couples class at the church Maidie and Neville had joined—Maidie wanted God on her side in this gamble, marriage—pointed out that Neville was a Comfort Person and Maidie was a Goal Person. "That's a tough combination," he'd said.

"Maybe you don't get along," the woman in Virginia said.

"Obviously, at the moment," Maidie answered. She wondered who paid for hot lines. Who did they help, army wives? But *they* had each other, drinking coffee and twiddling thumbs while their husbands marched in circles. Maidie imagined a nowhere-to-turn corner, a dead-end cliff at which hot-line operators put up roadblocks and kept people from flying over. Maidie felt bad—what if someone worse off was trying to call now? "I'd better go."

The woman said, "I do my best. We all have limitations."

Maidie said, "But it helped so much to hear your voice," and hung up, realizing she couldn't use this phone call even as a joke to tell at cocktail parties, because how could she admit to a moment so depleted she'd told a dull-witted stranger her husband had run away from home? Honestly, Maidie thought, it was kinkier than phone sex, this impulse to divulge her troubles in public, in arenas where only Oprahic is spoken—a late-twentieth-century dialect fostered on TV and characterized by the use of phrases like *codependent, shared energy, touching the pain of others.* Jack had been driving and thinking, he explained four days later. Thriving and drinking, Maidie thought. He'd lied because he felt sure Maidie wouldn't understand, and she needed to trust that. He got fired: Maidie's fault for phoning, he pointed out. The manager had said, "Your marriage is your business, son, but don't use me as an alibi." Jack never got another job—he hardly looked for one—at least not in the final two years Maidie stayed married to him, working at the Civil War Museum.

But Maidie hated remembering that. Now was *now*. She'd been in Arizona long enough to situate herself. "Looks like you've been here forever," Rex said as he'd stepped into Maidie's house the first time. She'd unpacked her worldly goods, but her memories stayed disarranged: the past with its weak links to the present, and the vague suspicion her life was serial, not cumulative.

"Maidie?" Rona said. "You look peaked."

"I need to stand in the shade," Maidie said. But the perpetual sun, the deep-dyed, faithful sky, the winter that passed like a fugue to be clean forgotten, were what Maidie liked about Arizona. The climate, she said, her public version of why she'd be likely to stay here after having lived in six of the fifty United States in twelve years. Where are you from? people asked. Minnesota, she'd say. Or: all over. She'd list the places she'd been. People stopped listening. Who could blame them? Maidie's neighbor in Virginia, Dodie, had watched Maidie pack the U-Haul and said, misty-eyed, "Promise you'll write." Maidie froze a smile—like she'd been caught eating dessert before everyone else. "Sure," she'd said. But she'd thought: No way. In terms of a six-state flight out of tight spots, an exodus to an obliterating place where blessings fall like hail, you haven't been so important. But she wrote down the address anyway.

She'd turned hollow, having fired and rehired the staff of her life so often, having said so many times: That person is no longer a part of me, to be replaced. Once, she'd told Rona, "The best part of moving is it makes you aware the world is full of new people you can love." A chain of those people, their shifting, convoluted opinions, snaked through Maidie's past. A neighbor who offered advice. A couple who treated Maidie like a daughter, or granddaughter. There'd been a pair in every state, but Maidie found the first, the prototype, in Minnesota: Eugene and Vera Fleiderhaus had made room in their lives for Maidie, a cove she'd sailed into to escape the noise of her sisters, her father's hard-edged digs. Maidie's mother wasn't gone yet, just drifting.

Maidie had spent winter days with Eugene and Vera, dabbing paint from Vera's silver tubes onto child-sized canvases. The afternoon light waned. Maidie's mother arrived at sundown. She wandered through Eugene and Vera's house, examining quaint lamps, fusty chairs, the antique laundry mangle next to the fluorescent-lit aquarium with its kite-shaped fish darting. Maidie's mother—a scarf draped over her taut chignon—stared at one of Vera's paintings, in which an androgynous creature waved its hands, four fingers on one hand, six on the other. "This is"—she searched for a word—"an impassioned comment on the uniqueness each of us has, still flowering." What the painting meant to Maidie was that each of us got to the same end but by odd means. Still flowering? Maidie pictured the ends of people's arms turning into bouquets, fluffy and symmetrical like feather dusters. Vera shrugged, embarrassed. Eugene said, "I like it, but I'm no expert." Maidie's mother said, "Sure you are, deep inside."

On the way home, she'd said, "Of all the marriages I know, Eugene and Vera's is the only one that's"—the car slid on ice—"fair." Maidie thought about Eugene and Vera's marriage. Comely. Equitable. Fair sky. Fair treatment. Maidie's mother's conversations were one-sided like that, proclamations emerging laterally, not straightforward. Short-lived enthusiasms pocked by her mother's latest favorite word: *autocratic, ego, impassioned.* "His problem is his monstrous ego," Maidie's mother said once for two months about Maidie's dad. Later, she talked less; she went into a room and shut the door. Later yet, she moved away.

By the time Maidie was standing in the hot sun listening to Rona talk about oil and water, a bad mix, terminal love, Maidie's mother had been gone so long Maidie forgot she was missing—no mysterious phantom aching and itching. Maidie made friends instead, a trial-and-error series. But lately Maidie meant to rule out the category of friend, advice giver. It hurt: she wanted it out, a tumor. Rona said, "Rex is well-liked, but maybe he has a pathological need to be well-liked, and you play into that."

Maidie also thought she'd better rule out the category of lover. The men she'd been with, one at a time, had seemed so able to say out loud what was important to them, or bound to be, sooner than Maidie could even consider what might be important to her down the line. A sense of intricacy—a premonition no question had answers as untangled as the first ones that thrust themselves forward—forced Maidie to wait and see, to let her notion of what was right and reasonable evolve. Meanwhile, a man drew up plans, remodeled the status quo, shifted doubt to the other side of the map, and Maidie was still thinking, sifting, a sense of foreboding swelling like a blister. Even so, Maidie tended to believe a man with a stiff opinion.

She said to Rona, "We all want to be well-liked."

Rona said, "But Rex sets out to charm people."

Maidie considered it. A coworker she'd introduced Rex to had described him as "impressive." Someone less specific called him "wonderful." Someone else said he seemed "deep." Rona's husband, Harve, had said, "If you land him, you'll have done good." The Rex Hurley Fan Club, Maidie thought. A few times lately, she'd glimpsed a rehearsed quality, maybe, a confirmed self-awareness—as Rex filled someone's glass, or took his hat off to say hello in a soft voice—that he'd be well-received. Maidie said, "Perhaps a person's best quality, overdone, is a fault?"

Rona said, "But you might be a bad mix too."

Maidie said, "If we are, then I am with everyone." The sun beat down. Maidie thought: Why this conversation? Why Arizona? Why Rex, which rhymes with hex? Her first husband, Neville, had left her. But she'd given up on her second, no refund. Rex seemed like a stand-in, his outward features unique but his deep-buried hopes and qualms and plans for Maidie unchanged: triplicate. Or not. Maidie once read an article that suggested children of migrant workers—with their nomadic lives, detaching, re-annexing—develop a buffering mechanism called "situational narcissism," which lets them see people as indistinguishable, replaceable. If Maidie was narcissistic, she decided, she'd better keep it under wraps until she fixed herself.

Rona pawed the air with her three-clawed gardening tool. "Maidie, you have tapes playing in your head installed by your parents." Maidie cringed. What was her head, a piece of electronics? Why this emphasis on parents? Maidie tried to protect herself from people who probed. Up to a point, she was flexible. Then, a rebounding bulwark, pushing back at the person who hadn't noticed her reservations and inklings, the implied wall.

No Trespassing.

A practical side effect was that at work Maidie seemed not brusque but competent. Last week, as she spoke on the phone to a museum director in Oklahoma while arranging to attend the Multi-State American Studies Conference there, he'd offered Maidie a better job. Maidie wrote the salary and benefits on a pad near her phone. A few days later, sorting through a pile of notes, Maidie had wondered what the message she'd scrawled in a hurry meant: "Jobe Okra-home." *There was a man in the land of Uz named Job.* Maidie thought of Job's afflictions: dead children and a bitter wife, his parched crops and boils, a rocky pillow spilling sleeplessness in every direction. No, Maidie shouldn't go to Oklahoma.

She'd arrived here, where life was still a science of loopholes.

Exits.

Late one night in Virginia, the phone had rung, insistent, and it turned out to be Laree, the roommate Maidie had lived with in a trailer house in a field of weeds outside Jackson Hole. That's where Maidie still pictured Laree, on the striped black sofa, reaching for the yellow bong on its cut-glass tray on the cherry coffee table. "Bongs with coffee in the a.m.," Laree used to say, sitting Indian style, wearing a short blue dress, her hair parted in the middle, stuffed behind her ears, making her face a shiny triangle. She laughed. *Laree.* Maidie stood in the rented house in Virginia—she and Jack had lived there two years—and reminded herself that Laree's dress, circa 1975, would be rags now, a trace in a dump, a Wyoming midden. Laree might wear her hair short, live in a squat house decorated in state-of-the-Wal-Mart mauve with teal accents, a country duck here and there.

"God," Laree said. "You were hard to find."

Maidie said, "Laree?"

Then—after so many years—Laree said, "How are you, girl?" And moved on to her own answers to the same question. "Me. Not so good. He's driving me nuts. Nuts. Wait, he can hear."

Maidie didn't know who "he" was. "Phil?" The name popped out of old recesses: Phil, the father of the baby Laree never had. The phone line crackled, intermittent, the way Maidie remembered it did in Wyoming, wind blowing against the wires. Surely they had underground cable now? "Where are you?" Maidie asked.

Laree said, "Wyoming, silly. Not with Phil. But I'm stuck again. I am a true-life geek magnet." Her voice dropped to a whisper.

Maidie didn't understand. "Are you afraid of him?"

Laree said, "No! He's a geek. Understand? I wanted to say hi. Maidie, I thought we should stay in touch. How are you, girl?"

Maidie thought how to answer. "Same here," she said. "Nuts."

In the next room, Jack's TV made its potshot angry noises. The day before, he'd flung a pan of steamed mussels—a luxury they shouldn't have afforded with Jack not working—against the TV until every perfectly cooked morsel of flesh and juice had pelted the walls just painted forest green because, Maidie had said as she'd painted the TV room walls herself, she and Jack were ready to stay now. *Stay.* This is also what she said to dogs that harassed her when she walked to work. She'd picked up the black shells, their shriveled innards. The mussels-flinging had occurred because . . . Maidie didn't know. This time, she could trace faint origins to, first, a trip to the grocery store, where Jack had insisted on an orderly shopping cart—small canned goods up front, large here, dairy products down here—but it all got jumbled in the bags at the checkout stand. Then Jack and Maidie had skirted the aisles of a video store uneasily, settling on a 1963 western because it had action, which Jack required, and an old-fashioned historical quality, since Maidie would be watching it too. A compromise, Jack pointed out.

Oof. Bang. Crash. That was just the movie.

Maidie had served dinner on a tray. Some Indians, Jack said, Comanches, for example, deserved to be slaughtered because they'd been heartless themselves, slaughtering. This ran counter to Maidie's perception of most Native American experience in the West. How did he know? Maidie had asked. Books he'd read. Which ones? she'd asked, doubtful. She stopped when she saw his face transformed by the TV: altered, indoctrinated. The shooting and stabbing, the corpses, guts in the sand. A familiar taste, adrenaline, flooded Maidie's mouth. He threw the pan of mussels at the wall next. This was the two minutes preliminary to the fight.

But two years of living together had led to the decision to marry Jack.

Jack's mother once said, "I don't feel you're compatible." (A bad mix, maybe?) "Though he does try hard to treat you well."

Newfangled

In Virginia, Maidie finally called 911—months after Jack threw mussels at the TV. She answered the door, blood in her mouth, two broken fingers, her black-and-blue left breast hoisted into her bra as if into a sling. She didn't show her breast to the cop, no. But he pointed his flashlight at her mashed fingers, her sloppy mouth, and said to Jack: "You might not get along with your wife. But certain behaviors aren't, well, civilized."

"My advice," Laree said, "is to shake things up. Yikes."

She dashed off the phone.

She's in Wyoming, Maidie thought. But with what last name?

Counting her maiden name, Maidie had three. Giddings. Kramer. Bonasso. Maidie wished she'd thought of keeping Giddings when she married Neville. It would have been strange, of course, to keep Neville's name when she married Jack. *Druthers,* she thought. *If wishes were horses.* She shouldn't have married at all.

The sun beat down. Rona said, "You need to erase those old tapes."

Tapes, again. And Rona.

Maidie should have known better: Don't befriend a neighbor, because it's like having an affair with a coworker: the forced contact afterward, proximity when you want out. But Maidie had caved in. This year, Easter had seemed sadder than Christmas, family sounds floating though open windows, people passing on the sidewalk with baskets, tricycles. She didn't have to think very hard to remember times when she'd tried to ingratiate herself with a neighbor, a coworker, a date, worrying each gesture, each shift of the moon, might mar the chance for temporary . . . love? No. Company.

But she could start over.

In an escape hatch. A sanctuary. Oklahoma!

Already she was imagining the prairie, its weeds and steady wind, the blood-red sunsets, oil wells dotting the horizon like

25

religious icons. And the flat, naked miles: even in the city, a hushed dearth of populace. Maidie pictured the sidewalks, the vacant houses, a highway stretching empty and endless as after-life.

But she'd read just the other day—in *Glamour,* was it?—not to throw out a friendship the minute it seemed insufficient, but to embrace the aspect of the friend you'd liked in the first place and ignore the part you didn't. This applied to Rona, surely. But to Rex? To Arizona? Maidie had turned up here, the arid zone, because she'd run away from darkness, dampness, wed-lock, to solitude, this mildew-resistant state. Another piece of advice she'd garnered in the last year was this: Just because you know you're somewhere you have to leave doesn't mean you have to leave in the next five minutes. She'd heard it at a branch of AA designed for spouses of drinkers—the only free advice Maidie could locate in those flat-broke last days in Virginia. "You need to get a job or move out," she'd told Jack. He said, "Try and make me," and folded his arms over his chest. He wasn't an alcoholic, but Maidie kept that to herself as the other members spoke and prayed. And she concentrated on the med-itations about serenity by thinking of Jack's anger as liquor, his addiction she couldn't fight. Let Go and Let God. And Maidie would think she wanted a drink herself: Let Go and Let Vodka.

She wondered if Jack had been born angry—offended by his first gulp of air. During the two-month, subdued courtship in which he'd convinced Maidie to take a chance, move in with him, she'd mistaken his single-mindedness for repressed, un-coiling purpose. Desire. Five years later, scanning the *Norfolk News,* she read a profile of the typical abusive man: he was ge-netically programmed to respond with action, not language; his childhood had likely ended too soon, abruptly; he'd been knocked around by the time he was ten; as an adult, he was un-employed. Maidie set the newspaper down. She had psycho-social facts, an analytical perspective, but she still didn't understand Jack's anger—where it had come from, how far it might go—and probably never would.

She got away.

To this job, with a small moving allowance too. She said to Rona, "I can't stand in this sun a minute longer." Rona smiled, her brown eyes as sympathetic as chocolate. Maidie said, "I have a lot to do before I leave for Oklahoma." She got in her car to go back to work. She sensed conversion, a meltdown, the personnel in her life about to shift again. She was durable. She'd reconstituted. She'd sliced and diced. She wanted to *stay*. She didn't. Which one, what people, would finally be her life?

The first people who were Maidie's life as far back as she could remember—the first sensory tableaux impressed on her like a seal in wax—were her mother (her mother's lap and arms swathed in voile, her soft perfumy bosom), also Eugene and Vera Fleiderhaus, and, in the offing, Vera's mother, a stick figure in a red kimono and stage makeup, her eyes black and furred, her lips carmine. She hobbled, poking with her cane at roots and stones embedded in the green lawn that spread to the lake like felt on a billiards table. Maidie's mother stood, and everyone moved, a gentle swell, toward Eugene and Vera's house, where, according to Maidie's memory, her father was at the sink, spot-cleaning his trousers with lighter fluid because a june bug had squashed on them. Lucy and Thea were shrieking—Lucy racing and skipping near the fence, Thea just born and squalling for the breast, or bottle, Playtex most like mother herself. Vera's father, a knobby old man in a hat, tinkered with a bamboo fishing pole.

As they moved to the house, Vera's mother called out, raspy like a crow, "How dare you leave me here. Who knows what trouble I might stir up?" Everyone billowed back to enfold her, take her in.

Eugene and Vera were like Maidie's grandparents.

For instance, Maidie's dad had said about Eugene, "This man is like a father to me." He'd pontificated about Eugene one Sunday when everyone—Pastor and Mrs. Larssen included—ate dinner at a big table in the Bauer House Family Restaurant. "He taught me everything," Maidie's dad said, patting Eugene's back but staring into Pastor Larssen's eyes. It has to do with God, Maidie thought. *We plead guilty of all sins, even those we do not know.* "I owe him," Maidie's dad continued. And Maidie wondered if he owed Eugene a favor. He did owe money. Eugene was selling his insurance business to Maidie's dad, little by little, a low price. Out of the goodness of his heart! "And so we're obliged," Maidie's dad said when they visited Eugene and Vera's house.

Behind their house was a field—rusty hubs of wagon wheels lay strewn across it, also cusps of pails, old kettles, axles, all of them rust-burnished to a sparkling color, *cordovan* according to Maidie's Crayola crayons, the dictionary of color. Maidie had walked in this field with Eugene and Vera, Eugene pointing out artifacts, once even unearthing a huge white bone, like driftwood, only pearly. He said a great battle had been fought there long ago. Maidie's mother said later, "Really? I don't think so. Perhaps someone lived there. Maybe it's a cow bone?"

Eugene winked, mysterious.

"You!" Maidie's mother smiled, shaking her handkerchief at him.

Next to the main house stood a clapboard guesthouse, its entire circumference a porch and, inside, pine cupboards, a funny old stove in the middle of the floor; Vera's parents stayed here. Every summer, they rode the Northern Pacific from California to Minnesota.

When Maidie was seventeen—living with her father and sisters, who seemed to be of a more resilient, decisive breed of human than Maidie, and with her stepmother, Neena, whom

Maidie hated at first sight, which was actually a long time before, when Maidie's father was still married to Maidie's mother but hovering near Neena like a moth near light—she felt vaguely bereft and, though she didn't understand it yet, orphaned. One cold January night, she rode with a boy named Joel Scribner in a car to Tornado Lake, where Eugene and Vera's house stood locked, impregnable. Maidie and Joel managed to pry open the rickety guesthouse; they went inside, made love on a bed, a pocket of musty covers, Maidie meanwhile thinking how no one had slept here in years, that everyone who had was dust now, bones and cottony boll-weevil hair. Joel, making love to her, had long brown hair like silk threads, muscled shoulders, a worried face. Though she didn't love him, she felt sure—based on the scant knowledge she had (his brother had died last year, his father years before)—she could.

But that summer day long ago, they went inside for Kool-Aid. *Nectarella,* Vera's mother called it, a brand name from her past. "I don't remember Nectarella in this bright-purple color," she said grumpily, sitting in a rocking chair with swirly designs. She let Maidie play with her bracelet—a jade-encrusted circle of emblems that looked like cameos but with Cleopatra's head. She pointed this out. "See? The Queen of the Nile, not some Victorian simp." She also had a cream-colored makeup suitcase that sat on its back, opened into a satin-lined pyramid containing gold vials of rouge and powder. She used to be an actress, before they talked in movies. Sometimes Maidie thought that if she were making a movie, she would never have Vera and her mother related. Vera wore her hair in a gray helmet, bangs level with her eyes, silver glasses that pointed up like crooked tears, a color-spattered flannel shirt, with trousers. Vera painted pictures, but the man in California who used to sell them for her twenty years earlier, before she moved to Minnesota to marry Eugene, stopped trying hard, and now she wasn't famous.

When the Kool-Aid was gone, a discussion followed in which

Maidie's mother decided that Vera's father, with his bad knees and weak heart, shouldn't fish off the pier without someone to call for help, and since Maidie was the oldest child, Maidie should fish with him. Eugene fixed her up a pole. Maidie's mother walked with Maidie to the lake. "There you go, dear." Maidie loved the long bamboo pole, the way it tilted over the water like a palm. They stood together for . . . an hour? Maidie spoke: "They don't seem to be biting." And: "Enjoying your visit?" He wouldn't even turn his head. Maidie wondered if he was deaf, or angry they'd sent a child to watch him. She looked at his patchy skin, his shoulders stooping inward. At the time, she'd thought there were two kinds of people, young and old. You were born that way and, apart from gradations, didn't change. Then Maidie noticed the sun glimmering like red wax on the carpet of lilies that stretched across the water. The crickets started chirping and, next, the frogs, their thrumming rubber-band ragtime, like the Gershwin record Maidie liked her father to play, consonance and dissonance, harsh notes crying out for soft answers.

Thirty years later, Maidie spotted a Gershwin tape in a sale bin at a gas station and bought it—along with a tank of gas and Coca-Cola in a cup called "Big Gulp." She played the Gershwin tape that evening as she sat on her patio watching the paloverde trees in her backyard twist in the night breeze, in seeming rhythmic deference to the first gorgeous chords of "Summertime." The trees I have left in my life, she thought, remembering the long-gone summers in Minnesota, the whispering oaks, maples, elms, and pines. She stood up, walked into the living room, hit Power/Off. She turned on the TV instead, a comforting, preventive dose: plugged into the national mood, absorbing the same broadcast as everyone, she couldn't be crazy.

Or sad. So she thought, watching the Miss Universe pageant, Bob Barker's stand-in stressing that it wasn't a beauty contest anymore, beauty was inside. The sparkly, full-bosomed women licked their teeth, shook their hair, answered questions about humanity's future. Miss Canada talked about physical fitness. Miss U.S.A. came from a toxic family and overcame it. "If I can, you can!" she said. Miss India wouldn't make the next cut, Maidie felt—she'd said something too complex about overpopulation. When Miss Peru spoke through an interpreter about the importance of familial love, Maidie felt pleasureless, queasy: she wondered if she had PMS. A Purina commercial came on next—a gangly dog bounding through a linoleumed kitchen. *Because they love us,* the voice-over said. A simple answer: Love a dog.

But six years old, on the pier with Vera's father, she marveled at the sun, the quiet lap of waves, the frogs' perfect hymn. Then another noise interrupted the frogs. It groaned; it croaked. It set Maidie's teeth on edge. Of course—she sneaked a look at Vera's father, motionless as a statue—it could be him. Did he have a stomachache? No. Maidie felt sure it was frogs, maybe tree frogs, whereas the first were lake frogs. This idea seemed pretty to Maidie, each frog with a tree of its own, or a lily pad, a silky green mat with a bloom for an ornament so beautiful it was an endangered species. But then Vera's father passed wind so lewdly, with so much satisfaction, that it became obvious, indubitable. Maidie had been operating under the assumption that, with their sloppiness and foul-ups, only children passed wind, not understanding yet that sloppiness and foul-ups are what children and old people have in common. Maidie laid her pole down and climbed up the long, spooky stairway that cut through the green grass and trees.

Indoors, everyone was settling down to watch the cartoon version of *Pinocchio.* "Did you leave Vera's father on the pier?" Maidie's mother asked. Maidie nodded, and Vera went to bring him in. Maidie's father and Eugene were talking about a new car called a Beetle. Eugene admired its efficient design. Maidie's father said, "But if small cars take off, they'll hurt the economy, my insurance premiums most of all." Maidie liked the idea of a car named a Beetle, also the beginning of *Pinocchio,* the story swinging upward, happy, the klutzy puppet who came to life loved by an accidental father. The father is flesh, lots of it. Pinocchio is wood. Love solves that. Then Pinocchio starts blowing it, lie after lie. He could stop himself if he wanted. Maidie looked at Lucy to see if she felt scared. Lucy stared at the screen, engrossed, beatific. Then Vera came inside, making a racket as she helped her father sit next to her mother on the sofa. And Lucy yelled, "Stop it, all of you! I can't hear Pinocchio."

Maidie's mother scolded. "Lucy!"

Maidie stayed hopeful. What kids' show would have a dead puppet? What was a dead puppet? A real puppet. She felt embarrassed: Lucy, who was only four, was thrilled. Still, as time passed, Pinocchio's limbs seemed more fragile, like hinged toothpicks, his smile forced. His circumstances? A fat man for a substitute father, who might look scrubbed and generous on TV. But old men in real life are grouchy and smell like mothballs. So what if he carved Pinocchio? Maidie looked at Vera's father. Couldn't he say hello? Outdoors, the sky darkened. The forest behind the house seemed gnarled, and the depths below the green surface of the lake lethal. "I don't like this show," Maidie said.

"Button up," her father said.

"You're being rude," Maidie's mother whispered.

In the next room, Thea woke crying, loud.

"For Christ's sake, Elaine," Maidie's dad said. "Get the baby." Suspense.

When Maidie was nineteen and living with Laree, she had to leave the house on the nights Laree stayed up watching *Rosemary's Baby, Last House on the Left, Let's Scare Jessica to Death.* Maidie didn't understand: watch a movie about people with endearing habits, relent, love them, then watch them get hacked to pieces or impregnated with evil sperm? And those

long nights in Nebraska . . . Neville was supposed to get in at
2:00 but, after a few months, stayed out drinking with other orderlies, nurses too, and by 6:00 A.M. ended up at The Kettle,
talking about nothing, smoke and claptrap, to drunks. Sometimes Maidie went to find him. Most nights, she paced. Outside, the prairie—infinite and peaceful by day—seemed like the
ocean back when sailors thought the earth was flat, with edges,
drop-offs. And she watched their old TV—mechanically impaired so that images and faces, even on a Christian talk show
called *Truth as I See It,* beamed out crooked, like *Batman* when
the villains cook up death. So Maidie tuned into the radio,
country music, its homely moral (if you sin and feel bad, it's not
sinning), and sewed small, bright flowers onto pillow slips.
How much worse does it get? What's worse than the black
night? Dawn, if you haven't slept.

Six years old, Maidie stood up. "I don't want to watch," she
said. Pinocchio was sinking in water, the whale's mouth wide
open.

"Sugar honey, hush." Maidie's mother tipped Thea back and
forth.

"Elaine!" Maidie's father turned in his chair, his face tight.
"We all have jobs to do. Yours is to keep the baby quiet."

Lucy said, "Make Thea shut up."

Thea loud, louder.

Sometimes, when Maidie's dad said we all have jobs to do,
Maidie's mother gritted her teeth and asked where her paycheck was. Maidie's dad gave different answers. Once: "Who
else would have taken you in"—he paused—"under the circumstances?" Maidie's mother turned pale, like she was sick.
But most of the time he sounded sad: "I don't know what else I
can possibly give you."

Thea squalled, her face mottled.

Maidie stood next to Vera's chair. Vera turned her head; her
eyes focused behind their silver frames. Maidie said, "Thea's

face is dark red." Vera nodded. "Almost vermilion." Maidie thought this was funny. She laughed. Then something knocked her head, the dreaded finger. Maidie's dad reached his arm out—he liked the sneak attack—then *snapped* his big fingers on your temple. Maidie's mother didn't like it; he did it to Lucy once when she was so little her head bobbled. Mostly, it embarrassed Maidie. Her dad said, "Amuse yourself, but not here."

Vera's mother and father were asleep, upright but tilted, their mouths gaping like dead people's, skull faces. Vera said, "Come on, then." And she led Maidie through the house—lit in just one corner by the TV—and down a hall, up a flight of stairs. Vera pulled on a light string, and they stood in the room where Vera painted. A pungent smell of turpentine. And trifles everywhere. A short Venus de Milo next to a Roy Rogers lunchbox, a tobacco can, a red-handled spoon, a plaster fish blowing pink bubbles, a filigree crucifix (IRAE) next to salt and pepper shakers that said, together, God Bless (salt) This Mess (pepper).

Vera sat on a stool. Maidie remembered how, once, Lucy sat in Vera's lap uninvited, no warning, and Vera's arms floated up like they were filled with helium; she shifted, a look on her face as if a small animal had sneaked in. Maidie looked around—the stillness, the clutter—and understood she liked Vera's room the same way she liked music or stained-glass windows. Things combined, their complicated side effects, were better than one thing alone. A statue of a lizard seemed to watch as a woman on a ship made of seashells sailed toward a fruity pitcher. Maidie looked into Vera's face and, in that instant, committed herself to loving Vera for—how long?—forever. She'd start slow, make Vera receive love willingly. Then Maidie's dad came in. "Plain Jane," he said. "Movie Star." (Which one was she? Maidie wondered.) "Time for your beauty rest." He twirled Maidie over his head. For a minute she nearly laughed loud, like Lucy. Maidie's mother stood in the doorway, inscrutable, relieved, half happy.

* * *

Sporadic. Intermittent. Half happy. Maidie sometimes wondered if her father's improved mood, rolling upward and sunny, his daybreak smile, was better than anyone else's—a tonic like dandelion wine—because of the gloom that preceded it, the months and weeks Maidie watched his face for a sign some small change had relieved him. Lucy's memories didn't match Maidie's. "He wasn't so bad," she said, an adult now. Maidie wondered: Had he got to static despondency, the last rung down, by the time Lucy was old enough to remember? Thea, who'd known him only downtrodden, would shout: "Dad! Cheer up!" She shouted it from the steps of the church on her wedding day, her dress bunched in her hands, banged-up knees exposed above the pumps she clomped around in like horseshoes. "Cheer down," he quipped back, the ironic style he'd settled on to deflect attention from his basic fact, misery.

Who knew what he did home alone? Maidie wondered.

She went back to Minnesota for the wedding (wedding*s*: Lucy and Thea got married in the same ceremony), with her own new husband, Neville, in tow. They'd traveled by plane, the first time for both of them—Neville clutching the plastic armrests, his brow furrowing as the flight attendant explained oxygen masks and flotation cushions. The engine roared. The wing flaps raised up. The wheels clumped, whirring, across the tarmac. Neville grimaced. Maidie, on the other hand, liked sipping cool drinks in a high-velocity living room, contained but lofty. Small distractions below—cars, houses, people, life, death—blurred by, undetected. When the plane stopped, Maidie didn't; her torso flew.

They went to a motel and dressed for the wedding, Neville in a suit he'd worn just once, to his own wedding three weeks earlier. Maidie hadn't invited her family. "A small ceremony," she'd

said over the phone. No one mentioned wanting to come— not Lucy, Thea, her dad. Her ex-stepmother, Neena, sent a quiche dish. "I use mine a lot," the card said. Maidie had wanted just Neville's family, the muted, genial tone of them. "Golly!" Mr. Kramer would say in response to anything. "Golly," he said when Maidie and Neville said they were getting married. They wanted the wedding at the family farm. "Jiminy," Mrs. Kramer said, "we'd better mark the day on the calendar." Maidie had known Mr. and Mrs. Kramer a few weeks, Neville a few months. She'd pitched marriage as he lay on the floor of the trailer in Jackson Hole, watching the Three Stooges. She'd said, "Partners, see? I'd be your friend with whom to face life's battle. We could live in Nebraska." Wyoming seemed used up. She'd grown bored with her job, with classes at the junior college, with Laree, who, having aborted Phil's baby, cooked and cleaned for him and spoke always about what he liked. Phil really likes green beans, she might say. "Okay," Neville agreed. "We'll get married."

They moved to his hometown, Weeping Water, Nebraska.

The minister pointed out in prenuptial counseling that it helps for a couple to have something in common—the same minister who later hired the expert to say in front of God and all his parishioners that Neville liked Comfort, while Maidie liked Goals. Driving home from the church, Maidie asked Neville what he thought about the minister's doubts. Neville shrugged. "We have things in common," he said. Maidie asked, "What?" He said, "Music." Maidie contemplated. She listened to country stations then, true; everything else shredded her nerves like cheese, like raw knuckles. But she and Neville didn't like the same songs. She hated lyrics about great happiness. Love my country, my wife, my ancestors, great life. She liked a song to say something simple: for instance, that homegrown tomatoes were good, in fact better than love. But did it matter? The wedding was on. Then over. Neville stood near Maidie, polished, groomed—a groom, still—at Lucy and Thea's double wedding in Hector, Minnesota.

Maidie had turned respectable and settled in Nebraska, she felt. In her mind's eye, she saw herself from the edge of the crowd in her blue dress, accessorized with a white purse and shoes, and imagined the other guests saying: That's the older sister from out West. They'd configure a life for her, perhaps better than the one she lived. They'd picture her nested, a frame house, a garden, a quilt-making business on the side, rows of stewed tomatoes in Mason jars on larder shelves. This is what Maidie hoped for once Neville got organized and saved money from his orderly job—*orderly:* she liked the tone of it—and Maidie from her two part-time jobs and the better job she'd get when she finished college.

Thea had tossed aside her veil and stuffed her hair, blond and floaty like a corn tassel, through the hole in the back of a white cap that had the name of a golf ball, PING, in front. At the rehearsal dinner she'd worn a black floral dress with a black cap that said FENDER STRATOCASTER in red letters She worked at the Golf Pro shop twenty hours a week, the rest of the time in a local band, stomping across the stage with a microphone, shouting out slogans like *Take me, Make me, Hit me with a good shot.* Her husband drove a Pepsi truck and played guitar. Lucy's husband—she'd known him since high school—drove a white truck with a compartment refrigerated to minus 70: frozen bull sperm. He covered three counties, pulling up at farms to hop out, open the freezer compartment—steam wafted up, icy—remove the sperm, slide on a plastic glove, stick a long tube into a cow's butt, pat her, and say, "Okay, Bossie." (Lucy had talked Maidie into riding with him once.) But on his wedding day he wore a tuxedo with red lapels; Thea's groom too. Neena sat across the room, the banished ex-stepmother.

Maidie wondered if any of Lucy or Thea's new in-laws had asked about their mother. "Is she still living?" Neville's mother had asked Maidie the night before the wedding. They were washing dishes. Maidie considered answers. "I think so," she said at last. Neville's mother nodded. "Let's let the big pans soak."

Maidie's dad said, "I see Neena had the sense not to bring a date." He handed Maidie a drink, a cocktail napkin tucked beneath it. He tilted his head, smiled, wiggled his eyebrows vigorously.

"What?" she said. And she realized her father was flirting.

With her. She was twenty-three then, the approximate age of the women he'd targeted his whole life. Maidie remembered sitting at his favorite table in the Bauer House Family Restaurant, sixteen years old and looking away as he pinched a waitress maybe only ten years older than Maidie. He'd stopped talking to Maidie—directly, that is, looking into her face and waiting for her answer—by the time she'd turned into a preteen, a short, lumpy version of a woman. Until now. He probably didn't know how else to act, she thought. She patted his arm. "You look handsome, Dad." He said, "You too—much prettier than when you were little." Maidie stared across the room at Neville dancing with Thea—the Twist—Thea's white skirts and slips frothing like egg whites, and Neville in his brown suit. How unsettling, Maidie thought, to watch a tall man capable of dignity squat, contort, twist. He mopped his brow with his satin decorative handkerchief—clownish, grandiloquent. "I didn't know your little sisters were so much fun," he'd said, moments earlier. Maidie wondered if he meant he should have held out for one.

Dinner was served—pizza. The groomsmen charged into the golf course pond in their tuxedos. Maidie's father gestured across the dance floor. "So this is your husband? He seems . . . comfortable."

Maidie said, "What's that supposed to mean?"

Lucy floated by, wearing her veil flipped back like a hood. She said, "Lighten up, Maidie. He means what's-his-name is mellow."

Mellow. A word associated with amber liquor, also people who smoke pot.

Maidie had quit, after barely trying it. She'd smoked with Laree—in the morning sometimes—then headed down the highway to work, a big roar surrounding her car, her body, her soul, like a giant was asleep and snoring behind the next hill, the wind his steady breath. The blue sky. The red buttes. Flecks moving in the distance: tractors, cattle, men on horses. And everywhere sunshine and hay, a cheerful yellow color like egg yolks. But once Maidie got to her job—filing papers on the fifth floor of the courthouse—the roar turned into a buzz, a gnat's headache. And people who lined up on the first floor for licenses, blood tests, water samples, birth certificates, made her ache. She overheard:

A woman: I thought this was the year we'd try to be happy.

A child: Where will Daddy live, Mom?

A man: We did try.

The woman again: It was football, our downfall, I swear.

Eventually Maidie told Laree, "I'm allergic, I think." To pot, she meant, its magnified afterimage: life's flaws reproduced, swollen.

But a few days after her wedding, she'd agreed to take psilocybin mushrooms, a wedding present: Neville's cousin had wrapped a double dose in pink paper with flocked bluebells. Maidie meanwhile had enrolled in another college class—this time, they wrote essays by consulting a book with subject-matter units: for instance, Death & Dying. Elisabeth Kübler-Ross talking about stages of grief. Ivan Illich reconsidering his life from the deathbed perspective. William Raspberry saying death was inevitable but one's last living days were an arena of choice. The teacher, who seemed to drink too much coffee, hopped around and said that if we avoided someone's death, didn't want to see it, attend it, perhaps we hadn't accepted our own; we thought, maybe, we had forever. Death & Dying—the unit—hovered in the sky above Maidie's way of thinking. A clot, a tangle, a cloud. It hung over her wedding. From this day forward, as long as we both shall live. Maidie closed her eyes and tried to picture death: she saw a navy-blue field with icy stalactites. It wasn't cozy.

They'd taken the mushrooms carefully, in chicken soup, then climbed a ladder to the roof of the garage because Neville wanted to lie on the shingles and stare at the sky, he said. Nature, he said. In tune with my being. Death & Dying, Maidie thought. And she couldn't stop thinking. A navy-blue heaven with jagged edges. A grave, a box. Death seemed tight and dark all of a sudden. She said, "Neville?" The feathery ends of tree branches wavered. She said, "Neville, what do you think it will be like after we die?" Acorns fell on shingles. *Lllmmmph. Mmmm.* These were the sounds Maidie heard next. Neville lay on his back, hands behind his head. He was wearing his thick glasses, a blue terry-cloth robe. "Do you think about it?" Maidie said. "Life after we die. I mean, nonlife . . ." She floundered. "I can't say I do," he answered. She kept up. "If you did, what might you think?"

He said, "I'd think I was glad my stomach didn't hurt."

He rolled over on his side and moaned. His stomach rumbled. They went indoors. The rest of the night, he slept and moaned.

Maidie wandered through the house. Finally, she drank a glass of whiskey. Like Nyquil, she thought. So you get the rest you need.

Another glass. Another.

She drank at Lucy and Thea's wedding too. Neena crossed the room. Lucy said, "Hey there, Wicked Stepmother." She smiled. A joke.

Neena smiled back. "Bill," she said then, in a tone like: pothole, ice patch, snake. She turned to Maidie with her lawyer's smile. "How are you? Tell me about your wedding." Maidie started to describe the sunny day, Neville's grandmother's gladiolas a splash of color against the green, hazy fields. They'd borrowed tables from the Sunday school. Neighboring farm women had brought bowls of meatballs, buttermilk pie, melon salad, macaroni, iced tea. Mr. Kramer took his fiddle out of its velvet-lined case. Neena wasn't listening. "For Christ's sake," she said.

Mr. Kramer had a sweet voice; a yodel.

The song he sang: *It's a hard life, wherever you go.* And the old people had danced, bumping and gliding across the gravel driveway.

Onstage at the Golf Club, Thea folded the skirt of her wedding dress high, tucked it in. She tromped across the stage, the microphone cord a whip. "Hey, Lucy," she hollered. "Come up here."

Lucy smiled. "No."

"I think I'm going in," Lucy's husband said, taking off his jacket.

He meant the pond.

Thea sang. She belted out a stream of garbled words: *Thunder and pain. What's-a-matter-baby? We belong to the night out!*

"I'm turning into a pumpkin," Maidie's dad said.

Back at the motel, Maidie took off her shoes, her dress, earrings, hose, makeup. "Didn't you think," she asked Neville, "it was odd? Turning a wedding into a small-town prom, all that charging into muddy water, as if to say nice clothes were something you had to debase as soon as possible. And pizza. I'm surprised they didn't serve it in cardboard boxes." She turned around. Neville lay sleeping, a mound like a walrus under white bedsheets, his new suit a ball on the floor. This time, Maidie didn't wait to see if she'd sleep too. She put on jeans, tennis shoes, her coat. She drove back to the Golf Club. She didn't want to see anyone—and no one noticed when she took two bottles. She liked both colors. Sparkling, clean-white liquor:

like rubbing alcohol, elixir, liquid ice. Also smoky, dark liquor, chestnut, topaz, mahogany, the colors of a plush-lined study.

At the motel again, she turned on the TV station that broadcast printed snippets of news along with music: a narcotic mix of violins, tranquil bass lines, and—if there were vocals at all—singing like neutered angels. *A kiss, still a kiss. I got plenty of nothing. Hush now. Skip that lipstick, don't explain.* Maidie wandered up and down the motel sidewalk, the door open, Neville inside sleeping. How startling after the fact, she thought, Lucy's and Thea's wedding. How empty, like a book she'd opened to find blank pages inside, to have seen no one she knew, except of course the brides and grooms, Neena, and her own father. Whom had she hoped to see? A former schoolteacher? Pastor and Mrs. Larssen? Eugene? Vera? Dead or gone, all of them. Other lives, other kingdoms. She remembered a time, driving to Eugene's family reunion: supposedly, a little girl just Maidie's age would be there, and Maidie was being toted along to play with her. The aqua sedan crept forward—Eugene drove slowly—and Maidie sat between him and Vera on the aqua-checkered seat, admiring the bulbous chrome fixtures on the old dashboard.

Tonight she chose brown liquor because it went with the burgundy peignoir Neville's sisters had given her for a wedding gift. So she traipsed up and down the motel sidewalk in silky slippers, "scuffs," the ribboned, satiny ties of her thin robe fluttering like streamers behind. It was late, all the motel room windows dark except hers. She had another drink. She wished she had a sparkly, crystal glass, not this plastic cup. She sat on the hood of the car and wondered if Neville was a narcoleptic. She poured another drink—*those lazy, hazy, crazy days,* the TV sang—and wondered if she'd turned into an alcoholic. No. She was calming herself. She'd started drinking just since entering the stripped-down state of matrimony in which one bare fact glittered: she was more alone with Neville than without him.

The problem with drinking alone, Maidie came to see, apart from the obvious red flag—only bums and losers do it—was that once you'd drunk the drinks, you didn't have anything to do, or someone with whom to do it. At this point, she thought, you could make love. Or dance. If you lived near a lake, you could swim—if you could wake up your husband, that is. She sipped and looked at the faraway sky, the electrical wires bobbing and swaying.

*T*hinking and drinking, a brief history.

Sometimes Laree drank and Maidie followed suit, Laree's chattered directives. Drinking added up to dancing in the living room, Laree rushing across the room to pull a record off the turntable when the danceable song ended. "No, no," she'd cry if she set the tone arm down on a song that wasn't hot and swingy. Dancing made Laree relaxed but ecstatic. Her cheeks flushed red; her eyes shone. Maidie felt awkward, like at the one high school dance she'd gone to: too aware of her partner's impossible-to-follow torso gyrations, not to mention the floaty, uncivilized conversation.

Later, with Neville in Nebraska, Maidie really drank. One late night, walking around in black stretch pants, a silk tunic, a pair of '30s platform shoes she'd bought at a thrift shop, she listened to Billie Holiday, whom she'd discovered in the same thrift shop. She had the house decorated with Depression-era knickknacks too. She wished she had a cigarette holder. *Don't explain. You're my joy and pain.* For once, Neville came home on time. Maidie, in her diva costume, froze. She thought Neville might say: Sit down. Tell me what's bothering you. Or perhaps: You've gone insane. He said. "It smells like air freshener in here. Glade." And went into the next room to watch the crooked TV.

With Jack in Virginia, she learned to stay on her own end of the house with a full goblet under the halo of a lamp. She read magazines cast off by her next-door neighbor, Dodie, who subscribed to twenty-two because she hoped to win the Clearing House Sweepstakes. *Parent. Spy. Premiere. Travel & Leisure.* Fascinating particles of information! Frank Lloyd Wright had a temper. Queen Hussein was a mixed-up girl from Connecticut. Rita Hayworth was oversexed and her hairline had been altered. Back when Jack had a job, he'd come home wanting to talk about it, *sales.* He instructed Maidie to say that. What does your husband do? He's *in sales.* If they talked too long—Maidie offering encouragement as Jack said that he was smarter than his boss and thus felt constricted taking orders—or if Maidie suggested Jack hadn't considered his boss's perspective, the conversation blew up, a cyclical detonation. Once, Jack kicked a bag of groceries, his shiny wing-tip cleaving a purple onion into segments. Another time, he threw a hunk of cheese at Maidie's hatchback car as she drove away. Realizing she sounded almost ready for the Ricki Lake show, Maidie said, "You have to find a way to express anger." Repairing, sweeping up, apologizing, Jack agreed.

In Arizona, at first Maidie didn't drink. The day she arrived—having driven across eight states to get to Tucson, which seemed vast and partitioned with streets like runways—she pulled up in front of the house she'd rented and carried boxes inside. When she stopped to figure out how to move the big pieces of furniture off the trailer, a burly, smiling man came out of a house across the street—Harve, Rona's husband—and offered to help. Maidie's ears rang with the sound of vehicles she'd passed on the interstate, *thwip,* a loud reminder her car was a raft on a canal intended for barges. She stood on her porch—a *patio,* she supposed—and listened to strange noises. Uninsulated by hills and loamy ditches, traffic sounded flat, sonic.

She remembered the nights she'd stayed up, drinking. To avoid feeling separate from Neville, estranged yet wedded.

With Jack, to keep him away from the inside where she had, not secrets, but sore spots, lumps from the past. She'd told Jack once about waiting to tell her dad she was leaving home for Wyoming. Her dad put sunglasses on, flicked ice cubes from his cocktail into her face. "Cool out," he'd said, proud he'd learned the new slang. She'd packed and left. Downshifting his 4x4, Jack said, "Everyone's had bad times. My worry is that my wife isn't . . . Well, what should I say? Well-balanced." It hadn't helped to shout back like Barbra Streisand in *Nuts*. ("I'm undone, you filthy bastard!") Maidie learned to lie low, play possum. She drank cheap wine from the corner store with a plastic bull tied to the bottle: Toro. Jack barricaded himself in the TV room. Maidie ignored the gunshot blasts, the exploding cars, the melodramatic crest of synthesizers when bad guys got cornered.

She tiptoed, hid the wine, walked to work at the Civil War Museum, her jaw tender; she ground her teeth. At home, bills piled up faster than rings from soda bottles multiplied on the table next to Jack. Once, Maidie opened the TV room door. Five versions of Jack's résumé sat on the floor. He hated *sales* now. He flicked the remote control Off at her. He needed to take a sales job for stopgap, Maidie pointed out. He threw the receiver of the fax machine he didn't use anymore except to fax résumés. It hit Maidie in the face. Then he threw a punch. She remembers the rickety bang against her skull. In fact, all blows to Maidie's head had sounded like someone knocking on a hollow door. Maidie started applying for jobs that paid better. But as soon as she was interviewing for them at a conference in Washington, D.C.—boning up on notes while staring hungover into subway tracks—she understood she was planning a streamlined breakout.

To Tucson, this time. Where, the first night, stone cold sober, she slept on the patio on her old sofa from Virginia. Would she have drunk Toro if she knew where to get some? Yes. She woke when the sky turned coral. Doors slapped open. Traffic zoomed.

Someone somewhere brewed coffee. Maidie went inside and un-packed. She had to be at her new job the next day, at the Museum of Domestic History and Home Economy, where she'd sort and exhibit the seemingly trivial evidence of past lives: hat-pins, colanders, bootjacks, unwieldy gynecological instruments (circa 1880), old photographs, prams, and churns. She was chief curator, the only curator. The man who hired her, Garth McHugh, explained at the interview in Washington that certain people wanted to rename the museum: the Women's History Collection. "We might have to," he said, twitching his cheek muscles. "Surely a woman your age—I suppose you're a feminist—understands our pressure to suit semantic nitpick-ers." He'd outlined the salary, the moving allowance. "Is there a hubby?" *Hubby?* "No," Maidie had answered. And pictured herself in her new life, a sealed methodical environment in which she'd label, shore up, and realign each scrap until it found—and remained in—its fated niche forever.

Maidie sat in her office, its shelves stocked with archival sup-plies—Mylar photo protectors, nonbuffered tissue sheets, deacidified storage units, five bottles of Dust-Off Plus. And cu-rios that had drifted from their display cases: a replica of Mount Calgary grafted onto a geode, a gentlewoman's prayer book, a Mexican paperweight shaped like a pyramid, with a disembod-ied hand inside. And donated items that seemed irrelevant. An antique dentist's chair. Forty-two glass dogs. A pair of cowboy boots Willie Nelson wore when he penned "Crazy"—they'd be-longed to a trustee, who was also the granddaughter of the founder. Alma Kayser Willoughby, a rich widow and a Cofer College alumna (class of '13), had endowed the museum. So when her granddaughter, Cass, donated Willie Nelson's boots and a pedestal on which to exhibit them, no one had felt com-fortable even verifying their authenticity, Garth McHugh had explained. But Maidie, chief curator, should get rid of them; no one would complain, he added.

Maidie doubted it.

She remembered her stepmother, Neena, shouting at her law clerks: "You've reached your acme of incompetence!" This acme-of-incompetence terminology came from a book, *The Peter Principle,* which stressed that unqualified people got promoted until a corporation failed or a plane crashed. Maidie didn't dwell on the idea. Her so-called career had eventuated, a fluke; she was a fast reader. When she was a child, she'd gotten grounded for reading instead of cleaning house or cooking, or listening to her father talk about gumption or her mother quote Voltaire: "Marriage is the deathbed of Love." When she turned twenty and took a sociology class at the junior college, she'd liked the textbook. *Lost Rituals.* School wasn't as hard as getting Neville to sleep at home at night. In Arkansas, when Jack came in from work blustering, Maidie's research kept her distracted. Once, she wrote twelve pages about a late-nineteenth-century fad, Karezza, sex without orgasm, ongoingness without closure. Her point had been that it represented a collective fear of the next century, the next phase. Her baseboards weren't cleaner afterward, no pot boiled on the stove. But the red scrawl at the bottom of the page said *Brilliant and insightful if tentative.*

You were supposed to talk to teachers about school. "I see you lived in Nebraska," a professor might say. "How was that?" All Maidie could think was what Neville had looked like falling down drunk, his pants around his ankles, how sloe-black the sky seemed at night, or the curious aftermath once he moved out and Maidie still visited his parents. "Gloomy," she'd said. The professor put her transcript in a drawer. "Did you have a question about the exam?" Once, Maidie got a B on a paper, which is close to a C, which in graduate school is failing. The professor handed it back. Maidie read the comments and winced. A student she hardly knew said, "Your problem is you have no private life." He meant Maidie showed her emotions in public, or that if she'd had some hobby besides reading, a B wouldn't be tragic. At any rate, Maidie met Jack a few days later at the student union, at a Sam Peckinpah film festival. Maidie seemed like an earth mother, only smart, he'd said. The two of them hinged together like acrobatic tumblers, Frick and Frack. In two weeks, he bought Maidie an engagement ring on the ten-installment plan.

But in her new life in Tucson, Jack excised, Maidie sat at her desk. Disorder buzzed: too much, too soon. It still took three tries to turn on the kitchen light as opposed to the ceiling fan or outdoor lamp. Yesterday she'd gotten halfway to work before she realized she had a blue pump on her left foot and a black pump identical in every other way—she'd bought them at a two-for-one sale—on her right. At work, dust and clutter, and a floating dread that tainted the display rooms like a moisture-borne pollutant: how could she make a respectable collection from this uncatalogued queerness? She needed money for acquisitions, she decided, staring through her office door at quilts, cutlery, kettles, crockery. She needed to write grant proposals.

She reached for the *Foundation Directory,* remembering that Pillsbury Corporation had funds for "historical projects increasing a sense of community." Maybe because Maidie was used to thinking of Pillsbury in relation to baking, not fund-raising, she felt hungry and exhausted, and she remembered a day, years earlier, when she'd come home from school sick and convalesced on the living room sofa, sunlight tilting through windows. Her mother stepped out of the kitchen to complain about TV soap operas—long-lost twins and secret lives. Jingles for products blared. Mr. Clean. "A mental defective"; she'd waved a spoon. The Ty-D-Bol boat in the toilet. "Absurd." The Pillsbury Doughboy. "Who would buy flour because of a nincompoop who looks like Albrecht Metterau?" Who was Albrecht Metterau? Maidie had asked. "Someone from long ago." Her mother frowned. "Not even from this country."

The bell on the door chimed, and Maidie looked up, expecting her new assistant, whom, Maidie reminded herself, she'd have to be careful not to befriend, a temptation given Maidie's frame of mind—*displaced*—and her penchant for making women friends fast, volunteering her life history in minutes. But she looked up and saw a man, six feet two, with a craggy face, gray-blue eyes, a ponytail the color of a chrome bumper. He said, "I was expecting Midge."

Midge? Maidie wondered if this was the name of an insect specific to Arizona. Last night a bug with legs so furry they'd seemed coated with mascara had landed on Maidie's chest as she'd sprawled on a chaise longue. Splat. She'd been admiring the sunset, the distant mesa, slipping into a bemused state, I-can-live-here. She'd sprung up, flicked the bug off. Garth McHugh had offered this desert advice: Don't put your hand anywhere you can't see. He meant attics and crawl spaces, of course, dark closets.

"The lady who runs this place?" the man said.

"I run it," Maidie said. She pointed at her nameplate.

"I see," he said. "The curator." He said it wrong. Cure-i-tor.

"Cure-ay-tor," Maidie said.

"Very official."

Maidie wondered if he was kidding about her schoolmarm correction. Or was he quarreling? Then an ophthalmological hallucination, a blurry dust puff, limped across the room. A small dog with an uneven gait was plodding diagonally, correcting himself, plodding through the display room into her office.

"Guapo." Embarrassed, he scooped the dog up. It stared at Maidie, tongue lolling, eyes milky and blank. "He's old," the man said. "His name means 'handsome.' He used to be, a long time ago."

The dog wasn't handsome now. With his hunched shoulders and inscrutable face, he looked like a prophet who'd lived too long and begged to die. The man introduced himself. "Rex Hurley." He shook hands as if he'd been tutored by Dale Carnegie. "Here's the list. I've backed my truck up to the door." He turned to leave.

Maidie read the list:

- all Mexican dinnerware (24 pcs.)
- 1 churn
- 1 spinning wheel
- 2 trundle beds
- 1 tin pie safe
- three crocks
- 1 nutmeg grater
- 1 pearl-handled Derringer

"What?" she called after him.

He turned, exasperated.

Then Garth came through the door. "Lad!" He clapped his hand on Rex Hurley's shoulder. "I thought I saw your truck!" The front door chimed again, again, and two more people came in. A tall woman in a silk blazer and trousers, black boots, red lips, her blond hair draping her shoulders. "Hello there," she said. Next to her stood a short man—a boy, a student?—his head half-shaved, paint spatters on his sweatshirt, wearing a pair of horn-rimmed glasses fastened at the corners with safety pins.

Rex Hurley turned, his dog braced in the crook of his arm. "I came to get props," he said. "I already made arrangements with Midge."

Midge? No one had told Maidie anything.

Garth said, "I see introductions are in order." He started with Rex. "We rent some of our pieces to him," he explained. "For movies, westerns. One of our major sources of revenue—the proverbial gift horse we don't look in the mouth." He smirked, relishing the exercise of influence, the lowered boom. "This is Maidie Bonasso," he told Rex, "the woman we've hired to run the museum. You'll deal with her now. Midge quit in a snit."

"She was touchy," Rex said.

"This is your student assistant," Garth told Maidie. "José Eduardo González." The boy with paint spatters and mended glasses nodded. "Art major," Garth said, eyebrows raised.

The well-dressed woman stepped forward. "I'm your liaison with the Cofer College History Department," she said. "We'll coordinate."

Coordinate?

"Dr. Zora Coles," Garth said.

"Call me Z." As Maidie shook her hand, she noticed a tattoo just under the cuff of Z.'s blouse.

José González moved to a corner, arms folded. Scowling?

Garth turned to leave. "I have a meeting."

Rex Hurley was examining a display—patent medicine bottles.

Z. smiled at Maidie, a red smear over perfect teeth, a compulsive, unspontaneous smile that lasted a second too long, like Miss America's. She said, "I'm thrilled we'll be working together. I'll help you with everything—everything there is to know about living in this repressed city with short skyscrapers, which is no place to be single. Do you know what my last date said? 'You career women are so stricken.' But would you like to go out for a drink?" That smile. "To yoga class?"

Maidie said, "Now?"

José Eduardo González *was* scowling, emitting a low-pitched snarl.

Z. didn't seem to notice.

She said, "Sometime, then," in a fluty voice, waving and making a practiced exit with a dip, a near genuflection with a self-congratulatory air—like she'd succeeded in some small way by making this brief but unrequited overture to friendship.

Maybe she'd read she should, somewhere. Ann Landers? "Dear Ann. I'm single and new to this city and so lonely it shows. Signed, Stricken in Tucson." Ann would suggest outlets, venues: meet people at work, church, laundromats, never in a bar. "Dear Stricken, Get off your duff and say hi. The worst you can get is rejected."

"José?" Maidie said.

He didn't answer. He was cleaning a corner of the display room, piling paperwork here, trash there, artifacts on an empty cart.

"Mr. Hurley," Maidie called out. He turned around. "I'd like to make a more detailed record of what you're renting this time."

His eyes took inventory around the room: 1 gun case, 1 churn, 1 pie safe. "Maidie Bonasso," he said, "is a pretty name."

By the time he'd loaded his truck—an old blue flatbed—Maidie's office clock said four fifty-five. "Please write your hours here," she told José, handing him a time card. She started looking for, first, her purse, which turned up under Guapo, who was asleep, and, second, her keys, which weren't in her purse. She shook it, cocked her ear for the jingle. José—filling out his time card—said, "Maidie," and, clearing his throat, "Miss Bonasso?" She looked up. "What?" She checked the pockets of her dress, but she would have noticed her keys there. "What, José?"

"No one calls me José."

She said, "What do they call you?"

"Lalo," he said, "for Eduardo. Both my brothers are named José."

"I thought you were."

"Me too," he said. "That's why they call me Lalo."

"I see," Maidie said, but she didn't. "I can't find my keys."

José—Lalo—searched through the trash.

Rex Hurley stood in the door. "Are they in your car?"

"No," Maidie said. She never locked herself out of her house or car, lost a gas cap, left a bill unpaid, bounced a check; these were points of honor. ("I don't worry about keeping the money straight, honey," Neville once said. "You do such a good job.")

"Let me check," Rex Hurley said.

Maidie searched her office shelves, the tops of cabinets.

Rex returned. "I hate to say this, but they're in your ignition."

Maidie went outside. Her car sat in the blacktop lot, its keys dangling near the steering column, José—Lalo—growled again. He said, "We need to try to get inside," and walked to Maidie's car, faced the window, put his palms on the glass, and seemed to force it down in a gently physical, Houdini-like fashion.

"Careful," Rex said. "You can break it."

The window rolled a half inch, then an inch.

Then the glass crunched, crumbled: safety glass, a sheet of silver cracks erect, then limp, powdering the blacktop, Lalo's shoes, the driver's seat . . . Rex Hurley said, "Excuse me, but I don't think you should drive—not in a dress on top of glass chips."

Maidie stopped to think.

You don't leave your car in a new city, its cracked window a soft spot, an invitation. She looked at her car, her shell, her traveling mollusk home, its beige interior cushy and familiar, threatening to spill out onto the pavement. Lately, she'd promised to pray more. It had started like this: Spring evenings, she'd walk the streets of Norfolk, too worried to put the key in the lock and slip in until Jack was distracted or, better, sleeping. She'd said: God, open a byway, show me a route, a sliver of direction. It seemed to have worked, and so she vowed—driving to Tucson—to repeat the same unobtrusive prayer here from time to time, for God not to refashion his blueprint but to monitor, advise: she didn't want slack cut, easy breaks, just insight, a hot flash. In the parking lot, she waited.

But all she could think of was a crime she'd seen on last night's news. A man had fought with his wife and made her stand at gunpoint in a septic tank. It was clean, he'd pointed out, because it had just been dug. He shot her, then drove around weeping, a picture of her she'd had taken at the state fair propped on the dash in a heart-shaped frame with an inscription that read: You Are My Everything. Maidie had gotten obsessed with the news, maybe; it came in clearer than prayer. As she looked at Tucson's skyline, squat and angular, she thought of *The Technological Sublime,* which was the title of a book that described the peculiarly American notion that all change is an improvement, that the Hoover Dam, for instance, is a monument to achievement not because it pumps hydroelectric power but because at the peak of its iconographic sway it was improbably newfangled. Maidie looked at Rex Hurley, at Lalo standing between his bicycle and Maidie's shattered window, embarrassed, as though the window belonged to him, a debt on the boilerplate of their emerging professional acquaintance. Of course, you don't leave *yourself* cracked open in a strange city either. A Kleenex lay squashed in the passenger seat of Maidie's car. Maidie hadn't cried on the trip here. No. She'd had hay fever, second thoughts, a trailer of old furniture, but new plans, her road atlas flapping open like an instruction manual on the seat beside her.

Rex said, "Well?"

Maidie looked at Lalo; in fact, she could hear him.

She would have to say something about this growling.

*L*adylike, Maidie's mother never growled, but one morning, burning her fingers on the griddle as she flipped pancakes, she said, "Shh—sugar!" Then, "Shit." Then she smiled sweetly and said she didn't like her daughters walking to school between steep snowbanks, the sun not yet risen, and nothing hot inside their stomachs. She grew up in Madagascar, where water never froze and teachers made house calls. But the other pupils—Negro and Polynesian, Maidie gathered—went to a government school with grass walls. That morning, her plaid bookbag scraping the side of her fleece-lined boot, Maidie led single file down the scooped-out Minnesota sidewalk to the lit door of the brick school where Lucy and Thea went, kindergarten through fourth; she dropped them off, then walked to the steel school with big windows, fifth through eighth. Her toes curled up to stay warm, to fight numbness. Misery is optional, Maidie's dad said.

As she stood at the crosswalk, waiting for car headlights to beam past, Maidie pretended she lived in Madagascar and went to a grass school. Morning, predawn, would be welcome, a cool chance to sneak up on heat. Cold couldn't be sneaked up on. When school let out for recess, Maidie wandered through the white landscape, marveling at its impersonality; you'd die if you stayed out too long. In Madagascar, Maidie's mother had lived with her dad, who mined quartz (which is used in radar equipment), also water sapphire, garnet, amethyst. Maidie's mother pointed out these rocks in Webster's dictionary, a glossy page. She told Maidie about a lemon tree in the backyard, the paths around it strewn with mining waste—a gravel made from amethyst. Could this be true? Maidie didn't know much about her mother's father. He'd planted that lemon tree and spread pathways with jewels. "Where was your mom?" Maidie once asked her own mother, who answered, "It was just my father and me, pathetic, and the housekeeper." Maidie crossed the icy street and went inside to school. Mrs. Funderburk sat at her desk, reading.

In the cloakroom, Maidie hung up her muffler, mittens, and coat. Once, her mother told Maidie about a time when she'd been sewing and looked out a window and saw the first white boy she could remember. Who'd taught her mother how to sew? In Madagascar, the sun set orange. A cactus sprawled like a paddle-legged starfish. Poinsettias bloomed. "At home," Maidie's mother would say, "we have poinsettias. And red daisies." But her father sent Maidie's mother into an upstairs room when people came. She said, "I was young, locked up, no social life. It could happen to anyone." What could? She sat on the window seat, light through the lace curtains making a veil pattern. "It'll be different for you," she said. "Boat parties, football games, dates to the autumn dance." Maidie nodded. American teenagers on TV went to happy occasions in pairs, two in the front seat, two in back.

Maidie's mother stayed in Madagascar until she was seventeen, then moved to Hector, Minnesota, with Pastor and Mrs. Larssen.

"I was a girl," she'd said. "That lemon tree. Those pathways glistening under moonlight. Enchantment." She used that word. Maidie had studied it in Vocabulary, along with *enraptured,* which meant "captured, but pleasantly so." All the same, it was sad for a young girl, Maidie's mother said, leaning forward, the lace pattern on her face flickering into a shadow. She reached for Maidie, pulled Maidie into her lap and kissed her, hard pecks, as if her mother were soothing herself a long time ago, Maidie realized, being both the mother and the little girl, kissing herself.

Her father was dead now. The day Maidie's mother found out, she cried and drank clear-colored liquor, furious, gulping air.

In the cloakroom, Maidie took off her snow boots.

Once, Maidie had sat with Vera Fleiderhaus in her room above the garage, Maidie painting a small canvas—a picture of a helicopter she'd drawn with a pencil, and now she was dabbing inside the lines with paint—as Vera talked about how she and Eugene had driven to California in the aqua car, three days and nights, to go to her father's funeral; he'd died sitting on the sofa, eyes wide open. For two whole hours, Vera's mother didn't notice. They'd brought Vera's mother here—to Minnesota—to live.

"Death," Vera said, "is a deadline. So you choose a life for yourself." Maidie considered it: death, a deadline. They painted until the sun fell. Then Eugene came and told Vera he'd driven her mother to town to fill a prescription, and she'd wet herself in the drugstore. Maidie and Vera went out to the clapboard guesthouse, and Vera pulled her mother's jersey dress over her head—over the slim brown cigar in Vera's mother's red mouth. Vera pulled off her mother's girdle, wet, tight. Her mother struggled, the girdle knotted around her legs. She said, "I wouldn't need one if I hadn't been such a fool as to have you."

Later, Maidie's mother came to take Maidie home. In the living room, she slipped off her coat. "Thank you," she said, when Eugene offered tea. She sipped, dainty. But her eyes widened because Vera's mother had hobbled through the yard, her cane probing the snow. She came through the door wearing a purple bathrobe. "Tea," she said, "is a pretense. These people drink liquor. I'll have a snort." Eugene said, "We all will." He handed out drinks—7-Up for Maidie—in glasses shaped like camels.

Vera's mother sat on the couch, stretching her legs. "I'm being held hostage in Maine," she said. Vera said, "It's Minnesota, Mother." Her mother answered, "You think that's an improvement?" Maidie's own mother stared at the ceiling. "You look cagey," Vera's mother said. And she poked Maidie's mother with her cane. Maidie's mother's drink jostled. She said, "Thank you."

Vera's mother said, "I thought I'd have a daughter more like you. Why not pass along some of your cosmetic tips to Vera?"

Maidie looked at Vera, her funny hair and glasses.

Would she mind?

Vera's mother was leading Maidie's mother through the house. "You have a glamorous arch to your eyebrows." Maidie's mother looked in a mirror. "Really?" Vera's mother—like a cat who won't allow caresses, overtures, but initiates them—stood behind Maidie's mother, stroking her cashmere shoulder. "Here." She reached in her pocket and pulled out a bottle of perfume a great director had once given her, Vera's mother said. (It smelled bad, Maidie's mother said later; she took it to be polite.) Eugene and Vera sat on a love seat. Maidie sat across from them. Vera's mother was laughing, cackling, high-pitched. "Star quality," she said. They had their hands on each other's shoulders now. Vera's mother, her corpse face with makeup. Maidie's mother—her mouth frozen grinlike, eyes glassy— nodding, mechanical. Later she'd say Vera's mother had rude manners and smelled like pee, but for now she masqueraded, laughing.

Vera told Eugene, "Thank you for taking Mother to town."

He shrugged.

Vera said, "She's difficult, but she gives me—I don't know— connection." Maidie wondered for a minute. Connection? Un-interruption, she decided. Vera speared an olive in her cocktail. "See how sad, so empty I would be. If I didn't know my mother." Eugene's eyes flickered into Maidie's. In the next room, Maidie's mother said, "Glamorous, really?" And Maidie understood Vera meant Maidie's mother, in the next room, seemed sad.

So empty. At school, Maidie stood in the bare cloakroom, looking at her lone coat on its hook, hat above, boots below—a draped statue of a schoolgirl. Then past the classroom, its desks and chairs poised, and through the windows where, outside, the sun came up behind the edge of the world, its gray light spreading. Mrs. Funderburk stood up, cleared her throat. The students filed in, noisy, talking about TV, also new-and-improved plastic sleds that went so fast they risked your life, everyone said.

* * *

Maidie was driving Rex Hurley's flatbed with a big load: two trundle beds, a churn, a pie safe, a spinning wheel, all Mexican dinnerware (24 pcs.), assorted miscellany, and Lalo's red bicycle strapped down with rubber cords. Lalo, in the passenger seat, reached to pull Guapo away from Maidie's feet, which pumped the gas pedal, the clutch, the brake. "Slow," Lalo said. "Do you know what you're doing?" Maidie downshifted. Behind her, wearing a pair of thick jeans he'd changed into at the Women's History Collection, sitting in the brushed-off seat of her car—on insidiously minute glass chips, he'd pointed out—Rex Hurley followed. Maidie said to Lalo, "Since you and I work together, we should maybe consider the way we communicate." Lalo turned, eyebrows raised. "Uh?" a question. Maidie asked, "Sometimes you make a growling sound?" Lalo looked wary, shook his head: he didn't.

Maidie said, "You do."

He groaned, but Maidie let it go.

And wondered how she'd ended up here. But the answer was the same as to the question of how she'd ended up with anyone—ex-husbands, ex-friends: by an odd mixture of disregard and overweening caution. Maidie had realized it wasn't prudent to lead Rex Hurley home, where she lived like Diane Keaton in *Looking for Mr. Goodbar,* alone and, to the untrained eye, lonely. So maybe because Lalo reminded Maidie of a guard dog, with his throaty disapproval regarding social vicissitudes he didn't endorse, Maidie had suggested Lalo ride with her. She'd realized, barreling down Speedway Boulevard, past unfamiliar gas stations, stores, neon signs (Girls! Girls! Girls!), that she had no sense of where the bad neighborhoods began and the good ended, also that it might have been better to ask Rex Hurley to take her to a car wash with a vacuum, and also—having guarded against Rex by bringing Lalo—that

Maidie was leading not one but two near strangers home. On the
other hand, neither of them seemed as likely to be a threat as a
pest, a messy nuisance on the periphery.

Bad planning. But she didn't have to explain it to anyone.

Jack, for instance.

Or Neville.

Behind her, Rex flashed his headlights and pulled over.
"Where's he going?" Maidie asked, braking. The big truck
shuddered. GONZO'S STORE, the sign said—like a 7-Eleven,
only rustic. People sat on the steps in ragged clusters. A plant
called Spanish Sword grew in rusty barrels next to the door.
Lalo cleared his throat. "I suppose he needs a snack," he said,
meaning Rex Hurley. Maidie and Lalo went inside. In fact, Rex
Hurley was buying lottery tickets. "Twenty-three million
tonight," he said. He bought one for Lalo, one for Maidie.
"Welcome to Arizona. I thought you might like Gonzo's. For a
small place, it has a good microbrewery selection." He paid for
two six-packs—Black Dog Wheat Beer and Bigfoot Ale—as a
line of ants climbed across the cash register. "You probably
don't have these where you come from," Rex Hurley said,
"though I don't know where that is." He frowned. "Poison ants.
Chock-full of poison." Maidie looked at Lalo, who didn't indicate agreement or disagreement. The man behind the counter
said, "They're out of control because the owner uses organic
pesticide, which just makes the ants catch a buzz and—excuse
me—mate faster."

The beer looked cold. Mate faster. Maidie felt thirsty. She
looked at Rex, hoping Garth McHugh—who'd seemed to admire Rex, clapping his shoulder, exclaiming "Lad!" (*Lad?*)—
had good instincts.

She was standing next to a display of *Oui,* she realized, also
the *Sports Illustrated* swimsuit issue. She moved away. "Ready?"
she asked. But she was thinking about Jack and Neville, Jack
with his stashed cardboard box of pornographic videos Maidie

had found in the cellar in Fayetteville, Arkansas, as she put away Christmas decorations one January; and Neville's magazines with their protuberant photos and inane titles, *Cherry, Sexo, Babe-a-loo!,* under a piece of loose carpet in the bathroom closet.

Once, Maidie had watched a few minutes of an X-rated movie—the only theater in Jackson Hole had decided to face down the recession by showing a G-rated movie at seven and an X-rated movie at nine. Laree worked there. "Come and get your pizza from Pizza Laree," the owner would say over the PA, regardless of what might transpire in the movie: a bear might be wandering in a blizzard, or eight people might be having sex in a "daisy chain." But one night, when Laree was sick and Maidie covered her shift, Maidie watched as a wimpy man stood in a harem and touched dozens of breasts. It wasn't the breasts that offended Maidie, but bad dialogue: "Oh," the Walter Mitty man said, touching a woman's nipples, "just like elevator buttons." At any rate, Maidie left Neville's magazines under the rug, Jack's videotapes in the cellar. Later, she asked where they came from. Neville had a simple answer. A guy he worked with gave them away because his wife made him. Jack hit the roof, the wall actually, a minor crack, plaster shifting. "It's my private business," he said. Maidie didn't point out that she hadn't foreseen a crate in the fruit cellar would be private. But these memories returned headlong—she didn't like to think about the past.

Or the future it implied: if you had two husbands and neither of them liked to make love . . . Neville never did. He'd rather sleep, smoke pot, play solitaire. And though Jack liked lovemaking in the beginning—in courtship, the two-month-long period in which he'd never lost his temper once and bought Maidie perfume, flowers, and (explaining that in terms of his "dream woman," she met nine out of ten parameters) a diamond engagement ring too—as soon as they were living together he talked about sex differently. "If only you'd hold your neck stiffer, more like this." Or, "I wish we could do it outside, in a natural setting." Or complaining: "If you'd act nicer, maybe." The point, as Maidie saw it, was that if two ex-husbands had wanted a wife for domestic reasons and a photo or video for carnal, wouldn't all men, maybe? As Maidie got back in the truck and fired it up, she felt like asking someone. Of course, she didn't.

Lalo got in beside her.

Maidie pulled onto the boulevard, big trucks and low-riders blurring. Above, the sky stretched and glimmered, vapor lights and fading sun, orange and lavender. Wind whistled through the window as Maidie turned into a side street and heard cicada, a wheezy roar. Maidie's landlady in Nebraska, Opal Johnson— Maidie and Neville had rented the apartment above Opal's store, The Antique Outlet—once explained that a cicada lives a short life in service to its last singing day, raspy in the morning and, by night, strident, insistent, dying. Maidie had heard cicadas for the first time in Nebraska, and again in Arkansas, a spooky portent. She thought for a minute about the white house and patch of lawn she'd left behind in Virginia. Jack wouldn't be able to afford it now. He'd try house-sitting, he'd said the day she left. House-sitting where? He'd have to figure it out, he'd said. She pushed away an image of Jack asleep on a cardboard pallet under a bridge. Nonsense, she told herself, driving past sandy yards dotted with cacti. Above, a color-mangled sky. The cicada sounded like an electric malfunction, wired, shrieking. Home, she thought, braking, Rex Hurley's turn signal a steady blink.

Snow sifted down, milky and vaporous. Maidie and her mother wore winter coats in the summer gazebo, looking through leaf-less vines at white sidewalks and clumpy trees. It was Saturday. "I'd only seen pictures of snow," Maidie's mother said, "until that time with the Larssens." She meant when Pastor and Mrs. Larssen—who were missionaries then—brought Maidie's mother here from Madagascar. Then Maidie and her mother saw Mrs. Funderburk shuffling across the yard, wearing a plaid jacket, a blue bandanna. She lived around the corner with her husband, the sheriff, who parked his big cruiser in the street. "Nice schedule," Maidie's dad said once, waving as Sheriff Funderburk went into his house. "Nice schedule if you can get it," he said under his breath, waving broader. In the summer, Mrs. Funderburk hung laundry outside, the sheriff's underwear, also aprons and towels with embroidered words: Salt, Pepper, Sugar, Spice. Maidie's mother practiced wash 'n' wear. She walked into her appliance-accoutred kitchen, imperious, punched this button and that. Even magic was old hat compared to machinery, the mechanical victory over dirt, Maidie realized; on TV, a perky witch levitated her sofa just to swoosh a vacuum cleaner beneath it.

Mrs. Funderburk knocked on the front door. Maidie's mother called from the gazebo: "We're here, celebrating the change of season." She lifted her toddy high, then reconsidered, frowned, slipped it under the bench. Mrs. Funderburk crossed the yard. "The beginning of winter is . . ." Maidie's mother hesitated. "Soulful." She smiled, her shiny mouth stretching across her face. Maidie thought Mrs. Funderburk seemed tall, like Paul Bunyan. She said, "I came to ask . . . looking over Mrs. Rahn's lesson plans, I see she scheduled you to give a speech about your childhood."

Mrs. Funderburk was the substitute for Maidie's *real* teacher, who had cancer everywhere. At the end of school the year before, their old teacher had told them they'd been assigned for next year to Mrs. Rahn, who was a famous teacher; she'd won awards. "She has bravely fought cancer for nine years," their old teacher said. On the first day of school in the fall, Mrs. Rahn talked about her eye that had been removed, pointing at the smoky lens in her glasses, saying how glad she was not to be blind. She didn't mention her nose, which fit nicely, Maidie felt. Only when Mrs. Rahn had a cold could Maidie tell: she seemed miserable behind the plastic, smothery nose, blotting it with a tissue. At recess once, a brat said Mrs. Rahn looked like Porky the Pig if you were insane, her nose shifting. Joel Scribner had held him by the back of his collar and said, "You learn some manners."

Mrs. Rahn told her students what they needed to know—for instance, before the principal came to give his speech. He stood in front of the class, holding his hands across his big stomach. "Mrs. Rahn is ill," he said. None of the students said anything. "She's going back to the hospital, so the doctors can help her. Meanwhile, you'll be getting a new teacher." The principal looked at Mrs. Rahn. "A bunch of little stoics, aren't they?"

"I already told them," she said.

Earlier that day, she'd cleared the top of her desk and stared out the window. Autumn. The blackness of tree branches, the missing leaves. Mrs. Rahn told the students that on Friday she'd go away. She was sicker than before, and scared, but also brave because she'd had practice being sick. Some students cried. Maidie felt dread and hubbub, panic and fury, winding like a spool in the room. She wanted to hit someone, that boy who'd said Mrs. Rahn looked like a pig and now cried loudest. Sitting down, Mrs. Rahn held her arms out—skinny sticks—and the students came forward. Mrs. Rahn bent her arms around them and said, "All my life, I've loved my pupils." Tears ran out from behind her gray eyeglass lens into the creases of her nose. That one boy dug his head into her ribs and kicked. "There," she said. "We need to compose ourselves before the principal arrives."

When Maidie told her parents that her teacher had to go back into the hospital, her father said, "She's dying." Maidie looked at him, his necktie loose, his crimpy hair and handsome face. "Not for sure, not yet," she said. Her father said, "They

call the new teacher a substitute, and that way there's better insurance benefits for the old teacher." Maidie's mother stood up.
"You have a cash register instead of a soul," she said.

Many people had died. First, Maidie's grandfather on her
dad's side, something wrong with his worm-shaped intestine, so
he couldn't digest food. Maidie and her sisters didn't go to the
funeral—they got new Barbie dolls, and Eugene and Vera came
to baby-sit. Next, Maidie's grandmother on her dad's side didn't
like being alive without her husband, and she came for a long
visit, slept on a roll-away in the living room, sat at breakfast with
her warts and limp face, saying she couldn't eat eggs, or pancakes, or cereal. She'd walk in the snow without boots. She
died, and if people told Maidie's dad how sorry they were, he
said, "God's will." He got mad at his mother a long time ago,
Maidie's mother said, and didn't forgive her. He'd feel bad later.

Sometime in the 1990s—when a British actress on a talk
show said, straight-faced, that what she liked about America
was being able to practice self-therapy by watching TV—Maidie's dad began to plumb depths, his nascency of grief. It was
suddenly mainstream to examine your past as an unlit corridor,
early impressions, triggers installed, and though Maidie's dad
had come of age when the only psychiatrist, mythical or real,
he'd heard of had made the doddery observation that the
malaise called seven-year itch was caused by sex—any farm boy
who saw Marilyn Monroe in a white dress knew that!—he
caught on quick. Sitting at a fold-out table in his Winnebago,
sipping vodka, his good looks still good, only girthsome, he'd
say, tears welling, "My mother never loved me. My father died
before he could pass on . . . pass on his wisdom about this hard
life." He cried openly, mopping his face. His wisdom, Maidie
thought. Maybe he didn't have any! Recently she'd read that
genes caused unhappiness. A man had studied twins, one raised
by parents who were by all accounts loving, the other by a bitter, deserted woman. Both were miserable. And both had ex-

actly the same freckle, the same whorl of hair on the napes of their necks. Congenital misery was as hard to counter as fate, but it could be managed.

You weren't supposed to knuckle under.

For instance, when Maidie's parents visited the school on Parents Night—the windows glaring black, the overhead light gleaming on desktops—Mrs. Rahn, who was wearing a belted dress of shiny silver fabric, rested her hand, fragile and weightless, on Maidie's shoulder. "Are these your parents, dear?" Lucy and Thea were racing and yelling in the waxed hallway. "Yes," Maidie said. Mrs. Rahn's hand felt like a wand, a knobby space creature's benevolent scepter. But later, on the way back to the car, jingling keys, swooping down to pick up Thea, Maidie's dad said, "Man, what an eyeful." At first, Maidie didn't understand. Her mother said, "What would you have her do—commit suicide because she's inconvenient to look at?" And Maidie realized that Mrs. Rahn was not just brave but duty-bound to keep living. Maidie's dad looked at Maidie's mother. "Maybe," he said. He wanted a fight. They got in the car, Lucy singing about Chef Boyardee, except in her version ravioli came from the sewer, was made of manure. The car headlights flickered on trees, on asphalt. Maidie's mother said, "Bill, would you love me if I weren't beautiful?" He scowled, sour-faced. "Are you?"

She scowled back. "A little."

"If you didn't know looks were important," he said, "you wouldn't have shown up that first night—fancy hair, tight dress."

Maidie's mother sniffed.

Maidie wished they would say "I love you," "I love you back." They used to, at five o'clock, when Maidie's dad got home from work.

"I could have been something," Maidie's mother said.

Maidie's father nodded. "But you chose this."

Maidie's mother said, "You don't believe me." She turned in

her seat. "Girls, listen up!" Thea sat, glum. Lucy stared at the passing sky. The car hummed forward in the dark. "Understand what your father's saying. Earn your keep. This is your future—marriage is maid service with prostitution thrown in."

Lucy said, "What's prostitution?"

Maidie's father braked the car. "Stop it, Elaine."

At the time, Maidie thought prostitution was chasing someone else to accuse him—a judge and criminal, for example.

That's what she told Lucy and Thea at home.

They went to bed.

Maidie lay in the dark, the sound of Thea's puffy baby snores steady as a meter. At night, Maidie couldn't stand two doors in her room. One, a square big enough to admit a child or gnome, led to the attic. The other led to a closet, narrow and grave-sized. By day, doors were doors. At night, they were conduits for secrets, rude forces, a vapor or an ancestral ghost that might arrive, foul the air, ruin everyone. This is what Maidie thought. At dawn, she found her mother in front of the picture window downstairs, fully dressed, cigarette smoke furling like cobwebs as the sun rose over the stripped trees, the dim streets.

So a few weeks later, when Mrs. Rahn sent a note, spidery longhand on blue-lined paper—"You mentioned your childhood in Madagascar, and I thought about the changes you've seen, life here, life there, and I wonder if you will be kind enough to share your experience with the students and make a contribution to their education no book or film strip could, by coming as a speaker to Social Studies class?"—Maidie's mother, still angry because Maidie's father wouldn't say he'd love her if she were old or ugly, because marriage was really accusations and housekeeping, because she could have been something, a teacher or a speechmaker, sent her own note back: *By all means,* she wrote, *indeed.*

Still, no one mentioned it again, because Mrs. Rahn got sick. But now Mrs. Funderburk—her surprised, stern face like Olive

Oyl's, like Alice Kramden's—loomed over Maidie in the gazebo, snow outside falling like flour through a sifter, and Maidie got excited. Her mother would come and Maidie wouldn't have to devise questions, or stitch together her mother's scraps of fact about Madagascar into a series of events in the right order, a story with *reasons why,* a process Maidie found harder than real sewing, harder than long division, first getting her mother in the mood for questions, second keeping the details straight. Instead her mother would sit on a stool near the chalkboard and say, "Let me begin at the beginning, long ago, when I was little."

But her mother looked nervous. Mrs. Funderburk smiled. Maidie's mother said, "I don't think of myself as having much to teach."

Mrs. Funderburk said, "Tell the students about your childhood in Madagascar exactly the same way you tell your own children."

Which was—Maidie thought—by telling them nothing, a remembered hour here, a recollection totaling three minutes there. Maidie's mother was stitching a cloth; she knew someone named Albrecht; the lemon tree in moonlight made her feel captured, but pleasantly so. Her life, its upshot, could have happened to anyone, by which she meant to say, maybe, that if an identical series of errors happened to someone like her, that person's outcome would be hers. What? Maidie's mother's father was mean. Maidie's mother's mother—though there must have been one for at least the first thirty seconds of her life, that braying, floodlit instant when the doctor held her by the feet and, slap!, said Welcome to the Living—never seemed to have existed in any material, in any but the most cloud-wrapped and unshapen way.

The same way you tell your own children.

Maidie's mother knocked at the edge of the schoolroom door in her coral-colored coat with brown fur, her transparent rubber boots, which slid over high heels and buttoned across the ankle. She carried a shopping bag with handles. "Class, this is Mrs. Giddings, Maidie's mother," Mrs. Funderburk said. The class applauded, clap, clap, a sound like water running. Maidie smiled and sank deep into her chair. Joel Scribner, who sat in the next row, smiled back, a happy, serious grin. Maidie's mother was removing her coat, handing it to Mrs. Funderburk. She braced her palm on a stool, unhooked her boots. As she pulled her scarf away from her neck, it caught in the flip of her stiff hair. The students watched as, arms over her head, she tugged it loose, then smiled, her cheeks rosy from the indoor heat. A girl who sat next to Maidie lurched in her desk. "That's your mother?" she asked. Maidie nodded. "Wow," the girl said, sinking back down.

Then, before she premeditated—before she considered the lie she would tell, what the point of the risk might be, interest earned—Maidie blurted, "She has a baby in her stomach," a brassy whisper like sandpaper, like Judy Garland singing, *Oh, Love Is Soft!* but it sounds rough. As soon as Maidie said so, it seemed true. "A baby there?" a girl next to Maidie asked, so loud that even Joel Scribner turned around, also that boy, that brat, and two other girls. They looked to the front of the room, at Maidie's mother's flat, smooth stomach under her mohair dress the shimmering color that, in Crayola crayons, is *periwinkle.* A scientific marvel, Maidie thought, her mother's stomach slim as an envelope but with a baby inside, a boy who would hurtle out thick as a billiard ball. How would he hurtle? It had something to do with belly buttons. When he arrived—poing!—he'd be like Lucy and Thea, poking, running, leaping. Or boylike in a new way, considerate, helpful, and everyone in the family—Maidie's dad, her mother and sisters—would shift places and act differently, better. And he would look exactly like Joel Scribner.

Of course, there wasn't a baby. But Maidie's dad complained about being a man in a house of girls. It curdled his brain, he said.

Maidie's mother held up charts she'd made with her crooked handwriting. "A primary export is coffee," she said, nervous. Mrs. Funderburk interrupted, explained that Maidie's mother was talking about Madagascar, an island where she grew up, and this was Social Studies. "Go ahead," she said. "Coffee," Maidie's mother repeated, "is an export, also the vanilla bean and pepper." Maidie's mother reached into her shopping bag and pulled out a can of Maxwell House coffee, a brown bottle of vanilla, the pepper shaker from the stove. "Also mining," Maidie's mother said. At this point, she held up her hand, pointed at a garnet ring. Then Maidie's mother got out her jewelry box and held up a brooch and more rings; Maidie had never seen them. She stuffed them back in. She shuffled posterboards. "Madagascar used to be part of Africa, but it is now two hundred and fifty miles west, which is how much it moved."

That bratty boy said, "Islands don't move, ma'am."

Mrs. Funderburk said, "Button up, Duncan. Whole continents move."

He rolled his eyes. "No way."

Then Maidie's mother talked about the kings who were native and had a special quality that made them stern, violent, and mean enough to rule. The first French king was a pirate. But they chased him away and went back to stern Negro kings, also a queen who made people swim through crocodiles if she thought they were lying. A modern Frenchman took over later. "But in 1958," Maidie's mother said, "the French left, and Madagascar became a republic."

No one said anything.

Her mother dabbed her forehead. "It used to be called the French Orient."

"Are you Oriental?" a boy said.

Her mother shook her head. The class giggled.

"Negro?"

"That'll be enough," Mrs. Funderburk said.

A girl near Maidie asked, "Do you have relatives who are pirates?"

Maidie's mother frowned. "Of course not."

Mrs. Funderburk said, "Still, I wonder if there isn't some private detail—some particular insight we can't get from a book?"

Maidie's mother hesitated. "There were beautiful sunsets."

"A more personal angle?"

She said, "There were beautiful sunsets I saw from my window."

"Did you know some mean kings?" Duncan said.

"No," she said.

"What did you do for fun?" a girl asked.

"Nothing at all," she said, exasperated. "I'm finished." She opened her bag and gave the class a Madagascar snack—figs, olives, vanilla pudding cups, also Wheat Thins. Maidie's mother moved through the aisles dispensing paper plates, plastic spoons in cellophane wrappers, Dixie cups, napkins. Maidie still didn't understand Madagascar, what her mother had felt, worried about, and pondered there. Of course there was no baby, Maidie knew, staring at her mother's figure, the latex girdle, rubber-knit brassiere, and nylon slip having reengineered her from an ordinary down-sinking woman into this one: converted, ascendant, poised for the future. Maidie stared at her mother and had an instant of vision, a current of illumination that lit up the past, the island where all that had mattered was buried and left behind, and that made it important for Maidie's mother to make a new family here, blood relatives and friends borrowed to stand in, a lineage for now. Someone asked, "Did they have Wheat Thins in Madagascar, Mrs. Giddings?" She smiled. Behind her mother's brown eyes, Maidie realized, was a country of the dead and missing. "No," she said, "but they're very tasty with olives."

*   *   *

*I*n a whirl of exhaust, Maidie slowed in front of her house. Rex
pulled her car into the driveway. The sand in the yard stretched
frosty and silver, heat rippling, the earth letting out its sigh.
The pavement radiated through Maidie, who stood near Lalo,
thinking how hard it is in that first instant to tell hot from cold.
Heat sears; frost burns. On the patio, the hammock swung behind a mysterious screen of leaves. A cactus stood shadowy and
erect. The slow and sallow Santa Cruz River burbled under the
incandescent sky. The moon had seemed like a spotlight the
first time Maidie saw it rise into the pressureless black. If you
ignored the electric poles, cars in the street, a plastic hose
snaking across gravel—machinery and its output—would this
hypothetically pure sample of landscape look like the island
where Maidie's mother had lived from the time she was born
until she was seventeen and latched onto a way out? Maidie was
struck by how remote a time that seemed now—no doubt to
her mother, who lived in San Francisco, the last Maidie knew—
a time without industrial flotsam, with no Teflon, no polyester,
no Mylar. Just wind, fire, water, heat, glass, darkness. And a
pathway of jewels.

Maidie looked at the sandy yard, wrinkling into patterns. At
one time she'd thought about her mother every day, remembering her as more loving and graceful than Neena, as naive,
provincial, and terribly wronged by Maidie's father, who, in this
version, was a mustachioed, vain capitalist bent on impressing
the Joneses with his pretty wife, who'd turned out to be not
docile, an ingrate. And he hated *his* mother; Maidie remembered visits to the farm where he grew up, her grandmother's
hair net creeping down like a lumpy widow's peak as she stared
out the window and said in a mealy, guttural voice, "That's
where you were born, in a dirt house." Maidie's father answered: No, he was born in this house, but his oldest brother

was in fact born in that very spot, in a *sod* house! With just a memory of her own mother, no presence, Maidie had conjectured. When she was sixteen, she read everything she could about Madagascar; she checked out one book so long the overdue fees were more than the replacement cost, and she ended up owning it, *The Bloody Island.* All she could remember now was that its besotted-sounding author had complained about taking a foul-smelling shower in the dingy Hotel of Orchids, run by a half-French woman who'd plucked out all her eyebrow hairs.

Surely the landscape here, the cacti, the sand and wind, had drummed these questions up, Maidie thought; also a clacking sound like bones and far-off singing coming from her neighbor's yard, and bamboo party lanterns glowing on poles. A man emerged out of the dusk—a bulky mass that wasn't there and, in an instant, was. "Miz Bonasso," Harve said. Maidie noticed that certain native southwesterners avoided etiquette difficulty—the bungling and wondering if a woman you've just met is married, divorced, or what, and whose last name does she have?—by employing the all-purpose *Miz* (not to be confused with *Ms.*) to address all females over the age of twelve. "We're having a little impromptu to celebrate my daughter's engagement," he said, "and I wanted to invite you." A woman came up behind him. "Have you met my wife, Rona?" he asked. Then, leaning forward, getting a look at Lalo, he said, "Oh." He glanced at Rex Hurley's truck, parked in the street. As Rex walked up, Harve said, "I didn't realize you were having work done over here. Don't let me stop you." He clapped Lalo's paint-splattered shoulder. "Get on with it."

Lalo made that noise, growling, though Maidie realized she'd tuned in to the frequency now. Someone else might think it was wind in the trees, dry leaves rattling in gravel. Rex Hurley said, "He's not a flunky—he's a friend of Miz Bonasso's from work."

Rona slugged Harve. "You racist," she said. Except she pronounced it ray-shist. She told Maidie, "He's stuck in the fifties."

Harve said, "Ouch. Everyone has a right to their opinion."

Rona smiled. "Not if your opinion is stupid."

Harve said, "You've got a busted car window, girl."

Maidie said, "Yes, my keys . . ." But stopped. Too much to explain.

Harve said, "Everyone come and drink a little beer out of the pony, eat yourself some barbecue. My baby girl just got engaged. Everyone. You too." He clapped Lalo on the shoulder again.

Rex said, "You go ahead."

Maidie said, "Actually, I need to go inside."

Rona said, "To wash your hair?" She doubled over, laughing.

Harve said, "What?"

Rona said, "That excuse girls make if they don't want to go on a date."

Harve said, "Come when you like, Miz Bonasso, and bring your friends."

Rona said, "We do have an awful lot of food."

Lalo said, "I'll go. I'm hungry."

Maidie stared at him. Was she having acculturation stupor?

"Are you saving these?" Rex said, pointing at cardboard boxes.

Maidie asked, "Why?"

Guapo poked his head out of the truck and yapped.

"I'll cut a piece," Rex said, "to cover your window for the night."

A response, or a portentous lack of one, was necessary, Maidie felt.

Still, she didn't say—or do—anything.

Rex said, "Go on and have a nice time with your neighbors."

Was he acting like a foreman here?

A benevolent despot?

A cluster of intimates seemed to be collecting on Maidie—

like metal scraps on a magnet—before she'd developed wariness, her own defensive spikes and caution. She meant to be
choosy.

Rona said, "You must be famished by now, Maidie." And
Maidie, confused, wondered how Rona knew her name. Maidie
herself had probably told it to Harve the day he helped her
move, she thought, her brain dull. But it wasn't common, no,
Maidie, diminutive for Maida. Her thesis director—whom Maidie esteemed and admired—had always called her Maisie, like
that juvenile delinquent in the Henry James novel. Rona said,
"I don't see how you managed—moving one day, starting a job
with long hours the next." Maidie felt surprised again. Didn't
everyone work and move at the same time? Money doesn't rain
down from clouds. Still, Maidie thought, if you'd never had a
full-time job, you'd probably notice people who did, hours they
kept, friends they cultivated, the doilies and ferns they placed
on their windowsills. Rona said, "The house looks cuter than it
did with the last renters. We wish someone nice like you would
buy it." Maidie's stomach growled: hungry. As she walked toward bright lights and Rona's homemade food, Lalo stood near
Rex, holding cardboard as Rex sawed. Guapo crouched on the
truck bed under the streetlight, chomping dry dog food. "He's
handsome, very dignified," Rona said, meaning Rex, not Lalo,
of course. Or Guapo.

Maidie stood on the porch at Rona and Harve's. Agrarian-
nostalgic, Maidie had come to classify this decorating style: a
wreath, a milk can trimmed with calico, a picture of fluffy
sheep. Rona introduced her daughters. Evvy, the oldest. Cindy-
June, the betrothed. Two ponytailed children in tie-dye—a boy,
a girl—raced around in the dark yard. "They're Cindy-June's,"
Rona said. Maidie noticed that, under her own oversized tie-
dye, Cindy-June was pregnant again. If she got engaged pregnant, Maidie speculated, then the father of the baby wasn't the
father of the children, unless he had a reason for not getting

married until the third conception, Maidie thought, idle. No, Cindy-June was probably the matriarch of an amalgamate kinship unit, a family that was, in the Oprahic dialect, blended. "Congratulations," Maidie remembered to say. "About the engagement, I mean. Which one's your fiancé?" There didn't seem to be anyone the right age—just a man singing and playing spoons, who stopped from time to time to wiggle a tooth, and a sweet-faced gentleman with tufty hair like eiderdown, sitting in a plastic stackable chair next to a silver-haired lady with blue eye shadow.

"He couldn't be bothered to make it," Evvy said.

Cindy-June said, "She's jealous. Her biological clock is ticking."

Harve said, "Get yourself some food, Miz Bonasso."

Maidie, piling her plate with tamales, barbecue, and beans, felt amazed at how everyone, not just people conditioned by expensive "therapy," had adopted the new terms. That old man who edits the thesaurus must be hard put keeping up, Maidie thought, picturing his prim face on the book jacket. *Procreate,* copulate, make whoopee, screw, stop the biological clock from ticking. She'd become enamored of *Roget's Thesaurus,* its cozy taxonomies implying a fixed human history, that summer in Arkansas she'd written her thesis—"Labor of Love: Atavistic Work Ethic and 'Female Hysteria' in the 1890s"—with no one beside her friend from school, Mia, or her other friend, Marbella, with whom to discuss it. But Maidie felt annoyed about women in the 1990s imagining themselves ticking. Perhaps they'd gotten themselves, their insides, confused with that nuclear clock on TV a man used to shift the hand around on during the Cold War. A clock, a regulator, a machine metaphor for trouble: standard issue. Misery loves diagnosis, also hard liquor, Maidie thought, staring at a bottle of sun-hued tequila and a bowl of limes on Rona's table.

Maidie—sitting next to the couple Rona introduced as her

parents, Clima and August—cut her meat daintily in spite of the fact that she was starving, though not literally, she reminded herself. And she could hardly stop herself from rushing to unveil the side of her personality she knew encouraged conversation with old people, for instance volunteering the fact she'd worked her way through school, so suddenly, so unaccountably, that people no doubt wondered what that information—which did reveal old-fashioned perseverance too rare today—had to do with the conversation at hand. Or if someone generalized about the deficiencies of now, waxing fond about the old days, when people understood the difference between shit and shoe polish—and even though graduate work had trained Maidie to scrutinize firsthand memories, an old person's especially, as necessarily enhanced by the impending certainty that death is arriving, youth gone, and the memory of daybreak sweetest at dusk—Maidie found a way to agree. She believed in change, its ongoingness. But she also believed tradition and courtesy—and the appearance of tradition and courtesy—had molted away too fast. But of course she didn't take this tack right now. She said, "It's a pleasure to meet you. Do you live nearby?"

"Yes," the sweet-faced man said. "This street is named for my father."

Maidie said, "How nice."

Clima leaned over, waving a stemmed glass filled with yellow liquid. (Dandelion wine? Maidie wondered.) Clima said, "I always think that if people say 'How nice' they mean 'fuck you.'"

Maidie stopped eating. "That's not what *I* meant."

Clima said, "You have a gnat on your forehead."

"I ought to wash your mouth out," August said, but he went on slicing, chewing.

"Oh, not *her*," Clima said, waving her stemmed glass, "for God's sake." She leaned over. "What do you think of gay people? I personally admire their courage, though I myself am not gay."

"Of course you're not," Rona said, "and if you were, your sex life would be over anyway."

"Mother," Cindy-June said, "I said no arguing."

Rona said, "Today is the twentieth anniversary of Elvis Presley's death."

"Oh," Clima said. "I'll toast that."

Rona said, "I practically invented rushing the stage. This was our first date, the Elvis concert in Phoenix. Girls, your daddy was shocked—he wondered who on earth his cousin had set him up with."

Evvy said, "We know the story. You already told us."

Maidie said, "So some blind dates do actually work out?"

Rona laughed, an involuntary burst. "You could say that." She looked at Harve. "We sometimes wonder. I take it you've had a bad experience. I had ludicrous blind dates right after my divorce." Maidie didn't know yet about Rona and Harve's divorce, how Rona started dating and realized she was attracted to men only if they reminded her of Harve, who also had going for him the pointed fact that he was the girls' father. They revamped, new rules.

Rona's, this time.

"God, I'll say you had bad dates." This was Clima, who walked over to the table, filled her glass with straight tequila. "Who was that one who had his name legally changed to Liberty?"

"First or last?" Maidie asked.

Rona belted out a laugh again. "First. His real name was Larry. But, Maidie, tell us about your worst blind date ever."

The oral tradition flourishing.

Or trying to, Maidie thought, considering Evvy's bored response to the legend of her parents' first date. Maidie tried to picture it: Rona rushing past security guards toward Elvis. Did Harve stay in the back, hands on his hips, grim and rejected? Really, Elvis must have been svelte and vulnerable-seeming then, worthy of adulation. Someday, Maidie thought, Evvy would wish she'd listened. But as for Maidie's oral record, she couldn't describe her worst blind date, not uncensored to strangers.

So Maidie described a counterproductive but speakable—*discutable,* the French would say—date, which took place in Nebraska after Neville left, which is to say after Neville left Maidie alone with waffle and steam irons, Corning Ware and Pyrex, embroidered pillow slips and canned tomatoes, taking his clothes, one quilt, one pillow, the crooked TV, two bath towels. He didn't like helping with chores, he said, and he wasn't good enough for Maidie, once he considered it. (He'd obviously never heard the rule that it's best to make just one excuse or you'll sound like a liar.) After he left, all kinds of people—Maidie's landlady Opal Johnson, Neville's sisters, classmates from the college, fat ladies getting on the scale at the weight-loss clinic where Maidie worked part time—said her marriage had been a waste of womanhood and someone else would appreciate the pearls she'd cast before Neville, a swine, and they hunted up new men. One, a film critic for the *Omaha Sentinel,* had been described as short but handsome.

Maidie drove an hour in the August heat in her Rambler without air-conditioning because the film critic thought there'd be better restaurants in Omaha than in Weeping Water—which wasn't exactly true; there was that place with fried oysters and red tablecloths—and when he answered the door, Maidie registered "short" but not "handsome." Also: hungry, hungry. "I get low blood sugar," she explained to Rona on the porch at Cindy-June's engagement party. But the film critic couldn't find an entrée without meat, cheese, or eggs at the restaurant he'd selected, so they drove back to his house, in the first, original Omaha suburb, its countertops and doorknobs custom built for the previous, taller-than-average owner, a good buy, he explained as he made wheat-germ cocktails in a turquoise bulbous machine, its name emblazoned in red letters, VEGA-VITA-MIXER. He bought it at a yard sale. He didn't eat at restaurants often, he confessed. Did Maidie understand the suffering endured for leather in her shoes?

Maidie looked at her brown brogans. That poor cow, she thought suddenly; fish and chicken too! She was hungry and, worse, obsessed that she'd seemed as odd to Neville as this man did to her, and maybe Neville had married her out of politeness because she'd proposed. But he could have said no, she thought tearfully. And the film critic started chasing a moth through his fluorescent kitchen, leaping past tall counters, past his Golden Age of Machines mixer, looming like a monument. As he swatted the moth out the door, he asked her to spend the night, so she could attend a fur protest in the morning. Telling this story to Rona, Maidie omitted the part about having been the one to propose and Neville accepting out of embarrassment, but she did pantomime the batting and cavorting. She re-created the scene: a short, serious man chasing moths in a big kitchen. Rona laughed, mopping her face. Harve said, "Damn, girl. You could be on TV."

"It's not that I'm prejudiced against vegetarians," Maidie explained, in case a vegetarian was present. "It's just that he seemed . . ."

"Like a pure type," Clima said.

"Exactly."

There'd been another date around the same time, not blind, exactly; Maidie felt she *should* like this man, director of the Weeping Water Arts Council, who'd bought two tickets to a James Taylor concert in a natural amphitheater outside Omaha. Though he wore black socks with cream trousers (a bad sign, Maidie felt), Opal approved—Opal who'd once suggested Maidie make every prospective date show a credit report, a blood test for venereal disease, a urinalysis for drugs, and the results of the Minnesota Personality Inventory, which had diagnosed one

of her daughters-in-law as frigid long before symptoms mani-
fested themselves at home and, too late, Opal's son had married
her. The Arts Council director even bought a present for Maidie
at Opal's Antique Outlet: a mourning brooch, a dead person's
hair braided with delicate thread. Maidie didn't admire mourning brooches—in fact, found them morbid—but she had
pointed out to him that they'd been fashionable hobbies in the
1890s, fancywork upon which ladies kept their hands, their
deep wishes and fears, anchored.

But that awkward night at the Omaha Holiday Inn: Singing
in the Snow, Maidie thought, confusing Bing Crosby with Gene
Kelly, and skating across carpet toward the round bed as the
Arts Council director groomed in the adjoining bathroom.
They hadn't yet slept together, but Maidie knew it impended,
what with the round bed, the sliding doors at the foot of it leading to a snub balcony. He came out of the bathroom wearing
shaving cream on his forehead, a fact upon which Maidie had
been prepared not to comment. He said, "I suppose you notice
I have shaving cream on my forehead. I find it works as a facial."
He also said her dress seemed revealing. No, chilly. Did she
want his cardigan? Disconcerted—experiencing *negation* and *re-
versal* regarding her previous desire to go to the concert and,
worse, onto that round bed—Maidie got a black eye by walking, blind, into the open door.

But—she reminded herself, looking at Rona, Harve, Evvy,
Cindy-June, Clima, and August, at the tooth-wiggling, spoon-
clapping man no one had introduced, and, near the table, tucking it in, Lalo—if she'd told that story here, so naked-making
and revelatory, it would seem as if she sometimes had sex with
blind dates. And maybe she shouldn't have performed the
moth-swatting either.

Still, people had laughed and clapped. Rex, on the edge of
the porch, smiled, shaking his head. In the telling, Maidie knew
she'd seemed smart, wicked, and impervious now if, after all,

she saw fun in those past bad judgments. Also, her cocky stance, her face mobile like a comedienne's, her lipsticked mouth at intervals bold, then fragile, her hands flying like lightning bolts chattered out the ends as she made pronouncements on—what?—blind dates, grandeur in petrified decline, life's contradictions, the great fissure between what's been desired and what's proffered: this was her personality drop-forged by too much late-breaking news, bad surprises, odd locations, slim acquaintances, and short chances to present herself, her life a series of blips and appearances. Accordingly, Maidie confessed her past instantly, refitted for the people at hand, collecting a crowd around her like a stockpile of cans in the larder in the face of famine. You don't actually open the cans and eat; you're comforted by their presence. To *have* is why. She'd cast off, and away, later. And so Maidie found herself with strangers on the rim of the third coast, a rock-littered strip of land near the Mexican border. Rex seemed to be staring; he'll show up at the Museum of Domestic History and Home Economy, a pest, a midge, she thought confusedly.

"Have you tried the tequila? It's like cognac." Clima offered her glass to Maidie, who—hypnotized by light refracting through the yellow glimmer—took a sip. It tasted like gold, amber, like rare and ingestible perfume. Clima pointed at the label. "See, it has a lucky horseshoe. Don't ever settle for less."

"It *is* good," Rex said. "It still causes hangovers, though."

Clima ignored him. "Rona! Where did you put those dainty glasses?"

Rona brought Maidie a stemmed glass. And mentioned how worried she was about the wedding—cooking for it. And how would she keep the grandkids out of mischief? "We can't afford not to have it here. I don't know two bits about weddings. Do you?"

"A wedding in your home is hard," Maidie said, savoring the yellow liquor, thinking what she might say and still omit private facts, her own weddings. Maybe she should get a *z* in her name, like Zsa Zsa and Liz: *Maizie*, inducted into the Society of Women Who Collect Husbands. Chief Curator at the Museum of Multiple Divorce.

"Ouch!" The man playing spoons stopped, rubbed his jaw.

"Buster, why don't you go to a dentist?" Rona said. "He loses a tooth almost every time he eats here," she told Maidie.

Buster held a lumpy tooth in the air.

Rona said, "I had to use a cattle prod to get Harve to the dentist." At first, sipping, Maidie thought Rona had said, "I had to use a cattle prod to get Harve to the wedding." Because Maidie had weddings on the brain, she thought. She stared at Rona, who was saying, "Buster, I'll make Harve take you to the dentist," at which point Maidie guessed Harve and Buster were related.

Harve said, "Miz Bonasso, my brother here has an auto body shop." He gave Maidie a card with a picture of a tow truck, a bumper for a mouth, headlights for eyes. HAPPY BUSTER'S AUTO BODY. And a slogan in iambic pentameter: *Rusty, Crusty, Dull, or Dented, Just Forget It, Happy Buster Puts "New" Back In*. But Buster didn't look happy: because he's losing his teeth, Maidie decided.

"Do you replace car windows?" she asked.

"Yup, I arrange for auto glass," Buster said.

"Why is a home wedding hard?" Rona asked.

Clima, shuffling past, refilled Maidie's glass.

"Because at home you'll work too hard," Maidie said. "My advice is to keep it simple. Sliced ham, dinner rolls, fruit salad—as opposed to salmon in pesto sauce with baby asparagus. You'll want to see the wedding, not just serve it. Get someone to supervise it—not someone in the family or the wedding party."

Rona looked at Maidie, eyes narrow. "I see."

Maidie looked back, noncommittal, like: No way in Admiral

Byrd's white frozen hell will I cook for your daughter's wedding
banquet and tend your illegitimate grandchildren. But polite at
the same time. "This is delicious," she said, meaning the
tequila.

Rona said, "The barbecue? Harve makes it. But we can't have
that. He needs to walk Cindy-June down the aisle. You have
practical ideas, though—like a professional wedding planner."

This is what a fat lady at the Weeping Water Weight Loss
Clinic had said. Maidie, working part time as she finished her
bachelor's degree in sociology and wound up the details of her
divorce from Neville, had suggested to the fat lady that all food
at her reception be prepared in advance. Maidie remembered
how Neville's mother had missed the vows, the *I do, I do,* because she was frosting the cake. "You're right," the lady had
said, and later, effusing about how helpful, insightful, Maidie
had been, she suggested Maidie finish her degree—in sociability, she said—and subcontract with the local bridal shop to plan
receptions. But Maidie was planning a departure, to earn her
master's degree at the University of Arkansas. What might a
new degree and location lead to? Progress. Maidie subscribed to
Hegel's theory: The future ripens into what it will, and should.

Lalo was standing at the table. He could at least sit down,
Maidie thought. Harve slapped Lalo's back—for the third time.

"Were you ever married?" Rona, a question.

"Was I ever married?" Maidie said. "Yes."

She could have said no, she realized. And it wasn't necessary
to repeat the question like a game show contestant. She turned
to Lalo. "Why don't you sit." And Rex. "You too." How quickly
they'd become *known*—she'd met them four hours ago; Rona
less than two. Maidie didn't want to know her further, deeper.

Yes, Maidie wanted friends for odd Sundays, the clock ticking, the refrigerator droning, Monday looming, all the spooks
of Sunday past: a family in front of the TV, watching Walt Dis-
ney's fireworks, a story about pain and separation, hearts frozen

in the snow, but in the end, a hearth, a table, a cluster of brave, loving people who happen to be related. Meanwhile, Maidie ate ice cream with cinnamon or, if her mother felt inclined, popcorn produced by the shiny popper she'd received as a wedding gift from Pastor and Mrs. Larssen, its red coils glowing like the inside of a volcano, a contained glimpse of hell. Maidie's father sprawled in the recliner, a king, a sultan, Lucy and Thea on the floor, facing the TV; Maidie's mother sewed. Still, you can't show up at someone's house on Sunday and slip in for the gathering and murmurs, the happy flurry. People don't want guests on Sunday. Christmas morning either.

And if you say to so-called friends, in private, what has mattered and can't now, what has been tossed overboard on the way here—Maidie remembered a history lesson about the horse latitudes, the part of the journey in which bogged-down sailors threw horses over the side of the ship to gain speed—friends heard not the context and reasons, only the compromised details, which they'd pass on to strangers. Then Maidie went places, and people she didn't know already had a category for her: Multiple Divorce. Hard on Husbands. Impossible to Love. Maidie gulped tequila.

"More?" Clima asked.

"More?" Maidie repeated. But it came out "More!" Clima poured.

"You had your wedding at home?" Rona asked.

Maidie thought: I had my wedding at home. Twice.

First, the hopeful, pretty one in Nebraska. Later, in Arkansas, Mia and Marbella hanging garlands of peonies on the white fireplace, like for a funeral. Maidie was pregnant, *had been* at least: the baby a "fetus" no longer "viable" (which is to say, dead in her stomach). They waited, Jack at work, picking fights with his manager, then asking for forgiveness by pointing out he had a family tragedy under way; Maidie at home, with Mia and Marbella. At some point, the baby, nonviable, would pass on, and away. Maidie would resume forward motion. But the baby wouldn't. If it stayed longer, the doctor said he'd take pharmaceutical measures first, surgical next. Maidie had set the wedding date when she turned up pregnant. Then the future, Maidie's pregnancy, turned nonviable. Maidie stayed afloat with woozy protective hormones until the baby passed itself away.

She'd considered calling the wedding off but somehow confused it with the dying, dead fetus, and preparation became ritual. She painted the kitchen walls, scrubbed the rest with a mop. Marbella described Maidie's behavior as estrogen-induced. Maidie's body, believing itself pregnant, forced her to tidy the hovel. "Like a cave woman," Marbella said, "who doesn't want the baby sleeping in dinosaur shit." This atavistic housewifery took place in front of the plate-glass window, which faced the neighbors' plate-glass window, only six feet away. Maidie sometimes saw her life as the neighbors' movie. When Jack got angry, throwing a lamp at the wall, a paperweight at antique china on the shelf, and, once, Maidie herself at the window casement, Maidie wondered, in the collect-herself split second when Jack's tantrum stopped, if the neighbors had seen—the mother folding laundry, children climbing like monkeys over the sofa, the father smoking, reading. If they did, they didn't say. They invited Maidie to church. Talking to them, Maidie referred to Jack as her husband even before he was: My husband is grilling burgers, and we're still unpacking. May I borrow some matches? My husband's car, blocking your driveway? Let me move it.

The night of the wedding, Maidie wondered if they could see in. Did they think Maidie was marrying Jack for the second time? Jack wore a suit, Maidie a dress that, even when she picked it out, had seemed like curtains. But she hardly liked anything, her contractions starting for a day and stopping for four. Pharmaceutically urged, the fetus went away three nights before the wedding. Maidie stared out the window, toying with a jigsaw puzzle that lay in pieces on the table. Dawn came and, with it, bustle in the neighbors' kitchen, the mother making pancakes in the green bathrobe she got for Christmas (Maidie had seen her shake it from its tissue-wrapped box), the children sleepy in pajamas in the half-light, poking scoops of food to their mouths. Maidie's dad showed up the day of the wedding. "I want to be here," he said. And later, very drunk, "I want to be at all your weddings." Mia cried. Marbella made faces behind Jack's mother's back. "Every woman loses something necessary to happiness," Jack's mother said as she stirred olive–cream cheese dip. "Not just you." Maidie was considering this: had the baby been necessary to happiness? Then the judge said it was over. The light meter, set too high, made Maidie's eyes seem red in every photo.

"Yes," Maidie said, "a home wedding."

Like a home perm—it might take or not, and it's always messy.

But Rona was listening to Harve, who talked about Elvis. "It was Priscilla who ruined him," Harve said, "not that Doc Watson."

Rona said, "You mean Colonel Tom Parker."

Harve said, "His death coincided with the end of big automobiles."

Rona said, "What?"

"That's right. Elvis dies, and no one wants a big car anymore."

Rona said, "You're saying it was cause and effect?"

Harve said, "I am not. I find it interesting, is all."

Time to go, Maidie decided.

She knew the sociological explanations for personalizing a celebrity death. But she wished more people knew, so they could hear how stupid they sounded, projecting private futility onto a human-turned-symbol, a far-off death momentarily explaining the enduring sensation that life's essence has evaporated. The morning before John Lennon was shot, Maidie, Laree, and Laree's boyfriend Phil Kristofferson had driven eight hours to visit a place called the Garden of Eden, a cluster of forty-foot statues a farmer had built, hoping to explicate Genesis as a message about William Jennings Bryan and the labor movement: a statue of Adam toiling with a scythe, Eve suffering through childbirth (Maidie can still remember Eve's cement grimace). That night, the news came emergency-blipped over the TV, and Phil ended up outside the motel, saying John this, John that, holding a lit match in the air until Laree, unpredictable since she'd had the abortion, went outside and slapped him. As Phil slapped Laree back, Maidie remembered that song about rock-and-roll heaven and thought how most people the song mentioned as sitting out eternity at the right hand of Rock-and-Roll God had died near a toilet, or in some likewise uninspirational pose. She stood up. "Thanks for dinner."

Rex stood up too. He called to Lalo. "If you want to leave your bike on the back of the truck and get a lift home," he said, "I'll be there in a few minutes." Lalo—loading barbecue and potato salad into a plastic sack Harve held—nodded. At the curb, Rex said to Maidie, "I don't think he's lived here long."

Maidie said, "His ancestors have—longer than yours. He's not an illegal alien. He's a college student, for Christ's sake."

Rex, patient, said, "I didn't say he wasn't. But I don't think he's lived in the United States very long. I'm saying ask him."

"What for?" She'd stopped under the yard light to stare at a cluster of orange daisies. A cactus—a prickly pear—crouched nearby. In one of Maidie's remote brain folds, the memory of a captioned photo persisted: *Blood-red sand gives sustenance to the prickly pear.* Maidie also remembered that the prickly pear had been imported from Mexico to Madagascar to fight erosion and, like most species grafted onto strange terrain, became a weed, a curse; islanders chopped at it with machetes. Maidie wondered again if Arizona, minus its technological clutter, seemed like Madagascar. Coral sand, short mountains, and—Maidie watched Harve scraping leftovers into a sack for Lalo—unofficial apartheid. Maidie had tried imagining her mother's childhood in Madagascar so often that the image she'd settled on seemed as real as a photo: In a white schoolgirl blouse, her hair pushed back from wistful eyes, she stares out the window of an upstairs room. Is she locked in? Is the lemon tree's scent lovely? But this picture is concocted. So is the picture of Maidie's mother in California today: Small creases making her movie star eyes more starry, she wears a silky exercise suit and sips wine at a table near the ocean. Maidie blinks, her mother vanishes.

Maidie stepped into her yard. "Careful," Rex said. Her heels sank. She heard raucous laughing. She looked back at Rona's porch, at Harve and Buster clinking glasses to the absent groom, their foreheads gleaming like twin onions. Rona called Cindy-June's children inside to bed. Lalo walked to Rex's truck. Guapo yapped. Clima tried to practice artful conversation one last time. Over the scraping, tinkly sounds of dinner being wrapped up, hauled in, she called out, "They say young people today grow so tall because of growth hormones factory farms inject into cows. Do you agree, Harve?" Harve didn't answer. Maidie reached her front door drunk, *lit,* she decided, her insides as lucent as tequila in a bottle. Like being stoned: enlarged misgivings. She'd lie awake tonight, worrying: she did or didn't, should or shouldn't have, might easily have avoided. . . . The night would pass without sleep, brainwash, and in the morning she'd arrive at work disheveled, her Freudian slip hanging a half inch below every pedestrian, workaday truth she spoke.

What would she think of as she lay awake? Detachment. She'd been detached: unyoked, removed. Sometimes she'd detached others. She'd do it again, if she had to. She thought of her sister Thea singing a particular song, tipping the microphone stand: *I'm so . . . I need your . . . I'm special! . . . I'll get your attention!*

You don't get attention by asking, Maidie thought, though Thea seemed to. Really, the truth was inside the contradiction. A removal was relief, the onset of the chance to never again depend on connection, never again swing like a clapper inside an indifferent bell and break, clatter, on the floor. In the meantime, Maidie would need a temporary set of friends she could slough off painlessly when the time came. And touch, that undulant veneer. . . . Some likely night, she'd accept an impersonal caress, though she hoped the stopgap, the (im)person caressing, would understand that, thus far, Maidie had been untended, undermaintained, and therefore had never been *engaged*, not really, not like a clutch against a gear, or a pre-bride in love. But someday—she believed it and didn't—she'd fix herself.

Death, a deadline.

And Maidie remembered Vera tracking time, making sure her plans got laid, chances seized. She'd died early anyway, of cancer, lying yellow-skinned in the coffin, her hair combed wrong—the undertaker had flattened her bangs back with pins. Maidie's mother cried into a handkerchief, her head covered with a pleated cellophane rain hat. The church smelled like wool. Later, chocolate-colored mud streamed through cemetery roads. Later than that, Maidie's mother made everyone in the family take off shoes at the door, and she carried them, smearing the front of her cerise dress coat, to the bathtub, where she knelt and scrubbed the shoes with a fingernail brush. Her hair fell over her face, her gaudy makeup. She looked haggard. Maidie's father stood over her. "Enough, Elaine!" Maidie's mother said, "Eugene was too sad to tell the undertaker how to comb Vera's hair. He was too sad to even comb his own," she said. For the funeral, she meant. Vera's mother had sat in her wheelchair, her mouth sagging, her white hair snarled, and asked, loud: "Who's in the coffin?" Maidie's mother had slipped forward to the coffin and used a comb from her purse to fix Vera's hair right, familiar.

Brown water spattered the porcelain. Maidie's mother scrubbed. Her shoulders heaved. Maidie's dad said, "You weren't that close to Vera." Maidie's mother answered, half English, half French. "My heart," she said and, a few minutes later, *"mon dolor."* And winter began, the long transmission of pain. Maidie's mother cried when she broke a plate, when Thea outgrew her shoes, when snow melted, a hubcap fell, potatoes burned, the storm door gaped, the news reported burglary, a baby cried in the church, the paperboy's dog chafed against its chain, a page fell out of the dictionary, and TV commercials about scattered families reuniting by phone aired. Maidie's dad didn't understand. Years later—centuries, Maidie thought, standing on her step in Tucson next to Rex, whom she knew even less than her mother had known Vera—Maidie understood only that everyone her mother lost had somehow become a corpse, Vera's. Maidie looked at her own front door, dark windows, and pushed the memory back.

Where would it go?

Maidie used to tap on her mother's door, whispering: did she want a sandwich, a glass of water? If her mother didn't answer, Maidie pretended she wasn't there, no one was, the room vacant. Maidie came home from school one day, and her dad sat at the table—too early, he should have been at work—and said her mother had taken a bus. She'd write a letter later. Maidie shrugged. "I didn't spend much time with her." Which was true then. Her mother had been meeting with Pastor Larssen in his study a few times a week. She'd been questioning *meaning,* she told Maidie: what was she meant to do, produce, care for? She hadn't found happiness—her own she was supposed to give back. She had a bottle of blue Valium for night, yellow for day. She'd been baking apple strudel, brown betty, Sally Lunn cake, coconut macaroon pie, for Eugene, who stayed home, sad himself. When she did write a letter, it said: *I miss you, but for a woman who sees and feels too much before her allotted time, solitude is excellent.*

Maidie opened the door.

Rex stood with his hands in his pockets. He cleared his throat. "This is a nice old part of the city that hasn't been rediscovered." Then he was gone, calling good-bye past his shoulder. Maidie watched him disappear; his taillights vanished. She shut the door and stood for a minute facing the peephole, the glass bubble that provides warning against strangers, bald notice the world shouldn't be admitted. She closed her eyes and saw Clima, Rex, Rona, August, Cindy-June, Lalo, Evvy, Zora Coles (her lips), Garth McHugh (his mustache), blurring, all of it, wavery and gray like TV's last broadcast: "The Star-Spangled Banner," the Goodnight-a-Prayer, then *blank, buzz*. Did TV still sign off for the night? Or did talk show hosts raise their rabble until dawn? Maidie sensed Rex Hurley's truck still rumbling underneath her, as if she were driving, navigating Speedway still. (Or was it Buster's business card truck, its headlight eyes and toothless bumper?) Maidie didn't want to be a wife, no, but she didn't want to be alone either, a moldering root, a buried resource. Her own garbled prayer was about making it all the way just once, to the altar, no, but past a state of dormant uncertainty leading to . . .

What?

*B*obbing and swaying in the hammock stretched between olive trees near her patio, Maidie realized she had momentum, the habit of speed. She'd stopped moving, but the landscape didn't. A shuddering halt: *drag*. She missed the hypnotic whine of gears grinding, towing a load, gravity weighing in, reasons to stay. Then, exertion. Aerodynamic loft. Maidie missed that, also air slapping through open vent windows in her car as it wobbled onward.

Go.

To Norfolk, Virginia, to clear out the last of her refuse with Jack, divorce papers and recriminatory final remarks. The week before Maidie had moved out, there'd been an explosion in a federal building in Oklahoma. Maidie stood behind Jack's chair in the forest-green TV room, Jack more consummately entranced than he'd been since the Gulf War. Cameras zoomed in on stalwart survivors, the mangled remains of architecture. A journalist intoned about devastation and aftermath. Oklahoma seemed like a faraway planet, hills and dells like moon craters, residents stoop-shouldered and blinking, lights cast by news crews washing everyone's face pale, glinting off eyeglass lenses and startled expressions until people looked like they had silver disks instead of faces. The governor orated. A choir sang. *Almighty, we grieve.*

Go.

To Minnesota, maybe.

Because if Maidie didn't get in touch with her family—what they thought, said, did, new twists and protracted loyalties— they might sift through the dregs one last time and Maidie's place in the dim pattern would vanish. Once, at the Nebraska State Fair, Maidie had her fortune told with tea leaves. *I'm getting a clear sense,* the woman in the kimono said, *of your transparency.* Could Maidie prevent demotion in the ranks of Deserves Attention if she planned ahead? No. But she would feel the future arrive, her own willpower intersecting with complex alliances and protocol and better prepare herself for the days ahead exploding into weeks, months, a lifetime during which Maidie would grow less substantial, unanchored, flighty. Dear Family, Maidie might write on a postcard explaining that Arizona is hot, dry, clean, as opposed to cold, sticky, complicated. I miss you, but for a woman who has seen and felt much, the absence of, well, mildew is excellent. Maidie pictured her dad, dawdling and lonesome. Lucy, her closed, impatient expression. The death of pleasure, this is, her face would say. Thea grinning broadly, gums revealed. If we haven't found the fun, Thea would say—

Go.

Maidie's mother was still in California, Maidie supposed—a vacation turned permanent. In Hector, Minnesota, the bus depot used to be the Sinclair station, a white building with a dinosaur on top. A gray suitcase must have sat on its end on pavement. Maidie's mother must have worn her blue coat and matching shoes, her wide-open, dark eyes, small creases—from smiles? from sadness?—like delicate punctuation, parentheses, around her mouth. Her own father hadn't loved her much, Maidie's dad once told Maidie, Lucy, Thea. They were sitting at the Formica table in the kitchen. Maidie's dad had cooked dinner: scrambled eggs and bacon, also Sara Lee cupcakes with glasses of milk for dessert. "How much?" Thea had asked. "How the hell would I know?" Maidie's dad had answered, spooning out eggs. He was talking about milk, or cupcakes. Thea was talking about love: how much had been too little? Maidie said, "How much did they love her, Dad?"

"Who?"

"Mom, when she was little?"

He'd said, "Beats me. Maybe five minutes total. Now eat."

Maidie remembered her dad tried to bring her mother home. He'd taken a plane to California. Somehow—maybe he rented a car—he drove to the beach house that used to be Vera's mother's. Maidie's mother was staying there. But the last time Maidie said so—that her dad had tried to bring her mother home—Lucy disagreed. They were in Arkansas, in a Denny's near the airport. Lucy tamped her cigarette in a plastic ashtray. "No," she said. "He took Mom divorce papers so he could marry Neena." Maidie didn't believe it. He was sad when he came home. He did marry Neena, though. All the rest—Maidie's mother's hair and skin, her fragrant lap, her silky voice—lives on in one of Maidie's dreams like in a cramped, neat apartment where nothing shifts.

Go.

Going out to the patio one Friday afternoon to swoosh a vacuum cleaner hose along chaise longue cushions, Maidie saw Rex Hurley parking his blue flatbed in the street. He got out, walking toward her with a bottle of good tequila, a horseshoe on the label. "Housewarming," he said. "I noticed you liked it." Maidie smiled. "Thank you." Rex stood for a minute in the dappling, unsteady light. Was there something to say besides thank you? Maidie wondered. The weather had turned cool. "Maybe you'd like to join me for a drink," she added. She went inside for stemmed glasses. As she and Rex sat on chaise longues, sipping, Rex looked at a tin placard advertising Golden Boy Tobacco that Maidie had hung on the adobe wall above the patio; she'd bought it at Opal Johnson's Antique Outlet. It showed one man resting on a hay bale as another man heated up blacksmith tools. The legend read: *Make New Friends. Keep the Old. Those Are Silver. These are Gold. Brows May Wrinkle, Hair Grow Gray, Friendship Never Knows Decay.* Rex smiled. "That's a comforting thought."

Maidie smiled back. "If clichéd."

He frowned. "Then why do you hang it up?"

"It's an antique," she said, annoyed, "a record of a different time." Still, it was homey. Or saccharine. Maybe when people lived in the same town their entire lives, they'd needed aphorisms to resign themselves to friends they couldn't avoid.

Rex was talking about the mountains. "To the east, we have the Rincons," he said, waving. Getting out of a car across the street, Clima and Rona seemed to think Rex was waving at them. Clima called out: "Salutations! Bottoms up!" Rex lifted his glass and nodded. "To the north, the Santa Catalinas," he told Maidie, gesturing again. Across the street, Buster and Harve got out of a truck with a six-pack. Harve waved. "Good evening, Miz Bonasso. Rex Hurley, nice to see you again." Maidie and Rex waved again. "I'm familiar with these tourism facts," Rex told Maidie, "because I was the chamber of commerce president for ten years, in the seventies." Maidie nodded. Rex was wearing khaki pants and a striped seersucker shirt. "Did you have a ponytail," Maidie asked, savoring her drink, "when you were chamber of commerce president?" Rex blushed, a mottled, half-purple color, puce. "No," he said. "I was almost another person then."

The sun sank behind the hills.

Maidie stared at the bottle. If you live alone, you probably drink alone, she reasoned. But maybe only wine or beer. "Will you stay to dinner?" she asked Rex, suddenly intent on refilling her glass. *Drinks are on the house!* her dad used to say when Eugene and Vera came to visit. Maidie had always pictured people on the roof, clinking glasses, convivial. But when Rex and Maidie went inside, Rex carrying the bottle, Maidie the glasses, she opened the refrigerator and realized she didn't have anything to serve except bread, onions, broccoli, liverwurst—old maid's fare. "I've never eaten much liverwurst," Rex said. Maidie said, "It was one of our family traditions—in terms of lunch meat," she added, confused. She'd left the TV on when she went outside to vacuum the chaise longue cushions, a PBS show about wolves. Lawrence Welk was on now, flicking a white baton. Maidie's dad used to point out that Lawrence Welk was born on a farm five miles from where Maidie's dad was born. Lawrence Welk's parents didn't speak English. Maidie's dad's parents didn't speak much English. Maidie's dad, like Lawrence Welk, was an example of how far gumption might get you, he'd emphasized.

Maidie chopped broccoli. Rex seemed to be saying he'd gotten divorced after thirty years of marriage. Thirty? Maidie smeared bread with mayonnaise. Now he was talking about Christmas Eve a long time ago. . . . He'd gone to a bar to bring his father home, but before his father would leave, he made Rex stand on a stool and sing "Rudolph the Red-Nosed Reindeer" three times. Rex refilled Maidie's glass. Maidie liked this drink, its elevating effect, as if she were in a third-story room painted yellow. The sandwiches sat on plates until the bread turned stale. The broccoli, flaccid. A night bird outside the window shrieked, and Maidie felt a strange urge for bones, breath, flesh. Besides husbands, she'd had just two lovers: Joel Scribner; also, Phil Kristofferson's brother, who one night watched TV with Maidie while Phil and Laree made love in the next room, the bed thumping against the wall. Phil's brother had seemed engrossed, driven, and who was Maidie to say no? She hadn't wanted to be exclusive, superior. It had been a democratic impulse, she decided. She stared at Rex. She worried he'd think she was bold, amorous, a siren luring a staid man toward rocks. But she crossed the room and stood next to him.

Rex stared at Maidie, his blue-gray eyes startled. Then he kissed her, his face pressing so hard she thought their skull bones might crack from pressure. He was out of practice. She gave herself up to it, temporary kissing. She hadn't had much touch, handling, tangibility, not lately except for Jack's shoving and punching, broken dishes and furniture. Kissing was like crying, she decided. It could swamp you. It wasn't a good plan, this kissing that felt like stirring mud. There, there, Maidie said to herself, her breath coming in sobs. "Is the bedroom at this end of the house?" Rex asked, his voice warbly, but he steered Maidie that way as though it were impolite, uncourtly, or a waste of a good chance to refuse a woman spellbound by kissing. They backed onto the bed, and Maidie remembered circumstances had changed. "Condoms," she said. She didn't have one. Neither did Rex. They fell asleep, tequila pumping through their veins, the color of sleep gold, she thought as she dreamed she'd swallowed a shiny needle which had passed through her windpipe fine. "But it will cause problems later on as your body politic struggles to accommodate it," a white-robed doctor was saying. Then a familiar dream about her mother.

She woke to the sound of Rex dressing. Swish, legs into his pants. Clink, his belt buckle. Light through the window was silver. Maidie got up, put on the clothes she'd worn the day before. She walked Rex past the sticky tequila glasses to the door. Outside, the vacuum cleaner lay in pieces on the patio. I must be boy-crazy, she thought, walking Rex to his truck. She remembered her mother setting a drink down, belting out a song, "Where the Boys Are." Eugene and someone else—Pastor Larssen?—had watched as her dress fluttered, light shining through its filmy material. Maidie's dad had looked away, embarrassed. Once, in a velvet jumpsuit she'd worn to a church meeting where she felt she'd been snubbed, she'd said, "Get hard-boiled, Maidie."

Rex stood in the street, his brow wrinkling. "Maybe you'd like to visit the San Xavier del Bac Mission, which is sometimes called the Sistine Chapel of North America?" he asked. Evvy, Cindy-June, and Cindy-June's kids pulled up in Evvy's station wagon, emblazoned with bumper stickers. VISUALIZE WHIRLED PEAS. They headed up Rona's sidewalk, Evvy carrying a box of Dunkin' Donuts. Rona's door opened. "Maidie," she said, "come for coffee."

Maidie had barely combed her hair.

Rona's door closed again.

"I can't," Maidie said.

"The San Xavier del Bac?" Rex asked. "I didn't mean today."

Rona opened the door. "The doughnuts are going fast."

"You'd better get a doughnut," Rex said. He fired up his truck. "We'll let it grow." *What* grow? "I haven't been in love much."

He drove away.

Maidie crossed the street to tell Rona she couldn't come. But Rona opened the door with a cup, a doughnut on a plate; she handed them to Maidie. Clima was sitting on the sofa. "I like a nip of tequila in my coffee," she said, "then nothing until sunset, when I have a gin rickey." Maidie's stomach lurched. It was early in the day. Still, on Saturday mornings in Nebraska, she used to go downstairs to The Antique Outlet and visit Opal Johnson, who'd talk about the tribulations her children had faced. Their names began with K. Kent, Kendall, Kara, Kitty, Kenneth. Opal once said she thought her daughter Kara had never had an orgasm. "Not that you have to every time. Sometimes it's enough to give your partner pleasure." Maidie had felt surprised—that you did or didn't, that Opal logged orgasms at all. Opal also said she felt closer to Maidie than to her own daughters. Too bad, so did Opal's husband. One day, repairing Maidie's stove, he said, "I saw your brown eyes, and I was a goner." Maidie was twenty-four, Opal's husband sixty-two, moving her way. "I've got to run," Maidie had said. At Rona's, she said, "I've got to run."

Evvy, wearing bib overalls and a fedora, smiled. Cindy-June held her daughter in her lap, examining her hair for split ends.

Rona said, "My girls don't like to come for coffee on Saturday morning either. But I insist on it so we can stay in touch. Maidie," Rona asked, "how long have you been seeing Rex?"

What could Maidie say? Twelve hours?

Evvy said, "Don't grill her. You're not related to her."

Rona smiled. "But I'm a romantic. Where are you from?"

"Minnesota," Maidie said.

Rona said, "Is that where your ex-husband is?"

Cindy-June said, "Mother!"

Technically speaking, Jack wasn't Maidie's ex-husband yet. "Virginia."

"But you got married in Nebraska?"

Wrong husband. Maidie didn't correct her. "Yes."

Rona said, "Everyone in your family is in Minnesota?"

Maidie said, "Except my mother."

Rona said, "Where is she?"

Maidie paused. "I haven't seen her in a while."

Rona's eyes narrowed. "That must be difficult."

"A long time ago it was," Maidie said.

Evvy said, "Mom, stop. Maidie will tell you about it when she's ready." Evvy turned on the TV, a news show about a famous man who'd been accused of murdering his ex-wife. For years, she'd called 911. He was on TV now, saying the bruises on his ex-wife's face in police photos were because she used to squeeze her pimples.

Cindy-June said, "He's a big fat liar."

Clima said, "When we were first married and I wouldn't take his advice—I wouldn't take orders!—August used to spank me."

Cindy-June said, "How kinky."

Clima said, "I wish! He was bullheaded. But I suppose every woman has a memory like that. You find out how far you'll push, what price you're willing to pay." Clima reached over and ruffled Maidie's hair. "I could have traveled all over like you."

Rona said, "Mama, you could not."

"If I'd gotten my driver's license sooner," Clima said. "I graduated from high school when I was fourteen. My teacher used to say I was a mathematical genius." Clima turned to Maidie. "Do you like Arizona? I myself hate the hot, unrelenting summer winds."

Rona said, "*Do* you like it here?"

Maidie felt hungover. "I like the heat," she said. She had the paranormal sense that Clima was near, radiating kinship. *Body politic,* the phrase from Maidie's dream, popped into her head, and the memory of Rex beside her, a bolster. And the recurring dream about her mother. No matter if Maidie was twenty-three and about to marry Neville in Nebraska, or twenty-nine and bearing up in a house with Jack, or thirty-five and transplanted to Arizona, newly bereft, she slid into sleep, and the past rose up. Maidie was always how old she was when she had the dream, but her mother was the same age she was back then— which is to say, close to Maidie's age now. In the dream, Maidie's mother has said some small, irritating thing. Maidie has *done* some small, irritating thing. "You need to do better," her mother will say, her brown eyes soft, disappointed. "You can do better than that." At what? Wrapping the end of a Christmas present? Sweeping a porch? Conducting a life? Making love stay? When her mother won't answer, Maidie can't help it, she hits her mother hard, harder. She doesn't quit until the flesh gives way, turns sloppy, wet. In the dream, flesh tears like leather, like stale bread. In the morning, Maidie wakes guilty, thinking *what?*

"Maidie," Rona was saying, "will you stay?"

Set . . .

*O*nce—*at a cacophonous neighborhood party in Norfolk*—*Maidie* sipped wine and recalled an article she'd read that had traced the decline of the new South, its narcissism and short-sightedness, to the advent of privacy fences, air-conditioning, and backyard decks; in the old days, people had clustered on front porches and called out affable salutations. Maidie pictured a woman in flowered silk, a paper fan palpitating the still air around her face as she leaned forward and told people on the sidewalk that, indeed, her gout was improved. *Friends,* Maidie thought as she stood on Dodie's redwood deck. The word sounded strange, like the time Maidie had written a report on archival supplies at the Civil War Museum, and after she'd checked the spelling on *bumpons* and *anastigmatic loupe,* words like *with* and *also* had looked odd. *Neighbors,* she thought: *nigh-dwellers.* Dodie's party had a theme, "deckadence." Chocolate was the main event.

When Maidie woke that morning, crape myrtle bursting fuchsia outside the window, Jack was in the kitchen with the double boiler, making mousse for Dodie, another daylong distraction to keep him from looking for work. Not that he could on Saturday, Maidie reminded herself, though when she'd come home unexpectedly on Monday, she'd found Jack skateboarding in the street. That was Monday. This was Saturday. Maidie moved on to relevant irritations: they couldn't afford the ingredients for mousse. But what did *afford* mean when every time Jack spent unbudgeted money, Maidie rearranged payments on outstanding debts, or postponed a dental appointment or haircut, and—presto!—chocolate and sherry, or Blockbuster videos, were paid for after all?

Maidie didn't want to go to the party. She walked into the kitchen and said so. Jack wasn't surprised, he said, because Maidie had abnormal social sense. "As self-contained as an egg," he'd said, smoothing the white apron over his navy-blue sweatsuit.

All day, Maidie had wondered: an egg?

She took a shower. Self-contained.

She blew-dry her hair.

True, she'd never made friends without feeling as if she were fitting her life around someone else's, amoeba-like, and then recoiling at the sense of her own pliability, pulling back inside.

Laree had turned into an authentic friend, yes, but if facts are admitted, allowed in, Maidie would never have scraped up acquaintance with Laree if Laree hadn't cultivated Maidie first, enthusiastically. Maidie ate lunch at the cafeteria across from the courthouse in Jackson Hole where she worked as a file clerk. Laree scooped tapioca, ladled pea soup, asked, "You from around here?" Then, "Married?" Then, shocked, "You moved here by yourself? Girl, I'm coming by after work to take you out on the town."

In college, lonely women gravitated toward each other in the seating arrangement. Some professors photocopied class-member phone numbers, to facilitate the formation of study groups.

Maidie never called anyone first.

But she'd liked her in-laws, Neville's parents and sisters.

Though not Jack's mother, really.

She'd liked ladies from work.

Mia, who'd moved to Arkansas from Georgia to start her master's degree at the same time Maidie had moved there from Nebraska. Lovelorn, Mia grew depressed when Maidie married Jack, because she, Mia, wasn't marrying. She left town after the wedding.

Marbella, a woman Maidie had hired to clean to clean house, back when Maidie and Jack lived in Arkansas and he still had a job. Marbella passed on dubious information about history (Catherine the Great had sex with a horse), about cleaning (you get spots out of a carpet with nail polish remover). About palm reading. "You have a short life line," she said. Maidie said, "Just out of curiosity, if you saw someone with a really short life line, how would you say so tactfully?" Marbella had answered, "I'm not sure. I've never seen one shorter than yours."

One role: best friend.

Many faces.

Changing fast and inexplicable, like in a soap opera when one actress retires and another steps in and the story line doesn't accommodate change: e.g., the second "Alexis" having a different hair color and standing three inches shorter than the first. Do her loved ones notice? No. Maidie noticed, trying to explain her past to Opal, to Mia, to Marbella, to Dodie. It split into infinite versions: tamer, gutsier, more wild, passive. None of them had a simple germ of a beginning, like the sled "Rosebud" in the movie *Citizen Kane,* an early deprivation to which everything miserable that happened got traced. Deprived early, depraved late. And every possible ending Maidie had envisioned, every settled point of reflection, moved forward fast. Sometimes Maidie invented an end to fit the present. In Nebraska, talking to Opal, the reward for hard times suffered was here. In Arkansas, talking to Mia, contentment had arrived. So Maidie said, and wondered. Had she told his part before? Contradicted herself?

She looked at Dodie's party guests: Dodie's friend from La Leche League, who danced the "shag" in a flowered dress; a woman from down the street, who wore gray suits on weekdays and exercise thongs on weekends; Dodie's husband, in a chef's hat, KISS THE COOK; a pinched-faced gentleman in khakis, who seemed annoyed no one wanted to see slides of his trip to Bolivia; Dodie's brother Quentin, clipping back wilted buds of petunias; a woman in a red dress, who'd drunk too much and exclaimed, "But does anyone in our age group have sex regularly?" Was the pervading sense that people who befriended Maidie belonged to an upstart tribe with odd customs due to the fact that friendship based on proximity was ill-suited to the transient conditions of this part of the century? Maidie watched Jack, his forced jollity, a smile that looked like a grimace, which he'd worn since he'd been unemployed, two years. He lit citronella candles for Dodie. "Thank you, dear." Normal social sense? If Maidie moved again, old friends would come from where?

*R*ex Hurley had come to dinner. He'd bought the groceries and Maidie cooked them: linguine, also clams she'd left steaming so long they'd turned gummy, hard. Maidie and Rex sat at the kitchen table, chewing, chewing. Finally, Maidie thought, swallowing: the clams went down, edible. "These are delicious," Rex said, smiling, his eyes luminous and deep. Either he didn't know how clams were supposed to taste or he was polite. Maidie answered him, irritable, "If you give me fake compliments, I won't know a real one when I hear it. These clams taste like shit."

His face clouded over. His eyes turned shallow. "I understand there are a thousand words in the English language that drag up the past for you. But I'm bound to use one once in a while."

Then he was polite and receptive again, making conversation along these lines: He'd run into someone today he hadn't seen in fifteen years, Rocky Romaine. The last time Rex saw Rocky Romaine, Rocky was married to his second wife, a seemingly permanent arrangement—they had two well-raised children, for example. But Rocky Romaine had turned up divorced again today, claiming the women's movement had brainwashed his wife, which was beside the point. "It goes to show," Rex said, "that all the time, people change." He stood up, carried plates to the sink. Maidie tried to fathom whether the story had been designed, dredged up, for *her*. Was there a moral? Or was Rex simply recounting his day? Once, he'd said he didn't understand how people her age made commitments—marriage, he meant—and reneged so quickly. Maidie had answered that people her age couldn't understand how people his age had stayed like hypocrites in bad marriages. He'd nodded. "That's the flip side." He'd stayed married thirty years himself. How? "We were both good sports," he'd answered. "We wanted to. Until the children were grown."

"I'm pretty simple," he'd said once.

What did *that* mean? Maidie wondered.

Definition 1. Not involved or complicated; easy.

Definition 2. Having little sense or intellect.

He scraped the plates, washed the dishes. He needed to make a phone call, he told Maidie. Sitting at the table, she poured herself another glass of wine. He pulled out a notebook he used as a journal, business and personal. He kept his checking account the same way, business and personal. *Rex Hurley, Inc.* He opened his journal—spiral bound, the date of its initial entry, *Aug. 7, 1996,* scrawled on its pink cover. Maidie had snooped through it. Under a numerical date—say *10-17-96*—would be notes about phone calls to return, a better recipe for pinto beans, a reminder to buy his eighty-four-year-old mother a new air conditioner, a mention of his dog's health ("Guapo not eating well—looks old"). And from time to time, philosophical scraps: "Life's too short to drink cheap wine." "Worry is a spasm of the mind." And Maidie had seen messages, too, about herself. "Maidie Bonasso called today—*first time.*" Or: "Maidie Bonasso, very tense! So we drove to Sabino Canyon, drank tequila, watched sunset." Right now, he opened his notebook, took out his long-distance calling card. "This will take just a minute," he said, smiling. Maidie forced herself to smile back—she liked him, yes, didn't want him to go away, not yet—and felt surprised, again, he hadn't noticed her disingenuous smile, fake.

The phone call he made was about a vintage Cadillac. "No," he said. "Your whole underside's rebuilt. The price is way too high."

Maidie glanced in his notebook:

"Dinner with Maidie Bonasso. Love mixes throughout my body."

She looked away.

She went outside to the patio. She thought about the last time Rex Hurley had spent the night here, *love mixing throughout his body.* Had he made that up? It seemed like a greeting card: corny. The last time he'd spent the night, they'd cooked dinner, eaten it, cleaned up. They made love, of course. When she fell asleep afterward, she dreamed she was driving on a cliff, which shifted continuously, like a snowbank or a dune of sand, a peak turning into valleys, valleys everywhere. She drove a white bus with female passengers, and punched the brakes, the clutch, the gas. Her skin stretched tight over her insides, which she had to protect too. If she slid off the cliff—and she didn't see how she couldn't, the peak declining into depressing gulleys, no matter how she navigated—she'd die smothered, a bag of desiccated brains and bone. Of course, she didn't. She woke, hollering as a chorus of women from the back of the bus—the friends she'd made and lost as she'd moved from state to state—called out contradictory and useless instructions for love. *Never humiliate a man. Stand up for yourself. Start out mean and get nice. Start out nice and get mean.* Rex reached for her, cupped his fingers over her mouth. "Shh," he said. "Easy." *A broken heart, patched, mends.* Who said that? Rex draped his arm over the cage of her ribs, and they fell back asleep, peaceful. Now he stood in the doorway to the patio, the lit house behind him.

A bag of brains and bone.

A peak turning into a depression.

A heart, mended. With what, epoxy? Above, the stars seemed dim.

"What are you thinking about?" Rex asked.

Straining to make her voice pleasant, not testy (*Maidie Bonasso, very tense!*), she answered. "Thinking?" she said. "Not much."

Hard-boiled, old, golden friends. New, silver friends. Maidie doodled this on a file folder at a trustee meeting as she listened to Garth McHugh, who looked like a silent-film star, his mustache and sardonic grin. He flexed his cheek muscles, staring at Zora Coles, her lips that matched her cinched-at-the-waist dress. In the small-talk moment before the meeting began, Z. had reached into her bag—a Ralph Lauren, she'd mentioned—and pulled out photos of her cat, also of Z. herself standing next to a red convertible, a scarf swathed around her head like Jackie O. "They're lovely," Maidie had said, then frowned. The photos were? Or the cat, car, and Z. herself? Z. smiled. "They are. Thanks."

Sometimes Z. reminded Maidie of a personality in a tabloid, Princess Di or Little Richard, her remarks so aligned with her sense of how she hoped she seemed—in Z.'s case, like a professor impaired but also empowered by the fact that when she was hired at Cofer College, all nine members of the faculty had allowed only grudgingly that the department's effectiveness, its nuanced purview, might be enhanced by a woman. There'd been a discrimination suit the year before; no women had been hired since Z. So it was easy to attribute Z.'s brittle surface, her defensive tremor, to the fact that she'd suffered, a martyr, for History. Once, Maidie ran into Z. at the store and—stalled by the freezer section, goose bumps rising on her arms—listened as Z. said a colleague had disparaged her research that proved the conventional view of woman as household angel had not disabled but camouflaged, even emboldened, the pen-wielding women politicos of the last century. An oversimplification, Maidie thought, wondering if the ice cream in her cart had melted.

But one day Garth asked Maidie to come to his office to discuss budget cuts and, when they were done, ushered her into a room where photo portraits of department members lined the wall. He pointed at one under which the plaque read: *Dr. Zora Coles, B.A., M.A., Ph.D., Cleveland State.* Maidie stared. Z. stared back, but her hair seemed less confidently arranged. A widow's peak dipped unflatteringly, and two babyish barrettes clamped the rest of her hair inert against her temples. Her smile—perturbed, disappointed—made her look like Thea when she was five and sorely, forebodingly tired. "That's why the old pricks hired her," Garth said. "They had to hire a woman. But she looked malleable." She still was, Maidie realized, a quivering pith behind a shell. Z. herself told Maidie she'd been raised by a great-aunt who disinherited her because she wanted Z. to become a Unitarian minister, not a professor. Maidie had a vision of Z. wandering, bundled, through a snowy, sooty city as she searched for the YWCA—though Z. might well have been disinherited on a sunny day. Even so, Maidie felt a jolt of sympathy—affection?—as she stared across the table at Z.'s perfect smile, which trembled.

On the other side of the conference room, the founder's granddaughter, Cass Willoughby, picked at the label on a bottle of Evian spring water. "Grandmother wouldn't approve," she said. She meant the dismantled state of the collection. Maidie had sorted the objects into categories: permanent, study collection, soon-to-be-discarded.

Garth had scheduled this meeting to discuss the public image of the Museum of Domestic History and Home Economy, to resolve its identity crisis, triggered by the American Association of Museums' refusal to grant accreditation, citing "serious deficiency" in the museum's "sense of mission." At the same time, the Cofer College Home Economics Department had changed its name to the Department of Family Science and foisted off the museum onto the History Department, where all ten members proposed to change its name to the Women's History Collection, but—if Maidie believed the memos Z. wrote—they agreed about little else. "This collection is merely," Z. had written, *"nothing more than* Alma Kayser Willoughby's autohagiography, class and race exclusions implied."

Maidie pictured Alma's portrait hanging in the display room—her slick hair shiny as sealskin, eyes visionary but hard. Every woman loses something necessary—Jack's mother said that. Z. was standing, preparing to read from *The Manual for Small Museums.*

" 'Museums suffer. . . ,' " Z. read.

They suffer? Maidie looked at Garth, who rolled his eyes.

" ' . . . from the delusion that to be historic,' " Z. read, " 'an object should be ascribed celebrity. A towel on which George Washington dried himself is likely a good towel of its period. Its value thus arises because it is a historic towel and not' "—Z. paused—" 'because it touched Washington's flesh. As a towel it is an object, as souvenir a *relic,* and so blind is the worship of *relics* that the very word has fallen into disrepute, a denomination for objects set up as targets for cloying sentiment.' "

Z. sat down. Maidie gathered that Z. thought Alma Kayser
Willoughby had set up her personal effects as targets for cloying sentiment. Horsefeathers, Maidie thought. And wondered
where she'd picked up the expression. From August, she decided, who—Maidie had noticed when she went for a visit—
tried hard to keep Clima from swearing. "Shit," Clima said.
"Sugar," he'd say. "Damn," she'd say. "What's wrong with
you?" he answered, frowning.

They'd invited Maidie over for cocktails. August swished
them in an old tin shaker as Maidie had examined every shelf
and cabinet: miniature teacups; salt and pepper shakers shaped
like outhouses, or windmills; a cat-shaped pitcher cleverly engineered so cream would pour out of its mouth in a tiny river; a
painted plate with a pink sky, black cacti, turquoise mountains
(SOUVENIR OF TOMBSTONE). But at the meeting, Garth and Z.
argued. Garth blushed, angry. Z.'s lips shifted, contempt.
Garth wanted to *screw* Z., Maidie realized (copulate, make
whoopee, stop the clock from ticking), but he didn't actually
like (esteem, admire) her. Cass Willoughby squirmed. Across
the table, the previous chief curator, Midge, knitted, raising her
eyes over her half-glasses. Would this meeting end? Maidie
wondered. She hated stasis: she pictured herself stalled at a busy
intersection, her car revved, waiting to fly. Swoop. Horsepower.
But sunlight screamed off the hood; the car fumed; and Maidie
worried about afterlife turning out to be an extension of the last
living minute.

Dull.

In the Women's History Collection conference room, Maidie
stared out the window at the gray sky and considered whether
to buy a Christmas tree this year. She thought about the box
stored in her laundry room, XMAS DECORATIONS. In it, a set of
ornaments that had belonged to Vera Fleiderhaus: twirly cylin-
ders, silver spirals. An aqua-and-orange globe with the Miami
Dolphins team insignia, a gift from Jack's mother last year; a

gold-plated sleigh, Avon Special Edition, which Neville's mother, solicitous, gave to Maidie that first Christmas Neville moved out. For the top branch, an angel in a brocade robe, with yarn hair and a face disconcertingly like Debbie Reynolds's. It used to be Maidie's mother's. "Ho," someone said. Maidie looked up. It was Garth—his rejoinder to Z., who'd just said, "The function of a museum is not to preserve hazy nostalgia for old men but to explore history." Z. had waved her arm as she'd said so, and her sleeve slid back to reveal her crosshatched green tattoo.

Cass Willoughby cleared her throat. "You think young people aren't interested in Willie Nelson's boots? Well, they are."

Z. said, "Don't make me trot out that conceit of Santayana's—that those who fail to study history are condemned to repeat it. Turning the shoes of a country singer into a fetish is not enlightening."

Cass stared.

Maidie spoke up. "I've found a nice place for Willie Nelson's boots," she told Cass. "An exhibit in the library in his hometown."

Cass frowned.

Garth looked at Z., at Maidie. He didn't look at Cass. Or at Midge, who was saying that the museum's mission was to record the history of needlework, to provide a taxonomy of stitchery. "Treble, cluster, picot," Midge said, nodding for emphasis. "This collection's function has always been to preserve the tatting, crochetwork, and embroidery of another generation, the tablecloths, ripple-edged towels, and ornate pillow slips that were women's artistic contribution." How poetic she sounded, Maidie thought, as Midge's champagne-colored hairdo bobbed and glinted.

Z. said, "Needlework is a *text* of women's lives."

Maidie sighed. Four people would never devise one plan. Besides, sitting at a table wasn't work. Maidie's response to discord was to memorize the extremes of an argument. Her mother's complaints about her father. Her father's about her mother. Z.'s claim the museum's goal was to record oppression. Garth's counterclaim the museum-as-curiosity-shop had attracted visitors in the past. Maidie pledged loyalty to both sides—venomously opposed—and to meanwhile remain untarnished by spite.

Maidie narrowed her eyes and watched Garth, Z., Cass, and Midge—the collision of four perspectives like falling stars crossing and recrossing. She thought: They'll redefine *mission* until the spring thaw. Not that it froze in Arizona. She stared out the windows at the peripatetic drizzle of the Arizona winter. Garth proposed to read a Statement of Mission from the Jocelyn Museum in Omaha, Nebraska. Maidie had visited the Jocelyn: plywood-and-glass cases, artifacts laid out like cans in a supermarket. A moment of claustrophobia hovered. Maidie felt as if she'd inhaled bleach, slid down a hole, a panic like a flutter of wings behind silk. She wanted out, beyond. I could get stuck, she thought, staring at Garth, Z., Cass, and Midge.

Garth laid down his folder and said, "Why don't we meet again in January?" Everyone stood, pushed chairs in, scuffled out.

At Maidie's office, Lalo sat in the corner, typing accession records from the handwritten log into the computer. Z. followed Maidie in. "I think we presented a united front, don't you?" She smiled. Maidie frowned; she didn't remember saying anything except that she'd found a congenial place in which to dump Willie Nelson's boots. "There are a lot of details to iron out," Maidie said. Z. said, "There are. But would you like to come with me? I'm driving to Phoenix to attend a seminar called The Group, for single professionals. We work on self-change, dynamism."

The Group? Self-change? Dynamism? Boxed wine, Maidie could have predicted. She glanced at her watch. "I can't today."

"Well," Z. said, nodding, backing away.

Lalo let out a moan, gravelly.

Maidie let it pass; he hadn't done it in front of Z. at least.

She said, "What's the matter?"

Squinting behind his glasses, Lalo looked at Maidie; he'd recently replaced the safety pins with two outsized screws. He was wearing a black T-shirt under a pink-and-tangerine striped vest that seemed hand-knitted. Just then, Midge passed by the window, waving, her smile bright under her silver coiffure. Lalo said, "It seems like there's pollution wherever you listen, or look."

Garth suddenly jutted his head through the door, flexed his eyebrows. "Kiddo," he said to Maidie, "if Zora Coles comes by, don't tell her anything. If she talks to you, take notes." He left.

"What do you mean?" Maidie asked Lalo.

Garth stuck his head in again. "She has us by the short hairs." he nodded.

Maidie nodded back; Garth left again.

Lalo said, "You do know what I mean—that's why you won't go anywhere with her. I feel the same way when I drive by a billboard."

Maidie said, "The same as what?"

"On a road, in the country."

Maidie was starting to follow this: Z.'s conversation seemed to Lalo like raw advertising in an otherwise nuanced landscape.

Lalo said, "When we're through, can you come to the student gallery?"

Maidie said, "I wanted to get a Christmas tree on the way home. Is tonight the only night? But congratulations—about the show."

Lalo said, "It's a green papier-mâché surface with a lump."

"What is?"

"The piece I named *A Day in the Life of Maida Bonasso.*"

Maidie said, "Goodness." (*Goodness?* She *had* been spending time with Clima and August.) "I'd better go, then." She felt

117

flattered at first. Then she thought: A green surface with a lump?

Lalo said, "Next week will be fine."

He turned off the computer, covered it with its plastic hood, slid rubber bands around the cuffs of his pants, and, a few minutes later, outside, unlocked his bicycle and sped away. The sun was sinking behind buildings. Maidie hated this time of year.

And day. But if the sky turned up cerulean and she managed to get outside in time, sunshine fell like a veil. Maidie remembered snow blowing horizontally in Wyoming, cold fog in Virginia, dug-in days in Nebraska, Arkansas's icy rain. Rex Hurley had been saying, lately, Maidie needed to visit Pia Oik, a ghost town near lava beds and the Organ Pipe Cactus National Monument, where he had a house: four walls and an electric socket, no roof or running water yet. But a galvanized tub of water set out in the morning heated up enough to bathe in by afternoon. Maidie pictured herself naked on a rock, feet submerged, hair pinned up, soap frothing over her shoulders as sunlight ticked down.

In Tucson, the light outside the window turned dim, the illumination from the fixtures in her office more brilliant. She finished a packet of paperwork—a statement of expenses, a one-page enumeration of Lalo's duties. She addressed the packet to the trustees, mailed it, locked up. A few minutes later, headed down Speedway, she noticed Christmas trees in rows outside Gonzo's Store. She pulled over. The man selling them looked like a biker—a chain looped from his wallet to his belt. He sat in a lawn chair, arms crossed over his belly. A fat man in a plaid shirt sat next to him, selling Louisiana sausages, boudin, out of an ice chest. Maidie looked at the trees; she wanted a spindly twig with just a fringe of green. Christmas in the desert seemed strange sprouting evergreen boughs, she felt, or decked with holly berries—all of which looked incorrect without snow sifting down around them, or beyond, outside the window.

She stopped, tilted a tree out. The man who looked like a biker said, "Seems like Charlie Brown's Christmas tree to me, Miz."

A sympathetic noise unspooled somewhere, a whimper. Maidie looked down. At her feet, a box of puppies. One leapt onto her foot. *Love a dog.* She hadn't, so far, loved Rex Hurley's Guapo, who smelled funny, barked all night—a hum like a motor only Maidie could hear, then a tortured yelp that made Maidie bolt upright. Blind, Guapo bit Maidie if she petted him. Maidie hadn't managed to feel love ("let it grow") with Rex either, but she found it hard to contradict Rona, Clima, Harve, Garth, and August, who liked Rex. Lalo—who didn't like much—liked Rex.

Once, at Maidie's, Lalo looked around, annoyed, and said, "Why do you have all these vessels?" Maidie had answered, "Vessels?" Lalo pointed to the antique pitchers, vases, and bowls that belonged to Vera Fleiderhaus, to Vera's mother before her, to Maidie's grandmother on her dad's side. Lalo asked, "Is it true women can't help liking round things with holes in them?" Rex, who'd gone to college before they even taught Jungian archetypes, said, "They're souvenirs of home life." Maidie supposed Lalo was enrolled in a class that applied French theory to gender issues and thus construed all aesthetic choices as the biological projection of the chooser: e.g., women, wombs, surround themselves with empty vessels; men like hammers and tailpipes, sausages.

Maidie bent over and picked up the puppy, his fat belly stretched pink; he wiggled his perfect, unscuffed nose. He churned and squirmed like a wind-up toy. The man selling boudin said, "Half coon hound, half border collie. He'll make a fine pet."

Maidie looked at the sign, FREE PUPPIES, and thought: Try and stop me. Who'd want to? She had no idea. Jack, she decided. Her mood sank. The last phone call she'd had from him, he was living in someone's garage, with a toilet and a sink in the corner, sending out résumés. But I want a dog, she thought, obstinate, staring at the box. Even to herself, inside her skull, she sounded defensive, like Z. complaining about a lack of datable men in Tucson. Still, Maidie thought, Ann Landers would advise yes: "Dear Recently Dislocated. Studies conducted at the Institute of Hereditary Moods indicate pet owners have increased zest for life." Maidie looked at the boudin man. "I think so," she said.

Unfolding his arms, the Christmas tree man said, "I knew it. I could tell by your eyes you'd do anything for someone down on his luck." Maidie stared. What was wrong with her eyes that they sent messages she'd do favors for losers? It was a sales pitch, she decided. In the biker world, a dog's welfare rated higher than a spouse's. "Hell, I like my dog better than my old lady," the boudin man said. Maidie put the black, eel-shaped dog in her car. He slithered under the brake. When she pulled him out, he turned, gave her a surly glare that made his face look oddly like Jack Bonasso's, and bit her, his teeth sinking like pins. She jerked her hand. "Ouch." The boudin man said, "You need to tap him for that. He'll quit when he sees who's boss."

Later, Maidie pulled into her neighborhood and parked. Across the street, Clima opened her door, waved. Maidie came up the sidewalk, holding the puppy. "What do you think?" she asked. Clima ushered Maidie inside. "It's cold." Then, pulling the puppy near, Clima said, "He looks exactly like my old dog, Trouble." August seemed worried. "That dog is going to get big," he told Maidie. Clima said, "Like my old dog, Trouble." August asked Maidie, "Have you ever raised a dog?" Maidie hadn't; but when Neena moved in with Maidie's dad, she'd brought an aging poodle named Strudel with her. Clima, nuzzling, asked, "What's his name?" The dog was thin, slippery. "Zip," Maidie said.

Clima set Zip on the floor. He walked two feet away and squatted, then shit a pile almost as big as himself. At a loss, Maidie said, "My God. Sorry." August said, "I told you he's going to get big." Clima waved a paper towel. "He's excited. He's had a nerve-racking day. But don't you wonder if the past tense of *shit* is *shat?*" August said, "As a matter of fact, I don't." The dog glared at Maidie, looking like Jack again, Jack when he got caught, cornered. "Am I supposed to spank him?" Maidie asked. "Not exactly," August said. He held Zip's nose to the floor. "Bad! Now take him outside and praise him if he goes there."

Outside, Zip nosed around.

Maidie said, "Good! Good!" She went to her car and got a bottle of wine she'd just bought, made from grapes harvested after dark for a supposedly piquant flavor. Inside, she handed it to Clima, who hated sweet drinks. Clima, smiling, girlish, said, "Do I like this?" Maidie said, "I think you do." Clima said, "I'm about to engage in happy hour. Join me?" August glowered, waved his hand as if to say a wife who tippled through her golden years was beyond his jurisdiction. He shuffled to the corner where he was decorating a short, artificial tree on an old stand.

"I forgot to buy my Christmas tree," Maidie said suddenly.

Clima said, "Dog food too. But at least you got wine."

Clima slid open the door that led outside. August said, "Maidie, leave the dog in here so he won't get lost." Maidie did, and followed Clima to the "crow's nest"—up three flights of stairs, Clima holding the rail with one hand, her etched goblet with the other. One stair step, one leg, one stair step, one leg. At the top—a deck perched on the roof's peak—they looked at the city, short skyscrapers glowing red, green, neon-edged, for Christmas. "How was the Museum of Housework and Drudgery?" Clima asked.

Maidie shook her head. "I don't understand my job. I can't

tell if I'm supposed to lead or follow. Obey or make decisions."

Clima said, "My theory is to act like you're taking orders but make decisions anyway. Carry them out. No one will even notice."

Maidie felt relieved to be on Clima and August's roof, staring at the sky instead of cooped up at home, but, at the same time, guilty for not using her time well. She could be wrapping Christmas presents or cleaning closets, buffing away dust on top of the refrigerator, rinsing bowls and pitchers—*vessels*—in soapy water. She'd been raised to believe a house should be swept and wiped down with ammonia once a week. Lutheran ablution. She needed to buy dog food. What had she thought, stopping for a tree but getting a dog? Clima said, "I don't feel like cooking. We could order pizza." She reached for the bottle, refilled her glass and Maidie's. She was wearing a gray parka with a tufted, fuzzy texture, a grandkid's castoff, Maidie decided; Joel Scribner used to have one. In a tree nearby, a cicada bleated, plaintive. The sky looked wintry—pale, stiff clouds.

Clima said, "August couldn't put up the outdoor lights this year because of his legs. They won't bend and go up the ladder."

Startled, Maidie wondered: did legs quit bending?

August was seventy-six. Maidie divided by two: thirty-eight.

Maidie was thirty-five, middle-aged if "middle" was applied literally, as opposed to in vague reference to someone older than her.

By the time Clima was middle-aged, Maidie calculated, she already had Rona, who was already dating Harve, the progenitor of Clima's grandchildren, one of whom had babies of her own now, albeit out of wedlock. These children, grandchildren, and great-grandchildren surrounded Clima in her old age, a multigenerational thicket. Rex Hurley was neither as old as Clima nor as young, as impatient, as Maidie, he pointed out. Once, he said, "I hope you won't mind taking advice from someone older, but it's better to wait and see rather than try to manhandle stray details." Maidie had been thinking out loud:

planning a weekend or the rest of her life. She'd bristled. "I'm surprised you didn't say *elder:* I need to take advice from my elder." She couldn't believe he'd belabor the age difference, fifteen years, after she'd spent weeks of conversational effort stressing shared experience, accenting the fact she was as wise beyond her years as Rex was youthful because he'd reinvented himself, his values, in mid-adulthood, in the 1970s, the same era in which she'd come of age. They were like-minded, she'd emphasized.

Then he acted like the supervisor. How could they maintain a companionable stance, no arguments about who/what was right/wrong, if he ignored that they had almost everything in common?

Rex had two sons: one a stunt man who lived in Elko, Nevada; the other an accountant in Phoenix. Before Maidie had acquired this late-breaking sense that she was postponed, behind God's schedule—a pressure that seems to have put plans about *next, later,* on hold, willpower pending—she'd been devoted to longevity. When she was married to Neville, preservation was her aim. She kept the pantry well-stocked. She insisted Neville see a doctor once a year. She fine-tuned routines. Did Neville prefer starch in his orderly's uniform? Flannel bedsheets or percale? She marked the calendar, X's for happy occasions, hoping to make happiness recur. Once, Neville had pounded the table and said, "All this preparation for later makes me crazy now." Still, she'd collected durability advice. Don't let the sun set on anger. Cook with the five food groups. Beware, love is fragile.

Later, with Jack, she revised her rules. Love was fragile, yes; she understood it differently by then. They'd maul love to death if they examined it too closely, passing it back and forth between the two of them until, like a sick child, it gave up and died.

When she was young, Maidie tried make her father act gen-

tle, her mother brave. Later, she tried to keep Neena calm and
therefore unlikely to slap someone, or laugh, tired, and say that
Cinderella's stepmother didn't seem as wicked as Cinderella
seemed paranoid. Maidie feels new, a dangerous, false sense
that—since none of these plans helped prevent institutions and
promises associated with the concept of *forever* from dissolv-
ing—her life, her function, hasn't happened yet. But time lum-
bers on, and Maidie is unschooled in the mechanics of even
seeming young, scrawling eyeliner here, lipstick there; her
brown hair smudges to gray. In certain casts of light, she's wary,
beaky, a spinster.

Clima said, "So we're not going to put up the outdoor lights.
And maybe this is the last year we'll have a Christmas tree."

Maidie shook her head. "No. You might have a tree next year,
or Christmas lights this year. I could come over and help August."

Clima shrugged. "It doesn't matter."

Maidie shivered. She felt the wine, ghostly and astringent,
slide through her veins like antifreeze through the coils of a
dark engine. "For heaven's sake," Clima told Maidie, "I'm ready
to give up the fuss about Christmas. My life is well-done, like a
roast. Stick a fork in it. Let's go inside." She waved the empty
bottle at Maidie. "I've always wanted, once in my life, to chuck
a bottle over my shoulder. Or to shatter a wineglass in the fireplace." Her face, surrounded by synthetic, matted fur, focused.
She lifted the bottle, flung it hard, backward. It swished
through tree branches and crashed. Clima smiled. "Don't tell."

Downstairs, she slid open the door.

Inside, August was stringing lights on the tree. Zip sat on the
floor, head bobbing, attentive, as he watched August frown and
search for the one burned-out bulb that kept the rest from
blinking. On TV, Dan Rather narrated: about homosexuals in
the military, Maidie gathered, because the legend behind his
head read DON'T ASK, DON'T TELL. Clima, who liked con-

tention with cocktails as much as some people like small pick-
led onions, said, "Homosexuals are born that way. They can't
help their preference. Did you have gay affairs when you were
in the army, August?"

Maidie wondered how August would change the subject.

He looked at Clima, jaw clenched.

Clima opened the cupboard, took out her bottle of good
tequila with its lucky horseshoe. She said, "I had a lesbian experience."

He said, "You did not."

Clima said, "We kissed."

August said, "People might be born homosexual, but a war
makes some."

Maidie said, "What?"

Clima said, "This was after I graduated from high school."

August ignored Clima. He looked at Maidie. "Everyone was
scared and too far from home," he said. "This was in Guam. It
wouldn't have been anyone's first choice. It was panic, you see.
What bothers me is the hypocrisy, then and now. They asked,
when I enlisted, did I like girls? Of course I liked girls! But as
soon as I got overseas, what happened? Eyes. I looked up in the
mess tent, or at a movie on Saturday night. Sad, lonely eyes. I'm
telling you because I thought with your education you could
make sense of it. I burned my journals, though."

Maidie paused. How could she answer?

August said, "I never told anyone else."

Clima poured tequila into her glass, oblivious. "As I was saying, I had a lesbian experience with a family friend. We kissed."

August said, "All women your age had those gushing friend-
ships."

Clima said, "You don't know what used to be in my heart."

August looked at Maidie.

Since, according to Maidie's bylaws of polite discourse, con-
troversy got broached in a way that forced everyone to, if not

concur, admit that discord was a human constant, she nodded and said, "The realization death is imminent probably makes a person reach for the nearest living creature." She wondered for a moment how uncandid she'd sounded. Sexual intimacy as a response to death just outside the tent flaps—wasn't that a plot from *M*A*S*H*?

She looked at August.

His eyes filled up. "That's exactly right."

He took a handkerchief from his pocket. Maidie thought he might cry. But he sat in a chair and mopped his face. What locked-up memories he had! Clima too. Maidie watched her sip tequila with a far-off stare. They'd carry their secrets to the grave, the abode of the dead, Maidie thought, regressing briefly into liturgical rote. Did most people arrive at death, regrets unsalvaged, hope for insight (in the nick of time) past due? Clima seemed to have had not enough raw experience, August too much.

Maidie traced most problems, tragic, pesky, wide-flung, idiosyncratic, to social context. Too much school, her dad had once said. One Christmas, he and Maidie sat in his kitchen and Maidie told him she was moving to Arkansas to start her master's degree. Sipping a martini so dry he'd used a cotton ball to waft vermouth nearby, he'd said, "Finding the why and wherefore won't make you happy." Maidie had shrugged. He didn't seem happy himself.

Still, she saw the press of history, its residual stamp, on Clima. Her sheltered upbringing in Ash Fork, her mother's and grandmother's strictures to let household order and wifely decorum satisfy and elate her. But Clima met August, moved to the city, and was just Maidie's age in the 1960s. She told Maidie once her favorite TV show was *Laugh-In*. Maidie considered it. The pursuit of transient euphoria. Yammering, unrepentant drunks. Sex-crazed dodderers chasing luscious waifs whose virtue didn't seem worth guarding. But new times arrived and rules changed again; at a certain point, Clima didn't.

When Maidie wrote her thesis, she'd found that skills women developed on the frontier had remained operational even after conditions changed: e.g., the solicitude it took to keep a child alive became—with the rise of mechanization, science, and leisure—excessive solicitude. Without a useful function siphoning it off, maternal wariness seemed like neurosis, a fascination with bad endings that hadn't happened yet. And motherhood a posture of self-sacrifice unrequited, culminating in the mothers' march on Washington for a national holiday in their name, also the "Dear Mother" fad (plaques, pictures, and cards extolling maternal selflessness purchased by a generation of heckled sons and daughters). Clima had never thought of herself as a dear mother, a household angel. Maidie gave Clima flowers for her birthday, and she said, "You're sweet. I'm not, though."

Clima shoved a phone book at Maidie. "Order pizza. I can't see. I've hated losing my eyesight. But menopause was wonderful."

Maidie looked at August, who petted Zip, who thumped his tail adoringly, then turned and glared at Maidie. That dog—Maidie blurted to herself—he senses I have no confidence. Then, embarrassed, she let the thought go. She'd mixed up conjecture about a dog's cognitive processes with platitudes about self-help, bad relationships. She'd had random, spasmodic brain patter in the Oprahic dialect. Smart Women, Foolish Pet Choices.

Later, Maidie drove while Clima sat in the passenger seat, holding Zip and sipping tequila out of her stemmed glass. They stopped at a 7-Eleven for dog food. "I'll wait," Clima said. At Pizza Hut, she got out, waved her checkbook. "My treat." She skidded on the curb and slipped, teetering. Maidie grabbed a handful of lumpy parka until Clima balanced. Kids sitting in front with boom boxes laughed. Maidie stared *Teenagers*. She used to hate the word. ("Teenagers," Neena would say, hands in the air, mock exasperated.) The teenagers glanced at Maidie, then away. She was as beyond notice as Clima—which shouldn't have been news, a revelation. But not so long ago, teenagers had looked at Maidie, her clothes and shoes, her "style," with respect, curiosity. When had Maidie gotten older, another gradation closer to fusty disuse? Later still—Zip crunching chow out of a bowl, Clima and August chewing pizza, setting it back down on dainty plates—Maidie remembered how, when she was little, she sat in church behind the Parkinson brothers.

Parkinson wasn't their last name, it was their disease, genetic tremors. Maidie admired the fragrant smell of candles, the silvery gleam of the communion cask, Pastor's Larssen's stole draped over his snowy white robe as he prayed. Luminous impressions. The zone of the living: a quivering, physical mystery. The brothers in the next pew grappled their red hymnals open, jittered as they stood and sang. They'd been born hearty, durable, their muscles and nerve-threaded spines supple. Time, an everlasting stream, bears entities away. First, poise. Next, certainty. Once, when Maidie was married to Jack, they'd sat in a café as an old man at the next table yelled at his wife, who was cringing, cowed—she'd forgotten he didn't want mustard on his hamburger. Maidie had looked across the table at Jack, sweet when he could force himself, when he wasn't hungry, tired, or anxious. Maidie realized old age would be an exacting trap, her marriage a sawtoothed replica of the one across the room: Jack, feeble, yelling about mustard, lint on his socks, streaky window glass.

In the dining room with Clima, August, and Zip, Maidie felt her mood sag. She nudged it up, thinking how she'd observed exemplary marriages too. But in the best there were compromises, trivial and grand. Neville's parents endured a dim, uncertain spell when Neville's father took up with a woman and Neville's mother toughed it out on a cot in the back of her fab-

ric and notions store. Clima hid bottles. August had sad memo-
ries. As years passed, there'd be diminished grace, leg power.
Less concern for propriety. And—mercifully so, Maidie
thought, remembering the derisive faces outside Pizza Hut
when Clima stumbled—less capacity to care if you looked frail.
Maidie saw that belief in limitless, unclaimed pleasure still to be
mined in distant hills faded. She tried to drum up enthusiasm.
For Pia Oik? For California's green coast? For paradise beyond?
(Heaven? Hawaii?) Maidie thought of Jack living in a garage on
Dodie's brother's stinted largesse. She pictured him making a
sandwich on a tool bench, sprinkling it with salt and pepper, a
space heater kicking out BTUs nearby. Though she knew she
shouldn't, she felt guilty for eating hot pizza on bona china
here.

"I have to go," she told Clima.

"Of course you do," Clima said. "Tomorrow's a workday."

"The dog needs to go out when he eats or wakes up," August
said.

In her own yard, she watched Zip. "Good! Good!" she said.

Inside, her answering machine blinked twice.

When she saw it, expectancy flickered: on the other end, she
hoped, a message from someone who'd drawn up plans, a blueprint for a future without garbled, bleak days. Please call if
you're interested it would say. But who would? Rex, with whom
Maidie felt annoyed because he'd said he couldn't fathom—"it
seems foreign to me," his exact words—how Maidie's family,
her past, could be stowed away? Maidie pointed out that storage hadn't been a choice. "It's been a choice not to write or call
much since," he said. His advice seemed as naive as the *Reader's
Digest.* Not everyone in These United States grew up in a House
on the Prairie, she wanted to say. She'd hated *Little House on the
Prairie;* it might have been 1885 on the TV screen, but it was
1985 in Maidie's living room, and Michael Landon had wept
copiously. A new heroic template: tender, or gutlessly self-

absorbed. A message from Rex seemed like an arrow pointed at a detour. But how else might love make a phone call and pry Maidie loose?

From the *doldrums:* dead-still ocean regions by the equator. Sailors threw cargo overboard to get through them, but never rum kegs.

She wanted to talk to someone.

Laree, who would be a stranger now—like the time she'd phoned Maidie in Virginia. Was she still married to a geek? If Maidie did talk to Laree, she'd have to explain her new state. Arizona. Separated, not divorced. And Rex, who slept next to Maidie, his limbs weightless, the sheets buoyant, the glaring lamp she left *on* if she couldn't sleep *off.* Rex didn't kick the covers out; the bed was easy to make the next day; a good quality, that.

She started dusting, a sock on her hand sprinkled with lemon oil, swish, swish. Crash. She broke a seven-inch pelican that said *Metlox, Made in the U.S.A.* on the bottom, an antique piece that had belonged to Vera Fleiderhaus. Or Maidie bought it at a junkshop because it looked like one of Vera's. Sweeping up its residue, a million pieces, carrying shards to the trash, she cleared her brain, no thinking. She used to feel robbed, complicit, if she broke something. Maidie loved her objects—pelicans, floor lamps, antimacassars, tufted footstools. She'd learned, though, to get the broken pieces up quickly. No crying over spilled china. She could go to a secondhand store the next day and find something almost as perfect. Maidie had arrived at the faith that there'd be plenty of forty-, fifty-, and sixty-year-old knickknacks to replace broken ones and keep her house stocked—a facsimile of a cozy home forever—no matter how many she broke.

Two phone messages—

The dog, Zip, farted. Broke wind.

At least, Maidie supposed Zip broke wind. She hadn't been a

pet owner long. Maybe she was drunk, her brain activating false synapses. Research conducted by the American Academy of Psychoanalysis had determined that women's sense of smell—through centuries of application in checking for spoiled, poisonous victuals, or a cookfire out of control, or inside a child's wrapper for signs of illness—was ultrasensitive and more connected to taxonomic thought processes than men's. Today more superfluous smells exist—exhaust, furniture polish, scented garbage bags, Renuzit—but experience is less likely to be ordered by smell. Olfactory overload. An early-twentieth-century medical textbook listed one symptom of "Female Hysteria" as "reports of malodorousness attributable solely to the patient's fancy." Women smelled something foul doctors didn't. Evolution occurs sporadically: stasis, then belated, lurching reaction.

Maidie opened the door. "Outside?" Zip dashed out. "Zip!" she called. He didn't recognize his name yet. If he got lost . . . Maidie reviewed the worst possible outcomes. She'd never find Zip and wonder the rest of her life if he'd been stolen by a crook who sold pets to medical research, in which dogs were infected with, say, cystic fibrosis and dosed with debilitating cures. When Maidie and Jack lived in Virginia, a recent immigrant had roasted a terrier and taken pictures of it in the oven; the film developer reported him. The judge cited culture shock and sentenced the man to a class in American culinary tradition. What if Maidie never found Zip? How would she tell August? "Zip!" Maidie called. A window slammed down. Rona and Harve's? Evvy and Cindy-June's? "Zi-ip!" Maidie called. And Maidie remembered a time in Arkansas when Jack had hit her and afterward, ashamed, had run out into a hailstorm. Hours later, after the newscast mentioned a case of fatal hypothermia, Maidie had walked through the streets, calling "Jack! Ja-ack!" A window opened. A voice said, "Is it an Irish setter you're looking for, miss?"

Rage swept through Maidie. Tension coiled in her stomach. A metal-flavored taste crossed her tongue. That dog! The entire five years she'd been with Jack, she had a sore throat, which, at first, she traced to the fact that Jack yelled and—after the first months, when Maidie had tried to rise above his yelling, sympathize, but not be absorbed by it—she gave up and yelled back. Her throat was sore from yelling, she guessed. She'd also tried to rise above punches, slaps, shoves. Then she gave up and hit Jack back once. He knocked her over. Then, stunned, alarmed, didn't lay a hand on her for months. But by the time Maidie got ready to leave Jack, she'd stopped even yelling. She was tired, worried. Money. Her throat was raw. *Stress,* a force that deforms bodies. Maidie moved to Arizona. Her throat felt fine.

But the rawness—the bad taste—had come back. She felt like yelling. Bad! She walked out to the patio, called loud, shrill: "Zip!" He leapt out of the weeds, snarling, spit frothing. Maidie backed up. She had anger inside, capped. Mad! Mad!

"Stay out, you bastard." She went in, slammed the door. To focus, she thought about the Women's History Collection. But first she went back to the door, guilty, and opened it. Zip slunk past, toenails clicking, an apologetic side glance. Typical. She thought, too, about a photographer who'd visited her office, a woman who'd taken black-and-white photos of stacked diapers, Mason jars in gleaming rows, white towels in neat piles, each photo morbidly dark except for key lighting accentuating bright corners, perfect creases, glistering edges, the blanched, livid color of cleanliness, transforming the appendages of household order into forbidding icons. Maidie wanted to buy the photos for the collection. Garth would find them inexplicable. And Z.: too unempowering a set of images for women we want to inspire.

Maidie remembered a passage from Virginia Woolf about all the dinners cooked, plates and cups washed, children grown and gone into the world. And evidence of this essential work? Vanished. Maidie started to picture an exhibit that didn't treat domesticity as evidence of enslavement but instead explored the linguistic opposition inherent in it. *Hand wrought* was prized—antique—in a mechanized era, and *streamlined* was a rarefied technofeat in a homespun era. Maidie pictured an 1897 kitchen next to a 1997 kitchen. A laundry room from 1968 near a wringer and mangle from 1910. A cache of letters that had made their way from the east coast to the west by way of Pony Express, next to an answering machine playing, "Beep. This is Dr. So-and-so's office, and your X-rays are back." She'd mix old pieces with new, stressing the survival of the past as a trace, a specter. No nostalgia. No reckless headlong embrace of the new-forged either.

She'd talk Garth and Z. into it by pitting it against an exhibit they'd hate. Someone had just offered to donate one hundred seventeen Barbie dolls; she'd propose the historiography of Barbie images first.

The early Barbies wore haute couture business costumes, brainy eyeglasses. Then Barbie transmogrified into a wispy gal pal. The old Barbie was stiff, haughty, de rigueur. She had dark ridges above her eyes, a design feature meant to suggest artfully made-up eyelashes and eyelids combined. Barbie looked like Laree, or vice versa, Maidie realized: that baroque, slanting gaze.

Maidie looked at the phone.

She could dial, first Information, next Laree, then say, This is Maidie Giddings Kramer Bonasso. I'm fine, yes. Next, a rendition of Maidie's days spent cataloguing diaries, antique curling tongs, coffee grinders, ripple-edged towels. Or writing a grant proposal to be read by the director of public relations at Pillsbury, a request for money masquerading as a poem: "History is a vehicle carrying living memories to the future." Laree might say, What about the rest of your life—you getting any? (A day in the life of Maida Bonasso.) I'm making friends, Maidie might say. Tonight I ate dinner with two of them—old people, however, who see life as limited, shrinking. Laree might ask, Why

Arizona? Had Maidie, for whom settling down had thus far been an impersonal disaster, *arrived?* The phone rang. Maidie listened to it ring. One, two. Her own taped voice, warbly: Leave a message. Then Rex Hurley, saying, "If you're there . . .'

She thought about Clima. *You're sweet. I'm not, though.*

About her mother in 1969, shoving aside a box of Post Toasties cereal to get at the whiskey sour mix, saying, "But you don't want me to give up things that keep me calm and happy, do you?" And, later, Neena phoning Mrs. Funderburk, whom Maidie liked to visit, asking, "Is the Little Match Girl, by any chance, *there?*"

Rex: "Are you home?"

Arizona, vast, dusty.

"Pick up."

Maidie didn't.

Her phone messages?

Number 1. "Call," her father said.

Number 2. "Chrissake," he said, "call. My news is urgent."

"*I* should have called first," Eugene said on a cold spring day, his glasses steamy as he stepped over the threshold, into the house. "I've been alone too long," he said. He took off his snow-dusted coat and shook it. Too long since Vera died, he meant. Too long: one year since she lay in the coffin, her hair pointed in the wrong direction, silver eyeglasses missing; one year during which she seemed to be *away,* visiting her parents in California, maybe. But her father was dead. Her mother lived in a nursing home in Hector because she wet herself. Maidie tried to picture Vera's body, milk white, moldering and narrow, her fingernails and hair still growing prodigiously (like people said). Or transformed, arisen: Vera would pass through the small door that led from the attic, sit on the edge of Maidie's bed, reach in the pocket of her flannel shirt, put her glasses back on, arrange her hair, correct, familiar, and draw letters on Maidie's back in the dark, spelling out the future, the nudge or tremor that would alter the family pattern next. Maidie's father, mother, Lucy, Thea, and Maidie herself, waiting for dislocation. Plate tectonics. Clack, roll. Reacting, they'd scatter.

Maidie's mother nodded at Eugene. "I understand *lonely.*"

Eugene smiled unexpectedly. "But I've met someone, and proposed."

Maidie's mother's face shifted. "Where on earth? Where on earth are my manners, Eugene? Of course, bring her here for dinner."

And in the next week of thinking, cooking, bargaining, doubting, she dithered over beef or pork, linen napkins or high-grade embossed paper, whether to wear her sleeveless black dress or her puce-colored suit, pointing out that in French *puce* means "flea," or anything the same engorged purple color. "You don't decide to marry someone because of the calendar," she said, buttoning her flea-colored suit. "Where could he have found her?" She stirred gravy. She pulled the tray of pudding— stemmed crystal cups in rows—off the refrigerator shelf and garnished each one with a maraschino cherry. Maidie's father, behind his newspaper, said, "There is something businesslike, at least transactional, about selecting a mate, however." The door-bell chimed. Maidie's mother poured coffee into the silver urn; it splashed her hand. "Ouch," she said, Maidie opened the door.

Eugene looked polished; he'd shaved closer. He wore his plaid suit with a red wool vest. "Good day." He gave everyone a pres-ent. Maidie, a book, *Treasure Island.* Lucy, a water pistol. Thea, a rubber-tipped spear. Flowers for Maidie's mother. Tobacco for Maidie's dad. "My intended," he said. Dell stepped through the door in navy-blue shoes with snow on the tips, her silver hair coiffed. Her skin, dusty and creased, looked like pie crust. Lucy and Thea scrabbled across the floor, stabbing, squirting.

Maidie's mother said, "Would anyone like an aperitif?"

"Appetizer, you mean," Dell said.

"Aperitif." Maidie's mother waved the sherry bottle.

Maidie stood by Eugene's chair as he explained that Dell came from the Iron Range. Maidie stared at Dell's silver hair, her crinkled skin. "Chisholm," he said, the name of a town. Next, he talked about Hector. Someone had opened a business that would hire fifty people. "This town has been foredoomed since the railroad pulled out," Eugene said, "and a billiards factory won't change that." Maidie's back tickled, magnetic. Something budged; Dell smoothed Maidie's sash. "How old are you? I have a little girl." Maidie stared at Dell's skin. She had a little girl?

Dell said, "Eugene, she's just Nikki's size. They'll be friends." Then she explained to Maidie's mother that she was raising her granddaughter. She touched Maidie's back. "She's sweet."

Maidie's mother's eyebrows went up. "I suppose."

"It's her upbringing," Dell said. Bald-faced flattery.

Maidie's mother frowned. She trickled the last of her aperitif into her mouth. "Dinner," she said, yanking the cork out of a bottle of wine, which sloshed muddy and black inside its green bottle but poured out purple, a liquid gem, into transparent goblets. Everyone sat at the table. Dell told a joke about a Norwegian couple, Ole and Lena, riding on a bus on their honeymoon with a lumberjack and the tire goes flat, and Lena isn't happy with her honeymoon, Ole either, something to do with the lumberjack's tire, which got blown. Maidie's dad nodded. "I see. Funny," he said. Eugene smiled, twisting his wineglass. "Interesting," he said, "the jokes they tell around Chisholm."

Lucy said, "Knock knock."

"Where did you meet Eugene?" Maidie's mother asked.

Dell tilted her head. "At our class reunion."

Lucy stood up, tapped Dell. "Knock knock."

"Our fortieth," Dell said.

Maidie looked at her mother. Wouldn't she stop Lucy?

Maidie's mother plopped potatoes onto Dell's plate.

"Knock knock," Lucy said.

Dell adjusted her face, sweet. "Who's there?"

"Boo."

"Boo hoo?"

Ha ha.

"Knock knock."

"Who's there?" "Old Lady." "Old Lady who?" "I didn't know you yodeled."

Then Thea, who didn't understand jokes, said, "Knock knock."

"Who's there?" Dell said, exasperated.

"Anybody."

"Anybody who?"

Thea shrugged. "Just anybody." Jokes were another brain level up; Thea wasn't there yet. Dell grimaced, smiling, weary pity.

After dinner, Eugene and Dell got ready to leave. Dell stood on the sidewalk, between snowbanks, the porch light making a yellow path to Eugene's car. "You need to eat my cooking next," she said. Maidie wondered if they'd eat Dell's cooking at Eugene and Vera's house, though Vera was dead now, altered. Or at Dell's, in the Iron Range; Maidie pictured a lunchbox-shaped house the metallic color of tinfoil, sitting on a pile of steel filings. "You haven't tasted anything until you've tasted my smelt," Dell said, Maidie's dad nodded, closing the door. "Smelt?" Maidie asked. "A small fish, tasty when fried," he answered.

Maidie's mother had the aspirin bottle. She twisted the cap off. "She works at the plant. That's where she hears those jokes."

Maidie's dad said, "I also get the feeling she's done some time at the corner tap." He stacked albums on the phonograph. Judy Garland shrieked, singing, "I happen to *like* New York!" And

Maidie thought about Dell, humping and bumping, trying to seem like the superintendent of dinner. "I'm a big fan of plain food," she'd said, blinking. Maidie's mother had humped and bumped back. And Dell's little girl? "She calls me Mother, but her real mother . . ." Here Dell rolled her eyes. What about the mother? And would the little girl move to Hector and live at Eugene's? Maidie had a sense of the inaccurate compliments a stepchild might endure: Maidie is so calm! Lucy has the face of an innocent! Thea is kind! Maidie sat on the floor next to her father's chair. "*This* is my *lucky day, lucky day!*" Judy Garland sang (stuck, damaged). Maidie's father shifted his feet to make room. "You're in the way, Thea," he told Maidie. A kid was a kid.

Maidie heard noises from the next room, open, close, slam. She found her mother sitting on the bedroom floor, her painted toenails jutting against the nubby brown ends of her nylons, her suit, its engorged purple color, stretching tight across her hips. Above, closet doors gaped open. She sifted through stacked boxes, neckties, handkerchiefs, whispery silk scarves. A forest-green jewelry box sat on the floor, its satin-lined lid open, glinting. Maidie thought about Madagascar, the gravel made of jewelry dust, pathways shining under moonlight. The jewelry box had a secret space. "A false bottom," Maidie's mother explained, "for keeping precious documents." She reached in, pulled out a snapshot. "Does he remind you of Eugene?" Maidie stared. A pale man stood in front of a black tree, his white shirt buttoned up all the way above gray pants. His nose, bell-shaped. His ears stuck out. His hair? Brown or auburn or gray. It was a black-and-white photo. Maidie said, "Not exactly of Eugene."

"He does me," Maidie's mother said, "the way he makes me feel. Not transparent. Not invisible. Valuable." Maidie's mother slid the photo back into the jewelry box, snapped the lid shut. Maidie pictured a sparkly silver window facing nowhere. A mirror?

Not invisible. Not transparent.

Valuable.

"Dell," Maidie's mother said, "I see right through."

A window without a view.

And Nikki, when Eugene dropped her off the next day for a visit, leaned close to Maidie and said, "Let's take a walk so we can look into people's houses." Maidie said, "Why?" But at sundown, when the sky got dark and the lamplight inside people's houses bright, they tromped through the snow and Nikki stopped in front of a lit, hypnotical window. "What are we looking for?" Maidie asked. "I don't know yet," Nikki answered. ("Deception. The robbing of graves." Maidie had studied the word *skulduggery* in vocabulary the week before.) A fat man stood by himself in his kitchen, eating potato chips out of the bag, staring into space, oblivious that his life, his house, was as see-through as an ant farm, inner machinations exposed. "I'll bet he smells bad close up," Nikki said, hands in her pockets, feet in the snow, legs stiff. A few minutes later, they stopped in front of the Funderburks' window. Mrs. Funderburk held a saucepan with a potholder, spooning mishmash onto the sheriff's plate. "I can't watch," Maidie said. "She was my teacher." Nikki said, "Her? You'd better watch. You might learn something." She laughed. She bent over, made a snowball with her bare hands, no mittens. "Ha."

She threw the snowball at the window and dashed away.

Maidie ran too. But not before Mrs. Funderburk looked up, startled.

When Maidie and Nikki got home, Dell was standing in the driveway, under the porch light, talking with Maidie's dad. "I don't want to be impertinent, but I'm a widow raising my daughter's daughter. I can't afford to make a bad financial decision. I've asked Pastor and Mrs. Larssen, nice people. Pillars, I can see. Mrs. Larssen and I struck up a friendship. She gave me the impression that Eugene is, well, solvent but stingy."

Maidie's dad said, "I can't say. Don't know. Thrifty, yes."

Dell said, "Thank you for your help."

"I haven't helped much," he insisted.

"Bah," Nikki said, sitting on the back-porch step, pulling her rubber boots off. "It smells like farts, it does, inside my boots."

Maidie went inside. "I don't like her."

Her mother was staring out the kitchen window at Dell. "I don't either." She reached for the whiskey bottle and poured. Maidie's dad came through the back door. His eyes met Maidie's. He flexed a smile. But Maidie's mother didn't see him. She said, "I tell you, Maidie, this time, I swear, I'll resist. Hold back, hold firm," she said, confused. Maidie's dad said, "Hold firm against what?" Maidie's mother looked up. "I meant it in a general way, that's all. I was giving advice. To Maidie. Hold firm against the future, dear," she said, bright, brittle, opaque, an imitation of optimism. "I'll take some of that," Maidie's dad said. He opened the freezer door, slid the ice cube tray out, pulled the lever. Crack, shatter. Ice chips flew, speckling the ocean-blue linoleum floor. "Whiskey, I meant," he said.

Maidie stood jittery on her stone patio one morning, staring at closed windows, locked doors. "Too much coffee, I mean," she told Zip, who sat at her feet, skittish, annoyed. She'd stayed up late last night, dusting tabletops, washing ceiling fan blades, spritzing dark corners with ammonia and Pledge. "Because the top of a refrigerator is the best indicator of whether housekeeping is going on or not, I always check hers," Maidie's landlady Opal Johnson once said about the refrigerator of a daughter-in-law she hated. Maidie's dad's approach, his imminence, had prompted this last hygienic spate, this whirling-dervish bout of purification. On the answering machine, he'd sounded spooked, out of joint, out of time. Whenever Maidie moved, she called and left her address and phone number, and he joked abut the corrections her section of his Rolodex had acquired, but he never called. When she got the phone message, *urgent,* she dialed fast, thinking he had cancer, or Lucy or Thea had crashed a car into a cliff and lay at death's gate in a chrome-rimmed hospital bed. No answer. She tried later. No answer. Two days passed. The phone rang. "In fact," he said. Maidie could tell by the sound he made—licking his teeth and savoring the taste—he was home alone, drinking.

"In fact, your old pa has retired," he completed the sentence. He'd lately cultivated a rural persona. He'd stopped listening to Perry Como, Judy Garland. He liked Willie Nelson and Johnny Cash now. The last time Maidie saw him, at her second wedding three and a half years ago in Fayetteville, Arkansas, he'd said, tipsy and portly in a powder-blue suit with a western yoke, he felt the need to be in touch with his roots. Maidie looked at his hair and thought of Grecian Formula, which, years back, his mother used, rinsing herself shoe-polish brown every Sunday. But he was talking about ancestral traces, roots dug deep in the dirt farm in northern Minnesota. Congenital memory. That ugly lump of a woman, Maidie thought when she looked in the mirror and saw that the slope of her shoulders, the heft of her bosom, resembled her grandmother's now, though on a smaller, hopefully more comely scale.

She'd seen him then, the father of the bride. In the interim, she'd called to say she and Jack were moving to Virginia. She sent holiday-induced cards and letters. She called and told him she was leaving Virginia, also Jack. He'd said, testy, "I don't understand." Maidie had just finished explaining to Jack for the second time that she was leaving Virginia, Jack too. She'd stood near the door in case Jack decided to flare up, a fulminating discharge. He didn't. Still, she'd juggled credit card debts, sorted her clothes into boxes, called the landlord, terminated the utilities, changed the oil and transmission fluid in the car, made minute computations as per the barely sufficient moving al-

Debra Monroe

lowance that was in fact not an allowance but a reimbursement. "What confuses you?" she asked.

"Why he stopped working." Jack, he meant.

"In that case, I'm confused too."

"He needs a job."

She nodded, but realized she was on the phone, invisible. "Yes."

"I don't know why you even got married."

Her anger roiled for a moment, caustic acid in a washing machine, gentle cycle. "I don't know why anyone gets married, period."

"You don't know why *what?*" His voice rose up. "I thought you'd gotten nicer." Then he faltered and flattened. He'd started sounding like that, over his head and sinking, only lately. When he was younger, he shut off conversations he didn't like. Snap, blank. "You sound hard and bitter like your mother."

Hard and bitter. Also glossy, impenetrable as she'd tilted back her glass, mesmerizing in dark lipstick, coral-colored hostess pajamas, gold lamé shoes. When she talked, her hands clapped around her face like thunderbolts. When she listened, her eyes gleamed, fathomless pools of receptivity: you wanted to swim. She had spitfire, disproportionate anger. A stuck mayonnaise lid made her furious. Or Maidie's father wouldn't say he loved her, so she didn't speak for days. She broke the silence, driving her Lincoln, wrangling the wheel. "God must have a plan for me, because my life's been shit pie à la mode so far, but I've been sweet and good in the face of it." ("Self-Sympathy as an Acculturated Feature of Maternity in Post-Industrial America," the title of paper Maidie once wrote. The professor responded: "Content substantial, even groundbreaking. May I suggest subtle semantic changes? Stop saying *self-appointed martyr.*")

When her father called Maidie to report the urgent news, he'd said, "Your pa is retired and taking his living room on the road." He'd bought a Winnebago, he elaborated; he'd be in Tucson tomorrow.

142

"What?"

"I'm calling from Kansas." *Thwip, Clank. Zoom.* Highway sounds. He wasn't home. He was at a truck stop. Drunk. "That's right," he told Maidie. "Kansas City, Kansas. I've got a nice surprise."

So Maidie stood looking at her windows, Zip whining, her father due, the patio dusty. But she'd finished cleaning. Done. In Nebraska, Neville once clipped a cartoon and taped it to the cupboard: Helga, broom in hand, swept farther and farther across a vast field, until Hagar, a speck in the door of his little hut, yelled, "That's enough, Helga! You can stop cleaning now!"—except Neville crossed out "Helga" and wrote "Maidie." Maidie imagined vacuuming her patio, sidewalks next, waving as she tidied past Rona and Harve's, Clima and August's, Evvy and Cindy-June's. "A clean neighborhood," the landlord said when Maidie had called from Virginia to inquire about the house. "No breaking and entering yet." Maidie picked up a branch and tried to pry open her window screen. Her keys were on the kitchen table; she could see them. She'd always congratulated herself that she never made small, daily mistakes, only massive, life-altering ones. Had the curse reversed? She'd make small mistakes now but transcend imprecision and miscalculation on the grand scale and marry someone kind and industrious, new and improved?

Or never marry again, a circumspect option.

Maidie needed to retrieve her keys, drive to Lalo's, then go to the office and finish paperwork, then back home to sit still as her father positioned himself in the pink-doilied living room and talked, confabulating. How was his trip? He'd point at a yellow legal pad, detailed notes about roadways, gas prices. His retirement? He'd saved since 1967, Lutheran Brotherhood of Man, good interest rates. His house? Its larder shelves and dresser drawers more orderly now than when he was married to either of his daft, inattentive wives. He didn't need one! He had a pocket calculator, a closet caddy, a hectic schedule of meeting impressive people who were impressed by him too. This was the typical conversation, give-and-take, Maidie thought as she nudged the olive branch under the aluminum-framed window screen. The screen bent. She yanked the branch back, threw it. It slammed against the house, clattering. "Sugar," she said. "Shit." She wanted to pull someone's hair. Zip whined, alarmed. But when she reached to soothe him, "There, there," he curled his lip and snapped, savage, fierce. She thought: I have bad taste in dogs too. "Morning, Miz Bonasso. You sure look pretty." Harve waved from the street, his work truck idling. "Thanks." She'd chosen carefully, a silk ribbed skirt, filmy tunic, shoes that looked like a little girl's Sunday school shoes but with exotic pointed toes.

"Can you help me?" she asked. "I've locked myself out."

"Be right there," he said. He pulled over and gleamed, smiling, a wide, friendly moon face. He reached for the screwdriver in his toolbelt. "Rona sends her love, I'm sure. Our best to your boyfriend. If you land him, you'll have done good."

Maidie stiffened. Rage again, disproportionate, bloating. She chose her words slowly. "If he lands me, *he* will have done good."

Harve stopped smiling, puzzled.

Zip growled, low and menacing.

Harve stepped back. "Take it easy, boy." Then he recovered his grace, magnanimity. "That's right, Miz Bonasso, you're a good catch too." And he smiled, jogged the window. "There you go. Hop on through. Careful of that nice dress. Have a good day."

"Thanks."

Her skirt caught on a nail.

She ignored it. A few minutes later, she pulled up in front of Lalo's, a former What-A-Burger he'd converted into a co-op gallery. Lalo slept and ate in the office and kitchen. In the cus-

tomer service area, paintings hung from partitions; sculptures
sat on Formica counters and tables. He'd mounted a black-and-
white sign, ramshackle, on the red plastic-tile roof. COOP
GALLERY. Maidie had pointed out the missing hyphen, but Lalo
cleared his throat, ruminated, said, "That's my sense of humor.
The building doesn't encourage, ah, habitation, lingering."
Maidie parked in front of the plate-glass windows and
honked—she'd started picking Lalo up when his bicycle got
stolen. "We're tardy," he said as he got in the car. Maidie sped
through town as Lalo opened his backpack and read from a
sheet of paper. *"Parere. Transparere. Disapparere."* Maidie stopped
at a light. "What?"

"A quiz," he said, "in Latin." He handed her the paper.

> *Parere*—to give birth
> *Transparere*—to be seen through
> *Disapparere*—to pass gradually out of sight
>   or existence

"Tenses," he said.
"Yes, tenses. Past, future perfect, like that."
He shrugged.
Maidie pulled into the parking lot, next to the WOMEN'S HIS-
TORY COLLECTION TEMPORARILY CLOSED FOR RENOVATION
sign. Inside, she sat at her desk and read the last half of the
Statement of Mission she intended to submit to the American
Association of Museums with her reapplication for accreditation: words and phrases about the persistence of memory, the
likelihood that what is recalled is understood only after years
pass, that extraordinary struggles of ordinary people are enlightening and worthy of examination. The essential responsibilities of the late-nineteenth-century household—be it a cabin,
a casa, or a tipi—are a template of responsibilities we face a century later. *Ding-a-ling.* The blue-shirted mailman delivered a

packet of flyers and envelopes. "Morning." He laid them on Maidie's desk. Someone came in after him. The phone rang. "Women's History Collection," Maidie said. "Kiddo," Garth McHugh said, "I want to pick your brain about something. But later." Click, he hung up. Maidie sifted through the mail. The return address on the envelope: Director of Public Relations, Pillsbury Corporation. Too slim, she thought; i.e.: *Many proposals seem admirably worth funding, et cetera, but alas and woe, our budget permits only* . . .

"Maidie Bonasso." Rex stood in the doorway.

Maidie said hello and gave him a smile, moderately sincere. She opened the envelope. Rex talked while Maidie read. "Lunch, La Luna," he said. "For lighter fare, Mother Earth Café. I'm leaving in three weeks, for three months." . . . *pleased to inform you your project is one—out of more than four hundred—to which Pillsbury has awarded a stipend.* "Mon Dieu," Maidie said.

Rex said, "Pardon me?"

"We got the grant. What did you say?"

"I'd like to take you to lunch."

Maidie looked at the clock. "I told you, my father is coming."

"I want to meet him."

"No." Her pitch must have risen like a high-wire trapeze act, or barometric pressure. Because Lalo stared, then groaned. Maidie felt trapped and annoyed. "Would you hush up," she told Lalo.

Rex said, "I don't see why not."

Lalo glared at Maidie. Mad? Confused? Protective? How could Maidie say, when he was so sphinxlike, disturbingly inexpressive? She said to Rex, "I'm not divorced yet. You have a ponytail. He's a Republican. You're older than me. He's difficult."

"But I want to. He'll like me." Rex looked hurt yet also patient, dog-tired and benevolent. Maidie remembered he was the depended-upon only child of an elderly mother, a fair-haired always-do-well. Also, what Rona said last week: "It seems extremely important—a problem area, if you get my drift—for Rex Hurley to make a good impression on people, hale-fellow-well-met. Do you see?" At the time, Maidie didn't see how wanting to appear even-tempered and dependable could be a problem. But she saw now: it could. Rona had said, "Of course, neither Evvy or Cindy-June ever brought home a man I thought was good enough." She frowned. "Not that Evvy ever brought anyone home."

Looking across her desk, Maidie told Rex, "I never brought anyone home who made a good impression. I had bad taste. Or luck. A bad track record. I haven't seen him since my last wedding."

"Could we have this conversation in private?" Rex said.

Lalo slammed a filing cabinet drawer.

"In the other room, maybe?" Rex said. But it was dusty, full of boxes, paint cans, lumber. Rex opened the door, and they stepped out under the turquoise sky, the wavering teal-colored trees. Maidie wanted to yell. What? "You're so . . . there all the time," she said, "like a fence post. You're only twelve years younger than my dad. You're not my type. You're temporary." She felt free, high, elevated. Her elbows seemed to flutter, her clavicles, like wings. Except her hands, clenched into fists, ached. A tin taste filled her mouth; her heart raced.

Rex straightened up. "Fine," he said. "But stranger things have happened than two people who aren't the same age fell in love. And you don't know I'm temporary. You can't tell the future."

She'd tried.

She'd bought a pack of tarot cards with an instruction manual. The seeker after wisdom selects a card for the person about whom she wants inside dope, the unrevealed future. Rex was the Hierophant, she decided, with his desire for social approval, his skill in outer forms of ritual; in the best of times, an inventor, in the worst, a superstitious hippie. When she tried to tell Rex's future, he'd said, puzzled, "I always thought of myself as a reliable owner of large estates, usually married," making a case for himself as the King of Pentacles, a card signifying wealth and power. But remembering the night Rex woke her to write down the lottery numbers he'd dreamed—he wouldn't go back to sleep until they turned on a light, found a pencil, wrote the numbers in the cover of a paperback novel, *The Alienist,* by Caleb Carr—she said, "You're the Hierophant." Since he thought she knew the tarot better than she did, he'd nodded, subdued.

She shuffled the cards, told his future. His business would take him to faraway lands, but a woman light on her feet and fond of movement, also deeply loyal though not reliable when crossed, might interfere. "You?" he asked. "I have no idea," Maidie said.

But she did.

She'd been loyal for years. Then a plan materialized, a cluster of immutable barriers and slim options tumbling like kaleidoscope fragments into place, a teleological mass wavering into visibility: the future. Maidie lived with Jack thirty-seven days, knowing. She read U-Haul brochures. She borrowed a road atlas from Mrs. O'Hara. She subscribed to the *Tucson Daily Star* and perused it in the easy chair as Jack walked past. He didn't encourage conversation about private qualms, subterranean compromise. Maidie might sit at the table with the calculator and checkbook, a stack of bills, and he'd walk by in TV-spectating attire. "I know it's hard," he said: which bill to pay, which to postpone, he meant. He patted her shoulder. She stood up. "It is." She wanted him to see the bills, her paycheck stub, the chronic discrepancy between. His mouth went hard; his eyes distant and smoldering. Maidie paid another month's rent and left him. She told him two days in advance. His response? He felt tired. He lay in the bed until she dismantled it, loaded the trailer, Dodie watching with teary eyes, naive about steel-clad truth, likelihood. "Promise you'll write."

"Maidie." Rex watched her. His face seemed to be unnaturally mauve-colored. Flushed. "Are you embarrassed by me?"

How could she answer (impossible!) except: Of course not. How could she say—civilized, decorous—I don't want to be seen with you, linked, associated, labeled as having any relation to you, not Rex Hurley's girlfriend, partner, kith, sweet thing, paramour. She stood silent too long. His skin turned back to its usual color. She said quietly, "I'm embarrassed I haven't landed somewhere more permanently." His face converted again—soft, revelatory. He looked like a child who meant to put the toys back exactly where they belonged. He didn't want to disgruntle anyone, least of all Maidie. Where was his reserve, inaccessibility, the vulnerable resources he held back, concealed? She wanted to grab him by the collar and slap him.

"It's you, Maidie and Rex." Z. walked up in a salt-and-pepper tweed suit. "Hi. Hi," she said, beaming. "Isn't this a gorgeous blue sky?" She stepped closer. "Maidie," she whispered. "I need advice about something, your insight, but later."

Insight. Maidie nodded and smiled. She'd switched into hide-the-fight mode. In Arkansas, but mostly Virginia, she'd regularly pantomimed sociable ease in front of neighbors and strangers. For example, a waiter approached the table with Maidie's waffles, Jack's sausage patties, set them down. "Is everything okay?" Maidie nodded, a dopey smile, as Jack kicked her under the table. He'd just called her a name in a harsh, barely audible whisper: "Stupid cunt." A housekeeping dispute. He'd taken money out of the "Rent" jar and spent it on a rowing machine. The word *cunt*, Maidie explained, had a distinguished history as the proper Anglo-Saxon term for the passage to the womb; in fact, it appeared *(queynte)* in manuscripts for royal entertainment in the fifteenth century. It became obscene in the Age of Enlightenment, when medicine appropriated Latin as its vocabulary.

"Later," Z. said. "I'll call. Enjoy the weather. Bye-bye." She waved, her scarf flopping rhythmically as she strode away.

"I won't keep you," Rex said.

(Pathologically interested in genial appearances, Maidie thought.) And she considered Z.'s cheery about-face, her unearthly patter about fair weather. And something old and indecipherable rolled over inside Maidie, like a worn-out carpet being pulled up and replaced. "Would you bring Guapo?" she asked Rex.

He turned mauve again. "I wasn't planning on it."

"I wondered," Maidie said. "My dad likes dogs, I think." Lately, he talked about the dog he'd had as a boy, Fido. Faithful one.

"He should meet Zap," Rex said.

"Zip," Maidie said. "I don't know." Zip had bitten two drunkards—Cindy-June's fiancé, Harve's toothless brother, Buster.

And as Maidie's dad's Winnebago lumbered up the street, Maidie wondered what Rex would wear, and say. If this were 1971, if her dad were still married to Neena, he'd act superior. "Nice fellow," he'd say about Rex, as he sometimes did about a rural insurance client, "but I could never be so simple." Maidie sat on a lawn chair and looked at the Winnebago's lit windows. Her dad pulled into the driveway, opened the door, jumped out. They embraced, Maidie's hands splaying involuntarily as if she had potting soil on them and didn't want to brush up against his suit. But he wore jeans, a red sweatshirt with a porcupine emblem. Across the street, Clima stepped off her porch and waved; August too. "Hello!" They walked to their brown sedan, August wobbly, Clima stately; she'd been in the tequila already, Maidie thought.

"My neighbors," Maidie explained.

"I have someone I want you to meet," he said.

Maidie's brain searched: who? She pictured no one. "Me too."

"You first."

"He's not here yet."

Inside the motor home, her dad introduced Paula, who sat knitting green yarn. About the same age as Rex, Maidie guessed; she had copper-colored hair piled up cocktail-party style, circa 1965. She wore jeans, a T-shirt decorated with calico flowers. "How do you do?" She smiled. Maidie's dad said, "Who's this I'm meeting?"

"A friend."

He nodded. "I want to meet all your friends."

Rex pulled up in his flatbed and stepped out. He was wearing a shirt Maidie hadn't seen before, eggplant-colored with pearl snaps, and creases as if he'd just unfolded it from a square package. Maidie hated purple, all shades. She'd read in the Lifestyle section of the newspaper that if you hate purple you'd make a good critic; if you love it, you're creative. Maidie loved carmine, burgundy, crimson—which meant she was aggressive, if frightened. Something made a terrible noise. An attack dog barked, rabid. Next, a high-pitched whine like a hallucinating cicada. Maidie's dad said, "Hell, I'm afraid of dogs."

Rex stepped up to the travel trailer. "Easy, Zap." He opened the door, came in, nodded. "I guess you have a cat in here."

Paula smiled and stood up. "He's a little ferocious now and then." She climbed to the mattress by the ceiling and pulled him out.

Zip sat by the door and whined.

"Who owns this idiot dog Zap?" Maidie's dad said.

Maidie bristled. To show up, she thought, no invitation, and criticize Zip—it's not like he'd paid for dog-rearing lessons!

Rex said, "He's smart, too smart for his own good. Maidie got him at a hard time in her life, and he's picked up some of that."

Maidie's dad said, "What?"

Rex shrugged. "Hardness. Fear." He liked abstract words, pat causation theories. A 1970s tic, Maidie decided, rolling her eyes.

Her dad pulled out a bottle of liquor. Rex said, "I met some Russians once, and they taught me about vodka's special social qualities." Her father stared at the bottle. "It is beautiful." He spoke to Rex. Women and children: seen, not heard. Maidie didn't feel seen. She felt negligible, light-headed.

Sheer.

Rex pointed to the east. "Santa Catalinas. South, Santa Ritas. Tucson and Tortolita Mountains to the north and northwest."

"You don't say." Maidie's father poured.

"Your daughter has a true friend, sir," Rex said, drinking.

"Don't call me sir."

"You are a little older."

"True."

"I look out for her," Rex said, "and will."

Maidie said, "I look out for myself."

Paula stifled a giggle.

Maidie's dad frowned. "No one said you didn't." But he reached across the table and patted Rex's shoulder. "I appreciate that, son." He stared into Rex's eyes. Rex stared back, unwavering. The cat climbed into Maidie's lap and purred. Maidie thought: My dad drives thousands of miles. I clean until dawn. To impress a cat. And she imagined her obituary: *Maidie Bonasso devoted her life to the study of family customs in another century, and many cats liked her.* "Dad." She made her voice smooth, careful. But even to herself it sounded tenuous and splintery, like Mia Farrow on national TV explaining that Woody Allen had eloped with his stepchild. "What brings you here?"

Her dad raised his eyebrows. "To see the country."

He didn't mention her house or yard. Rona and Harve commented on it daily. Harve: "You're a hardworking girl, Miz Bonasso!" And Rona gave her a little book about Holly Hobbie cultivating garden flowers, but her soul grows too. Maidie thought: He'd notice a KOA campground. He'd make a note on his legal pad: "clean, attractive grounds." Maidie stood up and poured a glass of lukewarm vodka. Her dad filled his glass and Rex's.

"You like dogs?"

Rex said, "I've had mine fifteen years. Hundred and five dog years."

"Amazing."

Maidie gulped.

"What impresses me," Rex said, "he has erections."

Maidie said, "What?"

Paula giggled again.

Her dad said, "Still? That's inspiring!"

Rex said, "It's not over until it's over, I suppose."

A pair of well-matched dunces, Maidie thought, snorting and gulping in an unfeminine way; but appropriate, she decided, given the conversation. "Stop making dog erections into philosophical precepts."

Rex said, "You're right. I'm sorry."

Maidie's dad said, "There's no reason to be crude."

Paula said, "You're the one enthusing about dog erections." But she laughed, knit and purl. "How was your Christmas?" she asked.

Maidie looked around. "Me?" Paula nodded. "I bought some old pieces of furniture," Maidie said, "stripped them, painted them a pale ocher color with aqua trim. I put new covers on sofa pillows. I've introduced ocher to complement the other colors in my living room, which are royal blue and maroon, periwinkle as an accent."

Paula frowned. "On Christmas Day?"

Rex said, "I wanted to take her to my mother's in San Vicente."

To meet his mother, yes, his sons. Temps. Maidie already had plenty of temps. Rona invited Maidie for dinner too; Maidie declined. "I was tired. I needed time," she told Paula now, "to organize." She was grinding her teeth, she realized. Rex was staring.

"Are you divorced yet, honey?" her dad said. "In my experience, whoever acts first comes out best. I wouldn't put it off."

Maidie's brain ran down a hill. Pink doilies. Royal-blue antimacassar. A ceramic tea table with periwinkle sprigs. A maroon chair. Jack wouldn't want those. But one compliment he'd always paid Maidie, on the phone to his mother in Florida: "She makes a low-rent dive look cozy." Neville, on the other hand, complained about Maidie's taste, held up a statue of a glass elephant with real ivory tusks. "I'd give this the boot," he'd say, pretending to kick. But since she moved to Arizona Maidie had begun whittling down bills she and Jack had accumulated. She'd have a raise in a month. Should she give Jack money? Was it fair to live semi-opulently here while he sat staring at garage rafters?

How did he keep his spirits up at nightfall? She looked outside. She saw the black and brilliant glare of windows facing a dark sky, reflecting internal light only, dim. She said to Paula, "These don't seem like the curtains that came with the Winnebago. They're pretty." They were, 1940s-style yellow and black stripes, matching divan cushions. And pert daisies in vases.

Paula smiled. "I redecorated. I made them myself."

Rex stood up. "It's been a pleasure." He shook Maidie's dad's hand. Her dad, wobbly, said, "Don't let me interfere with your routine." (Routine?) He was talking to Rex. Giving him permission to spend the night, Maidie realized. She rolled her eyes.

As they crossed the dark yard, Rex reached for Maidie's hand. Maidie looked at the black corridor of the sky, its mica peepholes, the distance no human traverses. She wanted some force—not gravity: levity—to push her back out of the long ditch into which she'd headed. She thought of Mia, in Arkansas, two days before Maidie got married. "You have someone to sleep against every night. You know where your body ends and the rest begins. I can't feel my limbs. They don't seem to belong to me any more than to the rest of the world." Her mahogany-dyed hair hung lank around her face as she cried. "I'm trying to find a metaphysical way to say I'm lonely." She packed boxes and crates, getting ready to leave. Maidie tried common sense, practicality Ann Landers–style. "You need to meet people," she said, "like I met Jack." Mia shook her head. "If it happened already, it won't again. If it happened once, it's a lie by now, a truism," she said, inexplicable when depressed. Maidie wondered where Mia with her widow's-weed hair was now. And how. Happy?

Rex said, "I like your father."

Maidie thought of her mother. ("I like *me*," her mother had said. Or, home from the beauty salon, her hair upswept: "I really *like* my neck.") Maidie answered Rex in the dark. "I noticed." A damp, vernal smell drifted in. Maidie closed her eyes and pictured lilies, a lake carpeted pale green. She stumbled in the dark.

Rex touched his fingertips to her back.

She opened the door. Zip clattered in behind, toenails over tiles. Even in the dark, Maidie sensed his betrayed glance. She'd been in the Winnebago with Paula's cat. Her father had called Zip an idiot, then raved about Guapo's virility. She reached to pet Zip, but he growled, moved on. Rex said, "Would you like a drink?" Maidie didn't want the so-called social aura attributed to vodka, the impetus to prattle glib niceties. "You don't say." "I appreciate that, son." "Your daughter has a true friend." "Make mine tequila," she said. Rex poured it, luminous and moonlit. They drank in the dark. "I don't want to stay late," he said, nodding as if pointing with his head at Maidie's dad's travel trailer in the yard. But he started to kiss Maidie in that accelerated, stoked way, like he was going north, Maidie south, and he wanted to stop her. He pulled at the barrette in her hair, clumsy. She yanked it out. He carried the glasses to the bed-room, lit a candle. "My father died when I was young," he said.

She thought: Too much talking.

"I wanted my father-in-law to like me," he said. "It's a mis-take to want something that much." His voice floated in the dark.

Maidie said, "This is no family to use as your substitute."

"Most important," he said, touching, persisting, "I've waited for someone like you." He kissed her, murmuring. Then off with his engorged purple shirt. Its snaps clicked. Maidie—in-gratiating, she knew—said, "For me? You waited?" She couldn't help it. She heard Lucy: Stop fishing for compliments, Maidie.

He said, "Someone like you. Your hair and face. Your favorite colors. The organized way you take care of yourself." He slid her skirt off, her tunic over her head. He set her down and removed her shoes, Mary Janes. The glasses of tequila glowed next to the candle. "Your large white breasts," he said. Then the sex. Slow touching, like that. Then Rex, all of him, the moment of grip and stall, electroshock therapy: a lightning-rod theory of time. This minute, moving and holding still, lasts forever, or as long as Maidie lets it. As long as she can stand it.

Afterward, returned to earth, inert, Rex asleep nearby, Mai-die drifted. How much I like it, she thought. How much I never found out with Neville. And with Jack, the words *sex* and *ser-vice:* synonyms. Also, that time with Joel Scribner in the guest-house at Eugene and Vera's, the frozen air, decrepit smell. Old people had lived, smoked, drunk, slept, dreamed there. They died, their bones bleaching the color of lichen. Joel, a pale, rangy torso, labored above Maidie. "You didn't come." Maidie said, confused, "But I'm *here.*" "*Come,*" he said, "like I did." Mai-die's mother had explained sex. "Overrated hoopla which can be," she stressed, "endured." Maidie closed her eyes and willed herself back to the fusty cabin, her legs floating like they seem to when she and Rex made love. But the walls turn flimsy, light-pervious. Maidie passes through them, hands and feet tingly. She's going up, between the banisters of the stairwell in her old home, ghostly in memory, unnavigable. She bumps the wall, knocks her head on the landing, crosses the threshold into her room, and floats toward the attic, which, like a false bottom in a jewelry box, holds a secret. Does it? Death is small and dark.

Rex Hurley rolls over. His loose hair flies into Maidie's mouth. Dry weeds. Dead protein. In the half-light, she watches him, face agape, pall-colored skin, knotty elbows and knees, his brittle ribs. Asleep, dreaming, he said, "Indians here two thousand years ago disappeared, no one knows. *Hohokam,* vanished ones."

Maidie woke all the way up. She rolled over.

Rex touched her breasts, legs, face. "I want to wear it out."

Maidie said, "What?"

"My penis," he said slowly. As if he hadn't said the word out loud much. "I want to make love to you until it wears off." Maidie started to say, No more conversations about penises: yours, anyone's. But she stopped when she imagined how Rex might look in the dark, wary, his eyebrows in a V. He smelled like sand and leather, skin in the sun. His breath? Like vodka and toothpaste—like peppermint schnapps, which Eugene used to serve in little cups in honor of new snow. Maidie remembered, its glimmering renewal. She moved her hands across Rex, gnarled, wan, familiar. Outside, her father and Paula slept under a thick quilt in the transportable living room, a cat at their feet. "In the next life, you see, it'd grow back," Rex said, his voice dropping over the night like a net, cobwebs, "and I'd find you." Maidie fell asleep again, thinking: Sweet. I could never be so simple.

What Z., in a lime-green minidress, gladiator sandals, wine cup in hand, said (scoffingly) to Maidie as Maidie dreamed: "All the Zen Buddhism in the world won't do for you what a good orgasm can."

*M*aidie's mother said, "Zen Buddhism forces you to seek knowledge with your intuition. Not scriptures, which are someone else's big idea, never your own." She held a porcelain coffee cup, little finger extended, a slice of cake on a fragile plate, as she said so to Mrs. Larssen, Mrs. Funderburk, and Dell, also the church cleaning lady, Mrs. Scribner, all of whom sat in a circle. Maidie stood, her face near her mother's shoulder. The other children—Lucy, Thea, and Nikki—screeched and skidded on new-waxed linoleum around the portable tables and tan folding chairs stenciled TLC (Trinity Lutheran Church). Joel sat in a chair, reading about crustaceous forms of life, crabs and so on. This was the Lutheran Women's League meeting to plan the annual bazaar. Maidie's mother—having had a faith crisis and advised by Pastor Larssen to study religion so she'd locate universality, transcendental comfort—was dishing up her latest pressing news. She was on the move from this religion to others: unslaked by Lutheranism, she contemplated Navajo sweat lodges now, Catholic transubstantiation, reincarnation, and the *Tao Te Ching*.

"I went to Saint Patrick de Sales," she said, "and I liked the incense and kneeling—and Latin, not knowing what they're saying. It's . . . imaginative." Maidie wondered if her mother meant the service was reinvented every time, or if Maidie's mother used her imagination to make up what the priest might have said.

Mrs. Larssen, a pale woman with a thin mouth and tortoiseshell glasses that seemed to be her most daring fashion accent, said, "Interesting. But"—she looked around, her eyebrows arched above her glasses—"we'd better begin the meeting." Dell blinked at Mrs. Larssen, who paused, stared, then glanced away.

Maidie's mother stood. "Excuse me, I have to use the rest room." She didn't have to rest or pee or wash her hands, Maidie knew. She needed to retreat, recover, get a new facial style of composure; she'd take a yellow pill and come out reassembled, detached.

When she left the room, Mrs. Larssen said, "I told Ethan these studies were a bad idea. She'd do better with the Bible or Catechism."

Dell said, "I haven't read either. As you know, I'm not religious, though I believe in God. But I don't hold with doubting and searching. I'd like to know how long she's been Christian."

Mrs. Funderburk set her cup in her saucer. "I never think it's courteous to talk about someone who's just left the room. Besides, there are children present—little pitchers with big ears."

Mrs. Larssen said, "Maidie, go play."

Maidie didn't. Dell's eyes locked onto Mrs. Funderburk; then she turned and faced Mrs. Larssen. Maidie remembered how— when Maidie, her mother, Lucy, and Thea first got to the meeting—they'd thought no one was here, the church vacant, cavernous. Then they heard murmurs in the basement and headed down. Two voices, furtive, hushed. Dell and Mrs. Larssen in the dark, waiting. "Hello, strangers!" Dell said in a sham-cheerful tone. She reached over and flipped on the light. The room flooded, flesh beige, toothpaste green—Sunday school decor. Jesus prayed on the wall in a blue garden: Let this cup pass from me. The others arrived, the meeting began, Maidie's mother left the room, and Dell said to Mrs. Larssen, "As you pointed out, she's not from here. How Lutheran can a dyed-in-the-wool African be? I saw some pictures in *National Geography*. Instead of crosses and stained glass, Africans have statues—for fertility. I mean, I never. Smut. I'd bury one ten feet deep if I ever laid eyes on it."

Mrs. Larssen said, "Well."

Joel Scribner's mother said, "Statues?"

Dell nodded. "Painted up—the tips of their things!"

Mrs. Funderburk cleared her throat. "You're misinformed. Madagascar is an island off the coast of Africa. There are Africans, yes, also Polynesians, French, Germans, Americans. Christianity has had a foothold there for a few hundred years, as Mrs. Larssen knows. Mrs. Giddings was born in the eastern U.S., I think."

Mrs. Larssen nodded. "That's right."

Dell said, "A lot of bad influence, any way you look at it. And more smoke than meets the eye—more little pitchers too, I bet."

Mrs. Scribner frowned, confused. Mrs. Larssen looked alarmed. Maidie herself wondered about pitchers; all she could think of was a row of Kool-Aid pitchers shaped like heads with ears.

Mrs. Larssen said, "It's time to begin the meeting. I'll get Elaine."

Mrs. Funderburk turned to look at Dell. "Your take on Mrs. Giddings," she said, clipping off her words, "is as accurate as your sense of geography. I don't suppose you're familiar with the psychological theory that suggests what you're worried about in your own life causes you to see the same in others? At any rate, I hear you just got married. Then congratulations are in order."

Dell looked uneasy, like she'd been poked but couldn't see the stick. Maidie thought: Mrs. Funderburk doesn't like Dell. Dell won't like Mrs. Funderburk now either. Maidie's mother never liked Dell, and vice versa. Dell and Mrs. Larssen like each other, though Mrs. Larssen is embarrassed to say so. Why was this true? Maidie knew from girls' cliques at school: it just was. If you're friends with someone, you share things, hate included. Maidie didn't have friends, except her mother, and Joel.

Dell shifted in her chair. "I'm a newlywed, yes. I guess it's too much to expect romance at this point in my life." She waved her cup the way Maidie's mother sometimes did a cocktail, sloppy and graceful. Coffee sloshed. "Eugene is a fixer-upper," she said.

Maidie said, "He can fix anything."

Dell said, "I thought Mrs. Larssen told you to go."

Maidie said, "Broken chairs, picture frames, flat tires."

"He's a handyman." Mrs. Funderburk smiled.

Dell said, "An old handyman—but I'm no spring chicken."

And Maidie's mother came back, reserved, drifting. In the old days, she had two phases. One, she talked chronic and rapid. Maidie's dad liked the comments on this and that, even if they made him tired. "I started to cook pork chops," she'd say, "and I thought, no, this man needs something refreshing, so I put together a cool cucumber soup." Or: "Did you see the prickly cactus in the window has a bloom?" He'd smile and nod: nice cactus, nice soup. Talking meant fair weather, good moods. Yelling and slamming meant she'd clam up behind a hardwood door soon. Maidie pictured her mother shut away in the bedroom, an abrasive, irritating grain of sand in there with her, which would later become a pearl. When Maidie's mother closed the bedroom door, Maidie, Lucy, and Thea made tuna fish, noodles, and mushroom soup in the same big pot for dinner. Or cheese, saltines, carrots, and apples. Or Maidie's dad brought chicken from the Bauer House Family Restaurant. These days, Maidie's mother was neither silent nor loquacious: the blue and yellow pills. It was her old personality, sealed off, contained. This sanitary, mildew-resistant, improved way of being was, for the most part, a reprieve, because Maidie, Lucy, and Thea knew their mother was anxious and confused, but they didn't feel so anxious and confused with her.

Once, Maidie, Lucy, Thea, and their dad sat in the kitchen, the bedroom door closed. Maidie's dad said, "Funny, they named the sixteenth President after a car." Maidie countered, "Funny, they named that rock in Massachusetts after a car." Maidie's dad said, "An ugly car too." Maidie went on, braver:

"They named the French Mediterranean coast after a Buick."
Lucy, kneeling in her chair, chortled. "Funny, they named a car
a Dart." She howled, laughing. What Lucy said wasn't funny,
but *she* was, tumbling off her chair. They all laughed. The bedroom door opened, and Maidie's mother came out, a silk kimono over a flannel pucker-sleeved nightgown, a combination
she wouldn't have countenanced in better days. The more depressed she was, concave to the world, the less visible. She'd be
undetectable if she weren't crooked, askew, clothes and hair, the
shape of her mouth. She said normal words at odd junctures.
She seemed convinced the way to grace, to afterlife, was to fill
silence. One day at school, Mrs. Funderburk read the class a
Greek myth: There once was a race of men so taken with noise,
vibration, patter, they forgot to eat and drink, and died. These
men came back to earth as cicadas; locusts, some people call
them, she'd said, and shut the book.

At the Lutheran Women's League meeting, Maidie's mother
said, "Charity is deductible," but she mangled it: "Charity is in-
eluctable." And retreated deep to her interior, prehistoric
memory.

Maidie thought: Africa. Fertility.

Mrs. Funderburk said, "Good idea. We'll stress it in the pub-
licity." She took notes on a pad. "Do you think we should have
the bazaar here?" She looked around the basement. "If we can
get the goods down here," Dell said, nudging Mrs. Larssen's ankle with her patent-leather toe. Maidie looked at Mrs. Larssen,
her thin mouth. At Mrs. Scribner in a frowsy coat, a fake cor-
sage with a plastic bell. Mrs. Funderburk, stern, unflappable, a
bandanna kerchief over her hair. Maidie's mother, wistful, wet
eyes. All of us down here, stuck, Maidie thought. "Go play with
the children," Maidie's mother was whispering, slippery-voiced,
nudging. "You're lucky to have little friends. Go."

Maidie walked across the room. Thea, playing tag, bumped
Maidie, landed on the floor, stood up, ran away. Maidie sat

down near Joel. He closed his book, boy-like, considerate. "Would you like to take a look?" He offered it up, smiling, a shivery grin.

In the car on the way home, Maidie knew she should ask only so many questions, or her mother would say, "Is this an interview? I'm not exactly Liz Taylor. Please leave me alone." Maidie said, offhand, "Mom, we're studying Africa in school. Were you ever there?" Thea was asleep. Lucy looked out the window her eyes clocking this light pole, that fence, that tree, landmark, landmark. Maidie's mother said, "On the continent, no."

"Were you born in Madagascar?"

She twisted around. "Who wants to know?"

Maidie said, low, "Me. Where were you were born?"

Her mother said, "Germany."

All Maidie could think of was dirndl skirts—but that was probably the wrong time period. "What about your mother?" Maidie asked.

Maidie's mother said, "You know she left home."

"What do you remember?" Maidie didn't expect an answer.

Her mother said, "That cherry smell, Jergen's."

Maidie said, "What?"

Her mother shrugged. "She must have used Jergen's hand cream, because every time I smell it, I think I see her out the edge of my eyes—brown hair, rings with big stones, a flowery dress."

Maidie asked, "What was it like with your dad?" And waited. Because when her mother got the letter saying her father was dead, she'd cried in a big, choking way and stayed in bed, taking cough syrup, lemon toddies. "Is she sad?" Lucy had asked. "Sad and mad both," their dad answered. "She can't bury the hatchet." He closed the door. Maidie's mother pulled up at a stop sign. "It was wretched and hard," she said, "but that's not now, Maidie. Now is a time of peace and light and harmony. Zen," she said. "It does help with my driving," Maidie's mother explained. The car lurched ahead, then died. Start, stall, stay tranquil. Zen, Maidie thought. Also: How long will I stand outside my mother's life, knocking and tapping? How do I get in? Maidie stared through the sloping windshield. Or away? Which?

*W*hich? Maidie wondered, standing at the end of two slow-moving lines in the Cofer College Bookstore, amid displays of books, paper, pencils and pens, beaded earrings, coffee mugs, teddy bears in hula skirts, also travel-sized packets of Tylenol, which is what Maidie wanted to buy. The man in front of her stooped over to write a check, and the clerk—with his crocheted beret and wispy goatee—asked to see an ID. He checked it carefully. "So you're a professor here?" Maidie thought: Hurry. The man who wrote the check had a bald head, a chest-length beard, a tweed sports coat with leather patches. The clerk said, "What do you teach?" Maidie's head ached. "Psychology," the man said. The clerk brightened. "Maybe you can help me. I'm thinking of getting married, and I can't decide between two girls." The professor frowned. "That's not up my alley. I run tests on lab rats, that sort of thing." The clerk looked downcast. And without the good sense to know he shouldn't ask about theories of marital compatibility while people stood in line to buy aspirin, Maidie thought, running late.

She looked at her watch.

Late for the office. Late for the airport. She'd called Jack. First, she'd called Dodie's brother, because Jack was staying in his garage. "Could you have Jack get in touch with me?" she'd asked. Dodie's brother said, "He has a phone now," and gave Maidie the number. Then they had what linguists call a "phatic" conversation: "How are you?" "Fine." "You like it there?" "Arizona? I like my job, and I have good neighbors— the usual." "You deserve it," he said, and hung up. Maidie remembered Dodie describing her brother as a virgin who'd interpreted that fact to mean he was gay but hadn't met the right man. Yet he tended to get crushes on unavailable females too, Dodie had said, registering her skepticism by waving open-palmed at the sky. Maidie tried to call Jack around 11:30 P.M., his time. Busy. She tried again at 11:45, and 12:00. Who would he talk to from his garage at midnight? When she finally got through, he said, "We can get a divorce, sure. But you come here with the papers. You were standing beside me when we got married. You can stand beside me when we get unmarried. That's all."

Maidie explained that a plane ticket was $470—she'd checked the prices. He could sign the papers and mail them back. He said, "I won't cause problems. I want to see you one last time."

So when Garth McHugh asked Maidie to his office so he could pick her brain (his phrase), she began the meeting by saying she needed a long weekend, a day or two off—one day to go, one there, one to return—to get her divorce jump-started. "Divorce." Garth held his chin in his hand. "A messy business, that. By all means, take a few days. Perhaps the weekend after Easter?"

Then the items he wanted to discuss.

"I want you to attend the Multi-State American Studies Conference, in Oklahoma City. I think you'll give the old boys a stirrup."

That's what Maidie thought he said.

"Stir them up," he said. "I can just picture it."

Maidie said, "Why don't you go?"

He shook his head. "I've lost my verve."

Maidie said, "Their museum has a collection of Choctaw beadwork. We can arrange a visiting exhibit. Midge will love it."

Garth said, "That brings me to the second item. I want to warn you about our situation, though I think Zora Coles can be converted."

Maidie said, "No one needs to be converted. The museum—I mean, the History Collection—will be better off if it accommodates competing passions and ideas." Meanwhile, she thought: Situation? Tedious, hair-splitting meetings, more like it.

"Nothing can accommodate competing passions," he said, grim. "The committee is made up of giants—you, Zora Coles, myself—and midgets—Cass Willoughby with her feather-brained Willie Nelson fixation, and Midge, with her embroidered towels. Midgets cause problems, iota by iota, drip by drop, water torture."

Maidie was thinking of midges, little bugs at dusk. Also Midge, her bright, darting eyes. She said, "Those two? Cause problems?"

Garth flexed his jaw muscles.

"You know best," Maidie said. But she thought that Cass and Midge—apologetic, fluent in the body language of low self-esteem (Oprahic)—weren't plotting. Garth was. They'd end up reacting.

"I lie awake at night worrying."

"About the Women's History Collection?" Maidie said.

"That too."

"Do you have a family?" she asked, irrelevantly, she realized.

He said, "I have remnants of a family. Now go on, take your trip. May I offer some advice? Crying and drinking won't help."

"What?"

"In my experience, staying up all night crying and drinking won't make a divorce easier."

"Thank you," Maidie said, and left.

And the Friday after Easter, she stood in line at the bookstore, buying Tylenol. "It seems like psychology is out of touch with reality," the clerk said, petulant, wrapping up the professor's purchase. The professor said, "I did once read that there are three conditions partners in long marriages share. Spouses have, first, a similar socioeconomic background; second, a similar educational background; last, similar energy levels."

That covers it, Maidie thought, her head throbbing. She'd had at least two conditions mismatched both times—unavoidably, maybe. Who could have a similar educational background? What man, like Maidie, had had no plans for college, no history of anyone in his family interested in college, and then decide to spend the rest of his life at, or near, a college because he, too, liked the kindly way teachers pass on essential information, launch students toward autonomy, achievement, time well spent? Maidie could read forty books, write fifty papers, take sixty exams, to court a teacher's approval. The rules were clear. Take notes. Hand assignments in. Ask questions politely. Get coherent answers. As for energy levels, who else so loved the sensation of a moving car, an uplifting plane, but kept house in such a rigid manner that what Maidie did home alone most weeknights was straighten her doilies or the angle at which pictures hung? Maidie tried to imagine being married to herself; she felt exhausted and took a Tylenol on the way back to her office.

She typed a list of duties for Lalo to complete—clerical work—while she took this trip to Virginia. Next, the trip to Oklahoma. Then they'd catalogue the last of the objects, and the carpenters would finish. In June, Maidie would host the grand reopening.

"Hello." Z. stood in the door, holding her minicassette player. She'd lately begun listening to ads in the personals section of Tucson's alternative newspaper, *The Rag,* and recording them on her answering machine and playing them back for Maidie: she wanted insight (her word) before she made a decision. At first, Maidie said, alarmed, "Isn't there someone nearer at hand?" And Z. had shrugged. "All of them are from Tucson," and suggested Maidie try voice-mail dating too. "Of course, you're seeing Rex right now," Z. had said, "but that's a transitional relationship." Maidie said, "Transitional?" Z. said, "On the rebound, impermanent. You don't have anything in common. And the age difference. Still, transitional relationships can be very comforting." Nothing in common? Maidie had wondered. A bad mix, maybe? She'd answered Z., tense and abrupt: "I know all that." Z. had raised her eyebrows. "Is something bothering you?" She said it again in the doorway, "Is something bothering you?"

"I have a headache," Maidie said, "and I'm leaving on this trip."

Z. said, "I've narrowed it down." She turned on her tape.

> Hello {a disembodied voice}. I'm an architect. I have custody of my two children, ages six and nine. My time is filled up with parenting and work. But I'm looking for someone who likes starlit nights and white wine. I have enough money, but I'm not rich. I like dogs, no cats; sorry. I want someone who's sweet, independent, creative, for friendship, maybe more. If this sounds good {he laughed, scratchy} maybe you should have your head examined. Or call me.

"Second," Z. said.

> I'm a painter interested in a stable relationship. My interests include political protests. I'm looking for a fun, dazzling woman to share my life and ideals.

Maidie said, "The architect."

Z. said, "I like the politically-minded painter."

Maidie said, "Whatever. I have to go."

Z. left, and Maidie went to the parking lot, where Rex waited in his truck. She handed him her keys, he was coming by her house to water flowers and feed Zip. "Hello," she said. He nodded, his eyes bloodshot, and shifted his miscellaneous gear to

the back to make room for Maidie. He was still mad, she decided. He'd wanted her to go with him to his mother's in San
Vicente for Easter. "Just the three of us," he'd suggested, "no
pressure." Maidie had answered, "No, thank you." All she knew
about Rex's mother was that she'd lived in the same ranch
house forty-one years; Rex's father had been born there. A
housing development had sprung up around her, concentric
rings of three-bedroom homes enclosed by a fence with an electric gate, the combination to which she could never remember;
she waited for one of the new breed of neighbors to drive up,
open it, and she followed through. Also, she loved tinfoil—it
still seemed miraculous and newfangled to her. Why didn't
Maidie go? Frugality. "I already have some older friends," she'd
said. Clima and August, she meant. Rex said, "I don't understand your logic."

And when she woke on Easter morning, the streets seemed
vacant, as if a high-powered force had sucked people out. Maidie went for a walk. Through open windows, she heard children
calling out to parents. In one yard, an old lady stooped and hid
colored eggs behind a saguaro cactus, laughing to herself. At
4:00 P.M., Maidie went to Clima and August's for a pork roast
cooked in a cast-iron pot on top of the stove, chunks of meat
and bald potatoes floating in gravy. Rona, Harve, Evvy, Cindy-
June, her children and fiancé, and Harve's brother Buster with
bad teeth, had gone to Texas to spend Easter with Harve's parents. Maidie had mentioned to Clima that she liked pork roast;
she'd been thinking of one marinated in raspberry vinegar and
stuffed with apricots she'd had at a restaurant once. But this
roast was homey; so were Clima and August, toasting Maidie
with bad wine in small goblets. "We love you," August said as
Maidie left. Since everyone else on the street was related to
Clima and August, Maidie decided, they'd forgotten Maidie
was just a neighbor, nigh-dwelling.

Rex said, "I understand that you don't feel ready to meet my family. But I don't understand why—when I'm leaving to work on this movie for three months—you're taking a trip. You can handle this part of the divorce through the mail, whether *Como-se-llama* wants to cooperate or not. Let me call a friend who's a lawyer."

"No."

Rex said, "He used to hit you. What if he tries to hit you now?"

Maidie said, "He won't."

"How do you know?"

Maidie said, "It would be too much trouble, too strenuous now. He hit me when he was still trying to make the marriage work."

Rex said, "That's twisted." Her logic, he meant. He looked tired. In the past, she'd seen only a flash of this hangdog weariness, five minutes here, ten there, never two whole days. This is what he looks like pissed off, Maidie thought. Neville had looked contemptuous. Jack, like a warden about to mete out lashes. Rex: like a basset hound. I've stood worse than this, she thought, incensed. This isn't worthy of reciprocal fury. She asked, "Are you mad?" Rex said, "I don't appreciate it that you don't tell me what you're doing—that you seem hell-bent on staying five feet ahead of me. I'm tired of feeling like I chase you."

Maidie saw Garth coming up the sidewalk.

"Hurry up," she told Rex. "I can't stand to talk to anyone just now." Too late. Garth leaned in the window and slapped Rex's shoulder. "Lad." Rex, with his phony kindness, leaned outside and slapped Garth back. "How's the professor business?" Rex asked. Garth said, "Taking the little lady to the airport, I see." Rex, oblivious, said, "I'm glad you're doing so well, Garth."

Garth left. Rex started his truck, pulled into the street. "I've seen marriages founder in the time it takes to shoot a movie."

Maidie said, "We're not married. Also, I'm not afraid to be alone."

"No," he said. "You're highly evolved that way."

At the airport, he carried her bags inside. "I'll see you in three days," he said. "Try to get some sleep while you're there," he added suddenly, so loud and authoritarian people standing in line to check bags laughed. He glared and walked away.

Maidie called after him, "Good-bye. Thank you."

And the trip? She intended not to drink and cry—not because Garth and Rex had advised against it, but because a good night's sleep, soft and woolen, would swaddle life in no-life, and Maidie would reason better afterward, after eight hours of unconsciousness had helped drape the unraveling day. But drinking and crying matched the weather. Hurricane Brandon, approaching North Carolina's outer banks, had turned the entire east coast into a monochromatic trough of gray. She gave up not-drinking when Dodie wasn't at the airport to meet her. She ordered a martini—its streamlined glass and compact allotment of alcohol—and looked out the floor-to-ceiling window at jets, steam rising off their silver wings, rain rinsing the orange slickers of men who toted baggage, drove small train carts, waved flashlights in semaphores. Dodie arrived, kissed Maidie hello, steered her home. Maidie, Dodie, and Dodie's husband sat in Dodie's kitchen, eating meat loaf and frozen beans, their watery flavor and Astroturf-green hue. Sulfites, Maidie thought, trying not to look out the wet window to the house next door—its lights burned—where she and Jack once lived.

How would Jack act? Dodie had said in a letter: ". . . not that I blame you for leaving, no. But I did go visit him in Quentin's garage and it smells foul there, like he's not keeping the place up. He's gained about twenty pounds. Poor man, I guess he doesn't have much to do in that smelly garage except eat. . ."

After dinner, Maidie said, "I think I'll go for a walk."

Dodie said, "In this rain?"

Maidie said, "I've been sitting all day."

She walked past the house she and Jack had rented. Its windows glowed yellow in the gray rain. Maidie remembered a time Jack had punched her in the kitchen and she'd dropped a plate. Afterward, as she swept up shards, the phone rang. Sometimes Dodie had called offering magazines, once a casserole because, she said, she figured money was tight with Jack unemployed. This time, Maidie had answered the phone and Dodie said, "Are you all right?" Maidie had looked out the window. She saw Dodie in her own kitchen, holding the phone, staring through two panes of glass at Maidie. "I'm fine," Maidie had answered, and hung up, and walked to the corner store to buy one of those bottles of wine with the plastic bull tied to it. She used to walk to the corner store daily. *How do I get out of here, out of here?* She bought another bottle tonight, took it back to Dodie's. She changed into dry clothes, and she and Dodie drank as the storm blew.

In Dodie's living room, Maidie muttered, unprompted, "Thou art my compass as I commit myself to the wild, rough sea," the first line to a prayer she'd once memorized. Her mind wandered ahead to seeing Jack in the morning. Dodie said, "Incidentally, Jack has lost weight. His coloring is better. He bought a new Chevy."

Maidie, angry, torqued, peeved, said, "How?" She'd paid off their mutual bills: they were all in her name. Jack had bad credit.

Dodie said, "His mother gave him the money. It was right, I suppose."

"What?"

"For her to help."

Maidie remembered Jack describing the day his mother had left him home to watch his little brother, who—six years old, mowing the lawn—sheared off all the toes on his right foot. Help.

"He has a girlfriend," Dodie said.

"Jack?"

"She came up here with his mother to visit. She's his mother's neighbor in Coral Gables. Or maybe his mother's secretary."

"How old is she?"

"My age," Dodie said. "Your age. Middle-aged. Jealous?"

"No." And Maidie started remembering Arizona. The fire-colored bougainvillea. The stalwart cacti. Clima and August in a brown sedan. The sky, a blue dome by day, a vault of stars by night.

In Virginia, rain drummed. Maidie went to bed on a sofa in the attic, a triangle-shaped room tall enough to stand in. Boxes of books and old clothes, Dodie's doll collection, and her husband's golf clubs, stood like blockish guardians. A garret, Maidie decided, remembering the part in *Heidi of the Swiss Alps* where Heidi languishes in the city, pining for home. Outside the tall window, lightning illuminated the branches of trees like snarled cords. Maidie couldn't sleep. She remembered when Jack had crouched to put a pot of beans in the oven and she wanted to shove him in, slam the door. Lying on the sofa in the spasmodically lit room, she felt ashamed and untrustworthy with her disregard for marriage vows: for better and for worse. Worse, Jack had knocked Maidie down, and when she tried to stand, kicked her breast with his wing-tipped shoe. She'd called 911. Helpless? Vengeful. She had public opinion on her side. Husbands shouldn't hit wives. *Time* said, *Glamour* too. The cop said so, shining his light in Maidie's mouth. In the days afterward, the word *breast* didn't make sense, too soft. *Tit,* its connotations of animal husbandry, the efficient harnessing of forcible nature, did. Left tit. Jack's brother's mangled right foot.

Jack's mother had sometimes left her sons to be tended by their grandmother, who'd made money bootlegging but hoarded it, and she beat them with a hanger if they drank milk out the top of the carton. Jack's brother was the bleakest, most fleeced by the past: his bad foot, his cocaine, prostitutes. Prostitution makes sense, Maidie thought. Love becomes transactional, an exchange, not phatic, a feeling. It has an agreed-upon beginning and end, a calculated risk attached. Maidie went downstairs and got the Toro bottle and, as lightning flashed, drank out the top of it. Morning arrived. No problem that she couldn't sleep now. Problem: past.

Problem: present.

Jack picked her up in his new Chevy Blazer. "How are you, darling?" He called her that only when he was winning an argument.

His garage quarters seemed orderly. Maidie said, "This isn't too bad. Dodie told me it was depressing and smelled funny."

Jack grinned, leery, lips stretching over his teeth, eyes humorless, the same look he'd worn in photos taken on the day of his favorite uncle's funeral. "The plumbing was backed up when Dodie visited," he explained. He pointed at a toilet, sink, and shower behind a partition. A chrome-legged table and matching chairs sat on this side of the bathroom. Shelves on the wall were lined with the neatly folded sweaters and pants Maidie had bought Jack with credit cards when he was unemployed, depressed, low self-esteem, etc. In the middle of the room a sort of central-garage altar arranged on an upturned crate, the TV and VCR. Near the door, an almond-colored stove and refrigerator, with dealer tags still attached. "I'm moving into a house with my girlfriend, Gina," he said, "and it didn't have appliances." Before she could stop herself, Maidie asked, "How will you pay for it all?" Her interest in Jack's finances (i.e., right, claim, share) was over, and not a minute too soon, she reminded herself.

He said, "I have a job."

"Congratulations."

"Sales," he said. "Burglar alarms this time."

"You'll be successful, I know."

He clapped his hands together. "Damn right."

As they sat at a table and looked at the divorce papers, Maidie logged her exhaustion: head and stomach bleary, empty; eyes scratchy, dry. "Would you like a drink?" Jack said. He scanned the divorce papers and signed where the lawyer had marked X. He poured two shots of George Dickel. He shoved a CD into the portable player. "I don't suppose you want to go to bed?" he asked.

Maidie nodded. "You're right. I don't."

Arizona! Arizona! she hummed. Jack drove her to Dodie's. She went straight up to the attic and lay down. Dodie brought her a bowl of chicken noodle soup and saltines. "Jack's not a bad person," Dodie said. "Neither are you. It was a volatile mix."

"Thank you," Maidie said, as Dodie went back downstairs. The empty Toro bottle sat by the trash, transparent, sticky. Maidie wished she hadn't drunk that shot of brown liquor with Jack; she sensed it in her veins, spreading to her muscles like ink. She couldn't find that groove of calm, that tunnel of soft walls and striped ticking, dark, eiderdown peace that passes into sleep, death's brother. Phrases, images, noises intersected in her brain, which she pictured as a big screen in an auditorium. *Kisses so good, so good,* she thought, metrical, nostalgic. She remembered how she'd once buried herself in the crevice between when her father, Bill, kissed his lovely wife, Elaine. Maidie had put her right hand on her mother's leg, her left on her father's, jammed her head between. They kissed leisurely above her, an eclipse, a kiss aperitif. Then the hearty course. Her mother and father didn't *like* each other, or their children, not consistently. But as Maidie hung on while they kissed, she understood she'd been conceived in love, raised up from it, and a certain amount of disdain and fury was its complement. Its outcome?

Rapid departure.

Love is born, exists, and dies. Maidie knows for sure.

Where it spends its afterlife, she can't say.

She also can't say where her mother's jewelry box went. Or

the two hooked rugs, red roses in the center of pale green, that used to lie on the bedroom floor? Or photos of Maidie, Lucy, and Thea that used to sit on a shelf? Or a lamp with a milky, bubbled texture from Maidie's mother's nightstand? Or a mirrored tray that held perfume bottles, doubling, an illusion? Neville Kramer's sister—the one who wore glasses with big lenses, her tiny initials embedded (gold) in them, her sweatshirts decorated with hot glue and glitter—once lost everything in a fire that started when her husband laid his jacket on a burner turned to Low Heat. Her home: gone glimmering. What did Neville's sister say? We still have each other. Maidie's own home: gone glimmering, up in smoke. Her hindsight blurred, sketchy. She doesn't even know where the furniture went. And when she visits Clima and August and looks at, let's say, a statue of an angel with eyebrows merged into a single line the shape of a tire iron, or at a miniature punch bowl with matching cups, she thinks of Vera's studio, its clutter and riches. Nikki and Dell went home to the Iron Range, presumably. Vera died. But Eugene slunk to where?

For years, Maidie imagined him traveling the rails like a better class of hobo, as he'd done in 1937 when he went to find work in California and found Vera instead. Maybe he went to California again and found Maidie's mother. And they lived happily, happily, a tail-end remnant, a last economical butt of family.

The last time Maidie saw Nikki and Dell, Dell had come to the house on a winter day to gripe about Eugene—as if Maidie's dad, having sold the marriage, now addressed customer complaints. "I'd like to talk about something private," Dell had said, jaw clenched. Maidie's mother swooshed the children out. Maidie crept back to the living room door, propped ajar, and heard traces of conversation. "Whoever's there," Maidie's mother said, "shoo." Later, at the front door, Dell stood with her hand on Nikki, who made apelike faces. Maidie can remember more: what got said one day, suppressed another, what exact slur or prompt instigated the chain of spite and counterspite, fury and resentment popping like rolled-up explosives. But remembering makes Maidie's head pound. Like when she cleans house and puts chairs and tables back painstakingly, making sure every piece matches. She feels dizzy afterward. (The smell of bleach and disinfectant?) Like when she organizes her clothes to see what flatters or doesn't, what coordinates or won't, as if a yet undiscovered combination might make everything right and bright still. Sorting, considering, tidying, sanitizing. It makes her sick.

So the past stays disarranged. Even though, according to neuropsychological theory, memory is self-ordering: events store themselves in relation to earlier events, categorize themselves thematically, are retrieved linked. But Maidie's memories seem like truncated notes in damp air, disintegrating. Or a rare textile run through the automatic washer, stretched and snagged, warped and shriveled. The sense that Maidie's past decomposes, turns to moldering dust as it no doubt will when she lies to rest in the black earth, is, she believes, the aftereffect of neglect. If she were better organized, more disciplined, she'd air out her memories like collectible relics, clean them up, and put them away in deacidified storage units, cross-referenced with index tabs.

Stress, the force that deforms bodies, deforms time, its recollection, as do alcohol and jaw-grinding insomnia (memory-distorting factors). Maidie's first bout of insomnia occurred one night when her mother thought it Continental to let Maidie finish dinner with coffee and adult conversation. Then someone shut off the lights. Time for bed! The pace of minutes slowed and accelerated. Tree branches outside Maidie's window pulsed and pushed. She had the idea that pleasant thoughts might help the night pass less skiddingly—less breakneck motion followed by creaking halts. She'd tune her mind to high ideals. What did she think about? She was seven; she'd just seen the Rodgers and Hammerstein *Cinderella*. She conjured her own wedding, the exact circumstances of the proposal, her egg-white dress, the trip up the aisle, the rice-pelting, the final moment she stood by a train with a bouquet, a mystery groom beside her. Good-bye, she called to wedding guests she'd dreamed up; it's been a lovely life here, but I'm off to a new one. The End.

In the morning, Dodie's husband drove Maidie to the air-port. Cars zipped by in the gray dawn. Strip malls swam around the edges of the road. Muddy, rinsed by sleep, Maidie stared ahead. "Queasy?" Dodie's husband asked. "No," Maidie said. It would be impolite to be queasy so early in the day, she figured; also, she could sleep on the plane. She got out at the airport. "Good-bye. Thank you. Tell Dodie it's been lovely, but I'm off to my new life in Arizona." Then onto the airplane and up, up at last. But the plane landed to board passengers in Atlanta—a byzantine, ill-designed airport. Rain fell. Forty miles away, tor-nadoes clustered. The plane stayed grounded for three hours and forty-five minutes. "Hurricane Brandon," the pilot said over the PA. "Its ambient mayhem." At least, Maidie thought he said that. After two hours on the runway—with no sense whether the plane would leave in five minutes or five days—Maidie stared at the beige plastic seats in front of her. They seemed to swell and press forward. She worried she'd fall asleep and drop her head on the pin-striped shoulder of the stranger nearby. She started to cry, quiet and steady like a mechanized pump.

She didn't want Jack back. How fortunate he had a new girl-friend. Maidie wasn't responsible now. She flipped through her life: nothing amiss. Still, she produced choked sobs at robotic in-tervals. She stood up and went to the bathroom—a bit rapidly, because the flight attendant rushed up and banged on the door. "Do you need ginger ale?" Maidie said, "No, thank you," and went back to her seat and mopped her face with a paper hand towel. Out the edge of her smeared vision, she noticed the man next to her reading *The Seven Habits of Highly Effective People*.

When the plane landed in Tucson, *drag,* Maidie disembarked.

She saw Rex's head five inches above everyone else's, moving forward. He wore a straw hat with a big brim, a sombrero/cowboy amalgamation made in Guatemala, he'd once pointed out. With his creased face and gray ponytail, he looked like he'd been cast as an extra in a movie about misfits living on the rock-littered, last-chance border. Since Maidie had been crying on the plane and had tried to sleep for two days and couldn't, it would seem—she thought, pushing into strange, dense bodies—that she hadn't taken Rex's advice, or Garth's. Don't cry or drink. Try to sleep. She looked at Rex's pointed hat and ran. She lugged her suitcases, strapped-down lumps. Like Joe Namath, or Joe Montana, she zigged around a woman with a baby stroller, zagged past a flight attendant trolling an overnight case, jogged alongside a tram for handicapped passengers that tooted down the hall. Maidie remembered the surge as the airplane had lifted at last through the blustery clouds to the other side, yonder, blue. The present, gone. The future, immediate. Exertion . . . blurred faces . . . muffled noise. Maidie ran until—like a tollbooth barricade dropping down, click—Rex thrust his hand through the crowd, cupped her rib cage. A man crashed into her and barked, "Damn," noncourteous. "I'm here," Rex said, "so stop."

*S*ometimes Maidie stopped, asked herself: What had she thought she was doing both times, getting married? She thought she was getting married. The first time, for example, she thought she was ceding a life in which only Laree noticed if Maidie came or went, failed or flourished. Then Laree got pregnant, had an abortion, and, in the guilty aftermath, cinched herself to Phil, day by day affirming the connection with team

spirit and brand-name zeal. She talked about the Bulls, Phil's
favorite team; Valvoline, Phil's oil; Boboli, Phil's pizza crust;
Arm & Hammer, his toothpaste. Phil said marriage took 400
percent, she said: two people giving 100 percent 100 percent of
the time. How that added up to 400, Maidie wasn't sure, but
she wanted to be immersed, up to her elbows in love's chores.
She'd trade 200 percent, easy, for the Vacancy, Room-to-Let
sense she worried she flashed, vulnerable, at new acquaintances,
the I'll-go-anywhere glance she thought she cast like a farmer's
daughter at traveling strangers. People buying groceries in
pairs looked happy. Houses with lit windows and people clustered at tables seemed warm. Neville, good-natured, smiling,
fat, esteemed by fellow orderlies and appearing to return Maidie's affection, hesitated just a minute when Maidie proposed,
then said yes and loitered around, husband-like, two years.

The second time, the decision had soul-hovered between her
heart and ribs, as opposed to brain-hovered between her ears.
Maidie stayed engaged two years, receptive to omens. The
striped tulips she planted came up in the spring, but a passerby
lopped them off. A stain the shape of a handgun appeared on
the hallway carpet, but Marbella expunged it with nail polish
remover. Maidie made her wedding plans pregnant, swollen
with hope, but when the ceremony took place she'd flattened
out again. Miscarrying or not, how could she cancel a wedding?
The night before Maidie married Jack, she dreamed she was
walking down an aisle, a veil—"bridal illusion," the nineteenth-
century term—frothing over her face. The groom turned out to
be a palsied graduate student Maidie sometimes drank with,
Steve Stulter, who'd perch on a stool and sardonically apply sociological tenets to thronging bar patrons. After five or six
drinks, he'd say, "You tickle me." Whether his tremors were the
result of alcoholism, or his alcoholism was the result of tremors
he drank to forget, was speculated upon but left undecided by
students who gossiped in the Sociology Department coffee

room. The judge said, "We join this man to this woman." Maidie, her heart racing as she woke up beside Jack in the dark, thought: At least I know who I'm marrying.

"*I* thought I knew who I was marrying," Dell said, at the front door.

Maidie's dad said, "He's never dropped a hint to me."

Dell waved her hand, impatient. Nikki waved her hand, impatient, then stuck her tongue out. Maidie's dad said, "I love and respect him." Dell said, "You're naive." (Or tried to say. She said, "You're *nave*.") Also: "He's queerer than a three-dollar bill." She opened the door. It slammed against the wall. Nikki stretched her lips out, crossed her eyes, stared down her nose. Dell ran out the door. Maidie's dad called after her, "Dell, Dell, don't forget Nikki." She came back and stuffed Nikki's arms into her parka, jammed a cap over her head, and left.

After Dell left, Maidie's mother said, "She's wicked."

Maidie's father said, "Or stupid. Small brain and big self-opinion. A bad combination. I take it Eugene didn't consummate their love." He glanced at Maidie. "Don't you eavesdrop."

But Maidie couldn't concentrate on brains and opinions, consummate love. She had two worries. One, an uneasy chafing, like a bur in the hem of her clothes, about how Mrs. Larssen had come by yesterday with cucumbers from her garden. Maidie's mother heard the doorbell ring and headed toward it, Pavlovian, her pink Melmac coffee cup tilted as she sailed ahead, dribbling. She opened the door. "Hello," she said, sleepy, blinking. Mrs. Larssen offered the cucumbers to Maidie's mother, who nodded yes in her aqua slacks and matching sweater, except that she had the sweater on backward; the rumpled tag poked out against her throat. Mrs. Larssen narrowed her eyes inside their tortoiseshell frames. Maidie's mother dropped her cup, splash. Next, the cucumbers tumbled chunky over the floor.

"I'll be in touch in a few days," Mrs. Larssen said, backing down the sidewalk. But Mrs. Larssen was a small worry compared to the fear Maidie had for her own soul because she hated Nikki so much she wanted to beat her to a marmalade pulp. We plead guilty of sins, Maidie thought (by rote, Pavlovian), even those we don't know.

"You see," as the grown-ups discussed private matters upstairs, Nikki had told Maidie in the basement, "your mother's a Negro combine." Maidie, Nikki, Lucy, and Thea were in the fruit cellar. Maidie, confused but not mad, not yet, said, "She isn't." Her mother had blond hair and brown eyes, like the lady in the Breck commercial. Maidie also wondered about combines, machines that chop wheat. "She did it with a Negro," Nikki said, sticking a finger from her right hand into a loop she made with the thumb and finger of her left. Lucy roared, laughing. *"You're* a combine. *You* do it with Negroes." She pushed Nikki into a row of stewed tomatoes. Nikki laughed. Thea, a tinkly echo. This was Hector, Minnesota, 1969. Maidie had seen one black man; he worked at the hardware store. Lucy, Thea, and Nikki ran through cobwebbed recesses of the basement, yelling, "You are, you do, you are, you do." Maidie went back upstairs to the living room, where she tried to hear the adults. But she'd learned a lesson. If someone says something rude, say it back. "You're a traumatized cripple," Jack Bonasso once said. Maidie said, *"You* are." He stopped yelling. "True," he said and turned on the TV.

*"T*rue," Maidie said, as she wiped her hands on a dish towel and flipped off the TV, which had been tuned to a PBS show about a Hollywood poster artist who'd once aspired to paint mountain lions and sequoia trees but, after thirty years of drawing avenging forty-foot concubines and evil yetis, couldn't. Rex had frowned and said, "If you ask me, they overemphasize that angle about the artist's bad childhood." Rex was nursing a beer, a

Red Dog Ale. Its advertising slogan: No Whiners. Maidie was
standing at the kitchen counter next to Lalo, deveining shrimp
for Cindy-June's wedding tomorrow. Maidie said to Rex, prim,
like an egghead, a teacher's pet, she realized, "The idea of emo-
tional shelter as a child's inalienable right is fairly new. It has its
roots in the Victorian era." Rex said, "The past doesn't affect a
person every day. It blows in once in a while, like bad weather."

Lalo cleared his throat and said, "But still . . ." Maidie, turning her back to pour vichyssoise out of the blender jar into a
tureen, rolled her eyes. Lalo had recently read a book called
Abundant Manhood and worried ever since that—because he
couldn't remember his father, who'd drunk himself to death in
Chihuahua, Mexico, when Lalo was five, and then he'd moved
to Arizona with his stepfather, who'd told Lalo to learn English
by watching TV—he hadn't been launched into manhood with
sufficient lore, or wisdom, unless he counted that time when he
was sixteen and went to Holland on an art scholarship spon-
sored by Fuji and the Study Abroad leader had been kind and
instructive, teaching Lalo, for instance, to buy hash. But over
her shoulder, sympathetic, Maidie said, "Go on." Lalo said, "If
food or a house is needed, parents don't have shelter either.
Still . . ."

He let it drop.

Maidie let it drop. Rex stood up and patted Lalo's shoulder.

The phone rang, and Maidie answered it. Garth said, "Can
we talk for a minute?" Maidie said she was cooking. She had *just*
a minute. He said, "Kiddo, the problem is that Cass is threatening to get the other Willoughbys together to contest the en-
dowment on the grounds we're having secret meetings about
the museum."

"The collection," Maidie corrected. "Cass called and said
what? Were those her exact words? She's contesting the endow-
ment?"

Garth said, "Well, it was more along the lines she didn't

think her grandma would like decisions we'd made, and I called her."

Maidie said, "Why?"

Garth said, "I call her a few times every week to drop hints."

Maidie said, "About what?"

"That a museum requires expertise, more than she might have."

Maidie said, "You said that?"

"Pretty much."

She paused. "You'd better not call her anymore, Garth."

"Maybe you're right," he said, and hung up.

Maidie thought: He spends his evenings calling Cass. Then calling me to worry about Cass. Does he have friends? A TV? A dog?

She went back to the kitchen and said, "That was Garth."

Lalo groaned.

Rex nodded. "I suppose you told him about the job offer."

Maidie wrapped shrimp hulls in newspaper. "I haven't." She tried to picture Oklahoma: an umber and smoke-gray horizon, she decided.

Rex said, "It's an opportunity. Whether you take it or not, an opportunity should improve your life. If Garth knows someone else thinks you're valuable, you'll be valued and respected more here."

Lalo frowned. "What are you talking about?"

Maidie explained that when she'd called to register for the Multi-State American Studies Conference, the man who took her call had turned out to be director of the Oklahoma State History Museum, and when Maidie asked him about arranging for a visiting exhibit of Choctaw beadwork, also about Native American artifacts she'd found here and had trouble labeling— cordage baskets, mortars and pestles—he'd said, "We need a Young Turk curator ourselves, someone with fresh ideas. I wonder if you'd be interested."

Rex said, "I'd give Garth McHugh the impression that while you're at the conference in Oklahoma, you're taking a look at that job."

Lalo said, "But you won't leave." A statement.

Oklahoma City, Maidie thought.

She wondered what the site of the bombed federal building looked like now. What did the aftermath of vanished lives resemble? The shreds of office cubicles—portable walls, rolling chairs, metal desks. The memory of lives lived out in those tidy corners. The day care center, its regulation teddy bears and bright mats, institutionalized shelter. Was it paved over, an acre-sized memorial to the chance that each of us stands in the way when arbitrary winds blow? She looked at Lalo. "I'm not looking for a job." She changed the subject by telling him about a woman who'd donated antique wedding dresses to the History Collection.

Maidie heard about the wedding dresses from Midge when they bumped carts near the freezer section in the grocery store one Saturday morning. Someone Midge knew socially, she said—"when my husband was alive"—who knew Midge was connected to the museum—"the collection, I mean"—had called and offered to donate the dresses. Midge waved her hand as she spoke, her hair glistening under the fluorescent lights, her smile committed to the sunny interpretation, the happy take. She said, "In times of social upheaval, textiles worn for highly symbolic occasions like weddings contain visual references to the past even while making radical innovations, and they therefore reassure us about continuity." Maidie stood near the ice cream and frozen fruit and shivered. She reconsidered the plans she'd made to exhibit techno-sublime artifacts next to handcrafted tools—e.g., a margarine tub next to a churn—with the vaguely formed attendant idea that the dichotomy of cultural expression inherent between them might imply. . . what? Exactly what Midge had said. That we face the unknown future while looking to the past for incomplete guidance.

Rex drained his ale. "That'll draw a crowd. Women love weddings."

Maidie said, "Do they?" Annoyed.

Rex said, "That's my impression. Should I order a pizza for dinner?"

Maidie said no and fixed three plates of food. She sat at the table with Rex and Lalo, dipping shrimp in cocktail sauce, slurping lukewarm vichyssoise, thinking about her role in Cindy-June's wedding: volunteer caterer. Ingratiating, absurd, this habit of proffering herself for every freestanding problem and half-baked solution. In graduate school, she'd joined thwarted committees. In marriage, she'd tried hard to bring Jack, Neville too, lost causes, up to snuff. So even though she'd guarded against acting helpful and servile around Rex, when Rona had described the food she intended to serve at the wedding—hot crabmeat sandwiches that would seem to require a small crew of people running through the neighborhood, commandeering spare ovens, showing up with potholders and steaming food on cookie sheets just when the vows were over—Maidie felt her diffidence slide away. Rona looked tired, overwhelmed. Maidie felt charitable and abject, generous but deferential. She suggested plain, elegant food made in advance, served cold; she offered to cook.

Rona had said, gratefully, "Would you?" Her eyes, the color of Hershey's chocolate, welled. She'd had a fight with Harve over whether they needed a new refrigerator for the wedding. Harve said they didn't. Rona ordered one anyway and asked Cindy-June's fiancé to help move the old one to the garage. Rona didn't like her future son-in-law. "Because he thinks he looks like Elvis Presley," she said. "The fat Elvis, in my opinion." Moreover, he didn't understand a little-known fact about the transportation of refrigerators. He and Rona were hauling the old one across the driveway when Harve drove up. Maidie was home at the time, windows closed, air conditioner humming; she was making notes to herself about the Women's History Collection, its grand reopening. She heard Harve yelling loud, rhythmic. She opened the door to listen. "It's called knowledge! It's called knowledge!" he yelled. Maidie had been curious: what was? Rona told her later. You can transport a refrigerator on its side, or crooked, or upside down. You can give it a concussion of sorts and set it up again, vertical, but you can't plug it right back in and turn it on. You'll wreck it. *That* was knowledge.

So Maidie ended up cooking. Sitting at the table with Rex and Lalo, she described her menu. Canapés with pesto and goat cheese. Wicker baskets lined with gingham napkins and filled with strawberries (an agrarian-nostalgic motif in keeping with Rona's antique milk cans and wagon-wheel chandeliers). Perfect stalks of celery jutting from crystal vases. Bread, cheese, small quiches, vichyssoise, shrimp. Mimosa, also plain orange juice. Harve had ordered a keg, Schlitz. Rex said, "Shrimp's a good choice. People in the desert love seafood. It's a rarity here."

Maidie looked at her shrimp and considered what Rex had said. Pale, wet meat inside a hard husk. The sloggy embryo in the center of a shell. Outside, for thousands of miles: sand, dry riverbeds, sand. Lalo said, "My mother makes soup by boiling fish heads with nopalitas." Nopalitas were cactus strips, Maidie knew. Lalo's mother pulled the thorns out with pliers, he said. The meat beneath the needles was tender. She kept a cactus patch in her garden next to flower planters she'd made by painting a toilet, sink, and bathtub yellow, pink, and blue (respectively), he said.

Maidie said, "She paints bathroom fixtures for planters?"

"She did," he said, pushing his glasses up his nose.

"One of your early influences," Maidie said.

He frowned.

"Industrial chic," she said. He still frowned. She said, "The

way you use mass-produced scraps for your art, like that furnace duct." She and Rex had just attended a show at the Coop
Gallery. All the work Lalo agreed to exhibit was experimental,
but Lalo's pieces—including *A Day in the Life of Maida Bonasso,*
the green papier-mâché surface with a lump—were incongru-
ously familiar, prefab scraps reassembled in startling juxtaposi-
tions. Forging the alien, separating the familiar (Friedrich
Nietzsche), Maidie thought, looking at a fiberglass-and-wire
furnace duct, tall enough to walk through. Lalo had convinced
the manufacturer to donate it; then he'd painted it aquamarine
and ornamented it with color Xerox copies of magazine ads for
prepackaged food: Cheez Whiz, Rice-A-Roni, Wonder bread,
V8. But Maidie's favorite piece was an antique leaded-glass
window mounted crookedly on metal rods in a ramshackle
frame; in the middle of the smoky ornate glass was a jagged, tri-
angular hole, and from the corner of the frame hung an old
pamphlet Lalo had found in a thrift store: *How to Make a House
a Home.*

Lalo stood up. "Thanks for the grub. I'll be back to help tomorrow."

Maidie was in front of the sink, up to her elbows in suds,
when Rex sidled up behind her, circled his arms around, put his
hands in the water. He tugged the dishcloth away. "It must be a
northern tendency," he said, swabbing a plate, "this continual
cleaning, your ongoing fear of dirt." He scrubbed a pan, kissed
her neck. How did Maidie feel, crunched against the sink, dish-
water slopping off the counter onto her dress, Rex's breath hot,
ticklish? She felt crowded and damp. He wasn't a deep thinker,
she felt. If he knew more about the recent history of marriage in
the Western world, she felt, he'd understand that physical desire, assistance with household tasks, and the will to understand
someone you love, won't suffice. Maidie felt the same urges—
sex, goodwill, sympathy. She'd felt them before; she would
again. But urges and good intentions don't make love *stay* (en-

dure, remain), or *stay* (stanch, support, avert pain). O God who could destroy the world with hail or conflagration, stay us.

There were marriage counselors in every downtown and suburb of every city in the United States. Every bookstore had a section for happiness instruction, marriage how-to. The Barnes & Noble in Tucson had a section: *Self-Help/Self-Ayuda*. Every night, the Spanish TV station broadcast a show, *Se Podrá Salvar Este Matrimonio?* A close look at a husband, a wife, their argument; at the end of each segment the moderator implied that, indeed, the marriage had been saved, salvaged. But Maidie wondered. Theology flowers when faith fails. And did Rex Hurley think he knew something Dr. Joyce Brothers didn't know? Maidie disentangled herself and stared. Rex said, "You're about to say something?" But she couldn't think what, or how to begin. He was leaving in the morning for three months. She kissed him. Some people no doubt think of sex as communication, communion. ("Each night, I give my body to my husband like a chalice," a woman once wrote to Ann Landers.) But Maidie thought of it as diversion, the person she made love to assuming she was placated as she retreated into pleasure, no pressure to speak, to Rex, to Jack before him, or Neville. And say what? That the pieces of brick and mortar crumbling, the chunks of sky falling, forebode impediments if not ruin?

Meantime, she basked in that languid moon urge. Aroused, admired, necessary, Maidie kissed Rex. He craned forward. She pulled away. She wanted this part—stroke, delay, desire—to last. She opened the window, and the night air blew in, cool, temporary. She heard Rex in the next room, turning on the shower. She took off her clothes and stepped in with him. Soap and wet skin, steam, silence. Maidie washed her hair. She washed Rex's, lather between her fingers. When they rinsed, got out, dried off, Rex sat on the chair in front of the mirrored vanity, and Maidie combed Humectin Humidifier through his hair to make it wavy and fortified. It hung in her hands like ropes; she liked its scent, half manufactured (Amino Fragrance Additive #6), half animal (wet and musky like the smell of skin or hooves or fur). Rex sat with his face propped in his hands, eyes closed. Maidie plugged in her hair dryer and aimed it at his head. She reminded herself of Rex's good qualities, the pros contraposing cons.

Pros. He was neat, clean, considerate, patient. He left her house in the morning without waking her, without a trace except the notes near the coffeepot she used to find hard to read:

> Dear soft, white M.B.,
> Enjoyed our love last night. Am off to Phoenix to
> see about more props. I fed Z. and let him outside.
> Please call C. and A. and tell them thanks for the
> bottle of nice tequila. All my love,
> R.H.

He believed in compromise: for instance, the one they'd devised for the three months he'd be gone working on this movie, *The Sunlit Ambush*. Maidie had promised to visit him *once*. He'd call every Sunday. If an emergency occurred—strictly defined, he stressed—he could get away: otherwise, not at all. "There won't be an emergency," Maidie had said, scoffing. Maidie's previous experience with emergency had been that she handled it herself. Her previous experience with compromise had been that she'd worked hard at understanding Jack's perspective, or Neville's, articulating it for each of them as if she'd been hired to, an advocate, and since Jack or Neville didn't do the same, she'd ended up underrepresented, her position defended not at all. For the moment—blow-drying Rex as he hummed tonelessly, eyes closed, her hands lifting his hair into the warm stream—she wondered if he was *fair*. If the two of them proceeded slowly, could they avoid flak, disillusion? So far, besides the discord they nursed about Maidie's defensive tone—attributable, Rex

felt, to the fact that she was still undecided whether she wanted
Rex, or anyone, as a lover—they had stepdog problems.

Whenever Zip was in the same room as Guapo, he snarled,
raced forward, sunk his teeth into Guapo's back. Guapo—seventeen years old and blind but scrappy still—yipped, then re-
taliated. Rex or Maidie had to step in and separate them. Most
nights, lately, Guapo slept in Rex's truck. Sometimes Maidie
woke out of a dead sleep; above the harmonic clamor of the cicadas, above the sound of the thwipping ceiling fan, its aerodynamic blade, she heard Guapo, protesting and lonesome. *Yap.*

Rex stood up. "Thank you for drying my hair," he said, an-
gling in the mirror, touching his fingers to his temples. He
looked handsome, like an actor playing an experience-battered
hero. He slid his arms into the sleeves of a green silk bathrobe
he'd bought for himself. "Isn't it pretty?" he'd said, unwrapping
it, the plastic and tissue; he'd hung it on a hook in Maidie's
bathroom. He wore it now as he put his arms around Maidie
and pressed in, swaying to the radio song—Roy Orbison?—lost
in thought, memories. Which thoughts and memories? Maidie
felt something hard press against her leg: Zip, wedging his
head between Rex and Maidie. "Stop," she said. Zip growled,
leapt in her face, lips curled, teeth bared. "Bad! Bad!" she said.

Rex stopped dancing. "This isn't a criticism, but that dog
doesn't know you're in charge. He thinks you're negotiating.
But you're not equals. You're not married to the dog. With a
dog that big, you need to lay down rules." Before Maidie could
consider her response—I didn't ask, thank you; or: Humans
don't have dominion over animals; or: He's difficult and he
looks like my ex-husband; or: What am I doing wrong?—Rex
kissed her. Her neck ached as she held rigid. They moved toward the bedroom, and Maidie cleared her mind, shoveling out
thoughts, anti-aphrodisiac, that de-escalate desire: the TV
news, for instance, the prediction of a drought lasting to the
next millennium, a few years. No thinking, Maidie thought as

she kissed Rex. Sex, for the moment, seemed like a skirmish against an opponent as Maidie struggled toward the other side, the goal. Afterward, she lay under the ceiling fan, the fine hairs on Rex's body wafting and circling.

She disengaged and got out of bed.

Before she fell asleep, she wanted to make a list of the menu for tomorrow; also, a chart of clothes she meant to pack for her trip—like a multiplication table, except on the vertical column she put days she'd be gone and functions she'd attend, and across the top these categories: "Dress," "Shoes," "Hose," "Jewelry." Maidie sat in her royal-blue-and-periwinkle living room, under a gooseneck lamp. Rex leaned over in the dark. "Come back to bed. I leave tomorrow," his hair tickling her face.

She sneezed, "I can't." And rubbed her nose.

Rex said, "I know you hate advice, but if you could stand some . . . you can't *plan* everything. You can't air-condition the world."

Later, Maidie would ponder the latter: You can't air-condition the world. Was this adage recent (technology as a metaphor for control) and regional (uttered by inhabitants of a hot climate)? Or had Rex stumbled onto profundity by himself? But she'd stopped listening by the time he said, "I know you hate advice." She was stalled, mired in fury, when he said, "if you could stand some." Like a guardian! He'd better disabuse himself. Like she'd sleep with a guardian; how perverted. She didn't need one! She'd come this far, mistakes proliferating, but they were her mistakes. She said through clenched teeth, "I can't."

Rex frowned. "What?"

"I can't stand advice from anyone." Her jaw ached. She looked like Norma Desmond, probably, her eye makeup smudged from the shower and lovemaking, the skin on her face taut and crepey.

Rex sighed. His hair, draped over his naked shoulder, still

looked luxuriously coiffed. He stood in the living room, his torso thick, pale—a statue of an imperfect man. He shook his head. Maidie could smell her own shampoo. He said, "I'm tired."

She said, "What?"

He said, "Of you! Listening to you. I'm protective, yes. I'm patronizing, maybe. It's my shortcoming. But everyone has shortcomings."

Maidie felt her eyes open wide.

"You don't have time to do this or that," he said. "You don't have time to say good-bye tonight, fine." He went into the bedroom.

Maidie heard shuffling noises. Was he packing? Packing what? She had this urge to follow him, pull items out of his hands and shout. But she stayed in the living room and concentrated on calmness, unflappability. She remembered the day Neville had moved out. He'd gone into the next room, to the closet near the double bed, as she'd stayed on the davenport, filling in blanks in a *Dell Crossword Puzzle Book*. "Sting symptom." Eight letters. "Purple bloom." Fifteen. "Partner of *beyond*." Five. "Did you get everything?" she asked Neville as he came out with his suitcase, a garment bag over his shoulder.

That was years ago—and Neville was a husband, not a part-time lover.

Rex came out of the bedroom, wearing his jacket, his shirt tucked in his pants, his hair still flying around, shiny and stylish. One of his pants legs was pulled down over a boot, correct, the other bunched above it, lumpy. He had his new bathrobe wadded under his arm; its belt fluttered behind him like a tail. He stood by the door. Maidie felt a surge. Catecholamines? She'd read the other day that the body floods with these fight-or-flight hormones, which stimulate the heart and tense the muscles to prepare them for danger; if you had too many catecholamines, you'd die, heart failure. Rex said, "I'm not your father. I'm not your ex-husband. But I have lived longer than you. You don't have to take my advice. But when I was little, the old people had a saying—'Even the poorest beggar might teach a wise man.' You could respect me enough to listen."

Maidie, sitting in a chair, wanted him to take his coat off and stay. She wanted him to go. She wished she'd never met him. She wanted to comb his hair, or change the subject. But she hated clichés, conventional wisdom. The muscles in her face twitched. She said, "I can't believe you compared yourself to a beggar."

"What?"

"I suppose I'm the wise man."

Rex said, "You're impossible."

Maidie wondered if, in humans, catecholamines activated vocal cords, not muscles. Because a spasm of words, a long, thin tremor of incivility, pulsed. Maidie didn't know any better than Rex what she might say next, until it was out: too late. Worse, she understood as the words flew by, autonomous, that her fury predated Rex. It had its roots in the Jack Bonasso period, in the Neville Kramer epoch. No, her fury began in Hector, Minnesota. No, in a sod house on a dirt farm. No, in a bungalow in Madagascar. Maidie tensed. Words clipped past, backfiring, but she gave herself up to them. Whatever she said, she'd stand behind it. She said, "Your problem is you have no staying power. You have no resilience." To whom was she speaking? A kind, instructive voice rose out of the ashes of the past: What you're worried about in your own life causes you to see the same in others.

Mrs. Funderburk said that.

Rex frowned. "What are you talking about?"

Maidie was still thinking about Mrs. Funderburk, her clear-cut instructions on how to succeed, warnings about problems to outmaneuver. "Get a move on," Maidie said, incoherent. Not cohering. Get a moovahn. Her throat ached. Was she yelling?

"Clear out!" She would never have said words like these to Jack; he'd have beat her spongy. Was this how Jack felt when he'd lost his temper, lost control? Sorry already but helpless: too late.

Zip, on the floor by Maidie's feet, cowered.

"Shoo," she said. To Zip.

Rex stood by the door. "I've never been talked to this way."

Maidie tried to read the stiff expression on his face.

"Mean," he said, "or maybe rude."

Maidie said, "Everyone should be, at least once—it'll increase your perspective." She wanted the moment over. She wanted him to go. Words kept coming. "It should be like the draft."

Rex said, "What should?"

"It should be mandatory that everyone should be talked to mean at least once. It'll get you ready for bad experiences in life."

Rex left; the door closed. His truck fired up. Headlights flicked on the wall, then beyond. The partner of *beyond?* Great beyond.

Hereafter.

He didn't say anything as he left: when he'd call, or return.

Zip whined.

Mandatory like the draft? Really.

She looked at the closed door. Rex was gone, for three months at least. She understood departure—the back of the person you knew diminishing to a speck. The trick was to get out first. If you failed to: buck up, hang tough. Don't play country music, not Asleep at the Wheel, Uncle Tupelo, Mother Maybelle. Studies had been conducted in which rats were exposed to different kinds of music. Rats mate to jazz, work efficiently to classical; to country western, they drink from tubes of alcohol and huddle, aggrieved. With rock, they grow angrier. Maidie put a tape in the tape deck: 10,000 Maniacs. She uncorked another bottle of wine and poured a glassful, also a small shot of tequila. She considered the next few minutes, and hours.

She could clean. Or read. Or she could use the phone, an outlet. She looked up area codes. Wyoming. She dialed information. "Jackson Hole." The voice said, "Name?" Maidie used the last surname of Laree's she could remember: "Kristofferson, Laree." A computer keyboard clicked. "Sorry," the voice said. "I have no listing."

Maidie hung up. She thought about calling someone else, Lucy or Thea. To say what? "I'm in Arizona. The weather's fine. I have a new job." Even if she stuck to impersonal facts—she once spent thirty minutes explaining to Thea what sociology was—at the end of the conversation, Lucy or Thea, whoever Maidie had called, might say: "You don't sound too good." Maidie would answer, "I'm tired." (Rex: "tired of you, listening to you," and that was before she'd blown up, spitfire in his face.) Lucy once said, "Duh. So stop moving always." What was the point of calling someone, Maidie thought, if everything you had to say was half secret? Lucy and Thea hadn't even met Jack, let alone Rex. Should she call her dad? The one piece of connubial wisdom he'd offered when she got married the first time: Don't be stingy with sex. Duh. He should have told Neville.

Maidie turned the music up and drank. A lamp on top of one of the stereo speakers rattled, vibratious. The wine went down fast, clear, repellent. Time passed stickily. If she drank alone, her speech slurred, she knew, but to whom was she speaking? She might lurch, but solitarily. She lived alone and was bound to drink alone, sometimes. Tipple. She tried to picture the man on the back of *Roget's Thesaurus*. She went to the bookshelf and got it down. There was Robert L. Chapman, chin in hand, stately, parental, a wry sense of humor in his eyes, Maidie felt. He had a clue. She looked up *intoxicated:* tipsy, tiddly, giddy, overcome. She was near the end, the bottle. "If it's not one thing it's another," she told Zip, who slunk off and hid.

She said to him, under the table, "As certain people have pointed out, you don't know I'm in charge." Zip seemed to cringe. "You think I'm mean? Or testy?" she said. "You've had it easy so far, relatively speaking." The next part she hardly remembered. In the morning, head pounding, her stomach whirring like a front-load washing machine, Maidie remembered having gone outside, throwing all the empty wine bottles she could find, then glasses she and Rex and Lalo had drunk from, *crash, splinter,* against the wall above the patio. Meanwhile, the house throbbed behind her, rock music. As she looked around the quiet street, the adjacent houses, their curtains drawn against the night, she had the vague feeling she was in a play about neighborly relations. *Our Suburb,* by Thornton Wilder. She was the narrator, outside, watching, making pointed comments. But she couldn't get on the other side with the people; she couldn't get *in.* She remembered thinking: Gosh, I'll have to clean up this broken glass tomorrow. Across the street, a door had opened. "Evvy, Evvy. Is that you? Evvy?" Rona calling. At least, that was what Maidie seemed to remember as she got out of bed enfeebled and made her way to the kitchen. Or had she dreamed it?

As she hurried to finish cooking for the wedding, she wondered if anyone had ever done essential work—heart surgery, or defending a life in war—hungover. Her stomach lurched as she chopped shallots. She looked out the window. Zip was asleep in the street. He glanced up as a car steered around him. Maidie went to the door and yelled, "Come here." He bared his teeth. She remembered an article she'd read about the history of child-abuse reform in New York. A woman had said about her son, "Yah, I would sometimes forget he was not, you say, *solid.*" Maidie yanked Zip across the street. She felt the collar gouge into his neck, fleshy, malleable. He twisted onto his rear legs and bit her—his teeth clamping her hand as she gripped his collar. She didn't care, the bastard. She yanked hard, harder. He clamped and gnawed, clamped and gnawed, eyes shiny, beseeching. Later, she'd describe it as a pacifist decision on Zip's part. He'd protested the way she wrenched him. He pressed his teeth down, stared into her eyes unaverted, but he never broke the skin on her hand. She yanked him into the yard and yelled, Bad! Bad! Terrible! Terrible! He gave her a furious, sad look and slipped inside.

She finished cooking: chopping and stirring, her hand swelling, aching. She knew if she saw someone else drag a dog through the street, she'd pity the dog. Still, what could she do, apologize? She'd worry about Zip later, get a new angle, start over. When she left for Rona's, he was asleep under the table, exhausted.

At Rona's, she checked on the frozen fruit rings for the punch bowls, also the four-tiered white cake with a plaster bride and groom, and the flat, smeary chocolate groom's cake. Harve leaned over the banister bare-chested, a striped horse blanket around his hips. Cindy-June's children ate cereal in front of the TV as Rona scooted a Dustbuster around them. "Grandma, stop!" In the window seat, her hair hanging over her tie-dye nightshirt, Cindy-June said, "This is so typical. My wedding day, and you're preoccupied with Evvy's problems. The story of my life!" And she ran upstairs, past her dad in his southwestern dishabille.

Maidie said, "How's everything so far?"

Rona said, "I have a migraine, and I'm grateful you're here."

Harve edged down the stairs.

Rona said, "So help me, Harve, if you stick your finger in that frosting again, I'll hit you on the head with this vacuum cleaner."

Harve rolled his eyes: women, hormones, weddings.

"I'll be back right before the ceremony," Maidie told Rona. "Try to get a few minutes to relax." Rona went upstairs. As Maidie set out napkins and silverware, she thought about how she'd come home yesterday with a box of mini-quiche crusts from Food Club, and Rona had stood in her yard in a straw hat. Maidie unloaded her car, and Rona came over and said, out of the blue, "I was remembering a time when the girls were little and I was divorced from Harve for two years." She pawed the air with her gardening tool; her eyes focused, far away. "I dated a nice man from Canada, who I met at church. But we saw *The Sound of Music* together and he cried at the end, when the von Trapps went over the hill, singing. Such a wimp. I couldn't kiss him, let alone sleep with him." Maidie listened, holding the box of frozen quiche crusts. Rona had said, "I wanted someone who was—I guess—masculine. I decided it might as well be the girls' father."

Setting out silverware, then candles inside decorative wreaths Rona had made by fastening cactus parts together with hot glue and trimming them with red bandanna ribbon, Maidie wondered if most marriages were made and maintained for reasons as shrinking and contractual as Rona and Harve's; also love, of course, which shriveled, swelled, dehydrated, rejuvenated. So Maidie imagined; she'd never studied it close up, long term. As she opened the door to go home and dress for the wedding, Rona leaned out a door upstairs, over the banister. She said, "There's something going on with Evvy. I'll tell you about it later."

Maidie came back at two forty-five with Lalo, in a crisp white shirt and bow tie. "My mother," he explained, "bought me these white shirts she thinks college students wear, one for each day of the week." He cleared his throat. Harve tapped the keg. He stood next to it with a plastic cup, sipping; he handed Lalo a cup. "Hey, Miz Bonasso, I see you brought your trusty assistant," he said, winking. When Clima and August arrived, Clima set a bottle of Herradura tequila on the table, stemmed glasses nearby. Rona came downstairs in the same T-shirt and Lycra bike shorts she'd had on that morning, her face puffy and sad. "It's hell," she said.

"What?" Maidie said.

Evvy walked through the upstairs hallway. A door slammed. Slam. Another door slammed. Rona rolled her eyes heavenward. "Evvy, and Daddy too," she said. She tipped her head toward August.

Maidie looked at him, his white hair poking up, static cling.

"He has to go for a biopsy, and he's so nervous his legs won't bend. He threw up the barium twice." Rona glanced at Clima. "And Mama's been drinking, because even though they fight, she's helpless without him." Rona pointed at the tequila. "Don't you encourage her. I know you drink with her sometimes. She's semi-alcoholic." Rona ran upstairs before Maidie could answer.

Biopsy? Semi-alcoholic? Maidie was a neighbor, not a relative. What was her place in the middle of this ritual strain and scattering umbrage? She felt edgy, with Rona mad at Clima, and Cindy-Jane mad at Rona for paying attention to Evvy, who slammed doors. Harve and August, next to the keg, looked distressed and skittish. Had Maidie somehow added to the tension? Then someone she didn't recognize walked in the door. She squinted: Buster in a toupee. His eyes looked dark, like he had mascara on. He bowed, suave. "I hope you got your car window fixed, ma'am." Toupee or not, he was missing those bicuspids.

Then the rest of the guests arrived. Maidie and Lalo stood behind the food table as Cindy-June's children came downstairs, flinging potpourri. Cindy-June followed in a white maternity shift, carrying sunflowers. The groom didn't look like Elvis—more like Jay Leno. The minister, a woman with buzz-cut hair, said not to let the sun set on anger; every couple has a mix of attitudes merging in a hard way, but a mix of attitudes mixing in a good way too. A sermonette in Oprahic. But not without wisdom. Harve slid his arm around Rona. They were probably remembering their own vows, twice taken. Cleave to another on life's path: that's what the minister said at Neville's parents' farm. Maidie doesn't remember much about the wedding in Arkansas. They had a judge, not a preacher. Maidie had wanted Mia to read a Borneo wedding myth aloud—instead of a soloist singing, that is—but Jack nixed the idea. When the vows were over, Maidie had an urge to carry the trash out. She stepped into the yard in her white lace dress and saw the family of four she'd sometimes watched through the window. They stared, hoes and rakes paused in midair, as she walked to the can, plunked down the Hefty bag, then went back inside for the ceremonial toast.

She heard snuffling. Lalo blew his nose in a handkerchief. "Are you sad?" she asked. "Allergies," he said. She wondered if Cindy-June might donate her white maternity dress and yellow sunflowers for the wedding dress exhibit at the Women's History Collection.

"I pronounce you husband and wife," the minister said.

Maidie started serving punch. Lalo, ladling vichyssoise, cleared his throat and said, "When you take that trip to Oklahoma, can you drive me to San Jon, New Mexico, then pick me up on the way back? My mother wants to see me. I can't pay for any gas. But I can keep your dog there in a pen, to save you money."

Maidie considered it. She'd planned to board Zip in a kennel, twelve dollars a day. Clima came by the table. Maidie handed her a glass of punch. "Is it spiked?" Clima sipped. "It isn't!" She dumped it back. "I feel a depression coming," she said, her voice quavering. "If August is sick, I can't manage. I don't know how he pays bills or gets us places on time. Getting on the interstate is like driving into an egg beater. I've been treated for depression before, you know. But I'm taking Elavil. I have high hopes." She drifted away, looking backward at the tequila.

Maidie said to Lalo, "You could keep Zip at your mother's?"

He let out a moan Maidie had come to recognize as contented. "Yes," he said. Keeping Zip with Lalo seemed smart, she

decided. Other than Clima and August, and Rex ("You don't
have time to say good-bye, fine"), Lalo was someone Zip knew,
as opposed to the lady at the dog kennel. Zip . . . Maidie
meant to treat him better soon.

Maidie and Lalo finished serving food. They fixed plates for
themselves. Evvy stayed by the door, her face curtained by her
long hair. Now and then, she'd look up, pop a peeled shrimp in
her mouth, swallow. As the music grew louder—"Don't Be
Cruel"—Clima danced, lifting her skirt and shimmying, her
slip fluttering, a parody of a striptease that disconcerted Maidie,
not because Clima might disrobe, but because of the expression
on her face, bleary, medicated. August sat next to Maidie in a
straight-back chair. "She can't stop once she gets started," he
said, his blue eyes exhausted, hair tufting fluffy on top of his
head.

Maidie stood up. "I have to go home and pack for my trip."

"Trip? Will you be back when I go to the hospital?" Maidie
towered over him. His eyes searched hers.

"When do you go?"

"In three days," August said.

She bent and gave him a scrape of a kiss. "I don't think so."

Lalo stood next to the table, packing leftovers into a grocery
sack; Maidie had talked him into helping in exchange for plun-
der. "Leave a little for Rona and Harve," she said. "And let me
think about taking you and Zip as far as New Mexico. It sounds
fine, though. I do have an appointment I have to keep before we
go—with that woman who's donating antique wedding
dresses."

Rona walked up. "Wedding dresses? I didn't get a chance to
shower or fix my hair," she said. "I had to get right out of my exercise suit into my mother-of-the-bride dress. Are you going
home?"

Maidie nodded.

"I'll walk out with you."

Buster came across the room. "I bought you something at a yard sale." He handed Maidie a paperback book. *A Glance at Madagascar.*

Madagascar? Maidie thought.

Buster said, "Because you're from there."

Rona said, "She's not, Buster! Her mother was." She took the book out of Maidie's hand and thrust it back at Buster. "Go away."

He retreated.

Outside, on the sidewalk, Rona said, "Buster must think you're available." She looked over her shoulder, lowered her voice. "Anyway, Evvy has—what do you say?—come out with it."

Maidie said, "What?"

"She's gay."

"Come *out?*" Maidie said.

Rona said, "She wants to have a baby."

Maidie thought about Evvy, sad, surly. "She's pregnant?"

"I hope to God not right now." Rona's hair stuck to her damp face. In the dark, she seemed like someone Maidie knew well.

"Evvy's planning to have a baby?"

Rona said, "I don't know how, exactly."

"More grandkids," Maidie said.

Rona said, "But Harve's not going to be that philosophical."

About Evvy, she meant.

Maidie said, "He'll get used to it, I'm sure."

She went home. It was time for Lawrence Welk. Or a drama in which Chuck Norris repaired lives with kung fu. Or a news show that used to be famous for investigative reporting but now broadcast celebrity interviews. As Zip slunk out from under the table, Maidie turned on the lights against the darkening day. She glanced at her legal pad, the two-axis chart for her trip. The TV droned. A squirrel scampered over the roof. She heard the half-sad sound of the party across the street, gone on too long. Buster thinks I'm available, she thought, irritated. She'd

seen him nodding. She'd thought it was the toupee, its unfamiliar feel. Still, she was past the age of consent; she'd come without an escort. Available. The TV anchorwoman described an
ex–football player who gave his wife a life-sized statue of himself. Later, he stalked and killed her. "When low self-esteem and
unconscionable ego fall in love . . ." Maidie sifted though channels, voices. Lalo had two fathers, she thought. Rona, two weddings. Maidie herself, two mothers, two husbands. What she'd
liked best about Neville was Sunday dinner with his parents.

The phone rang.

Maidie put the TV on Mute.

She wondered if Rex was calling to say what had happened
was a misunderstanding, and Maidie would say she'd misunder-
stood too. She'd shouted out insults that applied to someone
else, not Rex.

But who?

She picked up the phone. "Hello?"

In that split second of silence and breath on the other end, she
knew it wasn't Rex's breath or silence. Z. said, "I'm in the doldrums. Do you feel like going out?" Her voice sounded tremulous
and lonely. Maidie remembered the photograph in the History Department, the blue plastic barrettes, the childish frown.

Maidie's head ached.

She didn't want to go out. She wanted company. (From the
Latin *companio:* one who eats bread with another.) "I can't," she
said.

Z. deflated. "That's all right."

Maidie said, "How's the politically-minded painter?"

"He was a housepainter. A housepainter, and his politics are
completely arbitrary. He likes protests, all kinds. I think there's
a scientific term for that: paramania. Joy in complaints."

"What about the architect?"

"His ad is gone."

"Someone else will turn up."

"It doesn't matter. Most days, I know *exactly* how lucky I am," Z. said, "so I'm treating myself to a new tattoo." The one she had was of a printing press; she'd brought a drawing to the tattoo artist and he'd copied it. "This time, I'm thinking of a pen dipping into an inkwell labeled with the universal symbol of woman."

Maidie's first impulse was to say: Phallic! Don't put an explicit and permanent emblem of sexual yearning on your pale body. You'll hate it later. What did she say? "I'd sleep on it, Z."

"Good night. Toodle-oo."

The phone line flattened.

Maidie sat in a chair, overtired, watching TV, thinking she should have told Z. about the wedding dress exhibit, except Z. would have resisted. "Wedding dresses are apolitical," she'd say, Maidie decided. She pictured a Women's History Collection trustee meeting with Z. speaking out anti-bride, while Midge scowled and Cass said, "Weddings make me cry." This is what Maidie thought of as she fell asleep, but also *The Newlywed Game,* which was being revived for the nineties, the *TV Guide* said. Maidie once watched the old version, Bob Eubanks asking, "Sheila, where will Larry say is the strangest place you ever made whoopee?" "I'd have to say in the marriage bed, Bob," Maidie's mother said, passing through with an apron, a wooden spoon, a cocktail already and it's a school day. She didn't say that, Maidie thought, angry even in her dream. "I'd have to say I took it too seriously. I took it to my heart, Bob," Maidie's mother said. Maidie woke, TV faces twisting voiceless, attenuated, until she flicked the remote control at them, banishment. They vanished.

Go . . .

Sunlight beat down, astringent. Maidie loaded suitcases into the trunk of a glossy silver car, its exaggerated bulk and avionic fenders. She was used to her own Japanese-made car, a small beige traveling bulb. Lalo sat in the expansive back seat, strapped in, reading a book. Zip perched in the passenger seat in front, facing the windshield, his mouth stretched back, head grazing the ceiling. Maidie heard a whirring noise. She turned around. Rona, wearing pink slippers and a navy-blue robe, wheeled a plastic garbage can across the street. She said, "Maidie, where did you get that car?" Before Maidie could answer, Rona wheeled nearer and poked her head in. "Why is Lalo in back? Why are you sitting in back, Lalo, with the dog in front?" Lalo said, "He wanted to sit there," and shrugged. Lalo wore a black-and-red shirt with clock patterns on it: pocket watches, hourglasses, grandfather clocks, sundials, alarm clocks with big bells. He'd bought new black-framed glasses, already speckled with paint. "I enjoyed myself at the wedding," he said, "also your leftovers. Thank you." He went back to his book.

Maidie said, "I'm driving this car to Oklahoma."

Rona said, "It must be a thousand miles. Why don't you fly?"

It was eight hundred, in fact. Maidie had studied the Rand McNally road atlas this morning. But first she'd gone to the patio and cleaned up glass chips from bottles she'd flung against the retaining wall three nights before. She'd meant to sooner, but there was Cindy-June's wedding to attend, cooking and serving, the hangover through which Maidie had observed the family tit-for-tat, ingrained spite. The next day: rain. It rattled in drainpipes, pooled in ditches, dripped off the hammock draped like a rag between wet trees. Maidie stayed inside, thinking. Sundays on the movie set—she remembered Rex saying so—people did laundry. Maidie imagined Rex sorting, agitating, whites in one dryer, darks in another. He'd use the laundromat pay phone, maybe. If he did, he didn't call Maidie. She meant to clean up the glass the next day too, but she had to go to work to meet the lady who wanted to donate wedding dresses, and when Maidie got home, Rona had stood in the yard in a straw hat, waving a three-clawed gardening tool, asking personal questions. When would Rex come back? Maidie said she had no idea. Rona looked startled, speculative. She wondered aloud: were Maidie and Rex a bad mix?

Like oil and water?

Rex had a pathological need to be well-liked, Rona added. Maybe Maidie played into that? Did Maidie haves tapes playing in her head installed by her parents? How mad was Rex, Rona asked, when he left?

Maidie had answered, "Maybe just tired." The sun shone. Her scalp prickled. She thought how she had to leave in the morning for the Multi-State American Studies Conference, also her job interview. Oklahoma loomed roomy and empty as a warehouse, and Maidie felt trapped between Rona and a heap of broken glass washed clean by yesterday's rain, glinting in sunlight. When Maidie lived in Virginia and Jack used to throw furniture and sometimes Maidie herself at the wall, she didn't want Dodie to see. Likewise, when Maidie was home alone in Tucson and breaking wine bottles, also antique goblets Rex gave her for Christmas, she didn't want Rona to see. Rona was cozy or nosy; Maidie couldn't tell. She daydreamed while Rona's lips moved, speaking. Maidie worried. If her domestic disputes were with herself now, not a husband, if she stood in the sun watching Rona speak but couldn't listen, had she turned narcissistic? She'd moved from place to place, met new neighbors, husbands, colleagues, in-laws, friends, so many, so continuous. People had begun to seem as receding and one-dimensional as landmarks, conversation like job-interview backchat, a screen, not a transparency; a barrier, not communion.

If Maidie *was* situationally narcissistic, like a child of a migrant worker, nomadic and noncommittal, aware of people as if they were extras and not totalities of complex human sentiment, she'd thought to herself in the front yard, bristling, what could she do? Her mind flew to the past, which was known and managed, a contained story spilling into the present. It had a moral: Be ungullible. As Rona talked, she seemed like an actress stepping into a well-known role, imbuing it with personal tics and idiosyncrasies. The concerned friend: others had played it. Dodie, Mia, Marbella, Opal Johnson, Neville's sisters, Laree. Maidie felt claustrophobic, also clearheaded. "I have to go back to work," she told Rona, "to catalogue some vases and butter paddles."

That was yesterday.

Today Rona pulled her navy-blue bathrobe together over her chest. She tapped Maidie's arm. "I asked, why not take a plane?"

"Cofer College wouldn't pay for the ticket," Maidie said, "something to do with workmen's comp, but they gave me this car and an Exxon credit card." She sounded angry, she knew. It was the sense that Rona stood on the other side of a thick window. Also, the vast distance Maidie had only just fathomed: Tucson as far from Oklahoma as Mars from Venus, War from Love. After Maidie consulted the atlas, her first impulse had been to phone Garth McHugh and say, Hell no, I'm staying here. But she finished packing, then used her yellow legal pad to make a tentative itinerary. Albuquerque by nightfall. Tomorrow, she'd drop off Lalo and Zip in San Jon. She'd get to the conference in Oklahoma in time to attend a function billed as "Cocktails and Convocation."

Meantime, she'd get a brief fix of the straight, ramplike highway, a launching pad to oblivion. Oklahoma! In five days, she'd come back to her job at the Museum of Domestic History and Home Economy she was trying hard to recast as a Women's History Collection. Back to a maladjusted dog, a rented house, a neighborhood full of people related to each other who forgot Maidie wasn't. Rona said, "I'll keep an eye on your house. Give me a number in case of emergencies. Maybe your dad's number too." Maidie felt herself frown. She'd already locked up her house; her Rolodex sat on a hard-to-reach shelf in a back corner. "My supervisor knows where I'll be in Oklahoma," Maidie said, "and he has emergency addresses and phone numbers for me on file." In fact, when Maidie started her job at Cofer College and filled out forms that asked for next of kin, she'd written in her dad's name, and Lucy's, but couldn't remember their addresses or phone numbers. She'd promised to consult her Rolodex and bring the information in later. But with the museum to transfigure, a life to arrange, routines to establish, she forgot, and the comptroller threatened to withhold her paycheck until she did.

Rona said, "What if there's a fire or flood?"

Maidie looked at the turquoise sky. "If it floods," she said, caustic, "the conference is at the Hilton in Oklahoma City, downtown."

"Maidie! Near where the bomb went off?"

Maidie said, "Rona, I need to leave or I'll never get there."

Rona said, "Of course. Drive safe."

Maidie got in and closed the door. *Thwimp.* It sealed, vac-uum-packed: Maidie, Lalo, Zip, a bag of sandwiches, a road at-las, a box of Kleenex. In the trunk: two suitcases, a garment bag, a sack of dog food. Maidie drove to the edge of town as Zip crouched beside her, ducking and cowering at cars, bicycles, trucks, and motorcycles passing by. Woof! he barked at a dog in a neighboring car. The city Maidie knew, its familiar milestones, receded. Strip joint. Stoplight. Car lot. Vanilla extract factory. Gas station. Stoplight. Acres of pottery (BIG SALE TODAY!). The air force base. The Pima Air and Space Museum. Tucson Inter-national Airport. Maidie turned the air conditioner off, its ven-tilating hum. "Lalo, are you comfortable back there?"

Lalo, nothing.

"Do you think Rona is too inquisitive?" Maidie asked, chatty.

Lalo waited awhile before answering. "Yes."

Maidie said, "I thought so. I need to put up a barrier."

Lalo didn't speak. The odometer and the dashboard clock clicked onward. Then Lalo rumbled, cleared his throat. "Like my mother."

Maidie said, "Your mother puts up a barrier?"

"Sometimes a piece of string to keep chickens out of the gar-den."

Chickens out of the garden? Was this folk wisdom?

He said, "My mother is nosy."

Maidie said, "Oh."

"With me."

But was that the same? If a mother—not a neighbor—pried and scrutinized, surely she was devoted, not nosy? Maidie had no idea. She understood late-nineteenth-century mothering styles best; industrialization had made for a decline in the amount of time a man spent at home, which resulted in not just children in

need of a father but a wife in need of a husband, who thus redi-
rected her affection and interest into a cosseting, even sexualized,
style of mothering, which had become a profession—guide-
books proliferated—as well as a calling. The popular press de-
picted mothers keeping altruistic vigils over bassinets, or waiting
by windows, lamps in hand, for wayward sons. Research suggested that even post-industrial mothers felt a smothered resentment they channeled into pseudosymbiosis. They failed to
bond with the child authentically and increased outward signs of
affection, false empathy, thus confusing their desires with the
child's. A son, who is *other* and—not insignificantly—referred to
as "Little Man" in sentimental poems of the period, experiences
attraction-repulsion. But a daughter perceives herself as having
only a permeable division, an ever-elastic barrier between herself
and her mother, later between herself and the world.

Thus Maidie understood mothering a hundred years ago as
an extraordinary social and hormonal condition. Yet the twentieth century had created not just absent fathers but partly absent mothers, and a definition of extended family that now
included *ex-* and *step-,* even *ex-step-.* Maidie thought about Rona
confiding her worries about August's biopsy, Evvy's sexuality,
Harve's temper. Did Rona, Columbo-like, volunteer information to get some back? Or, invested in Maidie's future, did she
assume Maidie was invested in hers, that the two of them
weighed in for each other, support and countenance? Maybe
Rona extended concern to Maidie like a relative? Maidie
stepped on the gas, seventy mph. No. Maidie was a neighbor in
a rent house—unusually transient to boot. She said, "Lalo, how
does your mother treat neighbors?"

Lalo said, "When you ask me questions and I take a long
time to answer, which I can't help, you finish sentences for me,
and what I say turns out to be your idea, not mine. I'd rather
read a book, thank you." He held up *Abundant Manhood,* by
Robert Herndon.

"You're still reading that?" Maidie said, stung. Finish his sentences, horsefeathers! What else could she do? He was incomprehensible.

He read aloud:

> When contact between a father and his son ceases, the father exists for the son only in the past, according to what the father once did or should have done. Aborted contact makes for a parent who exists only in memory—as a vision of perfection, or a hated ghost.

Lalo paused.

Maidie was silent. Let Lalo have one of his own ideas!

"A son can rid himself of a father who is a ghost by renewing contact," Lalo said. Maidie watched him in the rearview, the hair on his head spiky, glasses riding crooked on his nose. "My father is dead," Lalo said. "Therefore I am off kilter. My mother's love is incomplete because her husband is jealous. A son needs a father to have an abundant life, the book says." They were on the open road. The car turned hot. *Thwip, thwip* . . . traffic. Maidie turned the air conditioner back on. She said, "Lalo, you need to get rid of that book because it's making you want something you can't ever have." He sat straight up in the back seat and spoke, lips moving, hands waving. But Maidie couldn't hear. She turned the air conditioner off again. "What?"

He said, "You don't have a hint. I haven't passed through my passage yet. I remember my father in a white undershirt with a cast on his arm—a sick man with a dirty cast. Next, I am watching TV in English, and I have a new father. I don't want to paint anymore. I should work with ashes, manure, or dirt, for now."

Maidie thought: Ashes, manure, dirt? This sounded vaguely familiar, like *Hamlet*. Zip draped himself over the console and stared up, sweet, breathing his moist dog breath in Maidie's face.

From the back seat, Lalo sighed.

Maidie patted Zip's head as he burrowed close. Maidie wondered how to respond to Lalo, passing through his passage. Menopause came to mind. Ashes, manure, and dirt. "Well," she said. She thought about stages of cognitive development, and the long-term psychosocial trend which seemed to dictate that each generation would take longer to mature, a barnacle-like connection to childhood maintained and clear-cut rites of initiation resisted. Maidie thought about her own connections maintained, initiations resisted. When Vera died, and Eugene remarried, maybe? Not when Maidie's mother left, because all along she'd seemed more absent than present, and more present—a fog, a vapor—once she'd left. Then Maidie's dad remarried and Maidie rejected Neena, staying across the street with Mr. and Mrs. Funderburk when Neena moved in. Later, Neena moved out. Maidie went to Wyoming, etc. Neville wanted a divorce, so on, so forth.

Lalo said, "That was hard."

Maidie thought: What?

Lalo said, "Telling you my inner life."

Zip kept leaning on Maidie, his nose against her neck. "If traveling makes you this happy, Zip," she said, smiling and accelerating, "we'll have to get you your own car." In back, Lalo started to snore. Outside, the desert passed by, the cacti like uniformed sentries. Maidie studied other families on the highway—for example, a boxy Chevy with suction-cup window shades in up position, father driving, mother sleeping, a baby in back batting at toys clipped to a plastic chain strung from one side to another. Just west of Las Cruces, Maidie passed the Chevy; later, the Chevy passed Maidie as she turned north, toward Truth or Consequences. In Socorro, she stopped at a wayside, where Zip acted embarrassed to squat and defecate with

Maidie on the end of his leash, but he did and seemed to bow afterward, gracious. Meanwhile, Lalo slept hard, talking in Spanish in his sleep all the way to Albuquerque, where Maidie pulled into a Best Western.

Lalo woke in the parking lot. Maidie let the engine idle. She said, "I wonder if we should sneak Zip in. If they have a no pets policy, we can say we didn't know." Lalo pointed at a wizened old lady in golf shorts trekking toward the lobby with a Lhasa apso: "Look," he said. Maidie said, "But that dog weighs maybe six pounds. Zip is a different breed entirely." In the passenger seat, Zip beamed. He laid his paw on Maidie's wrist. Lalo rubbed his eyes and said, "If you know what you want, why pretend my opinion matters?" Except he sounded warped, garbled, as he yawned and stretched. He wakes up scrappy, Maidie told herself on the way to the lobby. She said to the clerk, "A room at the far end."

The clerk said, "Pardon me?"

A room at the end of the motel, Maidie meant, far from the lobby so no one would see her in a field of weeds, waiting for Zip to squat. But Maidie tended to be elaborate when committing subterfuge. "May I have a room at the far end, because I'm an insomniac and the open space of the parking lot soothes me," she said. The clerk shrugged and checked her in. Then she went back to the parking lot, drove the car to the room, stuck the electronic key card in the slot. Lalo dozed in the back seat as Maidie unloaded. She set Lalo's luggage, which seemed to be a typewriter carrying case, on one bed, hers on the other. For Zip, she filled a plastic ice bucket with water and set it on the floor. When she went back outside, the car door stood wide open. Zip sat in the front seat, panting, patient. But Maidie couldn't find a speck or thread of Lalo, his clock-pattern shirt. Had he been abducted? Probably not. And when he returned, maybe he'd be in a better mood. Maidie took Zip inside. She sat on the bed and flipped through TV channels. An hour later, Lalo knocked on the door. When Maidie let him in, he said, "As many refills as you wish, in the motel-lobby coffee shop."

Maidie said, "Don't you worry you won't sleep?"

Lalo said, "Does that bother you? I can see it does. In that case I'll go for a long walk, or spend the night in the car."

Maidie didn't answer. She'd read a book on female managerial skills. Its point: Don't cry at work. Maidie didn't feel like crying, and she wasn't at work but in a motel room with Lalo, hangdog and resentful, over whom, however, she presumably exerted something. Lalo picked up the remote control and flipped through channels so fast images rolled, the audio burping and bleating. Maidie felt as if she were sharing a room with Jack Bonasso, who'd rather channel-surf than have sex. She'd read a study once that proved men channel-surf more than women; also that when a subject spends long periods of time in the same room as a channel surfer and is thereby exposed to someone else's erratic video montage, a narrative discombobulation over which the subject has no control, remote or otherwise, that subject becomes, in the words of one researcher, "chronically startled." At the time Maidie read the study, she didn't watch much TV. But she dreamed all the time about a trip to an important destination that kept getting interrupted. She'd lose her car, then hot-wire a motorcycle but lose the motorcycle, steal a bicycle and lose it too. She ran furiously to hop a train that would take her . . . where?

Maidie turned to Lalo. "Studies have proved that the passive participant in a shared experience of discontinuous video imagery suffers anxiety," she said, "so we need to stick to one program." Lalo tuned in to a PBS special on the childhood years of Jim Morrison, who apparently had an almost Wordsworthian memory of life before the womb, and this memory of pre-life set the stage for his adult years, during which he tried to break back on through. Next, on a CBS talk show, Loni Anderson said Burt Reynolds used to beat her. Maidie got under the covers in a T-shirt and leggings. She had miles to drive tomorrow, 160 to San Jon, 250 to Oklahoma. If Garth McHugh drove for two days to this conference every year, Maidie thought, no wonder he'd bailed out. Her anger roiled again, like a wad of trash in a dust storm, as she thought about standing around a conference sipping wine in plastic Solo cups, talking to strangers about her Collection of History, née Museum of Drudgery. In the motel room, Zip whined, snuffling for a scent, a reminder of the house in Tucson, home. "Sit," Maidie commanded. "You, Lalo, turn off that TV so we can sleep."

Lalo was already asleep.

Maidie got out of bed, took the remote control out of Lalo's hand, pushed Off. She laid a spare blanket over Lalo, who sighed. He was sleeptalking. "En this nación, es ilegal to beat up las mujeres. Qué cabrón!" He rolled over in the blanket and snored.

Zip whimpered.

Maidie got into bed. She turned on her right side, her left.

She rolled onto her back

Lalo snored, Zip too, the motel room a pneumatic dream chamber. Maidie fell asleep close to dawn. A few minutes later—morning—she woke and packed. "Lalo," she said, "get up." Half an hour later, they were on the road, sipping coffee in styrofoam cups. Tijeras. Moriarty. Milagro. Maidie stopped for gas, and Zip crouched next to her as semi trucks idled nearby like big beasts. Back in the car, Maidie drove. San Ignacio. Montoya. Tucumcari. Outside San Jon, Lalo said, "I apologize for my actions—both last night and yesterday morning."

Maidie was tired. "You're a bad traveler." She shrugged.

"Solamente when I go home," he said. "You'll see."

What Maidie did see when she pulled into Lalo's yard—except it wasn't a yard so much as the endless desert pressing against a square box covered in plywood painted the color of a pumpkin and, on its outside walls, huge black butterflies constructed out of old bedsprings wobbling in the hot, constant wind—was a place no one would call home. Would they? "Did you make those, Lalo?" Maidie asked, nodding at the bedspring butterflies, but she was thinking about Zip. If she left him here, he might try to follow and get lost, stolen, skinned alive. What had Maidie thought: that Lalo lived in a suburb with a green lawn, a deck, a privacy fence? She didn't want to leave Zip behind; she didn't want to leave Lalo behind either. Her first impulse was to drive away and negotiate details later. Lalo pushed his glasses up his nose. "I would never make something so sentimental," he said. "My mother made those butterflies." At that moment, his mother ran out of the house, her pink-striped dress flapping in the wind like laundry on a clothesline.

She was beautiful, her face the color of butterscotch, her lips the purplish color of a bruise, her black and silver hair knotted behind her head. She talked fast. "Lalo, Lalo, a nice car. Nice lady. Viajaste all the way in this?" She opened the car door and hugged Lalo. "Y un perro!" At which point Zip jumped on her. Maidie said, "Down, Zip. Bad! Bad!" Zip slunk away, embarrassed. Maidie looked at the house; it was about the size of her living room. Would Zip stay inside, then? She looked at the nearby highway. Cars sped past, lethal. Lalo's mother said, "Can you stay to eat? I have barbacoa, but you might not like it. También enchiladas, macaroni salad, also lime Jell-O."

She smiled.

Before Maidie could say, I can't, I have to keep driving, the front door opened, and Lalo's stepfather lurched out. He has a bad leg, Maidie decided. But when he got close, Maidie smelled liquor.

Looking back later, Maidie realized that as soon as he'd hobbled out of the house, she'd cowered like Zip at the sight of the semi trucks, their unfamiliar noise and girth; she'd scuttled backward, groping behind her for the car. Lalo's stepfather, his face bleary and shiny, yelled something about Maidie: *Gringa!*

He raised his hand as if to hit someone. Lalo's mother yelled back. Lalo's stepfather made a face at Maidie, who got into the car and opened her automatic window. "Enjoy your visit, Lalo. I'll pick you up on Friday." Lalo said, "I'm sorry, I don't think I should keep your dog." His face flattened into unfamiliar planes and angles—the caved-in shape that fit here, home. Maidie suddenly understood his usual plump, stolid expression, the contentment it implied. Lalo said, "Don't forget to come back." His stepfather stared: contempt. Maidie said, "In a few days." She had the urge to give Lalo money so he wouldn't get stuck here. "Don't forget your suitcase," she said. She got out, opened the trunk. When Lalo came around back, she gave him twenty dollars. "What for?" he said. "You never know," she said. "If you don't need it, you can return it later."

Maidie drove out of New Mexico into the panhandle of Texas, then into Oklahoma, thinking about how she'd quaked, then backstepped, in front of Lalo's stepfather like he was a space alien, and he'd noticed, offended. What had she feared besides his curses, his fist waving like a club? He couldn't be essentially bad, she told herself. We don't, in this century, subscribe to theories of essential badness; we believe in genes and experience; in Lalo's stepfather's case, bad genes, bad experience. Maidie remembered the day she met Lalo—José Eduardo. All his brothers were named José and that's why he was called Lalo, he'd said. She'd pictured the other sons still living at home, wearing white shirts, cheerful, filial. Where were they? Why didn't they help? All the same, Maidie realized that somewhere in California her own mother might tell a stranger she had three daughters, and that stranger would wonder where the daughters were, how they could be so callous, when—as Maidie knew, as she was sure her mother always knew—calluses are a necessary buffer, a hardy response to abrasion, erosion, wearing away.

What would she do with Zip in Oklahoma City? she thought suddenly. She couldn't sneak him into the Hilton, past a front desk, up an elevator. She tried to think about Zip's dilemma; she tried concentrating on the car, its dashboard communiqués, the highway, proliferating road signs. But she thought instead about Rona, who'd once described an accident she'd had when she and Harve first got divorced and she'd driven blind-mad, raging about how she'd never intended to raise daughters without Harve, who'd refused to conform to Rona's template of what a husband is and does, Rona's mind wandering but her body belted into a car moving down a foggy, winding road, and slam, screech, Rona's car ran into a horse, a horse's torso, which shaved off the top of the car, one clean slice, making it a convertible. Her seat miraculously folded and she fell back as the car cleaved in half. She lay there, immobile, until a driver stopped, a woman on her way to work in a dental assistant costume, peering down like an angel in a white suit, Rona had thought. Am I dead? She asked the woman, who said: We think we can't survive shock, but we do.

"We don't have much choice but to survive and try new angles, new directions," Maidie's mother said, ironing her floral handkerchiefs as Maidie sat on the floor, draping a filmy blue and pink one like a sarong around her Barbie doll's torso. Maidie's mother bent down, a tower leaning, and said, "If I can save you from things I faced too soon, I will. I was raised, as you know, without maternal influence, mother love. I want your life to be better. I want to know everything about you." Maidie had sat on the floor, thinking: You do? It seemed exhausting and impossible that her mother should know everything about Maidie when, so far, Maidie knew so little. Her mother stared at Maidie, her expression turning that first pale-green shade of anger, perturbation. Storm and tantrum to follow. She was prickly and poisonous outside but, inside, full of sweet, soft intentions. She said, "Maybe I love you more than myself. You know what that entails?" Maidie didn't; it sounded cramped and sticky. Maidie's mother said, "I asked, do you know what love like that entails?" Maidie answered; she had to. She said, "I do."

Maidie kept driving; she had to. Zip leaned close. When she got to Oklahoma City, she thought, she'd go to a motel on the outskirts and get a room near the parking lot like in Albuquerque, and no one would notice Zip. But he couldn't stay there all day, while Maidie attended lectures and panel discussions at the Hilton. Still, Maidie knew she'd make a plan. Rona had said the other day, "Harve thinks you're so resilient." Maidie had answered, "Really?" She'd wanted Rona to elaborate on Maidie's ability to recover her original shape after having been bent and stretched. Rona said, "He tells people how you go barefoot in the yard over rocks and thorns." Maidie had felt let down, realizing that Harve meant her feet, not her character. Driving, she wondered what Harve might say about her character. Maybe not much. In population-dense areas, people respond to overwhelming stimuli by keeping acquaintances inside rigid role definitions (a clerk is a clerk, a mailman a mailman), and interaction rarely transcends those roles. If Harve did describe Maidie, she knew he wouldn't say much besides: She seems kind to old people, hardworking, educated, house proud, easy to get to know.

These were the qualities Maidie let flourish like ornamental foliage—showy and impenetrable—to camouflage her failings, shortsightedness. For example, Maidie might be educated, having insight into family structure at the end of the last century, but she didn't have a clue about families at the end of this century, about the difference between loyalty and dependence, between self-sufficient and self-centered, between what a daughter should emulate and what she should rescind. She woke sometimes at night, thinking: She belonged to no clan. Her attention to old people obscured the fact that she hardly

ever called her father and her father hardly ever called her.
Hardworking? A step-and-fetch-it, more like it, a teacher's pet.
Easy to get to know? Socially precocious, maybe, verbally
shifty, her surface molting and melting each time the trees outside her window changed. Only a few pieces of furniture she'd
dragged behind in a rented trailer stayed the same—and the
sky, of course, stars intersecting into stars, great constellations,
a milky, murky way.

For years, Maidie's persona had passed for a personality. Her
surface saw daylight; the interior it hid didn't. Her strategy of
making an impression on strangers had hardened into habit, a
way of life that made her feel brittle and translucent, like a patterned window through which light may appear but details
don't.

The sky had turned blood red—sunset—when Maidie pulled
into the parking lot outside the Oklahoma City Hilton. She
cracked the window for Zip, then scouted the grounds, shrubs
and wilty petunias ringed in mulch, until she found a hose and
filled Zip's bowl. She dusted off, combed her hair, and went to
the lobby, where signs pointed to the Multi-State American
Studies Conference Registration Now Taking Place in the Kick-
apoo Ballroom. She walked up to a table covered with computer printouts and told a portly, bearded man, "I'm Maidie
Bonasso, curator of the Women's History Collection, Tucson,
Arizona." He looked up, shoved his hand out, and said, "Why
in thunderation did you change your name?" Maidie thought
briefly he meant hers, Giddings. Kramer. Now Bonasso, which
might not be ideal with its downtrodden, sad, and violent connotations, but Maidie felt determined to keep it, never to
change her name again. The man said, "You were the only Museum of Domestic History and Home Economy in the world,
probably. I always meant to come over and get a look-see. Do
you have old-model vacuum cleaners? I love those. Do you have
one of those old-time contraptions that looks like an electric

chair they used a long time ago to give ladies permanent waves?"

Maidie paused; so many questions. She said, "Actually, we do have old vacuum cleaners, and one Wave-O-Matic. You'd like our history-of-gynecology collection," she added, suddenly conscious of the dog smell on her hands, silty paw prints on her dress.

"I'm director of the Oklahoma State History Museum, Hamlin Dwinn," he said. "I spoke to you on the phone about a job. I put an asterisk next to your name this morning, waiting for you to check in. My pleasure to meet you, Miz Bonasso. Did you have a nice trip over?" Maidie nodded; nice enough. Hamlin Dwinn gave Maidie a name tag and said, "Are you staying here, at the Hilton?"

Maidie said, "I need to get a room somewhere else."

He said, "The museum owns a little house. Hill House, it's called. It used to be the mayor's, before they built him a mansion. It has bedroom suites; I saved one for you if you want it. I'll be spending my nights at home, of course, but a few conferees are staying at Hill House. A popular-culture specialist from Colorado, who travels with her cat, also my dearest friend, Zack Alcott, a folklorist from New Mexico specializing in cowboy poetry."

Maidie said, "I've been thinking of getting a motel room out on the interstate—and maybe a dog kennel for during the day."

Hamlin Dwinn said, "Excuse me?"

Maidie said, "I've ended up traveling with my dog, by accident." Maidie thought about Zip in the car, temperature rising. She started talking fast. "I need to go and let him out."

"Bring him to the house," Hamlin Dwinn said. "Amelia Rhodie's got her cat—she doesn't go anywhere without it."

Maidie said, "But my dog is big and has a bad temper."

Hamlin Dwinn said, "Sounds like my first ex-wife." He roared, slapped his knee, stood up. He walked Maidie to her car.

225

Zip jumped out. "Down, Zip. Bad!" Zip sat, embarrassed. "He's a fine dog," Hamlin said. Then he got his car and led the way to Hill House, a white, three-story Victorian. Maidie parked the Cofer College car next to a carriage house in back, and Hamlin carried Maidie's suitcase to her room on the third floor, between the grand front stairwell and the snaky, cloistered maid's stairs leading to the scullery. Maidie's bathroom was ten feet down the hall. Her bedroom looked onto a balcony. "You can't get there except through your bathroom," Hamlin said, leading Maidie down the hall, into her bathroom, past the tub and toilet, onto the balcony. "How eerie everything looks," Maidie said, because in the red-lit dusk, the grass and vines encircling Hill House looked swollen, emerald green. Downtown, shadowy geometrical buildings jutted up, arrows and shafts. Beyond the city, the infinite, beige horizon. Indian reservations, Maidie recalled.

She and Hamlin went downstairs to the parlor to meet the other conferees, Zip clattering behind. Maidie shook hands with Zack Alcott, suave, dark, mannerly, also Amelia Rhodie, a wispy woman wearing a shawl over a gray dress, and Mary Jane shoes made of black canvas and rubber. "I'm giving two papers," Amelia Rhodie said, instead of the usual "How do you do?" Maidie said, "Very impressive," which seemed correct, because Amelia responded, "Thanks, I'm pleased." About presenting her papers, Maidie gathered, pushing back that feeling she got when she met certain career women: Z., for example, her blond hair and pretty red lips—but her chronic low-grade anger, those sad eyes! Is this my future? Maidie sometimes asked herself but never bothered to answer. "I'm Maidie Bonasso," she said, "curator of a history collection. My training is in sociology." Sociability, Maidie thought.

Amelia said, "You're wearing that to Convocation and Cocktails?"

Maidie looked at her dress—a wash dress, her mother used to

call anything that didn't need to be dry-cleaned. "I'll go change."

Amelia said, "Take your dog upstairs with you. I'm afraid of dogs."

Maidie said, "Here, Zip. Come."

Amelia said, "I keep my cat locked in my room at all times."

Maidie said, "How nice." Like Clima would, if she meant "fuck you." And Maidie came downstairs a few minutes later in a black fitted dress, pearl earrings, hair brushed shiny, lipstick refreshed.

Hamlin Dwinn nodded. "I like to see women in their finery." Then frowned. "I hope it's still acceptable to say so."

The four of them left in Hamlin's car for Cocktails and Convocation: plastic cups of wine, grapes, cubes of cheese, also an intoned sequence of welcome from people loosely connected with the conference. The daughter of the Oklahoma State History Museum's founder, an elderly woman with stiff lavender hair, said, "My father would have been pleased to see this distinguished gathering. Perhaps he *is*. People say his ghost haunts the upper regions of the museum, the storage rooms housing study collections." She nodded; her dress fluttered. Maidie sipped wine. "I must take exception," the woman added. "Indeed, he had a sense of humor, but not one, I feel, that extends beyond the grave." She gathered her papers up and returned to her seat amid polite clapping. Maidie felt a fleeting thrill at the idea that Alma Kayser Willoughby might haunt the Woman's History Collection, angry about its name change. Her granddaughter had said as much. Hamlin leaned over, his aftershave wafting, redolent, and whispered, "I think she made a joke. It's hard to say."

Then the nephew of the mayor (the mayor for whom a mansion had been built? Maidie wondered) stood behind the podium and said: "Let us observe one hundred sixty-eight seconds of silence for any person who lost his life unjustly, but especially those who lost theirs when Oklahoma City made its acquaintance with terror." He spoke quickly, profoundly, in bold juxtaposition to the cozy rambling of the founder's daughter a moment before. Clatter and percussion followed: people setting Solo cups on the floor, kicking purses and briefcases aside, yanking the tips of folding chairs rudely over the floor before they found repose enough to pause, remember. Maidie felt uneasy, like when she watched a PBS program about Rwanda. Or about nineteenth-century Australia, home of aborigines for whom a single wave once in a while rolled in but the whole tide went out. Or about an island near Japan where inhabitants of pre–World War II Taiwan remain exiled today, pining for home. In short, Maidie felt numb and disabled, thinking: A nine-story building, one hundred sixty-eight lives, untold hopes and fears muffled by steel and concrete walls upholstered with noise-reduction materials intended to make the workday serene, bearable; then a split-second detonation, spite-bolted thunder.

If it had been Maidie's office, her own unwittingness, how ready was she? Some days, Maidie felt fit for the next phase, blackness and vacuity, or, if death extended life in the way religion said, the post-life she'd earned, her faults and wisdom eking onward. But more than the guarantee of deliverance to a better place, Maidie required the sure sense her time here had yielded as much self-improvement as possible. (Was self-improvement the evolution of free will?) Satisfaction is a guest who arrives for short visits, and Maidie wanted to die during one. The worst fate would be to die impatient. Maidie thought how any office worker—e.g., in the county building in Jackson Hole—might phone a friend, like Laree, and say: I see decipherable signs life is turning out fine. Then the blast. The insight, unremembered. When humans decided to share life, Maidie thought, to invent and uphold the idea of love, they laid themselves bare to grief. Several rows back, a baby cried like a siren, its lungs livid, red, flaring, Maidie imagined. Was there a way to commemorate the dead over which our own sense of brevity, time curtailing, didn't cast a shadow? Still, how wrong if, for fear we'd commemorate inaptly, helpless and uninspired, we didn't.

The language of grief is communal, Maidie realized an hour later, as Hamlin parked his car across the street from the bomb site, a fenced-in plot of grass slated to become a memorial park. As Maidie got out of the car and crossed the street, she paid attention. She'd end up describing it all to Rona later. Did Maidie meet anyone who'd lost family members? Rona would ask, her voice curious, lilting, but her face pliant and sympathetic. A few minutes later, she'd ask if Maidie had heard from Rex yet. She'd sound intrusive, but her eyes would console. Maidie stood near the fence people had trimmed with ribbons, toys, framed photos, cassette tapes, and laminated sheets of paper—poems, she saw, as she leaned close and read, private pain converted to conspicuous rhyme schemes, sealed in plastic and pinned to a fence. The language of grief must be translatable to all and therefore can't be original, personal, constricted, exclusive; the language of grief must be conventional, even clichéd, Maidie thought, as she considered the flat plot of grass, black-colored by night, all that had been plowed under: cells of activity, the beehive life, a clerk having a bad day (a headache, jury duty, a fight with a friend), a clerk having a good day (life turning out fine).

Maidie could hardly see to read. "MUTE REMINDERS OF CATAstROPhe," the choppy handwriting read. "SUFFER thE ChILD'S LOSt LIBERTY. AMONG thE EMBERS, AMERICA WILL REMEMBER. FATE'S whIMS. HOPE SPROUTS. SCORCHED LIMBS. WE IN the STRUGGLE WERE NOT OLD ENOUGH TO HATE, A BABY WAILS AT HEAVEN'S GATE." Maidie stepped back from the fence and decided to stop thinking, not to commemorate, not for a few minutes at least. "This outpouring," Amelia Rhodie said, her face suddenly next to Maidie's in the dark.

In the car, Zack was asking Hamlin, "Did you know anyone killed?"

Hamlin said, "My cousin's neighbor. Also, my secretary's husband's ex-wife was injured. And a man I golf with thought his son was killed, but it ended up he'd missed his appointment that day."

Back at Hill House, the meditation on life's fleetness was over. Lights turned on, bright, golden. Maidie sat on a red sofa, sipping a vodka tonic garnished with fresh spearmint leaves from Hamlin's garden. She regained her normal sense, her living perception that she had—if not forever—time enough to discover what she lacked and find it. She felt relieved this was abruptly true again. She shouldn't contemplate death as if she were sick or old, she decided angrily. Back when she was married to Jack, she used to read obituaries, drawn always to those with youthful photos and subtle explanations below: . . . *after a brave struggle with cancer . . . following a senseless act of violence . . . please make memorial contributions to the AIDS Hospice.* Jack would lean over and say, "You're morbid." Unhealthy, preoccupied with the unwholesome, he meant. Finally, Maidie agreed it didn't help to brood on death perpetually, even if certain Trappist monks slept in coffins every night to remind themselves of the end. Death was far off, Maidie thought, looking at the quaint parlor, the frosting-like scrolls on the fireplace, Zip asleep on the floor, chin resting on Maidie's foot. "He's a fine dog," Hamlin said.

"You're kidding," Maidie answered. But Hamlin wasn't.

Meanwhile, Zack was talking about feminist theory. "Cowboy poetry will be obliterated if we incorporate that," he said. "Urban studies will languish. A penis as a cultural motif is a resilient archetype you can try to amputate, but it'll spring back."

Amelia sniffed. "You needn't take it personally, Zack. We're not replacing the Washington Monument with a flowering labial cave, no. We'd like some variety, not just in cultural icons but in critical responses to them." She went upstairs to bed.

After she left, Zack said, "She's been married seven times."

Maidie said, shocked, "Seven?"

Zack nodded. "I've known her for years. I'm sarcastic about her theories, I know, but it's clearly how she makes sense of her past. Think how idealistic she must have been to keep marrying—hopes raising up, shot down, raising up again and again."

Maidie stared into her drink.

Hamlin said, "Two divorces is enough for me. If I married again, and it didn't work—three times! That would indicate a trend."

Zack rubbed his chin and stared. "I'm always intrigued by the papers Amelia presents," he said.

Maidie said, "They're informative, I'm sure."

Zack said, "No kidding, informative. She finds something in whatever she's working on that corresponds with her life—a projected semblance of what's eating her, like when a storyteller retells an old standard, and you find out more about the teller than the tale." Zack paused and raised his eyebrows. "I'm not sure it's as obvious to Amelia as it is to everyone else."

Maidie didn't think she liked Zack. She was deciding how to answer: maybe that business that what you fear in yourself makes you see the same elsewhere, everywhere? Mrs. Funderburk said that; so did most twentieth-century psychologists. What could Maidie say to shuttle the conversation beyond this prying interest in Amelia and her miscarried past? But what had Amelia thought when she'd said *till death do us part* the seventh time? Poor Amelia, who traveled with a cat. But Maidie traveled with a dog.

Hamlin cleared his throat. "My first job was in New York City, at the Circus Museum, which was housed in the old waterworks building—interesting in itself. The stranger the better, I think, as far as museums go. Say, have you seen the Garden of Eden?"

This was better; Maidie responded enthusiastically. "Yes, the cement Adam and Eve—the labor movement explication of Genesis."

"There's a Nut Museum in South Carolina," Hamlin said, "and the woman who ran it told me I'd come at a bad time, because the squirrels had gotten in last year. No kidding. I saw the Button Museum in Macon, Georgia. Of course, they're not museums—not accredited—just oddball collections begun by someone with an eccentric hobby. I meant to come and see yours before it turned respectable."

Maidie said, "We're changing our name from the Museum of Domestic History and Home Economy to the Women's History Collection because we couldn't get accredited as a museum—we got turned down." She understood as soon as she said so that getting turned down, squeezed out, was a poor reason to change a name.

Hamlin said, sympathetic, "What did the AAM trip you up on?"

Maidie said, "We had an insufficient Statement of Mission and no Statement of Permanence. I found our last application, and all that we'd gotten approved was our Emergency Evacuation Plan."

Hamlin said, "If old Garth McHugh doesn't appreciate you over there, I can top your salary and give you more flexible hours."

Maidie said, "I'm flattered you've thought of me."

Hamlin nodded. "Think it over. Let me know."

Would there be no interview, then, Maidie wondered, just this congenial round of drinks and proffered change of life? Hamlin dropped another sprig of spearmint into Maidie's glass. Grapes, cubed cheese, boxed wine, now vodka, this cloying mint—an odd combination of texture and flavor. "When did you eat dinner?" she asked. But Hamlin was talking to Zack—about the conference, Maidie presumed. "You can't cut corners—it's an expenditure you have to make, or do without," Hamlin said, stern. It turned out, though, he was making a point about aftershave: pay for quality or decline to wear any. Zack responded that he bought his at Woolworth's, knockoffs with mutated names—like Marco, a knockoff of Ralph Lauren's Polo.

What better moment to excuse herself? Maidie thought.

She went upstairs and sat on the edge of her bed in her white nightgown, petting Zip and munching crackers she'd brought in from the car. She considered the future stretching out before her, flat: Oklahoma. A house on the outskirts. A kindly supervisor with a sense of humor. A job curating the Oklahoma State History museum, its hodgepodge documentation of the effects of the past on the present and future, perfect. Tucson, and everyone in it, would recede. (If Rex would call, Maidie thought, grinding her teeth, he'd end this suspense.) Yes, Rex would recede—also Lalo, Rona, Harve, Clima, August, Garth, Z., Cindy-June, Evvy, Buster, Midge, and Cass. In time, of course, Maidie would get a new boyfriend and they'd fight; she'd get another neighbor like Rona and tell her too much, then complain she was nosy. Eventually, Maidie realized, the future wasn't sealed in a box, bubble-wrapped, ready to be taken out and used someday. Maidie needed a mission, a narrower sense of purpose—less distraction and multiple directions—instead of this everlasting hurtling away from situations she'd let squeeze her out. Maidie needed to be visible and permanent, not a translucent, fragile, exchangeable prop in someone else's show. Someday.

She turned on a lamp and looked at the conference brochure.

Morning Sessions

"A New Look at an Old Text: Nancy Chodorow's *The Reproduction of Mothering*," presented by Candace Fae Caine, Bowbells, North Dakota

"Sexual Mythology Surrounding Billy the Kid," presented by Zack Alcott, Roswell, New Mexico

Of course.

"Masturbatory Rhythms in Emily Dickinson's Poems," presented by Amelia Rhodie, Pueblo, Colorado

Really?

"Sane Sex Living: Celebrating the Centennial of Violetta Strocchia-Rivera's Crusade for Lawful Passion," presented by Amelia Rhodie, Pueblo, Colorado

Interesting. Maidie herself had studied Violetta Strocchia-Rivera, a nineteenth-century suffragette and general reformer of staid values. Maidie might have proposed a paper of her own, she saw—"The Study of Private Versus Public Life: 'Home Economy and Domestic History' as a Valid Repository of Artifactual Knowledge."

Knock knock.

"Who's there?"

Zack stuck his head in. "It's me. I've stayed in this house before, so let me know if you have any questions or need something."

His aftershave stank, Maidie thought. Her stomach lurched. Zip bared his teeth at Zack. "I can't imagine I will," Maidie said.

When Zack left, she glanced at her nightstand, at the squat, square phone on top, which looked bald, freakish, because in place of a dial or push buttons was an opaque disk. Earlier, Maidie had lifted up the receiver and listened. It hummed, but not a dial tone, not exactly. A phone on which you receive calls but don't send them, she decided. Not that Rex would know to call Maidie here. If he did, though, Maidie felt her anger might clar-

ify, turn luminary and mellow. So far she understood just this:
she'd gotten to know two already. Husbands. What made them
sad, happy, angry, if they snored, if they were tidy or sloppy, if
they were the source of trouble or its antidote. She didn't want
to, not again. Still, she remembered the night she and Rex col-
lided, caromed into bed; Maidie had lain beneath him, being
kissed, kissed, receiving. At the time, it hardly mattered who
was above her in the dark. She'd ascertained he wouldn't hurt,
pinch, batter, or poison her, and she hadn't had much kissing,
receiving, not often. Afterward, she found herself upside down,
feet near the headboard, head near the footboard, realigned.

Then Rex unsettled everything again, saying that if he and
Maidie got married he wanted to go to Mexico on their honeymoon and swim in a pool filled with roses, or mentioning
movies he liked, or what he was buying his mother for Christmas, or that he wanted to visit a museum about extraterrestrials. Maidie didn't watch many movies. She wasn't ready to meet
Rex's mother. Extraterrestrials? Stop. Mexico? A pool filled
with roses? Stop. Still, Rex wasn't a sex object, and she needed
to be respectful outside of bed and let the otherness be, or let
go. She wanted to call Rex and say so, her first phone call sent,
as opposed to received. But she couldn't with a deformed
phone. Besides, she didn't know how to call someone on a
movie location, so she went to sleep.

But she woke to faint tapping, fingernails clicking on the
door—a knock meant to be not quite heard. Zack! Maidie
thought. Had she locked her door? She sat up and soundlessly
turned the button in the middle of the doorknob. Zip growled,
sinister.

Maidie said, "Who's there, please?"

Silence.

"Who's there?"

Then, after the stillness, the hush-hush knocking, Amelia
Rhodie said in a voice as loud as if she were giving a paper: "Oh,

it's you, Maidie. Sorry." Maidie heard her continue down the hall, the floor creaking. Another clandestine tap on the next door, Zack's, which opened. All at once Maidie smelled after-shave—like he'd recently slapped on more. This rendezvous was planned, Maidie thought, though downstairs there'd been no flirting or foreplay, just a quarrel about feminist theory versus phallocentrism that made Amelia and Zack seem, in retrospect, like a long-married couple debating the merits of Tide versus Wisk. But why had Amelia crept past like a character in an Edwardian melodrama while Zack waited behind a door, doused in scent? Intrigue as aphrodisiac? One of them was married, she realized. Zack. They were being discreet. Spearmint, Maidie thought next. She pictured that Wrigley's gum commercial—twins on skates, twin old ladies, twins in red cars, twin brides and grooms. She thought of vodka—clear and greasy, like mosquito repellent. Also, cubed cheese, sour wine from a box. She'd seen a bowl of gray guacamole at Cocktails and Convocation. Thank God she hadn't eaten that. It all came back now.

She jumped up, bolted out the door, down the hall into her bathroom, past the tub and onto her knees in front of the toilet, which was sparkling clean, she noted. She threw up. Her ears rang. When she was done, she stood up and washed, looking at herself in the mirror. Her crescent face, her eyes shaped like upside-down smiles. She was still Maidie Bonasso, just more haggard than the last time she'd looked. She remembered a stand-up comedian she'd seen on TV who said if a man had a one-night stand with a woman who was over thirty-five, he needed to prepare for the fact that she'd look like Ed Sullivan in the morning.

Maidie went down the hall, back to her room.

The door had shut itself—locked.

She knocked her knee against it, jarring the doorknob upward.

236

No entry. She looked at the front stairwell. She could sleep on the sofa in the parlor, but she didn't have a blanket. She tried her own door again. Zip whimpered. She went back to the bathroom, past the toilet, outside to the balcony. She crept to her own window and tugged off its aluminum screen. But the heavy window beneath wouldn't budge. Zip whimpered beyond the glass. Stars shone; city lights blinked. Maidie comprehended with a start that Zack's window was wide open, because she heard voices. Male and female He created them, she thought, Genesis 1:27. Then she heard the wheezing up-down-up of bedsprings and decided to go back in and sleep downstairs, with or without a blanket.

But the door leading back in was locked too.

How could it be? she thought, rash, furious. She kicked it. How had it gotten locked in the first place, and why was Maidie always on this side, outside? she raged, meanwhile conscious that the universe didn't plan mishaps and that to act as if she'd been isolated, cold and lonely, on a balcony for cosmically significant reasons was sentimental—loving herself more than God could—if not acutely self-pitying. All the same, I can't sleep here, she thought. I could sleep in the Cofer College car, she thought, looking down at its gleaming silver shell in the driveway. By morning, she'd be bedraggled, foolish-seeming, when someone let her in, and too tired to attend the conference. Hamlin would take back his job offer. Did Maidie want the job? Did she want to move again? The noise through Zack's window amplified. "Ugh, ugh, ugh," he uttered, climactic.

Maidie calmed herself. She'd wait a decent interval, she decided, then knock on the window, standing so far back she couldn't be mistaken for a Peeping Tom, hold up the screen from her window and explain the situation and ask Zack to go down the hall and let her in. She waited a few minutes until all she heard was crickets, cicada, cars passing on nearby streets. She knocked. "Hello, hello?" She heard rustling bed linens.

Then Amelia came to the window, frazzled and languid, wrapped in a sheet. She said, "Maidie, what on earth are you doing out there?"

"I went onto the balcony to try to come through my window, but I'm locked out here now—I'd locked myself out of my bedroom earlier and was trying to come back in through my window," Maidie said, confounding, reversing the chronology.

"Well, for God's sake, come back in."

Maidie said, "Could you go down the hall and open the door?"

Amelia said, "Just come through here. It's late." Amelia pushed the window screen out. Maidie climbed in, past Zack, who slept soundly. Postcoital relaxation, Maidie thought. God's tranquilizer, Rex Hurley called sex. "Thanks," she whispered to Amelia as she pushed Zack's bedroom door open. But it didn't lead to the hallway outside Maidie's room. It led straight into the maid's stairwell, long and coiling. Never mind, Maidie thought, hurrying downstairs. When she found herself in the kitchen, its black and white tiles and shiny fixtures, she felt thrilled. She was looking through a drawer for a tool—a knife or screwdriver she could use to jimmy her lock—when she heard a noise, a key rattling in the door that led outside.

And that old lady at the conference thought the museum was haunted! Did no one in Oklahoma City sleep at night? The door opened and Hamlin Dwinn stepped in, hair springy and mussed. He wore jeans and what looked like a striped pajama top.

He frowned. "What are you doing?"

Maidie said, "I locked myself out of my room."

"That's too bad."

"You have no idea, " she said.

He said, "I have keys. I can open your door for you. But I came because of a phone call—an emergency. You need to sit down."

Maidie sat on a chrome-legged chair. Emergency? This was coming on fast. Was she supposed to be frightened? She was hungry and exhausted. She smoothed her white nightgown around her.

Hamlin said, "I got a phone call from Garth McHugh."

Maidie thought: An emergency in Tucson?

"Garth got a phone call earlier. He's been trying to reach us since this afternoon." Hamlin perched on the chair, his portly frame overflowing. "It seems there's been a death in your family."

Maidie said, "Who?"

"He didn't know," Hamlin said. "He thought maybe your father."

*O*ur Father gives us hardships to bear in the season in which we can," Pastor Larssen said at Vera's mother's funeral, with no mourners. Vera herself was gone, yellow-skinned before she died, and four years later her bones still under the snow, untransformed. Eugene lived in Wraith, Ontario, with his friend, Everitt. Maidie's mother lived in Vera's mother's house in California. Maidie and Mrs. Funderburk had come to the funeral straight from lunch—beans, corn bread, ham salad. Maidie was staying at Mrs. Funderburk's, in a narrow room beside the kitchen. Mr. Funderburk, the sheriff, would come in at five and say, "How was your day, ladies?" He'd play cards with Maidie—Old Maid, but he called it Old Maidie, a joke. Lucy and Thea still lived across the street; Neena was like a substitute, Lucy said: more fun, not so much work. Maidie herself would rather have a mother. But after her mother didn't come home, Maidie's father wouldn't talk about her; he talked about Neena instead. Mrs. Funderburk had sent a note home: *a bad time . . . if I can help . . .* Maidie didn't show the note to her dad but went home each day and picked up a change of clothes to take to

Mrs. Funderburk's, until most of her clothes were there; Mrs. Funderburk had always wanted children of her own, Maidie forced her to admit.

*F*orced to admit the violent, amputated idea of it, forced to let it in, Maidie thought: My father, dead? And all at once: If he is, if I can't backtrack this time . . . If I get a chance, Maidie thought, I'll sort out the past, I will.

"I have phone numbers you're supposed to call." Hamlin stared into Maidie's face, then lowered his eyes. He handed her a slip of paper. "Call this number," he said. The area code was Minnesota; probably Lucy's number. "If you can't get through, call here," Hamlin said, pointing at a number with an unfamiliar area code.

Maidie stared. "Is there a phone I can call out on?"

Hamlin pointed at one on the kitchen wall.

Maidie nodded.

"Are you all right?" he asked.

Maybe my father, maybe not, Maidie thought. Then who? "I'm starving," she said. "I ended up missing dinner last night."

Hamlin said, "I'll go get some food. You make the calls. Are you going to be all right? Should I wake up Zack, or Amelia?"

Maidie said, "I'll be fine."

Hamlin headed for the door, but Maidie stood up and said, "Could you unlock my room first, please?" As she followed Hamlin upstairs, she thought: He probably thinks I need some feminine hygiene product, or my address book or phone card. But in fact she just didn't like the door locked, Zip on the other side. Zip clattered out, joyous. He followed Maidie back down to the kitchen, and Hamlin left through the back door as she dialed the first number. Ringing one, two, three, four. Lucy's answering machine: "We're not home now, " Lucy said, her Minnesota voice, flat *o*'s. "Please leave a message." Why wasn't

Lucy home in the middle of the night, her husband either? Maidie wanted to call her dad (dead?), or Thea. Neena, even. She didn't know their numbers.

She dialed the second number, area code 415. Ring, ring, ring. It was the middle of the night everywhere. At last someone answered, grappling with the phone, synthetic crackles, plastic thuds. "Hello?" a sad, trembling, soft, rich vibrato voice said, a voice as plausible as dawn appearing like a strip of reprieve in a nightmare, a seam of light above the tree line, a voice as familiar as a cramped and stuffy corridor or a bent stairway in the house in which you'd been born. "Hello?" it said.

Maidie breathed deep. "I'm Maidie Bonasso," she said, "and I was told to call this number because of a death in my family."

"Oh." Her mother's voice. "Maidie, Maidie, it's you."

Maidie hardened. "Who is dead, Mom?" she said, the word old and outmoded in her mouth. *Mom.* "Please just say who's dead."

"No one you know," her mother said. "My husband, who would be your stepfather. But I wanted you to come out for his funeral. I've phoned all you girls. Actually, I reached your sister, and she called you. Right? I'd like you to come if you could."

"Come to a funeral? Where are you?" Maidie shivered in the big kitchen. Zip sat on the floor, licking Maidie's feet. Hamlin Dwinn came through the back door with a bag from McDonald's. "Moraga, California," her mother said. Maidie tried to picture it. She thought of the nonexistent memories she'd invented: a beachfront table, her mother in a pastel exercise suit, her face familiar but fine-lined, etched, her hair turned silver. Make new friends but keep the old, Maidie thought, irrelevantly. She looked at Hamlin, who mouthed, "Egg McMuffins—all I could get," and shrugged. "Are you all right?" he mouthed. "Are you coming?" her mother asked over the phone. "Do you want to?" her mother asked, as Zip whimpered. Maidie said, "I do."

* * *

"*D*o you," Mrs. Larssen had asked Mrs. Funderburk as Maidie stared into the casket at Vera's mother, a white-haired husk, "know the rest of kin?" Next of kin, Maidie corrected silently. She wanted to have two children, she decided, blocking out Mrs. Larssen's clinging-to-bromides, rude prattle. That way, if one died there'd be another to see her through to the whittled-down last days.

Back when Maidie's mother hadn't left on her trip to consider her life, back when she stayed in her room with the door closed like the false bottom in a jewelry box, keeping secrets and clues hidden, back when there wasn't a good time to come home after school, Maidie decided to visit Vera's mother, who was living in the new extension to the hospital, cinder blocks painted flesh tone. It was January. School let out at three-thirty. The sun set at five. The nurses wouldn't let a kid in, so Maidie stood outside the window and waved, red mittens against glass, and all around, the metallic, acid scent of snow. Maidie couldn't tell which was Vera's mother—the women looked alike with their blue hospital robes and stiff, wild hair. One leaned over in her chair, arms extended, and said, "Gutta, Gutta," like she was calling a girl's name.

Joel Scribner's mother, who cleaned the church and sometimes the hospital, came through the door with a mop and a bucket on wheels. She squinted through the window at Maidie, then cranked it open. "You don't need to visit, honey. She doesn't know you're here." All the same, Maidie remembered what Vera had said about having her mother nearby. "I know she's difficult," Vera had told Eugene, "but she makes me connected." Uninterrupted, Maidie thought, sitting in the church pew between Mrs. Funderburk and Mrs. Larssen, Pastor continuing about God's pain our birthright. The door opened, and

Neena came in and sat in the back pew. At the end of the service, she said to Mrs. Funderburk, "You've helped us out, but
it's time for Maidie to come home. She has a perfectly nice
home." Maidie went home, but she still visited Mrs. Funderburk in that dim hour when she turned on the overhead lights
and boiled and steamed, banging pot lids. Maidie lingered in
the kitchen, finishing homework, polishing silver, tidying Mrs.
Funderburk's sewing kit, and the phone would ring. "If our Little Match Girl is over there, send her home," Neena would say,
which was a joke, Mrs. Funderburk explained.

"If that's a joke, it's not funny," an old woman in a bolted-down
plastic chair in the Saint Louis airport said to a wisecracking
teenage boy who'd said he hoped their pilot wasn't hungover, in
case the plane they were taking needed to make an emergency
landing. "You act odd, not normal," the woman added, per-
plexed. Was she his grandmother? Maidie wondered, eaves-
dropping. His foster parent? But they weren't talk show guests
who'd surrendered their privacy in exchange for cash, Maidie
reminded herself. She turned her attention instead to the TV in
the lounge across the corridor, on which a talk show *was* playing, its perky, tomboy host asking guests about their plans to
marry in unusual places: at the bottom of the sea while scuba
diving, for example. Travelers sat on barstools, sipping. A man
shot pool—clack, roll, an autonomous white ball scattering
motley subordinate balls. Maidie smelled the airport smells:
fast food, fuel fumes somehow seeping past the windows, the
heady effluvium of industrial-strength cleaners in big buckets
blue-shirted custodians wheeled by. Maidie glanced outside at
planes silhouetted against the sky. In an hour, Lucy and Thea
would arrive, and together they'd board a plane aimed at California.

Thirty-six hours had passed since Maidie dialed long distance and listened to her mother's far-off voice extending its invitation to a funeral—a funeral that seemed like a wedding, since Maidie was just discovering the fact of her new stepfather, already dead. But if she speculated on her mother's life these long years, it made sense she'd been married. Maidie pictured her mother ironing a shirt, stirring cocktails, applying lipstick as she laughed, scoffed. She'd been conditioned to rely on men, to station herself near one who, in the economy of prestige and power, prospered. Male-oriented, the 1970s term for women who'd never developed any skills besides acting indispensable while cooking, cleaning, and flirting, through the pressure to wax happy about white whites, Congoleum linoleum, and nutritious foodstuffs had seemed to enrage her mother all the same. Even so—Maidie fumed and pitched in the Saint Louis airport, anger welling below the surface of her skin—had it never occurred to her to phone home once in a while and at least ask the people she'd left raising the daughters she'd borne, then abandoned, how they fared? Apparently not. Maidie moved on to smaller, manageable questions.

How long since she'd seen Lucy?

Nine years.

When Lucy started selling Vigortone feed products—riding along with her husband and convincing farmers to buy steroids and dewormers from her—she'd won a regional sales competition, first prize a trip to Graceland, and arranged to fly home through Little Rock, which was two hundred miles from Fayetteville, where Maidie lived then. Maidie drove to Little Rock and met Lucy at a Denny's near the airport. They sipped coffee and watched the planes rise, fall, float, a clumsy ballet. "Are you still in school?" Lucy had asked Maidie. "What does your new husband look like?"

Nine years later in the Saint Louis airport, which didn't look very different from the Little Rock airport, the woman in the bolted-down chair said to the teenage boy, "I'm not the right age to cope with someone like you." Maidie listened, cringing at the implication of *like you*: difficult, unnecessary, expendable. He looked bored, like he'd heard it before. Had he spent his life thinking he was in the way, every act and gesture calculated to earn his right to stay? Again, Maidie turned to questions she could answer. How long since she'd seen Thea?

Twelve years.

Maidie was living in Nebraska then. Neville had left home, saying marriage seemed too hard. Maidie went to Minnesota for Christmas, a plan formulated by Opal Johnson ("Hard times, you need family"), echoed by ladies at the weight-loss clinic ("Don't sit staring at a Christmas tree all by your lonesome"). Her dad drove in from Hector to pick her up at the airport. On the way home, he couldn't talk because the roads were icy and he needed to focus, he said. Neena was spending Christmas in Florida, he added. When they got home, Maidie looked at the house, smaller, less graciously furnished than she recalled. Thea came through the door, coat draped open, her husband behind her. "How are you?" she asked. Maidie answered in the patois of the just divorced: "This isn't going to be my easiest Christmas." Thea blinked. "Well, don't bring your bad mood here." Her stocking cap edged down. "We need positive vibes." She tipped her head toward Maidie's dad, concocting martinis glumly while the Statler Brothers sang "O Holy Night" on TV. Every holiday since, Maidie had stayed where she was—Nebraska, Arkansas, Virginia, now Arizona.

"I don't want you to come along if you don't act right," the woman in the airport told the boy. He answered, "Maybe your definition of *right* needs modification," his eyes cloudy, bitter.

Maidie turned away.

She wished she could ask Ann Landers what to say when she saw her sisters for this first time in years. Surely one of them— being long married and having attended family parties for in-laws—could initiate a gracious, easy conversation. Or maybe

they'd picked up phrases and gestures from friends and neighbors in Hector who invited people to funerals, weddings, anniversary parties, baptisms. Of course, Maidie had neighbors
who hosted family parties too, but she'd moved so much and
didn't know her neighbors well, and hence hadn't had extended
opportunities to observe customs and communication. But
Maidie's gut sense was that you let a time-honored, almost styl-
ized discussion begin, expand. It's been years! How's business?
How's married life? Do you like your job? How's the weather
where you live? After a while, uniquely personal details crept in,
and you might not get heartfelt communion, family sentiment
arising, but a tenor of genuine interest materialized. Tenuous
contact reemerged. Tenuous or not, you needed contact, Maidie
understood, or memories distorted themselves and long-lost
relatives became saccharine ideals or hated foes, Lalo's book
Abundant Manhood said.

Accordingly, Maidie's heart beat fast and out of rhythm as
she thought about her mother. How many years had passed?
Did Maidie remember her? Or did memories self-sustain, static
and ornamental like photos you recall looking at but not the ac-
tual day on which they were taken? And when did Maidie's
mother disappear? When she retreated behind a door, shrinking, demurring? When she boarded the bus and it slipped
away? When she stopped answering Maidie's letters and Maidie's sense of her face, her lap, her perfumed arms and hair,
faded? By the time Maidie's dad wouldn't say her name and
turned silent if someone would, Maidie's mother had become an
aught in the space she'd once occupied. Twenty-odd years
passed. Then Maidie spoke to her on the phone in the middle of
the night. If someone had asked ahead of time how Maidie
would respond, she'd have cited a book she'd read in school, *At-
tachment and Loss*: the person who attaches and loses too soon,
too often, becomes controlling, not cooperative, with emotions
more eloquent than felt. Maidie would therefore respond from a

distance, a cordoned-off remove where expectations won't attach themselves or inflict pain at the site of their removal.

On the other hand, she'd heard her mother's voice and felt the old contours of kinship, connection. We *know* each other, Maidie realized, the give-and-take, suspended love, reactivated. *Mom*, she'd said, a twelve-year-old's inflection in her voice and demeanor as she slipped instantly into the pretense that it was customary, usual, for a woman to divorce not only her husband but her offspring, her next or rest of kin, then invite them to a funeral twenty years later for a stepfather they didn't know existed. It was perverse, sensational. Maidie pictured it as a talk show. Host: Do you resent your mother for her long absence? Guest: She had her own life to live, which was no bowl of cherries either. Maidie had always known anger and resentment wouldn't help any more than hard liquor, providing temporary relief, yes, lapsed sensibility, then the ensuing hangover—consciousness, with all its excruciating minutiae, restored. If Maidie had to tell some other daughter how not to grieve, she'd say: Concentrate on the future. Keep your house clean. Refinish furniture. Take a class. Love a dog. Move on.

But the last day or two had lasted so long: first she was stranded on the balcony, then the jarring, garbled news someone (who?) was dead, then the phone call to Maidie's mother, wishes and fear buzzing. Maidie got through to Lucy at 7:30 A.M. Where had Lucy been in the middle of the night? Home. Her husband turned the ringer off and the answering machine down when he went to bed, Lucy explained. She was leaving with Thea for the airport. They'd fly to Saint Louis, then switch planes for Oakland, which was the airport closest to Moraga. Maidie could meet them in Saint Louis. "Be sure to get bereavement fare," Lucy insisted. If Maidie mentioned their mother's husband's name, Lucy said, which was Harold Foss, also the name of the funeral home where he lay in state, Bright Chapel, the airline would check with the funeral director, who had a list of relatives, and Maidie could get half price. "But we're not relatives," Maidie had said. Lucy answered, "According to airline policy, we are. This is the 1990s." Sitting in the Hill House kitchen, Maidie thought how people would have to stop saying that soon. This is the 2000s, they'd say instead. "How do you know his name?" Maidie asked, suspicious. Lucy said, "Mom told me, yesterday. I'll see you tomorrow."

Harold Foss, Maidie had told the travel agent.

My stepfather who died, she'd added.

A day later, she was on her way to Moraga, California, to a funeral that would be a family reunion too, she thought, albeit with odd props—prayer books, candles, pamphlets with titles like "Your Last Disposition." All Maidie could feel, standing near her suitcases in Saint Louis, waiting for Lucy and Thea, was that she missed Zip. He'd ridden next to her in the car for two days, then sat at her feet almost the whole time she'd been in Oklahoma. She felt she was losing body heat without him, which was irrational, and she didn't want to be one of those people who treated a pet like a child, carrying snapshots, telling anecdotes to emphasize Zip's cleverness. Still, Maidie pictured him in the tiny yard behind Hamlin Dwinn's condo. "It's small, but it's better than a kennel," Hamlin had said, with his kind, pink face. "I'll walk him every night." Maidie had felt dizzy, exhausted. "What about the Multi-State American Studies Conference?" she asked. Hamlin said, "I'll walk him when I get home. But shouldn't you call Garth McHugh and tell him your plans?" Suddenly, Maidie remembered the Cofer College car— and Lalo, marooned in New Mexico. She used Hamlin's phone to call Garth.

"How are you?" Garth had asked, his voice unctuous. He seemed to like the state of emergency he assumed Maidie had entered, the imperative details she needed help negotiating, directives reverberating down the chain of command. Of course, he doesn't know the deceased is a stepfather I've never met,

Maidie thought. Garth said, "I felt so bad when your sister phoned. Don't worry about the car; we can send someone for it. Just get on the plane. I'll file your family leave paperwork."

Maidie interrupted. "You have to call Lalo. Tell him I'm not picking him up. He rode with me to New Mexico, to visit his mother," she said. "He has a bad home situation." (Wasn't that the lingo?) "He'll be waiting," Maidie insisted, her voice rising. Garth said, "He can take the bus." Maidie said, "Make sure he has enough money. Don't leave him there. Send him money. I'll pay you back." And she didn't hang up until Garth promised.

Hamlin drove her to the airport, and she flew from Oklahoma City to Saint Louis. People scurried past, dragging suitcases. Maidie had the romantic idea—no doubt fostered by airline commercials—that everyone who flew had a loved one waiting at the gate. Of course, they didn't, or maybe they had a hard-to-get-along-with loved one. Statistically speaking, over half the adult population—i.e., half the adults here—had been divorced at least once. The teenage boy in front of Maidie had fallen asleep on the old lady's shoulder now, his face childish, soft. Maidie worried about Lalo. Garth would have called him by now. Lalo had lived in that house until he was eighteen, Maidie reasoned; he could endure a few days more. She thought about Zip, his mournful yipping behind Hamlin's fence as she'd walked away. She felt agitated, exposed. She remembered that bright-lit moment Hamlin came through the door and said someone was dead, maybe her dad. She wanted to pick up her bags and run, like that time she'd come back from having Jack sign divorce papers and got stalled on the runway in bad weather, and when she'd landed in Tucson she ran and ran, and Rex waited. I'm here, he'd said. So stop.

She wanted to call her dad, right now. She carried her suitcases to the row of phone booths and wedged herself between a man in a business suit and a fat woman in a caftan-style dress, wearing a silver necklace that clanked and rattled as she breathed.

Maidie felt crowded, pressed upon. She got out her phone card, called Information for the number, then dialed.

"Hello?" He sounded cheerful.

"Dad, this is Maidie."

"Where are you? What are you doing?"

Maidie explained. "The airport. Saint Louis. Waiting."

He said, "It was a bit of a shock, that phone call."

Maidie said, "No kidding."

He said, "I knew her voice right away. I always expected she'd call someday. It didn't seem to be my place not to put her in touch with you girls. Neena used to say it was best for you to forget. But now you're adults. You have to make your own decisions."

Maidie said, "Are you saying Mom wanted to be in touch and Neena wouldn't let her?" How relievingly simple this sounded! Like an old-fashioned movie where members reunite and the man or woman who separated them in the first place is Designated Evil.

"No. Your mother wanted a new start. She wanted one when she came to Minnesota too. I tried to give it to her. I made a decent living. But she always said I was a fool to scrape up greenbacks in a small town. Maybe I was. My own mother said I'd never be more than a plow jockey." Standing in the airport, Maidie thought: His own mother? A plow jockey? Wasn't he over *any* of that? "She had tough breaks early on," he added, "your mother. Her father wasn't fit to raise a daughter alone. I pride myself I did better than that. When she got old enough and fed up, she ran off with that barkeep—living above a bar when Pastor and Mrs. Larssen met her. So they said. She never said different."

"Why didn't you tell me this before?"

"Tell you what? I never knew what to say. Or if you were old enough to hear it. You mother wasn't bad. She just didn't have any practice staying put. I'm not surprised she turned up married—a few times, I bet. Weren't we all? Everyone has to make a life, Maidie. I thought Neena had a good idea—face the future."

But I couldn't help looking back, Maidie thought, standing between the caftan and the business suit. She said, "Dad, that time you went to San Francisco—which one of you wanted the divorce?"

He said, "Both of us. I'd thrown in the towel by then."

"What do you know about her life in Madagascar? Her mother?"

He said, "Her mother was raised in a poorhouse. Or by nurses. I never really understood. You'll have to ask her yourself."

Myself? Maidie thought, stunned, and she couldn't help looking back, at years that boiled down to days, hours, intimate minutes her mother had held her, her mother's scented arms and sentimental, yearning opinions about the gap between what she'd wanted and what she'd been apportioned. A geometrical theory of behavior—rebound, don't crack. A plate-tectonics model for living—shift, don't shatter. Maidie's mother had reproduced herself, her mother love and survival lore, in Maidie. Lucy and Thea always seemed to be in another room, symbiotic, self-sufficient. They'd race through, waving. Maidie, the revised, reduced version of her mother, waved back. She remembered the day her mother kissed her neck, Maidie's neck, saying she herself had been a lonely child, and Maidie felt that her mother was kissing a mirror, or an old photo of herself. "There's no one to blame," Maidie's dad said, his voice tinny, faraway. "We did the best we knew. Not many people divorced then. No one knew"—his voice trailed off—"how to do the least damage."

Maidie said, "Dad, for a minute, when I got the news to call home because there was a death in my family"—she paused—"for a minute I thought it was you, and I'm glad it wasn't."

He laughed. "Not yet anyway."

"Not for a long time."

"I have some serious news," he said. "Are you sitting down?"

Maidie said, "Of course not. I'm in a damn airport."

"You were nice a minute ago, then you take this tone."

How fast he deflated, took the hit and stayed depressed. He used to bounce back, she thought, resilient as rubber, tension a form of willpower that permitted him to act as if circumstances were fine even when they weren't, which was the conventional wisdom on how to raise children then. "Sorry. Too many surprises lately."

"One more," he said. "I'm getting married."

Maidie remembered the woman in the Winnebago. Paula. "Wonderful."

"But if it doesn't work this time, I'll be a three-time loser."

Maidie said, "No way, Dad. Cheer up. You're not a loser until you get married and divorced, let's say, at least seven times."

"Good God."

"But you won't. This is it. You'll be happy." It didn't matter if she believed herself. Words sometimes, not always, come true by emerging out of nothing, brain folds and lung air, winging out in phonologically accidental but epistemologically determined ways, carrying weight, gravity, assurance. Many anthropologists believe speech in ceremonial moments is an act itself, not a description of an act. "I love you, Dad. I have to go."

He sounded surprised. "I love you too. Say hi to Rex."

Rex?

Maidie turned around, to see Lucy and Thea hurtling toward her. Thea was pregnant, her trench coat open around a stomach the size of a tetherball. She wore a plaid cap, her ponytail poking out behind. Lucy was dressed like an important woman in a small office: a fuchsia blazer, black slacks, blond hair stiff with gel. "Thea, you should have told me about your stomach—your baby, I mean," Maidie said. Lucy intervened: "When? During one of your weekly phone calls?" Thea was asking, "What about Oklahoma, Maidie? I thought you lived in Arizona. Am I wrong?" Maidie edged toward the circle of flesh and luggage, then jerked back to her own vicinity. Flesh tears, she reminded herself, her brain full of brittle, noncommodious conversations she'd had with strangers in Oklahoma for two days, strangers in Arizona for ten months, strangers everywhere. She felt prickly outside, watery inside. Lucy and I have that in common, she thought, but Thea acts happy when she feels mostly sad. "Let's not pick on Maidie," Thea said, eyes wide, conciliatory. Lucy smiled, grim. Flesh tears and repairs, Maidie thought, forcing her own smile until it turned real.

Driving her snail-shaped car, Maidie remembered a street—viny tree branches, a yard with red tulips—or a corner—a Sirloin Stockade on one side, Dunkin' Donuts on the other—and she didn't know if she was remembering Fayetteville or Norfolk, or the city she lived in now, Tucson. But here was Speedway Boulevard with its strip joints and Gonzo's store. She parked her car, got out, and asked two men standing there, "Do you know where the Public Records Office is?" One man, dressed like a biker, said, "I've never heard of the Public Records Office." A man selling boudin sausages out of a cooler said, "But the courthouse is over there." Then Maidie turned around to get in her car, but it was gone. She borrowed a moped from the men at Gonzo's Store, but it broke down. She found a bicycle and pedaled ahead until she saw the building where she'd attended a two-minute hearing in which a judge had pronounced her divorced from Jack. She wanted to go inside, find the file on Lalo, erase his stepfather's name, clear up the future. But the bicycle wobbled and pitched, then tipped . . . "Move your seat to upright position," a flight attendant was saying, tapping Maidie's shoulder as the plane descended into Oakland International Airport.

Maidie leaned across the aisle to speak to Lucy and Thea. Lucy said, "Shh, I can't hear," her eyes flitting around. Was she waiting for instructions from the flight attendant? She probably doesn't travel much, Maidie realized. She asked, "How often do you fly?" Thea leaned forward and said, "This is my first time, but Lucy's an old hand." Lucy said, "I flew to Chicago a few times for Vigortone conventions, and that one trip to Graceland. My ears bother me when we land." She turned to Thea and glared at her for a significant duration Maidie couldn't fathom. She felt intrusive, leaning into Lucy and Thea's closed circle. Lucy said, "I almost forgot. A woman is looking for you."

Maidie said, "Me?"

Lucy was digging in her purse. "From Idaho."

Maidie said, "I've never been to Idaho."

Lucy said, "Really? Well, I didn't know." She pulled out a piece of paper and handed it to Maidie. "This woman called Dad, asking about you." She shot Maidie a sardonic, flattened-out glance. "When a situation confuses him, he turns it over to me."

Maidie read the note.

> Laree Garver
> 67 Prairie Hollow
> Boise, Idaho 83708
> Ph. (208) 245-3011

Laree—with a new last name, a new address. Idaho!

Lucy said, "She said she was your friend and that the last address of yours she had was in Virginia. Dad didn't know if we should give her your new address, because, first of all, he's paranoid, and you were getting a divorce, and he thought this was a trick, like your husband was using her to find you. Anyway, to protect your privacy, I got her address and said you'd contact her."

Maidie said, "Thank you. She is my friend. We lost touch, moving around, new last names—" The plane thudded to the ground, then rolled slowly to the gate. People stood up and un-loaded overhead compartments. Lucy exited the plane, Thea followed—maneuvering her stomach through the aisle like a piece of freight—Maidie third. They shuffled toward the baggage claim. Maidie asked Lucy, "Where do we go next?"

"Someone's meeting us," Lucy said. "That's what Mom told me." A woman on the edge of the crowd was holding a piece of tagboard with uneven handwriting: *Giddings Girls*. Thea stopped, pulled her backpack off, and held it in front of her like a small, swaddled package. "That isn't her," Thea said, wary. They all stopped and stared at the woman: a gray pageboy, a plump, good-humored face. She leaned oddly forward as she waved, like she had stiff hips. Lucy said, "Could be. I don't think so."

The woman rushed forward. "I'd know you anywhere! That hair." She touched Maidie's. "And your nose." She beamed at Lucy. "I'm your mother's friend."

Maidie thought: Oh. "Thanks for coming."

"Jane," the woman added.

Lucy unloaded the suitcases off the carousel.

"Your mother is going to be thrilled to see you," Jane said. "Hard times, you need family. But she's taking it well. She's a brick. I'd go to pieces if my husband keeled over like that."

Keeled over?

How long had she been married? Maidie wondered but didn't ask.

Jane said, "I imagine it's a shock."

Lucy set suitcases in a row. "Yes."

Jane said, "He was the picture of health, and that much younger than her—you just assumed she'd be the one to go first. She thought he had the flu. I don't know how she stood it in that grocery store parking lot, or those hours in the ER, waiting."

Grocery store parking lot? Younger? Hours in the ER, waiting? Maidie glanced at Lucy and Thea. What did they know?

Lucy shrugged. Thea seemed to be tightening the strings on her backpack. "We weren't that close," she said, without looking up.

Jane said, "No, he came into her life late—all of you in Wisconsin."

"Minnesota," Thea said.

"Minnesota," Maidie echoed. In the winter, the sun set early in Minnesota, snow covered the memory of spring like a precious root, and Maidie had picked Jackson Hole off the map like a lucky password, a streets-paved-in-gold destination. She'd headed out like a hobo, clothing, pots and pans, memories that had survived the weeding-out process, tied into a knot. Her dad asked where she was going, but not why, or what she'd do there.

"Here." In the parking ramp, Jane unlocked the door to a minivan. She drove through misty streets. Office buildings poked up, windows radiant like square suns. Maidie sat in front next to Jane, who said, "Your mother is becoming my dearest friend. I'm single now, and all my kids are back East. I needed someone to bum around with, and your mother keeps up on all the latest trends." Maidie thought: I bet. "I golf too," Jane added, pulling onto an expressway, cars and trucks slipping past, engulfing.

"Where's the ocean?" Maidie asked.

Jane jerked her head at the fog behind them. "There."

Land flattened. Houses became newer, shorter, cheaper.

"Mom golfs?" Maidie asked.

Jane said, "Does she ever."

They passed shadowy housing developments and—between them—flat fields with twisted, stunted trees tied to strings. "Grapevines," Jane pointed out. Maidie said, "Where's San Francisco?" Jane jerked her head at the fog behind them. "There." Thirty minutes later, she slowed in front of a grayish bungalow. She pulled up in front of the open garage, got out, hobbled through it, opened the door leading inside, and called, "Yoohoo."

Maidie, Lucy, and Thea got out of the van.

Maidie said, "Is it just me, or is this strange?"

Thea said, "It's not the absolute strangest. It's medium strange. It's not like he was a serial killer they interviewed on *20/20*."

Lucy said, "I don't know how she expects us to grieve for Harold Foss. We don't know him. I suppose we're here for moral support."

Maidie said, "I mean, it's strange she made contact now."

Lucy said, "Well, that."

Maidie felt her eyes narrow, zero in. "Have you been in touch with her and didn't tell me?" A rude, suspicious question.

Lucy said, "Don't start on me, Maidie. I know a few more details than you because when Dad gave her our phone numbers she got in touch with me first and put me in charge of the trip. All I knew until two days ago was that she lived out here—in that old lady's beach house, for all I knew. I'm not in shock, because I gave up a long time ago thinking she was normal. Neena was normal."

Neena? Maidie thought. What did I miss there?

"Lucy, stop it," Thea said. The wind whipped her ponytail. She turned to face Maidie. "We knew you'd be upset. We agreed on that ahead of time. You were her favorite. This is harder for you."

"Not her favorite," Maidie said. She'd been her mother's confidante. She'd tried to help her mother, like Jane did now. Maidie never blamed her mother. She worried she hadn't done enough to keep her. Maidie's mother wasn't normal, no; she'd suffered. She couldn't help leaving. In Maidie's collection of the past, archives of home, her mother was gilt-edged, not shopworn.

The door inside the garage opened.

Maidie prepared herself.

Her mother looked worse in that she was older—all those

years lost—but improved in that she had stylish, up-to-date hair, still brown like Maidie's but with artful silver streaks, and trimmed at the nape of her neck, tapering to her face. She wore a smooth aqua sweater, matching silky pants. Her face had settled into burnished permanence, her wrinkles a kind of natural cosmetic accentuating good, angular features. She raised her hands in the air, dramatic. "You're a sight for sore eyes." She turned to Jane. "Aren't they just like I said—beautiful daughters?"

They moved toward her, with suitcases. Their mother was saying, "You've met Jane. After all these years, I finally have a best friend—like Barbie with Midge—and what does her name turn out to be? Jane Doe. Isn't that hysterical?"

Jane smiled. "She gets a kick out of it."

Lucy said, "Your name is Jane Doe?"

"I married a man named Doe, and back in those days we didn't have the option to keep our maiden names, like you girls now."

Maidie said, "It *is* funny."

Her mother smiled. "We have the same sense of humor."

Jane turned to go. "I'll see you at the funeral."

Maidie's mother led the three of them inside, through the kitchen, into the living room. She said, "Lucy and Thea, take my bedroom. Maidie, you and I will share the sofa sleeper, but put your luggage in the bathroom." Then Maidie's mother turned and said, "It was marvelous of you to come," her smile strained. Maidie waited for forthcoming reasons, excuses, analgesics. What might their mother say? Maidie looked around. Thea seemed bored, obedient. Lucy, like she was taking notes for a project she'd been asked to supervise. And Maidie realized that since she'd left home, abdicating, Lucy had become the child on whom their father depended, and she was poised to play the same role here.

Maidie said, "How long were you married to Harold Foss?"

Their mother said, "Three years this August. But we'd been

258

together for nearly five years." And Maidie remembered answering questions about how long she'd been married to
Neville or Jack the same way, eking out years and months to respectable totals.

"He was a kind man," their mother said, "and just crazy
about me, which is a wonderful way to be married if you must
be. But from what I've read in books at work, it wasn't a
healthy relationship, because it didn't leave me much time for
anyone else."

Maidie took this in. "Where do you work?"

"I'm a receptionist at an office for five shrinks—the Pine-
hurst Marriage and Family Counseling Center. Jane's the office
manager and bookkeeper. That's where I learn these new terms
like codependent, which means 'ingratiating'—which I'm not,
thank God. I'm more narcissistic, if anything." She frowned.

Not ingratiating by a long shot, Maidie thought. But could
you be narcissistic if you knew you were? Maidie had the idea
you could be for oblivious moments, phases, but you forced
yourself out of it. You didn't resign yourself to narcissism as if it
were incurable, like lupus. "Is that a diagnosis?" she asked.

Her mother shook her head. "I read a lot."

"I'm glad you invited us to Harold Foss's funeral," Maidie
said. "But how can we help?" She was semi-aghast at her own
forthrightness.

Her mother said, "Let me think." Any vulnerability in her face
flicked by fast, a bird passing a window. "I never liked cutting
the ties entirely. People at work said I needed my family now,
and I thought that would be good—if nobody minded coming."

"We're here," Lucy said. "Can we help?"

"I have to pick out the clothes Hal will be buried in," their
mother said. The three of them went with her to the bedroom
closet and helped her select a pair of tan knit pants with durable
creases, a shirt, a sports coat, a string necktie like Roy Rogers
used to wear. "You seem to be coping," Maidie said, vaguely an-

noyed. She remembered the day their mother got the news her father was dead and stayed in her room, door closed, sobbing.

Her mother said, "I have my emotions under control. It's hard. But I learn new skills quickly. I work on computers now too."

"Did you miss us?" Maidie asked suddenly.

Lucy breathed in, sharp.

Thea was staring out the black, blank window.

Their mother said, "Thea, look at you! You're pregnant!"

Thea smiled. Their mother said to Maidie, "Yes, I did. But you deserved a home with two parents. I was at loose ends for a long time. You have no idea. I'm better, thanks to my job, also maybe Hal."

Lucy said, "Let's get these clothes freshened up."

"My marriage to Hal had good . . . proportions," their mother added.

She scooped Hal's clothes off the bed and carried them to a washing machine in a tidy room just off the kitchen. She opened a cabinet. On the bottom shelf sat Tide and Downy. On the top shelf, stray kitchenware: a punch bowl, a popcorn popper, a three-tiered silver tray Maidie remembered from when she was little. Her mother took that? How had she fitted it into her suitcase? Maidie said, "Mom, is that the tray we used to use on Christmas?"

Her mother smiled. "No, it looks like it. That's why I bought it."

Someone was at the front door.

Maidie's mother let in a heavyset woman carrying a large, aluminum-cartoned casserole from the grocery store freezer section, a plastic bag of lettuce leaves, French bread wrapped in foil. "Already buttered and sprinkled with garlic powder," the woman said, wheezing, setting it all on the table. "When me and Galen heard your pitiful news, we thought, Lord, and threw together this meal, thinking you'd have family in from out of town."

Maidie's mother said, "Betty, these are my daughters."

Maidie, Lucy, and Thea nodded.

"Betty and Galen are neighbors," she said. "They loved Hal."

Betty said, "I never knew he was sick."

"Me neither." Maidie's mother averted her eyes. "Thank you."

Betty said, "I'll be at the funeral." She went home.

Maidie's mother slid the food into the refrigerator, next to plastic-lidded bowls, rolled-up tubes of Pillsbury dough, jars of olives and pickles, ketchup, mustard, and margarine in pop-top bottles. "Betty's a dreadful cook," she said, folding down a built-in ironing board. She plugged in the iron and set out a can of starch. "So I'm going to be a grandmother. I'd lost sight of the fact I was old enough." She looked up. "Maybe I am one?"

Maidie shook her head no.

"Lucy?"

"I'm trying to get pregnant," Lucy said.

Thea said, "You have to have sex every other day if you want to get pregnant in your thirties. Your egg production thins out."

Lucy glared at Thea.

"I suppose," their mother said, spritzing, steaming.

Lucy said, "Maidie's a career woman."

Maidie said, "So are you. And Thea sings in a band."

Thea said, "I'm really a housewife. Maidie runs a museum."

Maidie said, "It's not accredited as a museum." But the distinction between "museum" and "history collection" was moot here. "It's about the history of home life, domesticity," she added.

"A museum about domesticity," their mother said. "How odd. But I remember you liked curios when you were little. And colors—you would correct someone if they said aubergine instead of maroon."

Maidie smiled. She liked being with people who remembered such obscure facts, gimcrack details that commemorate the past, which is a vanquished, barricaded country, a quarantined homeland. Maidie said, "You keep a shipshape house, Mom. Do you remember that time you came to school and gave a speech for Mrs. Funderburk's class and brought a bottle of vanilla, a pepper shaker, and a can of coffee, because those were Madagascar's main exports?"

She seemed upset. "I honestly don't. Mrs. Funderburk?"

"She lived on the corner. Married to the sheriff?"

"Maidie had a major crush on her," Thea said.

Their mother said, "We need to go."

A half hour later, they pulled up in front of the funeral home in Maidie's mother's car—or Harold Foss's, Maidie supposed. She sat in front, next to her mother. Lucy and Thea sat in back. Their mother slipped the car into Park. "I'll let it idle and run these in. You wait." She crossed the parking lot, the stiff, neat clothes on hangers draped over one arm, a pair of boots tucked under the other. "I guess we'll see Hal in his casket, tomorrow at the funeral," Thea said. A few minutes later, their mother came out, the door to the funeral home opening to reveal a rectangle of light inside, then closing. She stopped and pulled a scarf from her coat pocket—her dress coat, she used to say. She put the scarf on, blew her nose in a hankie. When she got to the car, she said, "It's nice you're here."

The door to the funeral home opened again. Someone stepped out.

Lucy said, "Is that the undertaker?"

It turned out to be a priest, wearing a red windbreaker over black robes, and a knit stocking cap. He tapped on Maidie's mother's window. She rolled it down. "Hi there, Father Pete."

He said, "I'm glad to see you're not alone."

She said, "I have my girls with me."

"Call me in the days ahead if you need me."

Maidie's mother said, "You already did help."

"I'm glad I could."

"When you sang that song," she said.

His face stiffened. "I didn't sing any song."

Maidie's mother looked like a little girl, her shoulders hunched inward, hands gripping the top half of the steering wheel. "You did too," she said quietly. "You held my hand and sang that the sun sets but rises, one door closes and another opens."

"That was a poem my mother taught me." He looked relieved. "But I didn't sing it. I recited it to you, in the ER waiting room."

She said, "Well, it sounded singsong—maybe because of all the Latin, the chanting you do. To me it sounded like a song."

He patted her arm.

As she drove away, Maidie asked her, "Are you a Catholic now?"

"I started out as one, you know."

Maidie thought about this. "When did you become Lutheran?"

"When I met Pastor Larssen and I wanted to move to the United States. I remember her!" Maidie's mother braked suddenly for a red light. "Mrs. Larssen—that sanctimonious old bat. Although Pastor was decent. He never judged me." She sped onward.

In the back seat, Lucy said, "Those two left years ago. We have a young, up-to-date pastor now, with training in social work."

"Was Harold religious?" Thea asked.

Maidie's mother said, "Somewhat. But his real passion was AA. It's very big here in California. I went to a few meetings with him. I enjoyed it. People standing up and saying what's bothering them, but no one tells you what to do. You're anonymous."

"Are you an alcoholic?" Maidie asked.

"Not really."

"But you liked the meetings?"

"The talking, yes, and you don't lose your privacy." Her mother pulled into the driveway, then the garage. "June used to be my favorite month," she said, "but I won't think of it that way now."

Inside, Maidie slid the casserole into the oven. "I have a question."

Lucy exhaled, exasperated.

Maidie's mother hung her keys on a rack by the door. "All right. But let's turn the lights on first." She clicked on a bulb in the hood of the stove, two lamps in the living room, the flying-saucer-style chandelier over the table. "But I can't promise to answer every question. Hal used to say I'm a private person." She went to the living room and turned on the TV. Maidie felt ill-mannered, asking a new widow so many questions. But her mother must have expected some, calling her daughters to her side after twenty years. They sat down to dinner with the TV on, Barbara Walters interviewing a Malaysian prostitute with a numb-looking face, who said, "I am not a virgin, but I try in my heart to remain pure." Maidie's mother unfolded her napkin. "Go ahead."

Maidie felt ashamed of her curiosity, like a child staring at someone in a wheelchair, blurting: What's wrong with your legs? But she couldn't help it. "Why did you turn back into a Catholic?"

"Well, Hal was. And I picked that funeral home because they hold the service but they don't expect you to go with them to the cemetery."

"How long have you lived here?"

"I lived in San Francisco until the early eighties. Do you remember Eugene Fleiderhaus? He inherited his mother-in-law's house and let me stay there until he needed money and had to put it on the market. That horrible woman he married took half his savings! Anyway, I left that house and moved in with a

friend, but it didn't work out. And I couldn't afford the rents
there, so I moved to Orinda, which is west of Oakland, and I
got a job bartending in the clubhouse at a new golf course, and
I met Hal."

"Golfing?" Maidie asked. Poor Eugene, she thought.

"Hal was the landscaper."

Thea said, "I work at a golf course too."

Maidie's mother smiled.

"Was Hal from California?" Maidie asked.

"He grew up in that place in Nebraska, Boys Town."

On TV, someone was talking about a cult in which people
held off government agents with guns. Maidie wanted to ask
her mother about the lemon tree in moonlight, the pathway of
jewels, the day she wove a red cloth and looked out the window
and saw a boy. Did he grow up to be the barkeeper Maidie's dad
had mentioned? How had Maidie's mother survived the years
before she met Hal, who'd provided a car, a home, proportion-
ate love, anonymity? Maidie said, "When you were a little girl,
who taught you how to weave?"

Maidie's mother raised her eyebrows. "My father's housekeeper."

Lucy said, "I hope I'm not prying. Did Hal have a heart attack?"

Maidie saw instantly that Lucy's question was more suitable.
Her mother slid into the sanctioned role: widow. "A massive
heart attack. I was taking him to the hospital. He died in the
car, but the paramedics tried to resuscitate him in the grocery
store parking lot. They took him to the ER, and I called Father
Pete. No one would say he was dead, but I could tell." She stood
and stacked her dishes. Maidie toyed with her food. Her
mother's husband had died across the car seat from her—she'd
loved him in a meted-out way Maidie didn't understand. It was
sadder than Christmas, this chance to be near her mother, yet
separated by plies, layers. Her mother covered the casserole and

salad, put them in the refrigerator. "I love Saran Wrap," she said
suddenly. "Can you imagine how much I love it? You grew up
with it, but to me it's modern, so convenient." She turned on
her heel. "Now tell me about your lives—that's what I need to
hear."

Maidie felt her resistance thicken like sludge.

Lucy said, "I'm married. I'm working my way up in a company
called Vigortone, which sells feed additives to dairy farmers."

Maidie's mother said, "Not steroids and antibiotics?"

Lucy nodded, "Yes."

"Won't there be legislation against that soon?"

Lucy said, "If there is, it'll hurt my commissions."

Maidie's mother said, "Thea, what does your husband do?"

"He drives a Pepsi truck."

"Maidie?"

"I'm a curator for a museum."

"Are you married?"

"I have been," Maidie said, "twice."

Her mother looked like she had when Betty carried the casserole in and said she never knew Hal was sick. *Me neither.* Maidie's mother had glanced away. *Thank you.* "I would've helped
you with that if I could," she said now. "But I didn't have any
ideas or information that would have made a difference. I still
don't."

Thea said, "Maidie, since we're doing true confessions, I want
to know what happened to that big, jolly one who came to our
wedding."

Neville.

"He didn't want to stay married," Maidie said. "He didn't
like helping with the household chores. He stayed out all night
sometimes." She tried to sum it up. "I don't think he was in
love."

"Why did you get married?" Thea asked.

Maidie wanted to answer. She remembered how she'd proposed to Neville. He'd acted puzzled at first, then cooperative, then resigned.

Maidie's mother was looking at Maidie intently.

"The second one?" Lucy asked. "The one Dad had bad vibes about?"

"Jack Bonasso." But Maidie felt protective of Jack here—his sad details. His grandmother with her coat-hanger retribution, his brother with the chopped-off toes, his mother who got hung out to dry early but toughened and survived to speak of it. Maidie said, "He had a temper, and he couldn't hold down a job."

Thea said, "You had bad fights? But making up was sexy?"

Maidie said, "Not really." She remembered an ad in the newspaper, a person offering to beam up prayers to heaven for deceased loved ones via a backyard satellite dish, two hundred dollars a pop. Jack had shown the ad to Maidie, amused. She'd thought it was cruel. "You have to hand it to the fellow," Jack had said. "At least he knows that if God didn't want them fleeced, He wouldn't have made them sheep." Jack had a similar opportunistic take on work and courtship: he'd finagle a job he knew he didn't have the skills to keep; he'd win over a woman without worrying about how to sustain her. Maidie remembered the big engagement ring, the ten-installment plan. "We were both lonely," she said finally. "I moved around a lot. I didn't meet people like you do if you stay in the same area— through neighbors or friends. I met other people who didn't have connections, who were far from home."

Maidie's mother was nodding, her chin tilted. "You said a mouthful."

Thea folded her hands over her stomach. "I see. Both times, they should have stayed boyfriends but you went and married them." As if "boyfriend" and "husband" were clear-cut categories and mistaking one for the other was excusable. "You must have liked the idea of being married," Thea said. "Was there ever anyone you were crazy about, your true love?" Maidie thought: Not yet. And understood why questions made her mother tired.

Lucy spoke up. "But it all turned out fine. You have a good job, a nice house. Dad likes your new boyfriend, that old guy."

Maidie's mother stared out the window. "We should go to bed."

Lucy nodded. "I don't know how you hold up."

"Practice." Maidie's mother smiled.

While everyone vied for the bathroom, Maidie used the phone to call Rona, who answered right away: "I've been worried sick. Rex has been calling here for you. He thought you'd be home by now."

"I'm in California. My mother's husband died."

Rona grew quiet. "No kidding."

"Everything's fine. I wanted to leave this number with you."

Rona asked, "Where's Zip?"

Maidie said, "It's a long story. I'll tell you later."

Rona said, "Daddy hasn't had the biopsy yet. He keeps throwing up the barium. We think he's allergic, but the doctor doesn't believe us. I'm worried he'll have a heart attack before he even gets to the surgery. Mama's drinking with her anti-depressants—not a pretty sight. We met Evvy's significant other. We like her."

Maidie said, "I'm glad."

Rona said, "You need to call Rex. He left this number." She read off a number with an 800 prefix; Maidie wrote it down. Rona said, "Call him tonight. He's been so worried. I feel for him."

Maidie was puzzled. "I thought we were a bad mix."

"Sometimes we're all a bad mix. Or I was wrong. It was a theory."

"We might be a good mix?"

"No one is all the time. Maidie, he's worried."

"I'll get in touch with him," Maidie said.

She hung up and dialed Garth McHugh first.

He said, "Kiddo, you need to call Rex. He left his number. I got Lalo's home number, but I haven't had much luck."

"Why not?"

"He's not there."

"Where is he?" Maidie asked.

"I have no idea. No one speaks English there."

"His mother does."

"Not much. *Lalo not aquí*—I got that."

Maidie was worried.

Garth said, "I have news. I'm in love." Maidie thought of a headline in a newspaper she'd seen lying around the airport: FASCISTS IN LOVE, about the just-published youthful love letters of Joseph Stalin. "You'll never believe who—it'll be a big surprise."

Maidie said, "How's the History Collection?"

"Locked up, I imagine. I haven't been there. You haven't been gone a week yet. Are you still planning on reopening this month?"

She hesitated. "I don't think we should change the name, Garth."

"What?"

"The name—the Museum of Domestic History and Home Economy."

"You'll have trouble getting that past the board."

Maidie thought about Midge, Cass, and Z. They wouldn't care. "It's part of our history," Maidie said, "even if it is lackluster."

"Be sure to call Rex. He's having a conniption. By the way, don't worry about the college car. I sent someone to pick it up."

He hung up.

She tried to call Rex next, but she got a woman's voice, a recording: "Rough Rider Productions. If you know the extension of the party you're calling, please enter it now, or leave your name and number and someone will get back to you." Maidie didn't have a concise message ready, so she hung up. She put on a dark T-shirt and leggings and got into the sofa bed with her mother, who was sitting up in an ecru lace nightgown, filing her nails. Maidie pulled the covers back and said, "We have to stop meeting like this." Her mother smiled. "You haven't changed a bit."

"Really?" Maidie hoped she'd go on.

She said, "Maidie, I always knew you were all right. You had a good father, and he married that plain-looking woman, who I'm sure helped him. He had a lot to give. He loved me—or thought he did. Mrs. Larssen got overinvolved. I was staying with them, the Larssens, you know. You can imagine it sounded good to marry your father and move in with him. But there was a tone to the whole arrangement—Mrs. Larssen's, I guess— that I should be so grateful. I should cook and clean and keep my opinions to myself." Maidie's mother was taking pills out of three different bottles.

"What are you taking?"

"Prescriptions." She smiled, complacent.

Maidie read the bottles. One was Elavil, like Clima had. Also Paxil and Ambien. Their names sounded redundant. Maidie wondered if their functions were. She said, "Maybe you're over-medicated."

"If I am, I'm allowed to be right after my husband dies."

Keels over, Maidie thought. "Sorry I intruded." She slid down into the covers. She wondered about August. Was he going to be all right, and if he wasn't, how would Clima cope? Not in the managed, sealed-off way Maidie's mother did, her averted eyes.

"If you're having trouble getting to sleep, Maidie," her mother said, "maybe you'd like one of my pills? The Ambien is very nice."

"I'll settle down," Maidie said. She held still, courting sleep. Soon she was having a half-dream in which she knew she could halt negative progress by forcing herself awake. In the dream, Jack was coming back for her. He pulled up in front of her house in a pickup with appliances in back: a stove, a washer and dryer, the dealer tags still attached. He looked like a man in an

ad for better electricity, improved wattage. She woke. Her
mother breathed steadily; Maidie pictured her submerged in
deep, slightly toxic white sand. An idea came to Maidie—a result of all the information implanted today: the priest at the funeral home, the TV show on prostitutes and refugees, a
brief-lived, clear vision like she'd read Thomas Edison used to
have. She'd figure out a trend, she thought: that most people
who believed the apocalypse was imminent had been beaten a
lot and were thus accustomed to seeing bright light around the
edges of things, being smacked in the head unawares, so the
idea of the surprise Second Coming seemed normal. But after
she put her theory in words like that, she didn't see how she'd
prove it, or how it would help anyone, and she went to sleep.

She dreamed Rex Hurley was in the kitchen in her house in
Tucson, saying he had an older brother, which was news to Maidie, and this brother got up every morning to contact Kitty
Wells on the Internet. "Kitty Wells is dead," Maidie was saying,
wearing her favorite bathrobe, drinking coffee out of a red-and-
white china cup. Rex was saying, "But isn't that what the
Internet's for?"

Then she woke to the bustle of three women competing for
one bathroom. Thea came out of the bedroom, already dressed
for the funeral, carrying a framed photo. "This is Hal." Maidie
looked at it. Hal was handsome in a sunburned, 1950s movie
star way. He was grinning under a canopied table with Maidie's
mother, who seemed to be looking at something beyond the
range of the photo. "It was in her drawer," Thea said. Maidie's
mother came through in a sleeveless puce-colored dress. "I put
it away when I came back from the hospital," she said. "I
couldn't bear it."

At the funeral, Maidie sat next to her mother, wearing the
same dress she'd worn to Cocktails and Convocation and Hamlin Gwinn had said, "I like to see women in their finery." But
now she had a run in her stocking, and had she known she was

packing for a funeral when she'd left Tucson, she would have brought better shoes. Hal lay in the coffin, an ashen, flaccid replica of the healthy man in the photo, and Maidie remembered someone saying a bad coronary made the heart blow out like a used-up gasket. People started coming in. Jane Doe. "My best friend," Maidie's mother leaned ahead in her chair and whispered, raspy and authoritative, as if she hadn't introduced Jane Doe just yesterday. "Betty and Galen, neighbors," she whispered a minute later. Six people came in together. "Friends from AA," Maidie's mother whispered. "They loved Hal." One elderly man approached Maidie's mother, wiping his eyes on a blue-trimmed handkerchief. "I couldn't believe it," he said. "Just when Hal was happy, after all those years of searching." Maidie's mother responded, stiff, aloof, terrified, Maidie saw. "Yes, it was sudden."

Maidie realized how necessary these normative gestures were to her mother. She'd summoned her daughters as widow's props: to make the funeral and the irreparable fact that Hal was dead seem real, not staged; to support, stanch, and stay her. She'd asked them to come because she'd known them the longest. There wasn't anyone else she could have asked except Eugene, and Maidie wasn't sure he was alive. The tiny chapel filled up with the priest, outsized and hierophantic in his flowing robes, swinging a censer, flicking holy water. A eulogy followed, emphasizing the deceased's better qualities. "Hal Foss was a hard worker for whom work was play," Father Pete said. "He liked machinery. It's hard not to think of him in heaven with a bulldozer and backhoe." Maidie tried to follow this but got a strange picture of heaven as a golf course, or a smooth lawn with a rock garden and a fish pond. Was this a California version of eternity, in which the afterlife comprises your profession, Maidie wondered, and would she be cataloguing vases and butter paddles there?

They sang a hymn, "Just as I Am Without One Plea."

It was a Lutheran hymn—Maidie remembered it. They'd had it at Vera's funeral, she was sure, and maybe at Vera mother's funeral.

She started crying.

She remembered the time she'd watched the Miss Universe pageant and Miss Peru had said that if she won the crown she wanted to travel the world, stressing how important family love was. Maidie—having imagined Miss Peru pining for her mother, father, brothers, and sisters, her humble home in Lima—had begun to cry. And now she was crying so hard at Hal Foss's funeral that her wooden folding chair started to wobble and creak, and her mother poked Maidie with her elbow, offering a tissue. "Calm yourself down. Do you need to visit the ladies' room?"

In the car on the way home, Thea said, "Do you remember the time we went to see a movie about how Yogi Bear accidentally boarded a train that took him out of Yellowstone, and he lost touch with Booboo, and Maidie got so upset she made us leave the theater?"

Maidie said, "I don't remember that, no."

Back at the house, people were eating Wheat Thins, cold cuts, cheese, olives, little dried chunks of dates and figs—bereavement fare. Maidie's mother turned her TV to a station that projected images of waterfalls and seascapes while playing synthesized versions of pop standards. Maidie recognized "Summertime" and a diluted version of the Billie Holiday classic "There Is No Greater Love." Than I feel for you, Maidie hummed along. Her friend from graduate school in Arkansas, Mia of the flowing auburn tresses, had once written a paper on masochism and self-loathing as a recurring feature in Billie Holiday's lyrics. Maidie went into the bedroom to phone Rex.

A woman answered the phone.

"I'm trying to reach Rex Hurley. He works with props," Maidie said.

"If you can hold on a minute, we'll connect you."

The connection buzzed, crackled, then Maidie heard laughing, wind whistling, a horse's whinny. "Props." Rex's voice.

"Rex, this is Maidie."

"Hold on." More noise. Clomping around. Slam. He said, "I'm so relieved to hear from you. I know we parted arguing and I didn't leave you my numbers. I tried to call you before you left for Oklahoma, but we got behind schedule and I was on top of a mesa—for two sixteen-hour days in a row. I did write you a letter."

"I'm in California, at a funeral."

"That's what Garth told me. Who died, exactly?"

"My mother's husband."

Rex paused for a minute. "You weren't close to him, right? You never talk about your mother. I'm not sure I thought you had one."

"She hasn't been in touch with any of us for years."

Maidie could hear muffled noise. Rex said, "Everyone has strange relatives. It's hard when you have one for a parent—but it does make you self-reliant. Still, I wanted it easier for my sons."

Maidie had forgotten Rex had sons—one in Arizona, one out of state. She'd put off meeting them; Rex's mother too. She said, "August is in the hospital—August my neighbor, Clima's husband."

Rex said, "You've had a lot to deal with in a short time. I've been planning to take a few days off here. I can leave my staff in charge for that long. When do you think you'll be home?"

Maidie said, "You don't have to." How would she get Zip?

Rex said, "What's bothering you?"

She said, "This is how you earn your living—just stay and work. Plus, I ended up taking Zip to Oklahoma. He's still there."

"What?"

"It's complicated. I was planning to fly back there and pick him up. I guess I still will—and rent a car and drive home."

Rex said, "Listen. We have three dogs, two dozen horses, and eleven buffalo on this set, from California. I'm sure we have the technology to get one dog from Oklahoma to Arizona. Let me talk to someone. I know you don't like depending on people, but you can this once. You can owe me and return the favor."

Maidie said, "You mean fly straight home? Let me think about it. I need to talk to the person who's keeping Zip at his house."

Rex said, "Who has Zip?"

"It's so confusing, bad planning." So far she'd had strategy— the habit of reacting, rebounding—not forward motion.

Rex said, "Get in touch with me tomorrow."

They hung up.

Maidie went out into the living room. Her mother sat on the sofa, Father Pete on her right, Jane Doe on her left. Betty and Galen were in the love seat. The AA people clustered together on folding chairs. Maidie might have been too tired to differentiate, but everybody seemed to have one expression: weather-beaten cheer. Optimism as anesthetic, she thought. She sat at the dinette table with Lucy and Thea, thinking about a movie she'd seen a long time ago, the story of a family who'd survived the Great Depression. At the end, they're singing in church as the light turns pale yellow, and the camera pulls back to include the remaining churchgoers. The audience sees this is no ordinary Sunday, because everyone in the movie is fully congregated now, arms linked around hymnals, even if they've moved away, escaping the dust bowl, or have died out of season. New techniques fulfilling the old wish to counteract and cure death, palliating the knowledge that life declines—*going, gone, has been gone*—glossing over the fact, that we don't fraternize with the dead, that they're not fleshy and full-muscled, not while our will and instinct keep us here, above ground.

275

When Maidie got into the sofa bed with her mother that night, she asked, "Is Eugene Fleiderhaus still living?" Her mother said, "Yes, I get Christmas cards from him. He lives in Canada with a fishing buddy." Pulling the covers around as her mother swallowed Paxil, Ambien, and Elavil, Maidie said, "Is he gay?"

Maidie's mother turned her head. "Goodness! Where did you get that?" Her expression changed. "I know. From that barfly who thought she was marrying a rich hermit. No, that was a fabrication, her nasty way of explaining a certain dysfunction. Eugene loved Vera, and she loved him—one of those ideal matches you hope you'll find if you keep looking. From my point of view, Eugene and Vera were the only people who had enough imagination and experience to know Hector wasn't the expanding universe."

Maidie thought how her mother had gone from Madagascar to Minnesota, now to California, halfway home. They lay under the covers, in darkness. Maidie said, "Will you tell me about your mother?"

Maidie's mother said, sharply, "Maidie, I'm exhausted. I can't bring any of that back. I operate in terms of today, tomorrow."

Maidie said quietly, "But I need to know."

"Why?"

"I just do, a little."

"She left home when I was six."

Maidie waited for more. "You remember?"

"Not much. Sometimes you remember just what you used to remember—but dimmer, like a photocopy of a photocopy. I used to remember how I once sat in her lap and it felt cushioned and slippery. Maybe it was her soft skin, or she was wearing clothes that slid around, a silk dress over a slip. She couldn't have been very old. She was sixteen when my father married her. He was hard—hard for a young girl to understand or please."

Which girl? Maidie wondered. The bride? Or the child she'd left behind?

Maidie's mother said, "The housekeeper who took care of me said she'd asked my mother when she was packing, did she think about the people she was leaving, how they'd feel, and she said no, just No. I admire that, her willpower. She was raised in a hospital for poor people—old and sick people, or disturbed. So the nurses loved her, a healthy little girl. I suppose she was used to all of them, and it was hard to settle down with just us."

Maidie comprehended this: a grandmother who was raised by nurses, a mother who'd been raised by a housekeeper, and Maidie, who'd been cared for by her own mother some of the time, also by Vera, Mrs. Funderburk, Neena, then later on Opal Johnson, and Dodie in Virginia, now Rona and Clima. She'd had high hopes for her in-laws too. Neville's parents had been curious and flattered about Maidie's enthusiasm: "We like you too," they'd answer, surprised. Mrs. Bonasso, Jack's mother, saw the clinging neediness and turned Maidie away, telling Jack that Maidie was weak. What a relief, Maidie thought, that she wouldn't have to make good impressions on strangers now. But she needed to check in more often with her father, who was real, not substitute, and her mother, who'd turned up in this partial, half-formed way with an address, a phone number. Maidie said, "I'd like us to be in contact now. Don't move without telling me." A wave of love, admission. "I'm glad we had the years together we did," she said.

Her mother said, "That's what I told myself. Other times, I hated myself, thinking I should have given you up sooner, like they used to make unmarried mothers do. But I can't fix that. You had your father. He was unhappy, depressed maybe, but not mean."

"It can't cost too much to fly between here and Tucson."

Her mother said, "You would come here?"

Maidie considered it. "For visits."

She sensed her mother beside her in the dark, her worried,

skeptical face. Her mother said, "I suppose we will visit back and forth now. We have the biggest hurdle behind us—getting reacquainted. But I don't know what plans you have, or how able I am."

She rolled away, tugging the blanket, letting cold air in; then she rearranged, tucking it in, laying her arm over Maidie, a formal, familiar gesture that lasted a minute longer than Maidie expected. Maidie thought of Lucy and Thea in the next room, surrounded by suitcases, their somnolent, joined breathing. The streetlight shone in slivered angles around the edges of venetian blinds. The clock face above the table glowed dull, round. The microwave timer blinked blue, and the ice-water dispenser on the refrigerator was a cube of light. Maidie thought about peepholes, answering machines, privacy fences. About Victorian tufted furniture and thick-walled parlors. A long time ago, her mother had looked out the window at shiny paths that led nowhere: she'd left home as soon as she could. Too much shelter, ease, and buffering, proffered too soon, would have made us less resolute, less aware when at last we settle into place, Maidie decided, thinking of her mother and sisters, any orphan following moonlit bread crumbs. Or Job, who'd lived for years on weeds and dirt, forced nourishment, waiting. Not the Maidie would wish homesickness on anyone, itinerancy, vagabondage, no. She fell asleep.

Maidie sat in the front seat next to her mother, who idled in front of Terminal A at the Oakland airport. Lucy and Thea unloaded. "I'll clean house today," her mother was saying. "Tomorrow I'll go back to the office." She kept her hands on the wheel. Thea came around to the driver's side and leaned in to kiss her good-bye. Maidie's mother said, "Thanks for coming, Thea. I would have managed, but I felt better with you here. And you'll be a good mother—much better than I was." Thea stepped away from the car. Maidie's mother called over her shoulder: "Lucy, good-bye, thank you. Stay in touch." She pulled the car into traffic. Maidie turned to wave. Thea was already lifting bags, moving inside, but Lucy stood on the sidewalk, staring after the car. "We should have gotten out and wished them bon voyage," Maidie said. Her mother said, "No. Once you're on the road, big farewells drag you down." Maidie remembered saying good-bye to Dodie in Virginia, who'd cried: "Promise you'll write." To Opal Johnson in Nebraska, who'd inspected Maidie's apartment one last time and written the check for the deposit refund, weeping: "You've been more like a daughter than a renter." Both times, Maidie had felt trapped, stalled. Her mother stopped in front of Terminal B.

Maidie gathered up her luggage.

"It's wonderful we aren't strangers now, " her mother said, in her linen skirt and leopard-print shell, her feet in slim loafers. But her hair seemed lank, too depleted to shine. Her mouth trembled like an old lady's. She was exhausted, Maidie thought: Hal's dying, the funeral, the unaccustomed family feeling. She'd die herself someday. Later, not sooner, Maidie hoped.

"If you move, promise you'll let me know where you are."

"I do promise—there. But I don't have reasons to move now."

Buses and taxis pulled up. Travelers scurried by. There wasn't much time for divulgences. "You mean you used to have reasons?"

Her mother sighed. "These days, I don't feel so—I don't know—invisible. Back then, I thought it was right to give up custody. I'd made bad choices. You were better off without my influence. Besides, you had a stepmother. What is the word everyone uses? Bond. You needed bonding. And after a while, we had the habit of being apart, and when I thought about seeing you I wondered how we could. And if you hated me? Lucy does, a little."

Maidie thought her words seemed well-chosen—as if she'd always expected to be asked to justify the lost years. But she was right. Separation had become routine, a treadmill. Maybe places she'd been and company she'd kept those fogged-in years in San Francisco as she'd vied for a safe niche were best kept outside a child's ken. "Lucy doesn't hate you," Maidie said. She couldn't think of anything else to say.

Her mother said, "She's like your dad—wasting her life, sad."

But the last time Maidie saw her dad, he wasn't sad. Lucy might not always be. Maidie asked, "What about me—am I like you?"

"Goodness. I don't look at myself, or think how I seem or act. But you do like to travel, and we have the same sense of humor."

Someone behind them honked. Maidie wanted to ask: Did you miss me? Did you sometimes ache, missing me? (Maidie wanted her *longing* requited, if not her love.) Did you know your departure was just the first crisis? Next, we had the aftermath, the vacuum in space and time you used to occupy. Bad weather blew in. We didn't batten down for it. We scattered. But Maidie didn't say any of this. The car behind them honked again.

Her mother leaned across the seat, a muscle in her cheek twitching. "We'll be in touch." Maidie nodded. Suddenly, she was glad to be getting out of the car. She wanted time to consider how much she'd believe her mother's theories about the past, assurances about the future. And would Maidie believe herself—her own reasonable but elaborate fantasies about reunion? For years, she'd stood outside other people's families, waiting to be asked in. Now she was in the middle of her own, and the rise and drop of hope and memory seemed fatiguing. "Good-bye," she said as her mother drove away. Maidie found her gate, checked in, settled down for the wait.

She was reading *Discover* magazine, an article about

pheromones. Researchers had asked women to smell sweat-shirts worn by a variety of men, and they found that sweatshirts worn by men whose genetic compositions were markedly differ-ent from the subject's genetic composition were generally per-ceived as having an attractive scent. "Rugged," one subject logged in. Also: "masculine," "sexy," "reminds me of my boyfriend." But a man whose genetic composition was similar evoked responses like "sweaty," "stale," "needs a shower." Re-searchers speculated that the biological imperative to reproduce in a genetically sound way—exogamously, outside one's own circle—accounted for this pattern. Men smelled good if they were genetically "other." Once women were pregnant, how-ever, responses reversed themselves: pregnant women perceived the smell of men with similar genes as pleasant and turned up their noses at the smell of men with dissimilar genes. When a woman was pregnant, the study seemed to say, exogamous genes were no longer biologically necessary, and the desire to be surrounded and protected by one's own clan took over.

Lucy and Thea materialized. "Our plane doesn't leave for hours," Thea said, "so we looked up Tucson on the monitor and found your gate." Maidie smiled. She wondered if she looked like her mother—gracious, weary, her cheek muscle twitching, too much family interaction after years alone. Lucy and Thea sat down. "Traveling makes me tense," Lucy said, arranging her suitcases in a protective circle. Thea rested her hands on her stomach and said, "Maidie, you never told us why you were in Oklahoma."

"I was at a conference, and a job interview."

Lucy said, "A job interview for Oklahoma? Don't take it. Ok-lahoma is the South. They eat hog skin, and okra, which is a weed."

Maidie said, "Everyone doesn't. Besides, I don't plan to move."

Thea said, "You don't?"

Maidie said, "I don't have reasons to move right now."

Lucy said, "Maidie, seeing you was the best part of this trip." Maidie was surprised: it was? Lucy glanced right, then left. Was she on the lookout for pickpockets? She said, "People in Hector always ask about you—how's my big sister? And I say you travel a lot for your career, so you're too tired to travel home."

Maidie was surprised at this picture of herself: a career woman exhausted by travel. She said, "Lucy, until recently I've been flat broke, working odd jobs and going to school. And I had a knack for picking husbands who spent more money than they made. I've never traveled much. I've moved a lot, trying to make a better life. But I like my job. I'll start coming home, promise."

Thea said, "Bring your boyfriend."

Lucy said, "Let us be the judge this time—if he's good enough."

Maidie said, "I might come when Dad gets married."

"What are you talking about?" Lucy said.

"Dad's marrying that woman, right? Paula?"

Lucy said, "He told you before he told me? After all I've done!"

Thea said, "Lucy's going to take over Dad's insurance business. Isn't that perfect? Can you picture her in twenty years?"

Lucy scowled. "I'm not down in the doldrums."

Thea said, "Of course not," soothing.

Maidie's plane was at the gate. She hugged Lucy and Thea good-bye. Thea said, "Love you." Lucy nodded. "That goes for me." Maidie gave them a smile, which turned genuine. "Same here."

She boarded, found her seat, buckled in. She pictured her house in Tucson, its hammock and patio, sand and cacti. She'd see Rex tonight. And Zip. Yesterday Maidie had phoned Hamlin Dwinn and told him Rex would be calling to fine-tune plans for getting Zip home, but basically Hamlin would take Zip to the airport—if that wasn't too much trouble? A transportable pen was waiting for Zip, and he'd fly to Tucson in a part of the hold engineered for traveling pets. Hamlin said, "I have another idea—you take the job I've offered, and I'll keep Zip until you get here." Maidie laughed; this was one of those remarks you treated like a joke. "I'd miss him," she'd said, picturing Zip's sleek face, his complex dog expressions. "Is he okay?" Hamlin said, "Are you kidding? We go for long walks at night. If you don't want him, I'd finally have a reason to get rid of the condo and buy a house." Maidie laughed again, hollow. "Rex will call you about Zip. When I get home, I'll give your job offer serious thought."

She meant when she got home, she'd turn it down. She'd been too tired to say so tactfully.

Her seatmate settled in beside her, an old man carrying a *People* magazine; the cover photo was of a pro-football player on his way to an arraignment hearing on assault charges, and he was wearing a mink coat dyed orange to match his hair. Maidie thought about this recent evolution beyond the era in which fame was a form of elevation, PR an articulation of ideals. Today's celebrities distinguished themselves by flouting perfection, not epitomizing it. People who otherwise declared themselves worried about the loss of traditional values bought the magazines and watched the shows that perpetuated the myth of aberration as authenticity. This fascination with exotic people who broke rules by which ordinary citizens abided was like the nineteenth-century fascination with freak shows. The appeal of "freaks," Maidie had once read, was that they were extrinsic. They came from the outlands and passed through middle America, here, gone. In times of rapid change, "freaks" allowed people to reassure themselves, by way of comparison— with a bearded lady, a tattooed dwarf, a man who'd married and buried ten wives—that they were still in the center, even if the center itself had shifted.

Her seatmate said, "Are you from Oklahoma?"

"What?"

"I said, Are you from Oakland?"

She'd heard wrong: Oakland, not Oklahoma. "No, I live in Arizona."

"Heading home, then?"

"Yes." But she didn't want to talk. It used to seem important to exert the side of her personality that would make an old man get off the plane, saying: I met a nice young lady! But Maidie wasn't young, and maybe she used to talk to strangers because she hadn't talked often enough to family. Maidie gave the man a polite smile and pretended to rifle through her bag like the distracted career woman Lucy had imagined her to be. She found the note Lucy had handed her when their plane first landed in Oakland—Laree's address and number. Maidie pictured Laree: a blue dress, hair pushed behind her ears, her face lit with curiosity. Did Laree regret her abortion, Maidie wondered, now that Laree, like Maidie, was almost too old to conceive? Egg production *thins,* Thea's word. When the plane leveled into flight, Maidie found herself staring at the phone mounted on the seat in front of her. Too expensive, she told herself. But she took out a credit card and punched in the number anyway. When Laree picked up, Maidie recognized her voice—flat, amused, husky.

"Laree, this is Maidie Giddings." Her maiden name.

"Eeeee! Maidie Giddings. Hooray!"

Maidie laughed, remembering she used to be embarrassed by Laree's sporadic enthusiasm. Maidie said, "The last time we talked, you'd divorced Phil and remarried. You were a geek magnet."

"Maidie, my second husband was so weird. Where are you?"

Maidie said, "I'm on a plane, coming back from my mother's in California. I had to go to a funeral. But I live in Arizona now."

Laree said, "You were at a funeral? No one you were close to, I hope. What happened to you in Virginia? You didn't sound good."

Maidie remembered Laree's late-night phone call. Jack had been in the next room, absorbing TV mayhem—amplified crashes, screeching tires, gunshot blasts. "My advice," Laree had said, "is to shake things up." Now Maidie said into the compact air phone, far above and past that: "I shook things up. I took your advice."

"I hope it was good advice. Hold on."

Maidie heard crying.

When Laree came back, Maidie said, "Is that a baby?"

"Yes, a little girl."

"You're married?"

"Not exactly. I got pregnant on my thirty-ninth birthday, on a date, our third date. Boy, getting back into the dating scene at my age—that wasn't easy. I called this eight hundred number in the paper, which advertised that girls didn't have to pay. I'd thought it was a computer dating service, but it turned out to be a hot line for people who want kinky sex—in this day and age. Can you imagine? With AIDS and all? I guess everyone uses a condom."

"Except you," Maidie said, laughing. "You mean you met this guy from that ad?" The man reading *People* looked at Maidie, uneasy.

Laree said, "God, no. It was a blind date. Except it wasn't blind by then, because it was our third. His name is Fritz."

"Fritz?" Maidie said. "Do you have a job?"

"I'm a waitress, at night. Fritz takes the baby."

"But you're not married?"

"We don't even live together."

"You love him?"

"I do. Maidie, if you're calling from a plane, this is costing you an arm and a leg. Give me your number, and we'll talk when you're back on the ground." Maidie had that split sensation she'd had when she'd left her mother at the curb. She wanted to hang on, and yet the past had resurfaced too quickly.

Maidie gave Laree her address and number. Laree said, "Maybe I can come for a visit." Maidie thought about taking Laree—and maybe her baby in a stroller—to the Pima Air and Space Museum, the San Xavier del Bac Mission, the Museum of Domestic History and Home Economy. She'd point out the Santa Catalinas to the north, the Rincons to the east. She'd introduce Rona, Harve, Clima, and August. And the next time Maidie started staring at the horizon as if it kept a secret she hadn't uncapped, a paradise at which she hadn't arrived, she'd call Laree. Or when she started cleaning house so vigorously she broke knickknacks, or smashing goblets against a wall because she couldn't tell if Rex was ingratiating or dear . . . When Maidie last spoke to him on the phone, he'd said, "I know what your eyes look like when you're tired, a bird's eyes." Yes, the next time Maidie wanted to clean out, upgrade, and replace, she'd call Laree for revised tactics.

"We'll talk in a few days," Laree said. They hung up.

The sky: endless turquoise.

The plane descended into Tucson and rolled to its gate. Passing through the chute that led inside, Maidie felt dizzy, enervated. In this flimsy white tube that rocked as passengers treaded through it, light seemed thin, caustic, a bleach that steeped them, stripping away superficial blemishes, leaving old ones visible, indelible. It was the same sun that beat down in Moraga, California, but it beat hotter here. She emerged into a crowd: a family wearing Day-Glo T-shirts that said HOOKED ON ARIZONA; a young gallant with a sheaf of roses; two girls with Mylar balloons that said WELCOME and GRANDMA. Maidie remembered Rex saying he didn't like plane travel, the rapid segues. She looked for Rona, who'd said she'd meet Maidie's plane, but Maidie didn't see her. She followed arrows, GROUND TRANSPORTATION, to find a taxi.

"Maidie!"

She looked up. Rona's daughter Evvy was hurrying down the

corridor in overalls and a gray fedora, her blond hair swinging. "Are you ready? Mom asked me to come and pick you up."

Maidie loaded her suitcase into Evvy's station wagon with its bumper stickers. VISUALIZE WHIRLED PEAS. IF IT'S NOT ONE THING IT'S A MOTHER. Evvy got in, started the engine. Maidie felt like she was speeding ahead still, momentous, though the station wagon idled. She wasn't sure what day it was. Saturday. She'd have tomorrow to rest, then back to work on Monday. Then the grand reopening in two weeks, June 25. Maybe the AAM had responded and the museum was accredited now, and its name didn't have to change. Evvy pulled out of the parking lot, out of the airport.

The streets looked like streets everywhere. Yards, houses, sidewalks, virtual neighborhoods. Maidie stared through the windows. Here was Speedway Boulevard; she focused until it looked right, familiar. Here was the store, Gonzo's, where Maidie had stopped to buy a Christmas tree and got Zip instead. Evvy said, "You must be tired. Mom said you've been through hell." Maidie's ears popped. She remembered something from a magazine, or one of those TV shows beaming out over passengers (how teeming and excessive information was), something about conversation and how the failure of one person to inquire after the other within twenty minutes was a sign of narcissism. Maidie didn't want to be narcissistic. "Tired?" she said, tired, robotic. "How about you?" Evvy looked disconcerted. Then Maidie remembered Evvy had just "come out with it," as Rona had said. Maidie kept talking, trying to make her remark seem innocuous. "We keep such a hectic pace today," she added, an awkwardly trite reflection, Maidie knew, and historically tunnel-visioned too. People had been complaining about life's pace for centuries.

Evvy said, "True. Right now I'm trying to simplify."

Evvy parked the car in front of the house she used to share with Cindy-June before Cindy-June got married, which sat next to Rona and Harve's house, which was two doors down from Clima and August's, which was across the street from Maidie's. Maidie stared at her house, an adobe box in the center of a silty lot, less mysteriously elegant than Maidie had pictured it this week she'd traveled—one night in New Mexico, two in Oklahoma, three in California. Meanwhile, a climatic change must have occurred, because tall, wiry weeds had sprung up at the sidewalk's edge, the patio's rim, and Maidie's house looked like a down-scale and especially dusty version of Michael Landon's Little House on the Prairie.

"Mom wants you to eat dinner at her house," Evvy said.

"Let me put my bags inside."

Maidie's house smelled stale, like mothballs or moldering cabbages—the way Eugene and Vera's house used to smell after Vera got too sick to clean. Maidie opened a window. Her answering machine blinked steadily. When she played back her messages, they were all from Lalo. 1. (Clearing his throat) I see you're not there. But I have something to say. 2. I can tell you're not there, but I want to tell you I don't need a ride. I've changed my life. 3. When you get this, I'm at a truck stop in Las Cruces. 4. Are you there? I don't see why hitchhiking is illegal. 5. When you're there, rest assured I'm home at the Coop Gallery. 6. Come to the Domestic Museum for a surprise.

Maidie went back outside and crossed the street to Rona's. The sun cast itself down, incandescent, and Maidie remembered that Arizona's first economic boom had occurred in the 1920s, when northern doctors sent TB patients here to convalesce, repair. She opened the door to Rona's, and people yelled: Welcome! Salutations! Hello! Crepe-paper streamers spanned from one corner to the other. Cindy-June, who looked more pregnant than when Maidie last saw her, her two kids, and her husband who looked like Jay Leno or the fat Elvis, stood near a table loaded with pots, bowls, and platters. Buster smiled, gap-toothed, sans toupee. Clima sat on a stool, her silver hair gleaming. August sat next to her in a rocking chair, a crocheted blanket over his knees. Rona smiled, her brown eyes shiny, liquid. Harve put out his hand and said, "Miz Bonasso. We're all glad you could make it."

Maidie said, "You shouldn't have gone to any trouble."

Rona looked confused. Then she doubled over, laughing. "This isn't for you. Not that we're not happy you're back, but you've only been gone a week." She straightened up. "But we did want you to celebrate with us. Daddy got through the biopsy, and his tumor was benign. He's weak, but he'll be okay. Mama has missed you. She's so used to your company." Maidie looked at Clima, who seemed happy but remote, appreciating the reprieve but facing the future: August would be fine, but only for a few more years.

Rona pulled Maidie to a corner. "So you stayed at your mother's house. Was this the mother you haven't seen for twenty years? How did it feel," Rona asked, her eyebrows darting up, "under the circumstances?"

Maidie considered her answer. "I don't think it's what you'd picture," she said. She was thinking of a made-for-TV movie, actors rushing into each other's long-lost arms, mutually gratified.

Rona said, "It was painful?"

Maidie looked around the room. Buster smiled and waved. Maidie remembered a talk show she'd seen about adopted children finding birth parents and vice versa. Some reunions looked tense but cathartic. Others seemed laced with blame, banishment, recrimination. "Maybe it was fairly typical," Maidie said. "My mother seems like a cousin or an aunt I haven't seen lately. Except she used to be my mother. It's like I had a mother and then I didn't. And now I have a partial one—one-quarter of a mother."

"I guess that's progress." Rona frowned, her vicarious fulfillment incomplete. Then she brightened. "You can't eat here."

Maidie looked at the table. "Why not?"

"Rex called and said not to let you. He's taking you to dinner."

Someone knocked at the door—a jaunty woman wearing a tank top tucked into patterned boxer shorts. When she came inside, Maidie saw that the design on her shorts was fish silhouettes, those fisher-of-men symbols people print on business cards and mount on car trunks. She had a twelve-pack hoisted onto her shoulder, Diet Slice. Rona said, "Maidie, this is Pamela, who is Evvy's significant friend. Pamela, this is our neighbor Maidie."

Pamela set the twelve-pack down and smiled.

Rona said, "I found those baby pictures of Evvy you asked about."

"I can't wait," Pamela said.

Maidie watched Evvy in the window seat. In one fell swoop, she'd told her family she was gay and brought home a true love, a helpmate, a potential daughter-in-law. She'd simplified: no secrets. But she'd complicated too. Now Pamela would come to know not just the adult Evvy, her cultivated good graces, but the fumbling, uncertain child she used to be, all the vestigial household strife—the shelter and apportioned freedom, push, tug, pull—still exerting force and effect. Evvy and Pamela had chosen and declared, a sacred, crucial transition. (Maidie would postpone her own indefinitely now: she wanted a *really* long engagement.) And Evvy and Pamela were making a second sublime leap of faith and engineering, joining not just each other but the amalgamating family, a jerry-built unit that—*believe!*—might endure, multiply, generate. Or tumble down as it took on dents, impressions, new alterations. Certainty wasn't required, or attainable. Evvy looked sober and chastened, but when Pamela sat down beside her, her face creased into a glad smile.

Rona said, "Mama quit taking her antidepressants because we told her she couldn't drink and take antidepressants at the

290

same time. So she opted to drink—which is fine if she drinks moderately."

Clima was pouring herself a thimble-sized glass of good tequila from the bottle with the horseshoe; she never settled for less. She said, "Maidie, come sit with me." When Maidie did, Clima said, "I myself have never minded the gays. Ann Landers has been saying for years they're like us." Maidie glanced across the room to see how Evvy and Pamela were reacting to Clima's declamation.

They didn't seem to mind.

Clima said to Maidie, "I was so afraid when August was in the hospital that I came home at night and walked through the house, holding the pillow from my bed and singing hymns. Not that you could have helped me, but I'm glad you're home now." Then Clima pulled back, stared at Maidie's face, and slapped it hard.

Maidie was shocked, stung. Her logic swarmed: Clima was mad because Maidie had been gone! Clima was mixing pills and alcohol!

August said, "What on earth?"

"A gnat." Clima reached over and lifted one off Maidie's cheek.

August scowled.

Clima said, "I could have been gay."

August said, "You could not. Be quiet."

Buster said, "No insult to Evvy or her friend, and I don't have a bias against the gays, but I get queasy if they touch in public."

Rona said, "We get queasy if *you* touch in public, Buster."

Harve said, "Everyone, be nice."

Evvy and Pamela stood up. Evvy said, "We have to run some errands." Pamela added, "But we'll be back. I want to see those photos."

Evvy rolled her eyes.

Clima sipped tequila. "Maidie, has Buster mentioned the circumcision?"

Maidie wondered again if Clima was mixing intoxicants.

Cindy-June said, "Mind your p's and q's, Grandma."

Buster said to Maidie, "You remember that book I bought at a yard sale—*A Glance at Madagascar?* I don't know where I got the idea you were from there. I thought you'd like it for a souvenir. Then I read it myself. It sounds like a fascinating place."

Clima said, "I'll say."

Buster said, "In some tribes . . . " Then he stopped.

In some tribes, what? Maidie wondered. August looked exasperated. Harve, oblivious. Rona was putting food in the refrigerator. Clima winked at Maidie. "They swallow it," she said.

Buster blushed. "Cindy-June is right. It's not fit to discuss."

Clima said, "Someone swallows the foreskin. Right, Buster?"

Rona said, "Mama, you're disgusting."

But Maidie remembered reading this, in her own book she'd checked out from the library and kept so long she had to buy it, *The Bloody Island.* "It's an adolescent circumcision," Maidie explained. "The swallowing symbolized that as the boy turned into a man, the memory of his childhood self would remain inside the elder who's raised him. But that tribe has been pretty much wiped out, if I remember. I don't think your book is current, Buster."

No one said anything.

Then Rona whispered to Maidie, "I think it's Pamela who will try to get pregnant, not Evvy."

Maidie nodded, wondering: how? But didn't ask.

"I didn't ask how," Rona said, worried.

Rex's flatbed pulled into the driveway, loud, fast, creaky—a familiar sound. When he first came through the door, he looked as beloved and reassuring as one of Maidie's favorite earthly goods, she thought, as comforting as a prized, polished belonging she'd moved from place to place, a forty-, fifty-, or sixty-year-old relic with which she'd furnished her house, a facsimile of coziness. Rex's kindly, other-generational ways—scooping an unasked-for second helping onto her plate, arranging her new-comer's tour of Tucson, advising her that she had one family, al-beit imperfect, and had better belong to it as best she could—had seemed uncomfortably oldfangled but steadfast too. She stared at his creased face and flyaway ponytail, his gray-blue eyes, and realized she'd been scraping against just the first layer, callously regarding Rex as a slighted convenience, an overlooked milestone, and under the surface she'd no doubt find a complicated miscellany, a hybrid of stellar qualities inter-mixed with foibles and excess: generosity and patience, yes, but spite and impatience now and then, too, and an occasional streak of melancholy or bewilderment, far more than the genial, forbearing one dimension she'd allowed herself to know.

Rex yawned, too tired to assume formal courtship mode. "How is everyone?" he asked, staring at Maidie. "Are you ready?"

"Have fun," Rona said.

Clima called out, "We love you."

Maidie said, "Same here." Crossing the yard to Rex's truck, Maidie had a brief spasm of worry she wouldn't have anything to say. Rex put his hand on her shoulder. "You must be tired."

Then Maidie saw Zip in the back of Rex's flatbed, hunched and nervous in a cage. Zip locked eyes with Maidie as she ap-proached, rhythmically thumping his tail as if to indicate he knew they'd been on bad terms, or he wouldn't have ended up in a cage, and that Maidie was on the verge of forgiving him. When she said, "I've missed you," Zip sat up, thrust his chest out. Rex unlocked the cage, and Zip leapt down. He didn't scramble or scurry. Stately, he stood next to Maidie and barked *basso profundo.* This woke up Rex's dog, Guapo, who stuck his head out of the truck window, his glazed-over, beady eyes blinking. *Yap. Yap.*

Rex said, "We'd better put them in the house if we're going to dinner." Maidie opened her front door, and Zip stuck his head inside, looked gratefully around, scooted under the kitchen table, and fell asleep. Rex put Guapo into the bathroom and shut the door.

Walking back to the truck, Maidie said, "Can we drive past Lalo's? He left a message he was home, but I want to make sure."

When Rex stopped in front of Lalo's a few minutes later—in front of the What-A-Burger turned Coop Gallery—Lalo was sitting outside in a lawn chair, wearing a white sleeveless undershirt with plaid shorts, clip-on shades over his black-framed glasses, and drinking a Heineken. Leaning against one of the Coop Gallery's plate-glass windows was the green papier-mâché surface with a lump: *A Day in the Life of Maida Bonasso*. The flatness represented Maidie's previous life, Lalo had once explained, and the lump the interrupting divergences and shifts that took place the day she moved to Arizona. Lalo stood up. "How nice you came to visit," he said, nodding at Maidie, shaking Rex's hand.

Maidie said, "You hitchhiked?"

"I left early," Lalo said. He took out his wallet and returned the twenty dollars Maidie had given him in San Jon. He cleared his throat. "I didn't need bus money. I feel sad for my mother. But I can't help her now. Say, I had the idea to give you this." He pointed at *A Day in the Life of Maida Bonasso*.

Maidie paused. "Thanks," she said finally. "But I think it's a museum piece, too imposing for just a house. I've always liked that one." She pointed at the cracked leaded-glass window mounted in a frame, *How to Make a House a Home*. "I'd like to buy it." She'd pictured it swinging from an olive branch above her patio.

Lalo said, "I have a surprise at the museum."

"We're on our way to a restaurant," Maidie said.

"This will take one minute."

Maidie looked at Rex, who shrugged. "Lalo could eat with us."

A few minutes later, the three of them pulled up at the museum in Rex's truck. He parked next to the original, granite sign, which said THE MUSEUM OF HISTORY AND HOME ECONOMY. Except a banner was tacked over it: *Women's History Collection Temporarily Closed for Renovation.* I'll never change the name to that! Maidie thought, feisty and overdramatic like Scarlett O'Hara. The museum looked strange but lovely, its adobe walls the color of egg yolks, its octagon-shaped windows that let light into the cloakroom shimmering in the twilight glare, its tile roof, which looked brown in the daytime, turning crimson as the sun waned. A hot, swift wind blew, flicking sand against Maidie's legs.

When they opened the door and stepped inside, the museum's peculiar smell buoyed up, that dank, velvety intermingling of chalk, Pine Sol, dampness, reams of paper, ink and coffee, a mishmash scent that tantalized Maidie, propelling her back into irretrievable time. She felt like pledging allegiance. Then she understood. The Museum of Domestic History and Home Economy smelled like school. School days! She remembered leaving home before the sun rose, following the sidewalk furrowing between snowbanks, the squeaking snow pack under her boots a reminder the thermometer was registering low, low. She'd drop Lucy and Thea at their school, then walk three blocks to her own. When she opened the doors, the smell of hush and order—happy, illuminated hours, teachers with kindly faces on tall bodies.

Lalo said, "Let me go first, for the surprise."

Maidie and Rex waited in the vestibule while Lalo went in. Rex rested his fingers on Maidie's back. "I suppose you're hungry." Maidie started to say she wasn't, not yet, then realized from Rex's face, the wan, white color his skin had turned, *he* was hungry, tired too, and these anxious solicitations were a covert way of nourishing himself. She said, "We'll go soon."

"Dearly Beloved!" Lalo said.

Music surged—brash brass, tinkly piano, metal brushes scuttling delicately across drum skins. Lalo turned up the lights, and Maidie saw that while she'd been at the Multi-State American Studies Conference in Oklahoma and Hal Foss's funeral in California, Midge's friend had somehow delivered the wedding dresses and various dressmaker forms on which to display them: six wicker, wasp-waisted, Victorian female ideals; one headless hourglass with pink rubber stubs for arms and a neck; one iron-and-steel dressmaker mannequin with hinged shoulders and a crank in back. Lalo turned the crank, and the form's bosom rose, full-busted; he lowered it again. "Adjustable," Lalo said, "to simulate all figures." Rex moved one of its metal arms to an ebullient, upward position, as though this steel bride draped in pearl-colored taffeta, her globelike head swathed with organza, were tossing a bouquet, waving farewell. Rex said, "It's like one of our articulating dummies. We use them for corpses in battle scenes."

Lalo cleared his throat and said, "Midge called me at home and asked me to unlock the museum so she could bring over the dresses. And then she called that woman who slept with a country-western singer and he gave her his boots—I can't think of the name."

"Willie Nelson," Maidie said.

"Cass Willoughby," Lalo said. "She dressed the dummies."

Maidie glanced at the portrait of Cass's grandmother: Alma Kayser Willoughby, with her flat hair and forbidding black dress. Maidie had read somewhere that because death was once so prevalent and mourning rites were so strict, some women wore black their entire lives. The music grew loud, a jazz version of *Lohengrin*'s wedding march. Maidie looked at a cream-colored dress with a low neck. She recognized Midge's handwriting on the note pinned to the wall behind it. "The nineteenth was a modest century," Midge had written, "though décolleté was briefly fashionable in the 1860s. Note the picot pattern of the veil." Another dress was made of white satin, but the rest were gray or brown, wool and linen. "Most brides opted for a practical garment that would serve them in the less ephemeral, more daunting days after the wedding was over and marriage commenced," Midge's note read. Maidie thought about the bodies that filled these dresses—sweat and perfume, desire and disappointment. The wedding march ended, and a soprano sang: *Though devotion rules my heart, I take no vows.* The museum turned dark except for the frazzled brides backlit by one of those electric candles people set in windows at Christmas, its bulb pulsing, a faulty connection.

The pop song ended, and Maidie said, "This is wonderful, Lalo, but we'll have to make small changes before the grand reopening."

"I know that." He growled.

They went back outside to get into Rex's truck. Dust swirled across the parking lot in short eddies. These are the hot summer winds Clima hates, Maidie thought. She looked down the street at a willowy blonde holding hands with a thick-waisted man, her skirt puffing as the wind gusted. "I'm so tired," Maidie told Rex, "that for a minute I thought I saw Zora Coles and Garth McHugh holding hands." But as the couple neared, Maidie saw that it *was* Garth and Z. Garth's face had erupted out of its fixed distemper into daredevil thrill. "I knew you'd be surprised," he said. Z.'s hair looked glossy, her face glowing, pink. "Maidie, you're back. I'm dying for a tête-a-tête."

Maidie stared. A florid tattoo was climbing out of Garth's crewneck sweater toward his ear; Z. had one on her left clavicle. "You have matching tattoos," Maidie said, uneasy.

Garth said, "I'm in love, but I haven't taken leave of my senses."

Z. said, "They're temporary. They wash off."

Maidie was relieved. Short engagements were a fairly new custom. For centuries, long engagements had prevailed.

Garth punched Rex's shoulder. "How's the movie? Are you shooting near Pia Oik? It must be hot as Hades this time of year."

Maidie tried to picture Rex's house in Pia Oik: well water, electricity, but no roof. Rex said, "I find shade where I can."

Lalo growled.

Rex said, "We need to go eat, right away. You're welcome to join us."

Garth and Z. promised to meet Maidie, Rex, and Lalo at the restaurant, which turned out to be a squat building five miles outside Tucson, nestled below foothills. Rex parked his truck, ushered Maidie and Lalo up the sidewalk toward the double doors. When he opened them, air-conditioning wafted up, cool, welcome. A porcelain bathtub filled with ice and raw oysters sat by the door. Diners at tables draped with linen tablecloths clinked glasses sedately. "I wouldn't recommend eating outside on the patio," the maître d' said, "because of the wind." Maidie looked outside. Canopied tables rocked and bobbed. Umbrellas flapped, twisting. "Outside, yes," Lalo said. "We'd like to be there."

They sat down at a round table.

Above their heads, pipes circled the patio and rained down mist—for coolness, comfort. "Like a grocery store produce section," Lalo said. "So peaceful." His face glistened round and happy, not wary and angular like when Maidie had left him in San Jon.

"But windy," Rex said, holding on to the bucking table, his ponytail flapping like a wind sock. A waiter arrived with a plate of oysters. Maidie was ravenous. The oysters slid down, wet, wobbly, delicious. As Rex poured champagne, he said Guapo was getting too old and sick for the movie-set lifestyle. "It's too unstable—too much moving around. I'll probably have to put him to sleep soon," Rex said, worried. Then Lalo told Maidie he had an offer for a job arranging products for advertising shoots. "Every day, I would make a still life that was artistic but commercial too. What do you think?" As the waiter described a special—one big platter, and everyone scrambles to eat—Garth and Z. came through the door, and Maidie thought about all the states in which she'd lived, the people she'd known, some of them alive and accessible still, others dead or misplaced. Z.'s dress billowed like Marilyn Monroe's. Garth's hair, longish on top where he combed it over his bald spot, whipped and twirled. "We can't eat out here in this weather," he said, jaw muscles grinding.

"Try to be spontaneous," Z. said, rolling her eyes as she did in trustee meetings when Garth failed to appreciate history's nuances.

"Ouch!" Rex clapped his hand to his mouth. He's lost a tooth, like Buster! Maidie thought. How inauspicious.

But the lump Rex pulled out of his mouth was purplish, misshapen. "A half-formed pearl," the waiter said. "People find them all the time, but this is the biggest I've seen." An airborne champagne glass crashed against the wall. Rex stared at the pearl—a hard case forged around infernal irritation—and Maidie got a glimpse of what his face must have looked like forty-odd years ago: rapt, attentive. As time passed, she thought, there'd be more funerals to attend, fewer survivors to provide the ancillary scraps of the past, communal recollection. So many potential states in which to settle, and Maidie wanted a sign, an omen, about which one, where to cease perpetual motion and make small adjustments that meant she was engaged here, attached to these companions, shared hours solidifying into connection, familiarity, so that the incomplete, snow-hazy, bygone days in which Maidie had been a solitary child would turn concrete at last, memorial. The wind blew like a furnace. The umbrella puffed skyward. The table floated until Lalo stood, pushed the umbrella into its base, the table and the unfinished meal back down.

Acknowledgments

Thank you to my editors, Becky Saletan, Denise Roy, Cindy Gitter. And to my agent, Colleen Mohyde. Also, Shen Christenson, Nan Cuba, Lynne Oaks, Don Carr, Tom Grimes, Dixie Blake, and Delmar.